SON OF MARY

Book 1 in the Crown of Thorns series

R. S. INGERMANSON

Ingermanson Communications, Inc.

To Eunice and our girls, Carolyn, Gracie, and Amy.

Although He was a Son,
He learned obedience
from the things which He suffered.
Hebrews 5:8, NASB

In those days and at that time
I will cause a righteous Branch of David to spring forth;
and he shall execute justice and righteousness on the earth.
Jeremiah 33:15, NASB

"Is not this the carpenter, the son of Mary,
and brother of James and Joses and Judas and Simon?
Are not His sisters here with us?"
And they took offense at Him.
Mark 6:3, NASB

WHO TOLD JESUS?

Who told Jesus he had to die?
Who told Jesus about the crown of thorns?
Was he born knowing he was doomed to the cross?
Did his parents tell him his destiny?
Did he read it in the prophets?
Maybe so.
But then again, maybe not.
We can't know for sure how he learned it.
Could it be that he discovered his destiny gradually?
The same way you and I do, step by step, working it out?
We read. We talk. We think. We pray. We listen.
Bit by bit, we find our way in the world.
The ancient creeds sing that Jesus was fully God.
But they insist that he was somehow also fully man.
As a man, he learned obedience, one step at a time.
As a man, he walked with God, talked with God.
Somewhere along that journey, Jesus came to know his destiny.
That he would be scapegoated by angry, frightened men.
That he would be beaten and mocked and spit on.
That he would die in shame on a cross.
And thereby rule as king forever.
Wearing a crown of thorns.
This is his story…

ACKNOWLEDGMENTS

I thank:

My wife, Eunice, who believed in me, always.

Chip MacGregor and Lee Hough, my agents who suggested I write a novel about Jesus back in September of 2004. Rest in peace, Lee.

Meredith Efken, my macro editor since forever, who talked me through sixteen drafts.

John Olson and Jeff Hilton, two friends who stick closer than a brother.

Tosca Lee, for telling me many times that the project must not die.

The Masterminds: Jim Rubart, Lacy Williams, Mary DeMuth, Susan May Warren, Thomas Umstattd, Tracy Higley, Tricia Goyer. Not forgetting our latest members: Brennan McPherson and Susan Seay.

Prof. James Tabor, who shares my obsession with the family of Jesus and all things Jerusalem.

Ted Dekker, for all those hours on the phone talking about Rabbi Yeshua.

Mel Hughes, my beta reader, who asked good questions.

Yoni Adoni, who helped me take my first steps in Hebrew.

My dozens of friends at Kehilat Ariel, who taught me Torah and the prayers.

My hundreds of friends in Chi Libris, who taught me to confront.

My thousands of friends in ACFW, OCW, CRCW, CIA, and SDCWG.

The Mount Zion Archaeological Dig, directed by Shimon Gibson, James Tabor, and Rafi Lewis.

The Magdala Archaeological Dig, directed by Marcela Zapata-Meza.

AUTHOR'S NOTE

This is a story set in a foreign place and time, strange to us in at least three ways:

- The land itself is not our land.
- The language is not our language.
- The way people think is not the way we think.

As for the land, I've created a few maps, based on what we know of first-century Judea, Samaria, and Galilee.

As for the language, I've given all characters names in Hebrew, Aramaic, or Greek. I've also salted in a few words from these languages. Just so we never forget that we are visitors in a foreign country.

As for the way they think, I've tweaked the way my characters speak. They put their words together a little different than you and I. Just to remind us that their brains are wired different from ours.

We can never understand these people completely, but we should remember one thing.

In their eyes, *we are the foreigners*.

We speak a strange language.

We think strange thoughts.

We come as guests into their home.

Welcome to their world, and enjoy the adventure!

WHERE TO DOWNLOAD THE MAPS

The maps in this book were custom drawn by the author for the *Crown of Thorns* series. These maps perfectly match the story. You can't find them anywhere else.

You can download the maps for free at ingermanson.com/maps.

Nobody lives forever, and neither do websites, so this offer can only be for a limited time. Best to grab the maps now.

AND A NOTE ABOUT X-RAY

The Kindle version of this book is customized using Amazon's X-Ray. Think of that edition as the Director's Cut of the book, with all kinds of cool goodies. See my web page "Why You'll Love X-Ray on Your Kindle E-books" for more info at: ingermanson.com/xray.

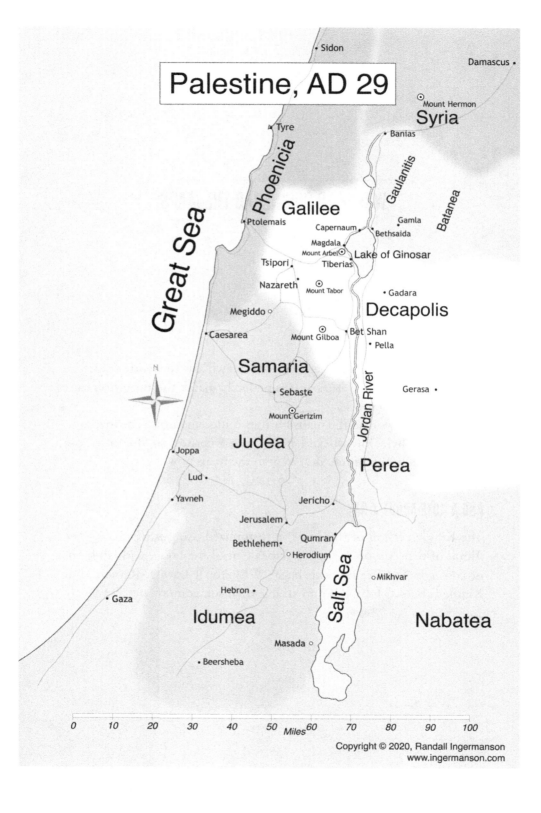

Palestine, AD 29

Sidon

Damascus

Mount Hermon

Syria

Tyre

Banias

Phoenicia

Gaulanitis

Batanea

Galilee

Ptolemais

Capernaum

Gamla

Magdala

Bethsaida

Mount Arbel

Lake of Ginosar

Great Sea

Tsipori

Tiberias

Nazareth

Mount Tabor

Gadara

Megiddo

Decapolis

Caesarea

Mount Gilboa

Bet Shan

Pella

Samaria

Sebaste

Gerasa

Mount Gerizim

Jordan River

Judea

Perea

Joppa

Lud

Yavneh

Jericho

Jerusalem

Qumran

Bethlehem

Herodium

Salt Sea

Mikhvar

Hebron

Gaza

Idumea

Masada

Nabatea

Beersheba

0   10   20   30   40   50   Miles 60   70   80   90   100

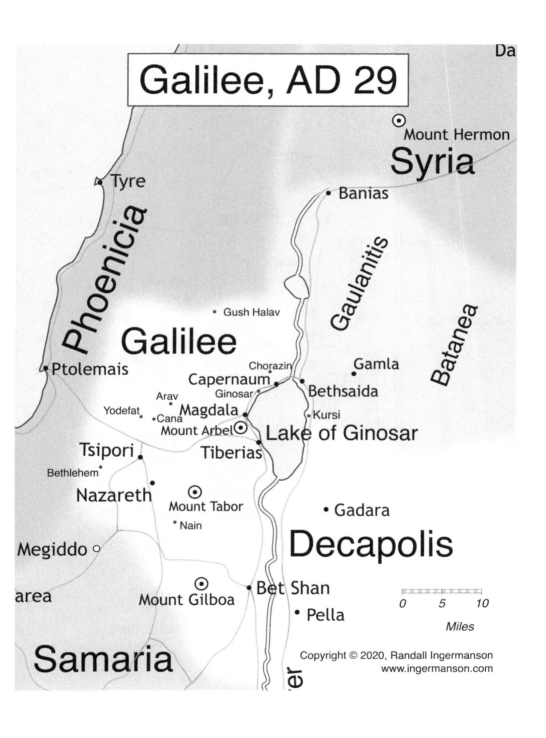

Galilee, AD 29

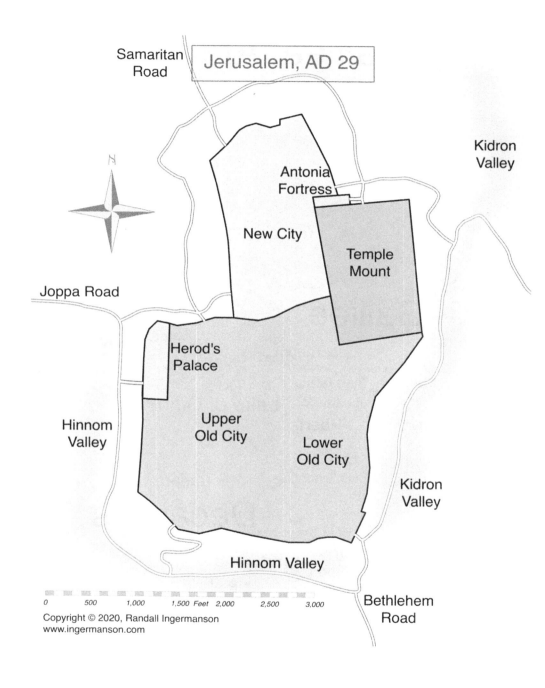

Jerusalem, AD 29

Samaritan Road

Kidron Valley

Antonia Fortress

New City

Temple Mount

Joppa Road

Herod's Palace

Hinnom Valley

Upper Old City

Lower Old City

Kidron Valley

Hinnom Valley

Bethlehem Road

0   500   1,000   1,500 Feet 2,000   2,500   3,000

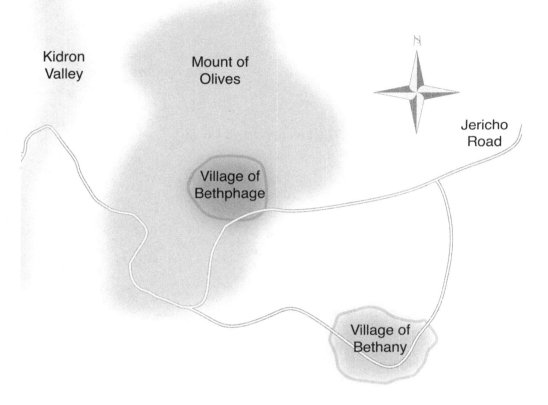

Mount of Olives, AD 29

Kidron
Valley

Mount of
Olives

N

Jericho
Road

Village of
Bethphage

Village of
Bethany

0   500   1,000   1,500   2,000 Feet 2,500   3,000   3,500   4,000

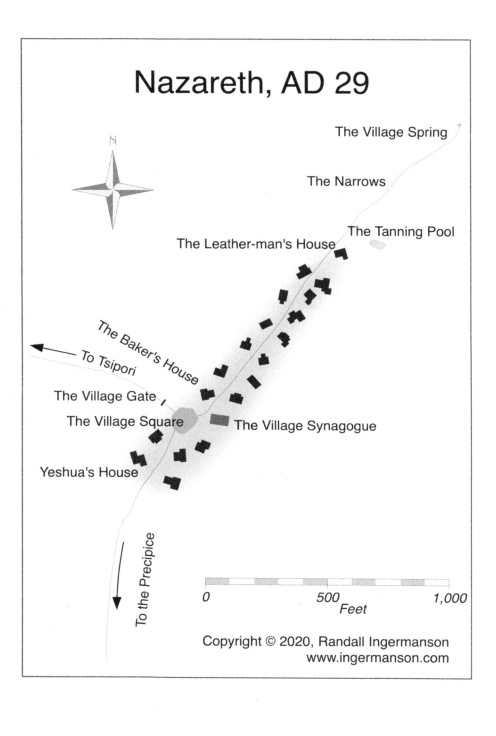

Nazareth, AD 29

The Village Spring

The Narrows

The Tanning Pool

The Leather-man's House

The Baker's House

To Tsipori

The Village Gate

The Village Square

The Village Synagogue

Yeshua's House

To the Precipice

0   500   1,000
Feet

PART 1: THE RING OF JUSTICE

Late summer, AD 29

Once there was an evil tale
An evil tale
An evil tale.
Once there was an evil tale
And Miryam was her name.

CHAPTER ONE

Miryam of Nazareth

My son Yeshua is making a scandal again.

He just came in the village gate holding the hand of a woman.

That is not done in Israel. It is a big scandal if a man talks with a woman. A bigger scandal to walk with a woman. Bigger yet to hold the hand of a woman.

But my son does all these things.

My Yeshua does not fear to make a scandal.

That is why I love him best of all my sons.

I am sure the woman is a sinful woman. A woman of shame. A *zonah*.

My son has brought home *zonahs* before. The village says it is a foolishness. I say it is a kindness.

Yeshua stops inside the gate to greet the village elders who sit all day taking their ease in the cool shade. He talks with the men and smiles kindly on the *zonah*, both at the same time.

The men do not look on the *zonah*, but they look on Yeshua and grin on him and slap their fat thighs and make a mighty roar on some jest he makes.

Yeshua turns and smiles on me.

It warms my heart that he smiles on me in the face of the village elders, who hate me. There was some man of HaShem who told me once that a sword would pierce my heart on account of Yeshua. That has not happened yet, and I beg HaShem it never will. When my son smiles on me, I can almost forget the matter of piercing.

Almost.

Yeshua pulls on the *zonah's* hand to come this way.

I am standing outside our house, which is at the south end of the village. Nazareth is long and narrow, one dirt street with stone houses on both sides. The village gate opens into the village square, not far from our house.

Yeshua makes a big smile on me.

He runs at me.

He lifts me in his arms and spins me around and around.

He kisses my left cheek. He kisses my right cheek. He kisses my lips.

A kiss and a kiss and a kiss, in the open street, as I am some man of honor and not the most shamed woman in the village.

My heart wants to break for my joy.

My son kisses me with honor while the village elders scowl on me for scorn.

Yeshua holds me long in his arms, as he is back from some far journey, instead of just gone for the day to Tsipori. He and his brothers must have found a good work there, because he smells like sweat.

At last Yeshua releases me. "HaShem has been smiling on you today, Imma. You look more beautiful than you did even this morning."

He says that every day, and it gives me a big joy in my heart. But lately, he says it more and there is a new look in his eye and it makes me afraid.

I think a day is coming when he will leave Nazareth.

HaShem has a mighty thing for Yeshua to do, and he knows it.

Yeshua wishes to do the will of HaShem, but he does not wish to leave me to the hate of the village.

My son loves me, but he loves HaShem more. If he thinks I am more beautiful today, it is not because I am younger. It is because he must leave me soon.

I think he weeps inside to leave me.

But even so, he will leave me.

And I am afraid. On the day he leaves me, I think I will die.

I do not think the village will stone me, but their scorn is sharper than knives. They will find a way to make my life a big agony, more than it is now.

I beg HaShem every day that he will not take away my Yeshua.

But I have forgotten my hospitality. The *zonah* stands near us, looking on the ground in her shame. Of course she is shamed. She is a sinful woman. Yeshua will find her a new life in the village, but the people will call her *zonah* until the day she dies. The stain of a *zonah* never scrubs out.

Yeshua says to me, "Imma, here is my new friend from Tsipori."

I hate Tsipori. It is the chief city of Galilee and stinks of garbage and piss and many thousand people. Yeshua says it is more than ten thousands, and not all of them are Jews. Some Syrians and Arabians live there, and even Greeks. Also, many *zonahs*. It is a wicked place. Yeshua goes there often with his brothers so they can find work. My sons know the craft of the *tekton*, so they can do any kind of stone-work or wood-work or metal-work that builders need. Each day a *tekton* can earn a silver *dinar*. We have a good living from Tsipori, but I will never love it.

The *zonah* stares on me.

She should stare. I am the most fortunate woman in Galilee. I am the most wretched woman in Galilee.

I make a smile on her. "My name is called Miryam."

She makes a smile back on me. "My name is called Shlomzion."

I say, "That is a good name," and it is true. The fourth part of the women in our village are named Shlomzion. There are so many, we give them each a nickname, or else there would be a big confusion.

My youngest daughter is named Shlomzion. We call her Shlomi

Dancefeet. She is to be married soon to a man of honor, but not in our village.

Yeshua steps inside our house and calls for my second son, who stayed home today.

A moment later, Yeshua comes out with two pots for water, tugging his brother's hand and smiling on the *zonah*. "Friend, this is my brother. His name is called Little Yaakov, and he is my strong right arm."

The *zonah* makes a grin, for Little Yaakov is a big man, more mighty than any of his brothers. But his grandfather's name was also called Yaakov, and so my son has been Little Yaakov from the day he was born.

Little Yaakov looks on the *zonah,* but he does not smile, and he does not speak to her.

I am glad on that. Little Yaakov's woman died of the fever last year, and I do not wish him to make a friend on a *zonah*. One son who makes scandals is enough.

Yeshua smiles on me. "Imma, you will come with me for a walk, yes?"

"Yes." My heart sings. This is the biggest happiness in my day, to walk with my son to fetch water. It is not done in Israel, for a man to go with a woman to fetch water, but my son does it because he loves me, and he does not care what other men think. My son is a *tsaddik*— a righteous man, a man of honor. A *tsaddik* does not make a worry on what is done in Israel and what is not done in Israel.

Yeshua hands the *zonah* a waterpot and me a waterpot. "Come, Imma. Did I remember to say you are beautiful?"

I smile on him. "No, you are a wicked son to have forgotten."

Yeshua laughs and kisses me again. In his laughter, I hear a far echo of his fear. And mine.

Just beside our house, a little way back from the street, my three daughters-in-law and my youngest daughter, Shlomi, are gathered around our firepit.

"Yeshua!" Shlomi Dancefeet squeals and runs to hug Yeshua.

She still hugs him as she is some small girl. When she is married, that will stop. The man she marries will not allow it.

"Shlomi!" Yeshua gives her a kiss and a kiss and a kiss. He lifts her up and swings her around many times. She was born a month after my lord Yoseph died, and so she is my last. Yeshua has been like a father to her. I see a big sadness in his eyes, because when she marries, she will leave our village.

Shlomi Dancefeet runs back to help my daughters-in-law with the cooking. They smile on Yeshua, but they do not greet him in public. They love him much, but they do not make a scandal on themselves.

Yeshua takes my hand again. When he holds my hand, I feel safe in this village. The men of the village hate me and their women spit my feet and their sons throw stones and their daughters sing cruel songs. But when Yeshua is with me, they do not. He is a *tsaddik* and a man of honor, and they fear him more than they hate me.

We walk.

The spring is far from our house, outside the north end of the village. It is a long way uphill, but when Yeshua is with me, it feels like a short walk.

When Yeshua is not with me, I do not go to the village spring.

We pass through the village square.

Yeshua shouts to Shimon the baker. "Father Shimon! Have you saved some rounds of bread for us?"

Shimon the baker is a fat man of sixty years who smiles much. He never smiles on me, but today he makes a big grin on Yeshua. "For how many mouths, friend?"

"Twelve," I whisper to Yeshua. Our family is ten adults, and the *zonah* is a guest, so she must have double. A *dinar* will buy bread for twelve, so Yeshua has just enough.

Yeshua thinks for a moment. "Four and ten."

There is a thing in his eyes I do not understand. Fear licks at my heart. Yeshua knows more than he has said.

Yeshua hands a *dinar* to Shimon the baker. "I will send Little Yaakov with more."

"You will not. It is an honor to sell you bread. I will send my grandson to your house with the rounds."

We walk all the length of the village and go out the north end. The wind blows from the east today, and the stink of the leather-man's piss-pool stings my nose. I wish it was farther from the village.

We reach the narrows and climb the stony path toward the spring of Nazareth. It is a good spring, enough for our village. HaShem, the Lord our God, the God of our fathers, makes water gush out from the ground. Long ago, our fathers built a stone pool to hold the water.

I dip my pot in the water and balance it on my head. The *zonah* does the same. She is a tall woman, and not young. She is more than twenty or I am a goose. There is a big hurt around her eyes. Tomorrow, Yeshua will find a house in Nazareth or some other village that needs a woman servant. No woman would be a *zonah* by choice, but a woman without a lord or father or brother or son can be a *zonah* or she can starve, and that is not a choice. I have five sons and a brother-in-law and a nephew, but sometimes I am afraid I might lose them all, and then what will I do?

Yeshua looks on me, and his eyes sing how he thinks I am more beautiful than I ever was.

Fear stings my heart like a poison. He knows some matter he has not told me yet.

"Come, Imma. Come, little sister." Yeshua takes my hand and the *zonah*'s hand and guides us back down the path.

The joy of my son fills my heart. Blessed be HaShem for my son, my greatest gladness and my greatest sorrow.

As we walk back into the village, our neighbor Marta comes out carrying a waterpot.

"Shalom, Marta! Are you well?" Yeshua says.

Marta does not look on him, and she does not speak, but she smiles as she passes by. Every woman smiles when my son greets her. Every old woman wishes he were her son. Every young woman wishes he were her lord.

And yet every woman of Nazareth hates me, because I shamed them all. Every woman wonders which man begat my Yeshua. Every woman wonders if it was her lord I seduced for no reason, when I was betrothed already to a good man. They hate me for a sinful woman. They hate me for a *zonah*. They hate me because I seduced a man for no cause, when I was not even hungry. They hate me because I refuse to confess my sin. They hate me because I will not tell who I seduced.

I am an evil tale.

I am the biggest evil tale that ever was.

A small village has a long memory. They would forgive, if only I would confess. But I cannot confess because I never seduced. They will never believe I never seduced, so they will never forgive. They have made me like the dust between their toes.

I hate Nazareth.

Every woman in the village has spit my feet. They would tear me to bits with their nails if they caught me alone, but I have always one of my sons by my side to defend.

Behind us, Marta spits the dirt.

Yeshua's hand tightens on mine.

For many years, I wept every night for saying yes to the Messenger. I could have said no. Then the women would not hate me. But then I would not have my Yeshua. And so, all these years, the women have thrown their scorn on me.

I will never forgive them. Never, ever, ever.

When my son redeems Israel and comes into his power, HaShem will make a justice on me. And he will punish my tormentors. That day is coming. I feel in my heart it is coming soon. For a little while, I must lose my son while he does a big work for HaShem, but then I will have him with me, until forever.

When we reach our house, my daughters-in-law are lifting a great clay cooking pot out of the firepit. I do not know how many mouths it can feed. When we are ten, it feeds ten. When we are twenty, it feeds twenty. This is the best of all times, at the going out of the day, when the women bring in the food and the men return from their work and we eat together and have joy.

We stand back to let the women carry in the food with care. Once, they dropped it, and we ate only bread that night. Only one time, but that was enough.

My three youngest sons are just now coming in through the village gate. They will never tell Yeshua no on the matter of bringing home a *zonah*. But neither will they walk within sight of her. My sons do not like scandals.

"Yosi! Thin Shimon! Yehuda Dreamhead!" Yeshua shouts to his brothers.

They turn to grin on us, but they do not walk this way yet. After my lord Yoseph died, Yeshua finished training them all in the craft of the *tekton*, and each of them finds work because of him. He also found men to marry my three daughters. When my youngest is married, I do not know what Yeshua will do, but I am afraid. Afraid and happy, both at the same time. Yeshua must do what HaShem calls him to do.

My sons still stand in the gate, talking with the village elders.

Now I see that some other man came in with them. He wears a worn tunic and carries a sun-faded leather pack on his back.

A traveler.

The elders all rise to greet the traveler.

I hear their excited voices, but I cannot pick out their words. I am old, almost fifty, and my ears are dull.

Yeshua's face is tight. I never saw such a face on him. A traveler means news and news means change.

I do not want my world to change.

Yeshua looks on me, and his eyes sing that no woman could be more beautiful than I am.

My heart wants to weep.

Yeshua hurries toward the village gate.

We will have an extra mouth for our evening meal. It is an honor to give hospitality to a traveler. Yeshua will ask for the man, and the elders will give him the honor. The village will gather in the square this evening to hear the traveler's news from the outside world.

It is a warm summer evening, but I never felt such a bitter winter in my heart.

CHAPTER TWO

Miryam of Nazareth

The stranger's name is Hanina. He is a Jew from Babylon who travels much. He sells oddments or works as a day laborer and walks wherever he pleases and does as he likes. We recline on mats around the cooking pot in our courtyard, eating stew wrapped in bread and listening to Hanina tell us all that he has seen. He has seen many things in the world, but tonight he wishes to speak only of one.

"Two weeks ago, I was in Jerusalem." Hanina leans back on his elbow and takes a mouthful of stew. "All the city was going down to the Jordan to see a great thing."

Every one of us leans forward. Our people go *up* to Jerusalem three times in a year to see a great thing, the Temple of HaShem. If Jews are going *down* from Jerusalem to see a great thing, then it must be a mighty wonder.

Hanina tips his stone mug and drinks the last of his beer. "Tales tell that there is a prophet again in Israel, a man named Yohanan."

My heart flutters to hear this news.

My sons all stare on Hanina. Their eyes sing.

"A prophet in Israel!" There is a big excitement in Little Yaakov's voice.

It has been many hundred years since a prophet spoke in Israel. Until HaShem sends us a prophet, we are still in exile. Even if we live in the land of Israel, we live also in exile, both at the same time. HaShem has not returned to rule in our land, as in days of old. Not yet.

But HaShem will return. I heard it from the Messenger many years ago. My sons do not know about the Messenger. I never told a living soul about the Messenger, because who would believe? But all Israel knows that when a prophet rises in Israel, it is a sign HaShem will return. HaShem will give us a king to rule on David's throne.

And the Messenger told me my son will be that king.

Hanina's eyes glitter. "I went down to the Jordan to see this prophet, this Yohanan, who is called the immerser. He looks like a prophet from old times, like Elijah, who killed the prophets of the *ba'al*. He tells our people that if we turn from our sins, if we turn again to HaShem, then HaShem will forgive our nation and return to us and be our king."

My sons' breath hisses in their throats.

I myself cannot breathe at all. Our people have looked for HaShem to return for many hundred years. We have prayed. We have suffered. We have been thrown in slavery to the goyim. We have cried out to HaShem. Now he will save us. Now HaShem will return as king. I heard it myself from the Messenger, and yet even I am surprised.

Yeshua studies Hanina's face with sharp eyes, bright as knives. "And where is this Yohanan?"

Hanina shrugs his shoulders. "If you walk south on the Jordan Way to Jericho and then go east by a walk of one hour to cross the river at the fords, that is where I saw him."

Yeshua's eyes turn inward, and I know he is thinking hard on the matter. There is another world behind those eyes.

My heart quivers.

My other sons ask Hanina many questions.

Little Yaakov asks what Rabbi Shammai says on the matter. Rabbi Shammai is the greatest sage in all Israel.

Yosi asks why Yohanan does not go up to Jerusalem, but makes Jerusalem come down to him.

Thin Shimon asks how they know he is a prophet.

Yehuda Dreamhead asks whether Yohanan parts the Jordan, as Joshua did in days of old, when he led our people out of exile from Egypt.

Hanina answers their questions, but I see my Yeshua is not listening. I see what he is thinking. A fist of iron grips my heart.

"Imma." Yeshua's eyes shine on me, bright as fire.

"No, Yeshua, please." The words strangle in my throat. "We have the wedding feast for your sister." I do not fear for the wedding feast. I fear for myself. Is it selfish to fear for myself, when HaShem has a big work for Yeshua to do? I do not wish to be selfish, but I am afraid. In days of old, they stoned seducing women. In the eyes of the village, I am a seducing woman.

"Imma."

All the others stare on us.

I am more afraid than I ever was. The Messenger said my son would bring in the kingdom of HaShem. That he would rule in power. That the exile of our people would end. I know my son must be taken from me for a little while to do a big work for HaShem, but I do not want him taken, not for one day.

"Imma, you know I must go and speak with this prophet."

A sword pierces my heart. The man of HaShem spoke true. To lose my son for one day is to die for that day. I have my other sons, but they are not Yeshua.

"Yes, Imma?" Yeshua's eyes tell that he is afraid for me. That he loves me more than his own life. That he would do anything within the will of HaShem to protect me.

That he must go.

I want to say no, to throw myself at his feet, to weep and beg and make him repent. But that is not the way of HaShem. I promised the Messenger I would obey. Therefore, I will obey.

"After the wedding feast," I say.

That is two months more I will have my son with me.

In two months, he can make a justice on me.

He can punish the village for me.

Then he can go and redeem Israel and bring in the kingdom and rule in power.

I only ask HaShem to make a justice on me soon, or else I die.

Yaakov of Nazareth

I love my brother Yeshua.

I hate my brother Yeshua.

Both at the same time.

We have finished our evening meal, and now Yeshua wishes to go speak with this prophet. Soon. I do not think he will wait two months. I think he wishes to go next week.

He must take me with him when he goes. He *must*.

The women begin cleaning the cooking pot.

We men take our guest Hanina to the village square so all Nazareth will hear the news on this new prophet in Israel.

All the village is already there, waiting. We do not get many visitors to Nazareth.

We sit in the square to hear the news all over again.

As soon as Hanina begins speaking, Yeshua stands and steps backward, away from the crowd. He waits on the edges for a moment, then turns and glides away on silent feet.

I follow him.

He walks north, past the house of Shimon the baker, past a dozen more houses. He passes the leather-man's house at the end of the village. He passes the stinking piss-pool where the leather-man tans his hides.

He enters the narrows on the way to the spring.

I drift along behind him, silent as Sheol.

At the spring, he sits on the ground and sighs deeply. We are one night past the full moon, and his face shows clearly. He is afraid.

I move forward into the moonlight. "Take me with you."

His eyebrows leap up, and his mouth opens in a perfect circle. "Little Yaakov! I … how can I take you with me? Our brothers need you. Our sister needs you. Imma needs you."

I shake my head and sit beside him. "You need me more."

"I need a word from HaShem."

I study him intently. "You think to redeem Israel, yes?" I never heard Yeshua say he is to redeem Israel. I never heard Imma or Abba say it. But ever since I was a boy of two, I smelled it in the air. I saw the way Abba and Imma looked on Yeshua. I heard a stray word now and again when they thought I was beyond hearing. I know there was some man of HaShem who spoke a word over Yeshua in the Temple once. All the family thinks Yeshua is to redeem Israel.

Except me.

Yeshua's face twists in doubt. "I do not know how to redeem Israel. The scriptures do not explain the matter. I need a prophet to explain the matter."

Yeshua is double-minded, that is his problem. He is fearful and womanish. He does not wish to fight. He does not long to take up the sword. How is he to destroy our enemy?

We have a special word in Hebrew to speak on an enemy of our people, an enemy that wishes to destroy our nation.

That word is *satan*.

In days of old, the enemy of our nation—the Great Satan—was Babylon. We had a weak king in those days, fearful and womanish, and he led us into a bad war, and we lost, and the Great Satan burned our city and our Temple. The Great Satan killed our men and raped our women. The Great Satan slaved our children seventy years.

Then HaShem brought us back from the Great Satan.

We have a big enemy of our people again, only now it is a different enemy. Now our Great Satan is Rome.

We need a strong king to fight the Great Satan, and this time we must win.

I do not know why Imma and Abba ever thought Yeshua should be king.

I do not know why Yeshua thinks he should be king.

But I know Yeshua is not fit to be king.

Yeshua is a good man, a righteous man—a *tsaddik*. I love him for his righteousness. He is good and kind. All the village loves him. All but a few.

But he is weak. He is fearful. He is womanish.

Yeshua must never be king. He must never be the anointed king of Israel, the son of David, which we call Mashiach.

Yet he thinks to be Mashiach.

If he tries to be Mashiach, he will take us into a bad war with the Great Satan and we will lose. The Great Satan will burn our city and our Temple. The Great Satan will kill our men and rape our women. The Great Satan will slave our children.

And that is why I hate my brother.

I sometimes think Yeshua has no *yetzer hara*—no evil inclination. But that cannot be so. Every man ever born has a *yetzer hara*. Strong men have a strong *yetzer hara*. Men like our father David the king, who was a man of strong deed and big passion. A man red with the blood of the sword. A man who took any woman he wanted.

Weak men have a weak *yetzer hara*. They are slow to anger and slow to look with desire on a woman. Maybe they sin less than other men, but they also live less.

I think the man of HaShem told a wrong tale. Or else Abba and Imma misheard him. Or else he was no man of HaShem at all. Yeshua has a weak *yetzer hara,* and he will never be Mashiach. The man who should be Mashiach is strong and fearless and quick to make decision. Also, the man who should be Mashiach must have no smirch on his name. Yeshua needs me, and he knows it.

I seize Yeshua's hand. "Take me with you! You are a righteous man, a *tsaddik*. Any fool can see it. You are a man all Israel will love. But you need a man to take up the sword and be your strong right arm. Take me!"

Yeshua smiles on me. "Little Yaakov, you are strong. You are brave. Our father was proud on you. Our mother loves you. Our brothers admire you and our sisters adore you."

I hold my breath. He tells me nothing I do not know.

Yeshua leans forward and gives me a kiss and a kiss and a kiss. "And I love you, my brother. You should have been the oldest."

My heart catches within me. Yes, I should have been oldest. I should have been the one about whom the man of HaShem foretold. I should be Mashiach, because I have the *yetzer hara* of Mashiach.

My fists clench. "Will you take me with you?"

Something flickers in Yeshua's face. Some decision, at last. My brother is slow to make a hard choice, but once he makes it, he has some little strength of will.

He stands. "Little Yaakov, come. There is a thing I must tell Imma and our brothers and our sister."

I leap up on light feet, and my heart beats a mighty rhythm on my ribs. My *yetzer hara* never felt so strong inside me. I wish I had a sword so I could take it to battle now. I wish my woman were still alive so I could give her a night of a big passion, enough to wake the whole village.

We walk back along the narrow path. I feel the sadness of my leaving heavy on my heart, but I know that in a month or six months or a year, I will return. We will return. As conquerors.

When we reach the village square, Yeshua calls our brothers.

They see the fire in my eyes and the face of quiet decision that Yeshua wears, and they follow us meekly home.

Our women are done with the cleaning. They sit on benches inside our courtyard, enjoying the moonlight. The *zonah* sits with them, and for a moment I notice the soft roundness of her body under her thin tunic.

Yeshua tugs me forward and waits for quiet.

Imma's eyes are bright with a big fear.

It will be hard on her to see Yeshua go. Harder to see me leave also, but she has still three sons. My uncle and cousin live in the next house. Imma will be safe.

Yeshua pulls Imma to her feet and gives her a kiss and a kiss and a kiss. When he speaks, his voice cracks with sadness. "Tomorrow I will go to hear a word of HaShem from this prophet Yohanan."

Imma screams and throws her arms around him. "No! Please! Not so soon!"

My heart shivers. I always had a weakness for the tears of Imma.

Yeshua holds her tight, kissing the top of her head many times.

At last her sobs weaken, but still she clutches him. Her knees have gone soft.

"I will not leave you defenseless," Yeshua says.

Of course we will not leave her defenseless. Our brothers Yosi and Thin Shimon and Yehuda Dreamhead are almost as big as me, with strong arms and thick hands. None of them has a *yetzer hara* to match mine, but they are men of courage and they keep their women warm at night. Our mother will be safe with these three to protect her.

Imma sighs with a big sigh and burrows her face in Yeshua's chest.

Shlomi Dancefeet has great tears streaming down her face.

The *zonah* stares with her mouth wide open.

"Imma, here is your firstborn son." Yeshua takes her hand.

He takes my hand. "Little Yaakov, here is your mother. Today and forever, you are the firstborn son."

Firstborn son? My head feels light and my veins feel on fire and my knees wobble. Yeshua has given me his place. He has given me all.

All but the one thing I wanted most. I want to shout *no*, but my throat is dry and my voice is stolen.

Imma wraps her arms around me. She lunges up and gives me a kiss and a kiss and a kiss. "Little Yaakov! My defender!"

My brothers crowd around me, pounding my back, shouting a big shout.

Shlomi Dancefeet leaps up and down, clutching at my hand. "Little Yaakov the Brave!" she shouts. "Little Yaakov the Strong!"

The *zonah* stares on me as I am a mighty warrior.

It takes the fourth part of an hour for the shouting to end.

At last, my brothers step back and Shlomi Dancefeet stops her dancing and Imma releases her iron grip on my waist.

Yeshua nudges his way forward and puts both hands on my shoulders. His eyes are haunted.

I never saw such a lonely man as my brother in this moment.

He leans forward and gives me a kiss and a kiss and a kiss. "HaShem made you for great things."

I do not know what to say.
I love my brother Yeshua.
I hate my brother Yeshua.
Both at the same time.

CHAPTER THREE

Yeshua of Nazareth

On the day I reached the fourth year of my age, I learned there is a smirch on my name.

It was Shabbat, and my father said I was old enough to go with him and my grandfather to the synagogue.

I thought it would be the best day in my life, to sit with my father, Yoseph the *tsaddik*, and hear the scriptures read. To say the prayers.

Also, to see my grandfather expound Torah. My father's father was a mighty man of honor in the village. His name was called Yaakov Mega, and he was president of the synagogue.

I was always a little afraid on Yaakov Mega, for he was a fierce man. He was counted wise by the village, for he could read the law and the prophets. Some said he had learned the whole Torah by heart. He could even write his own name.

Yaakov Mega looked down on me from his great height and said I must not make a disturbance in the synagogue and dishonor our family.

Abba said I would sit quietly and make an honor on our house.

Imma kissed me and told me to act like a man, not to squirm and shout like my baby brother. She went back in the house to feed Little Yaakov.

I took Abba's hand and my grandfather's hand, and we walked proud to the village square.

Our synagogue sits just to the east side of the square.

When we went to go in, one man of the village said no.

Yonatan the leather-man stood in the doorway with arms crossed on his chest. He said there was the smirch of the *mamzer* on my name, so how could I go in the synagogue?

All my heart was in a big confusion. I never heard the word *mamzer* before.

My father made a big scowl. "What smirch on his name? This is Yeshua, son of Yoseph, son of Yaakov Mega, son of David. He is a good boy and kind. Stand aside and let him enter."

Yonatan the leather-man made a shrug on his shoulders. "He is a good boy and kind, and all the village loves him. But it is a matter of Torah. Our prophet Moses says no *mamzer* can enter the assembly, not to the tenth generation."

I looked on my father and opened my mouth to ask what is a *mamzer*.

My father said, "He is my son."

Yonatan the leather-man said, "He was born in the third month after you took your woman into your house. Explain the matter."

I did not know what Yonatan meant about the third month.

My father's face turned the color of a brick. "There is no matter to explain. Yeshua is my firstborn son."

Yonatan the leather-man said, "Swear by The Name that you went into the chamber with your woman before the time and begat the boy."

"He is my son."

"Do you say you begat the boy?"

"He is my son."

"You are a *tsaddik*, and all the village honors you for it. Do you say your woman enticed you before the time, and you went in the chamber with her, against Torah? You are a righteous man, and I will never believe that is how it befell, unless you swear by The Name."

My father's hand was hot in mine, wet with his sweat. He looked down on me with a big sadness in his eyes. "He is my son." His voice cracked on the last word.

Yonatan the leather-man shook his head. "Yes, he is your son. The customs say he is your son if you claim him for your son. But still there is a smirch. Who begat the boy? Why will you not say? What if he is a *mamzer*? Then it is a big sin if we let him in the synagogue."

All the village stood around us with mouths hanging open, staring.

I did not know what was wrong with me. I did not know what is a *mamzer*. I did not know what is a smirch. All I knew was that I wished to run away fast and hide.

My grandfather stepped close to Yonatan the leather-man and stabbed a finger on his chest. "You are not the father of the father of the boy. I am, and I should decide the matter. The boy is Yeshua, son of Yoseph the *tsaddik*, son of Yaakov Mega, son of David. He is no *mamzer*, and he will enter the synagogue. Stand aside."

Yonatan the leather-man stood firm. "I did not say he is a *mamzer*. I said there is a doubt on the matter. Let Yoseph the *tsaddik* swear by The Name that he begat the boy, and that will make an end on the doubt."

His face became a blur in my eyes.

All the village murmured behind me.

"That is a good boy and kind. He will be like his father, who is a *tsaddik*."

"Yes, but would a *tsaddik* go in the chamber with his woman before the time?"

"He says the boy is his son. Therefore, the woman enticed him. We always knew she was lewd."

"Yes, but why will he not swear by The Name that he begat the boy?"

Yaakov Mega looked all around the circle of villagers. His face turned fierce and bold. He held up his right hand. A gold ring gleamed on his finger.

A shiver ran around the villagers when they saw the ring.

Yaakov Mega said, "I invoke the Ring of Justice."

I wanted to ask what is the Ring of Justice. I had seen his ring many times, but I always thought it was just a ring he got from his father.

Yaakov Mega said, "Yonatan, you make an injustice on the boy. Here is my judgment, and it is a righteous justice—that all the village together will decide the matter. All who accept the boy to go in the synagogue, show you accept by going in the synagogue yourself. Stand aside, Yonatan, to let them go in."

Yonatan the leather-man did not stand aside.

There was a long moment of silence, crackled and frozen as the moment before a lightning.

Shimon the baker stepped forward. "That is a good boy who will grow to be a *tsaddik* when he is a man. Stand aside for me, Yonatan."

Yonatan the leather-man stood aside.

Shimon the baker went in the synagogue.

Yoseph the iron-man went in the synagogue.

Hanan the sheep-man went in the synagogue.

Uncle Halfai went in the synagogue.

All the village went in the synagogue.

Last of all, Imma's father went in the synagogue. He spat the dust at the feet of Yonatan the leather-man when he passed him.

Yonatan the leather-man stood with arms crossed, glaring on me and Abba and Yaakov Mega.

Yaakov Mega raised his eyebrows on Yonatan the leather-man. "The village has spoken with their feet. Will you be the one man alone?"

Yonatan the leather-man made a hard look on Abba. "Why will you not swear by The Name on the matter? Until you confess your sin, that you were enticed by the woman before the time and begat the boy, all our women will give us sideways eyes on the matter."

My father said, "He is my son. That is the end of the matter."

Yonatan the leather-man spat the dust. And went in the synagogue.

We went in too, but I do not remember one moment of that first Shabbat in the synagogue.

All I remember is that I felt the Presence of HaShem, the Shekinah, wrapping arms around me, holding me close, making a comfort on me.

But even the Shekinah could not take away the smirch on my name.

When we left the synagogue and walked home, I did not walk proud. I felt a big hurt in my father's heart. I felt a big anger hanging over my grandfather.

Imma gave us a great smile when we went in the house, but her smile fell off her face when she saw Yaakov Mega behind me.

I rushed to her and gave her a hug and said she was beautiful. Then I asked, "Imma, what is a *mamzer*?"

She pulled me onto her lap and held me close and sighed with a big sigh. "A *mamzer* is a son of adultery."

I said, "What is adultery?"

All her body turned hard. "It is when some man does a wickedness on another man's woman."

I said, "Why did Yonatan the leather-man say I am a *mamzer*?"

Imma cried.

Abba took me from Imma and held me in his arms. "It is a lie, Yeshua. You are my own son, and no son of adultery."

I said, "What does it mean to beget a son?"

Imma said nothing.

Abba said nothing.

Yaakov Mega said, "You remember the matter of the goats yesterday?"

I remembered that I saw our goats acting foolishly.

Yaakov Mega said, "That is begetting."

I did not think that explained what is begetting. I opened my mouth to ask another question.

Yaakov Mega said, "We will not speak on the matter."

I said, "But—"

Yaakov Mega held up his right hand to show the ring on his finger. "I invoke the Ring of Justice. Here is my—"

I said, "What is the Ring of Justice?"

Abba spoke in a voice hard and tight. "Do not question your

grandfather, Yeshua. The man who wears the Ring of Justice has authority from HaShem to make judgment."

I did not see why I could not even ask a question.

Yaakov Mega said, "Here is my judgment. We will not speak on the matter of begetting. We will not speak on the matter of *mamzer*. We will not speak on this matter of shame, until forever."

So we did not speak on the matter ever again.

Ten years after that, Yaakov Mega died, and still we never spoke on the matter.

Another five years, and my father died untimely, and still we never spoke on the matter.

We had many goats, and soon I learned the matter of a goat begetting a kid.

Later, I learned the matter of a man begetting a son.

Later, I learned the matter of a baby born in the third month.

To this day, all the village agrees that Yoseph the *tsaddik* claimed me for his firstborn son.

In the eyes of the village, I am Yoseph's son according to our customs.

But in the eyes of the village, there is also a smirch on my name, because they say Yoseph did not beget me. They say Yoseph is not my blood father. They say Yoseph the *tsaddik* claimed me for his son for a kindness. They say Imma played the *zonah* with some man of the village, and therefore I am a son of adultery.

A few say that makes me a *mamzer*.

Most say it does not.

It remains a matter of doubt, for Torah does not explain what is a *mamzer*. Torah thinks the hearer will know what is a *mamzer*, and so Torah only forbids the *mamzer* to go in the assembly, without explaining the matter.

I am permitted to go in the synagogue. That was decided long ago. It may be the village will change its decision someday, but I am no prophet, and I cannot foresee what will befall.

But no man of the village gives me his daughter to marry. It is not for mislike on me. All the village loves me. It is because there is a doubt on the matter of *mamzer*. There is a smirch on my name, and no man would give his daughter to a man with a smirch, because then his grandchildren would carry the smirch, until forever.

While my father lived, all the village called me son of Yoseph. Afterward, the leather-man began calling me son of Miryam. He means I am son of a *zonah*. A son of adultery.

As the memory of Yoseph the *tsaddik* fades, the whispers grow louder.

The smirch on my name is growing.

After we buried my father, I asked Imma once who begat me. Only once.

She would not tell. She commanded never to speak on the matter again.

She said a day would come when HaShem would speak to me and explain the matter.

She said that when HaShem sends me to do a great thing, he will tell me the matter.

All my life, I have known that some man of HaShem foretold I would do a great thing for our people. We do not speak of it openly, but all the family thinks I will redeem Israel. And the sign I am about to redeem Israel is that a prophet will rise in Israel.

Elijah the prophet, who runs before Mashiach.

I do not see how a man with a smirch on his name can redeem Israel. The smirch must be taken away. I think the prophet must help me remove the smirch.

I have a secret I never told Imma, for it would crush her heart.

All my life, I have longed to know my blood father.

I loved Yoseph the *tsaddik*, who claimed me for his son.

The village says I am son of Yoseph, and this is true, but it is not enough.

I wish to know my blood father.

Yaakov Mega said I am son of David, and this is true, but it is not enough.

I wish to know my blood father.

Yoseph the *tsaddik* said I am son of Adam, and this is true, but it is not enough.

I wish to know my blood father.

Imma says HaShem loves me like a father, and this is true, for his Presence always surrounds me, but it is not enough. I would do anything to know my blood father.

All the words they say are smoke. I am desperate to know my blood father.

It is a walk of four days from Nazareth to Jericho. I have walked it in three. I am in a fever to see this prophet of HaShem, this Yohanan the immerser.

I will ask him how I am to redeem Israel, for the scriptures do not explain the matter.

Also, I will ask how to remove the smirch on my name, for I do not think I can redeem Israel when there is a smirch on my name.

Also, I will ask who is my blood father, for even if the smirch is removed, the question burns in my heart. Until I know my blood father, I am more lonely than any man ever was, whether I recline at the evening meal with my family or whether I stand with many ten thousand men of Israel in the Temple of the living God.

I wish to know my blood father.

I have begged HaShem all my life to explain the matter to me, but I am no prophet, and I do not hear the voice of HaShem.

I have felt the Presence of HaShem all my life. The Shekinah feels like a fire shining through a blanket. It is good, but it is not enough.

This prophet Yohanan must help me.

I wish to see the naked fire of HaShem.

I wish to hear the word of HaShem.

I wish to know my blood father.

CHAPTER FOUR

Yeshua of Nazareth

An hour before the going out of the day, I reach the place where Yohanan the prophet teaches. Many dozen men are going down into the river. Also many dozen women. I heard that men and women immerse here all together, and I wondered how it was done, for it is a big wickedness to expose your nakedness.

Now I see how it is done. They take off only their sandals and belts and go down in the water still wearing their tunics.

The Jordan River is slow as a desert turtle, and murky and green. You can walk in to the depth of your chin. Then you pull up your tunic over your head, and no eye can see your nakedness. You bend your knees and immerse all your body below the surface. After you immerse, you pull your tunic back on over your head and cover your nakedness.

When you come up out of the water, your tunic is clammy and greenish and clings to your body.

The water looks vile.

I do not think I wish to immerse. I came to ask the prophet for a word from HaShem.

I look all around and see a small man standing beside the river. He has stringy muscles and uncut hair that hangs below his waist, and he wears the ugliest tunic I ever saw. It is made of the cloth we call *saq*. I think he made it himself from the hair the camels rub off on the date palm trees in the spring. He looks like I always thought Elijah must look, for Elijah wore a tunic of *saq*. I think this must be Yohanan the prophet. The Shekinah glows faintly all around him like a pillar of fire. But the fire is masked.

My heart clenches. I need a man with the unmasked fire of HaShem. I walked far to hear a word from HaShem, and if this Yohanan cannot give me a word from HaShem, then I have left Imma crying at home to no gain.

Yohanan scowls on me. "Did you come to immerse? You should repent first of your sins and show works worthy of repentance."

"I came to hear a word from HaShem."

"Here is a word from HaShem. He will send a mighty judgment on Israel. Death and destruction and fire at the hand of the Great Satan. You will die in your sins unless you repent. You must repent soon. The ax is already laid at the root of the tree."

"I wish to know how to redeem Israel."

"You cannot redeem Israel unless you come from the House of David."

"I am a son of David."

Yohanan looks on me with hard eyes. "Even David could not escape the judgment unless he repented, for he had many sins. You should repent your sins and learn the way of *zekhut*."

Zekhut means righteousness. *Zekhut* means to take care of the widow and the orphan and the poor and the stranger and the prisoner and the *zonah*. I have done *zekhut* all my life. I look on Yohanan and shrug because I do not know what more *zekhut* I can do.

Yohanan makes a bigger scowl on me. "What is this shrug you make? If you have two tunics, do you give one to the naked?"

"You say so."

"If you have bread, do you give half to the hungry?"

"You say so."

"Have you done *zekhut* all your life?"

"You say so."

Yohanan stares on me long, his eyes burning with an angry fire.

I step close to make a beg on him. This is not what I came for, to hear a word from the Accuser. I came to hear a word from HaShem. My heart pounds like a mason's hammer in my chest. I must have a word from HaShem.

The Shekinah glows all around Yohanan. His eyes pierce me. "Who are you?"

I do not know how to answer. The village says I am the son of Yoseph, but I wish to be more than the son of a *tekton*. Abba said I am the son of David, but when men speak of the son of David, they mean Mashiach, and I do not know how to be Mashiach. Imma says HaShem is like a father to me, but when men speak of the son of HaShem, they mean the king of Israel, and I do not know how to be king of Israel.

"I am … the son of Adam." My words sound foolish in my ears. When men speak of a son of Adam, they mean any mortal, any son of man.

"What brings you here, son of Adam? Are you a prophet? You have the look of a prophet."

I shake my head. "I am not a prophet. I never heard any word from HaShem. All my village says I am a *tsaddik*."

He studies me, and a muscle flickers in his face. "If you are a *tsaddik*, why should you immerse with the immersion of repentance?"

"I did not come to repent, and I did not come to immerse. I told you already, I came to ask for a word from HaShem."

"Who are you to want a word from HaShem?"

I do not know who I am. That is my problem. I will never know who I am until I know my blood father. My wish to know my blood father burns in my chest like an open flame. My mother will never tell me, so I came to ask the prophet. But now he asks who I am, so even he does not know.

The prophet cannot tell who is my blood father, or how to remove the smirch, or how to redeem Israel.

My quest is all for nothing.

Yohanan's eyes look deep inside me. His gaze is sharper than any blade. "HaShem says you are a lamb of the heart of HaShem."

I stare on him. "What does that mean, to be a lamb of the heart of HaShem?"

Yohanan shakes his head. "How should I know? I told you what HaShem says. If you wish to know what HaShem means, then you should immerse and ask him yourself. If you are a *tsaddik*, you will hear a word from HaShem."

All at once, I am desperate to immerse. Not the immersion of repentance. The immersion of *zekhut*. The immersion of HaShem.

I feel in my heart that this is how I will know my blood father. I feel that if I do not immerse, I will die, for my loneliness weighs on me like a mighty stone.

I feel the Shekinah pressing near.

I kick off my sandals.

I lay down my waterskin.

I throw down my pack with my cloak and my food.

I unwrap my belt and put it aside.

I step down into the river.

I push my way out to the level of my neck.

I pull my tunic up over my head.

I immerse.

The water closes over my head like a grave.

I am alone in a great sea, more lonely than I ever was. 'HaShem, speak to me now. Speak to me or I die!'

The Shekinah comes nearer. I feel its heat like an iron-man's flame. It singes me. Scorches me. Burns me with fervent heat.

I am in a big agony, but I press in. 'HaShem, who is my blood father?'

My soul is on fire. I am destroyed.

I push closer. 'HaShem, speak to me!'

The fire grows to the brightness of many suns.

I stand before the Throne of HaShem.

And HaShem speaks. 'Who are you, my son?'

'Some say I am the son of Yoseph.'

'You are the son of Yoseph, but you are more than the son of Yoseph.'

'Some say I am the son of David.'

'You are the son of David, but you are more than the son of David.'

'Some say I am the son of Adam.'

'You are the son of Adam, but you are more than the son of Adam.'

'Then who am I? I beg on you to tell me whose son am I?'

HaShem rises from the Throne. 'Look on me, son of Adam.'

I do not look on him. It is not permitted for a son of Adam to look on the face of HaShem.

HaShem comes closer. 'Look on me, son of David.'

I do not look on him. Even Moses our prophet did not dare look on the face of HaShem.

HaShem stands before me, behind me, all around me. 'Look on me, son of Yoseph, son of Miryam.'

I look on the face of HaShem.

HaShem gives me a kiss and a kiss and a kiss.

The Shekinah is inside me now, burning like the sun.

HaShem sings the words of a mighty psalm, the psalm for anointing the king of Israel:

> 'You are my son.
> Today I have become your father.
> Ask from me
> And I will give
> The goyim for your heritage,
> To the ends of the earth for your possession.
> You will beat them with a club of iron
> To shatter them like shards of clay.'

The vision fades.

〜

I am again in the world of men.

My heart is on fire.

I am the son of Yoseph.

I am the son of David.

I am the son of Adam.

I am the anointed king of Israel.

But still I do not know who is my blood father.

I open my eyes and the world seems dim.

All my soul is alight with the Presence of HaShem. There is no time in the Presence of HaShem. Joy floods my heart forever, but also great sorrow.

I am not alone.

I will never be alone.

But I will be the loneliest man who ever walked the earth.

CHAPTER FIVE

Miryam of Nazareth

"I mma, he will come back soon. Maybe before Shabbat." Shlomi Dancefeet's voice cracks.

I shake my head. "If we are going to the feast, we must leave before Shabbat. We must leave tomorrow. Yeshua is not coming back."

My heart weeps inside me. My son Yeshua has been gone now five weeks. We have heard nothing. I am sure he is hurt. I am afraid he is dead. If he meets bandits on the road, they will not smile on his jests and become his friends, like the village elders. They will beat him and rob him and leave him bleeding.

"We cannot leave without him!" Shlomi Dancefeet says. "What if he comes back and finds us gone? He would be sad."

Little Yaakov shakes his head. "Uncle Halfai will tell him we are gone to Jerusalem for Sukkot."

Halfai is the brother of my lord Yoseph. He is firstborn, so he inherited their father's farm. Halfai always stays home for the feasts. A farmer cannot leave his farm unfarmed for a month.

We reach the village spring. It is the going out of the day, and my four sons have come with me and my daughter to fetch water. Four sons, but they are not enough. They are not Yeshua.

My daughter and I dip our waterpots in the spring. The water is fresh and cool, and we need it for the evening meal. We turn and walk down the path to the village.

My tormentors are ready for us. Two dozen women have come from the village, each with a waterpot. They grin with hate.

Between the village and the spring, the path narrows so only two can walk abreast. The women of the village wait for us there.

Little Yaakov and Yosi go through the narrows ahead of me. Thin Shimon and Yehuda Dreamhead come tight behind. We hurry past the women.

Marta, my own neighbor, spits my feet. *"Zonah."*

Rage stabs my heart. I did not ask for this life. I said yes to the Messenger, but saying yes is not the same as asking to be spit.

Old Hana the cheese-woman spits my feet. She has no teeth, and her lord is dead twenty years, but she has not forgiven me. She will never forgive me.

The other women mumble behind their hands. *"Zonah."*

It is dishonor for a man to strike a woman, so my sons do not strike the women. All they can do is walk close to me, all around. They have no honor to do more. Most of the men of our village are peasants, who own land and farm it. The men of our family are less than peasants, for we have no land. The men of our family are day laborers, finding work as HaShem provides. Our men are without honor.

All except Yeshua, who has a big honor because he is a *tsaddik*. Nothing can dishonor a *tsaddik*. If Yeshua were here, the women would not dare spit my feet and mumble *zonah.*

But Yeshua is not here, and I have no shield from the scorn of my village.

Every instant of the day, I ask HaShem to bring my Yeshua back. My son that I love more than life. For him I became an evil tale. My Yeshua, the joy of my heart.

I beg on HaShem to bring him back, but HaShem does not answer, and I am weary on it, and I am shamed that I am weary. The great women of old had a big trouble and were not weary on it. But I am not a great woman of old. I am a shamed woman, less than a peasant, less than a *zonah*.

When we reach our house, Little Yaakov's eyes are black with rage. "Tomorrow, we leave for Jerusalem, whether Yeshua has come back or whether he has not come back. If he comes to the feast, he will find us at the house we always rent."

My throat is so tight I can hardly speak. "And what if he does not come to the feast?" I lie awake every night in a big fear that my Yeshua is dead in some ravine with his bones pecked by birds.

Little Yaakov's face is set like stone. "We leave tomorrow. If Yeshua has come to harm, then HaShem will find some other man to redeem Israel."

My other sons nod, and their faces are hard like Little Yaakov's. They follow whatever he says.

"Yes, tomorrow we go," says Yosi. "Yeshua will make an army at the feast, and we will be first to join."

"The army of Yeshua and of Little Yaakov, his strong right arm!" says Thin Shimon.

Yehuda Dreamhead grins and waves an invisible sword in the air.

That is why we call him Dreamhead, because from the age of two he always lives in a world of invisibles.

My sons' women come in our house carrying the cooking pot. There are four of them now. Little Yaakov has a woman again—that *zonah* Shlomzion—the one Yeshua brought on the day we heard of Yohanan the prophet. It is not a proper marriage. No man would marry a woman who was a *zonah*. She is only a concubine, but she warms Little Yaakov in the night. She warms him well, for I hear her shouting in the dark hours. I think the whole village hears her shouting.

My son Little Yaakov ... sometimes I think the Messenger should have chosen him. Little Yaakov has the *yetzer hara* of his father David the king, a man of the sword, a man who had many women.

But I beg on HaShem that Yeshua is alive. There was never a son like my Yeshua.

Please, HaShem, bring back my son or I die.

Yeshua of Nazareth

'Shalom, stranger, you look tired.'

'Yes, I am very tired.'

'Who are you, and why do you travel alone?'

'My name is called Yeshua, and I am not alone. HaShem walks with me.'

'HaShem walks with you! Are you a prophet?'

'No, but do you not feel the Shekinah all around?'

'Only a prophet feels the Shekinah. Have you heard of that man of HaShem, that Yohanan the immerser? That man is a mighty prophet!'

'Yes, I met him many days ago.'

'Did you immerse with him?'

'Yes.'

'And he taught you to feel the Shekinah?'

'No, I asked him to tell a word from HaShem.'

'You ask much! Why would you ask a word from HaShem?'

'I wished to know who is my blood father.'

'You do not know your blood father?'

'My mother never told me.'

'Is she a zonah?'

'She is not a zonah and was never a zonah.'

'Then who is your father?'

'I ... my mother told me I am a son of Adam.'

'All men are sons of Adam.'

'And I am a son of David.'

'David had many sons, and they had many sons. Every man of Israel could be a son of David, yes?'

'There is one coming who is the true son of David, who will redeem Israel.'

'An idle tale! HaShem has deserted us.'

'HaShem will never desert us.'

'HaShem loved David, but he does not love us.'

'HaShem loves us like his own son.'

'When there were kings, HaShem loved the king and called the king his son. But that was many hundred years ago, and now we have no king. HaShem hates us.'

'There is a man HaShem calls his son.'

'You believe one is coming—'

'There is one now that HaShem calls his son.'

'A new king of Israel?'

'You say so.'

'I do not say such a big foolishness. Where is he?'

'Here with us now.'

'In this place?'

'You say so.'

'You?'

'You say so.'

'Fool, I do not say so! You say you are the king of Israel? You say you are the son of HaShem?'

'HaShem says so.'

'You? You have no king-look about you. You are shriveled as a desert carrion.'

'I should be shriveled. I spent many days in the desert.'

'Doing what in the desert?'

'Listening for the voice of HaShem.'

'Ha, you are a liar. You said you are not a prophet.'

'I am not a prophet, but I will be. I am learning the voice of HaShem.'

'But not eating at the table of HaShem, by the look of you. You are bony as a starving dog that steals from the village scrap heap!'

'I made a vow to do nothing unless HaShem tells me.'

'And HaShem told you not to eat?'

'No. But HaShem did not tell me to eat, so I did not eat.'

'You speak like one who walks beside himself. You look as you have not eaten in a week.'

'I have not eaten in many days.'

'How many days?'

'Forty.' My stomach stabs at me. I am more hungry than I ever was. If only HaShem would tell me to eat, I would fall on the ground and gnaw *the dead grass in the cracks between the rocks. I do not think I can walk all the way to Jerusalem.*

'And you call yourself king?'

My stomach tightens in a big agony. 'You say so.'

'I do not say so, fool! If you are a prophet, do the works of a prophet. Our prophet Moses made bread in the desert. If you are a prophet, make bread in the desert.'

I can smell the scent of bread baking when Shimon the baker makes rounds. It pierces my nose. I want that bread more than I ever wanted anything. 'If HaShem tells me to make bread in the desert, I will make bread in the desert. Otherwise, no.'

'When our father David the king was hungry, he took bread from the tabernacle and ate. If you are the true son of David the king, take bread from wherever you find it and eat.'

My head feels dizzy. I squat in the dust and think of home. If I were home, Imma would break off bread and dip it in a thick stew of lentils and chickpeas and onions and garlic. She would pour me a cup of good wine. She would feed me raisins and figs with her own hands.

'HaShem does not care if you take bread or no, you mad dog, you! HaShem is the King of the Universe, the king of kings of kings. He is not concerned on whether you take bread.'

My legs fail me. I fall on my side, clutching my belly. My whole body is hollow and cold. 'HaShem is ... concerned with all that I do, for he is my father and I am his son.'

'If you are the son of HaShem, then do the works of HaShem! If you are the son of HaShem, then speak to these stones and make bread of them and eat!'

I fumble for my waterskin and drink. It is the last of the water, warm and dusty and acrid. It makes me retch. I am too weak to retch.

'HaShem would not make you go hungry. Who called you the son of HaShem? Whoever said so is a liar!'

Fire floods my veins. HaShem called me his son. HaShem is no liar. All that HaShem does is good. 'In the book of the law, which Moses our prophet wrote, HaShem says this: "You must remember all the way that the Lord your God has led you these forty years in the desert so as to train you and test you, so as to know what is in your heart, whether you will obey his

commands or no. HaShem trained you and made you hungry and then fed
you the manna which you never knew, and which your fathers never knew,
so as to teach you that bread is not what makes a son of Adam live, but it
is the word of HaShem that makes a son of Adam live.'"

'*So you will starve and die, if HaShem does not command you to eat?*'

I can say no more.

'*You are more foolish than any man.*'

Perhaps I am foolish, but I will learn the voice of HaShem.

'*You are not Mashiach. You are not the king of Israel. You are not the*
son of HaShem.'

'*Leave me, you … Accuser. I know what HaShem called me. I know*
he spoke true.'

The Accuser laughs and then it is gone.

$\sim$

The sun burns hot and the wind shrieks in the rocks
above me.

Without the voice of the Accuser in my ear, I feel a little
stronger. I push myself up. Slowly, slowly, I stand. HaShem told me to
go to Jerusalem. Therefore, I am strong enough to go to Jerusalem. I
take the first step. I take the next.

On the wind, I hear the voice of the Accuser.

A cry of rage.

The Accuser will be back.

Next time, it will be stronger.

Next time, I will be stronger too.

CHAPTER SIX

Shimon of Capernaum

The boys of Jerusalem are eager to see the crucifixion.

That is a wrong thing, when boys are eager to watch a man die.

I came to watch, but not because I am eager. I came because I am wronged, and the man who wronged me is to die. I came so HaShem can make a justice on me. Torah says I must be avenged, so I came to be avenged. That is not being eager.

The evil man stumbles out of the city gate with a crossbar on his back. The governor's soldiers tied it to him with ropes. That is another wrong thing, that I will get a justice from soldiers of Rome. I wanted a justice from HaShem, not from the Great Satan.

I feel sweat on all my body. I taste bile in my throat.

My father stands on my left, sweating in the strong sun. He spits in the dust and leans on me.

My father is almost fifty years, and that is old. He should not have come, only he insisted that HaShem should make a justice on him. I beg HaShem will make a justice.

The boys of Jerusalem hoot for their glee and grab at stones in the dirt and run to meet the evil man.

The soldiers stand back and grin on the boys.

The boys throw their stones in the evil man's face.

His head jerks back. Blood springs out of his right eye.

They think that is a justice.

That is not a justice.

This would be a justice, if I got my brother back from the grave.

He was alive only last week. We had him with us. Our family was coming south to Jerusalem for the feast. We usually come by the Jordan Way, but that is a walk of six days and this year is hot. So we came by the Samaritan Road, which is a walk of five days.

The Samaritan Road is cooler and quicker than the Jordan Way, but it goes through Samaria, and Samaritans hate us.

Near the end of Samaria, we ran short of bread and beer. We stopped in a village to buy more. Samaritans are dogs and thieves, and they saw we are Jews, so they meant to cheat us. My father knows how to buy from dogs and thieves and cheats, and he kept a cool head and argued long with them.

I went around the corner from the others. I do not remember why, but I went.

The matter is hazy after that.

I know there was a fight.

I know I was knocked senseless. I am a good man in a fight, so they must have made a cheat on me. Some Samaritan must have hit me from behind.

When I came to my senses, I heard a bad wailing.

My mother, wailing.

My younger brother, wailing.

My father, wailing.

My older brother ... silent.

My older brother, Yehuda, had fallen beside me in the street, dead with a knife in his throat. Yehuda, the one we called Stonefist, dead. Yehuda Stonefist, stronger than iron, dead.

I do not know how it befell. I asked all the others, but nobody saw.

I hoped my friend Yoni saw the matter, but he says he did not. I will never know how my brother died.

Never.

We had to bury him in a pit outside the Samaritan village. We filled the pit with stones.

I walked the rest of the way on the Samaritan Road in a daze. My head hurt for two days and my eyes were cloudy and my thoughts were all a big confusion.

My pain is deeper than I know how to say.

I was always the second son. The second son is loyal to the first. Yehuda Stonefist was the oldest son. He was my brother and protector and friend. I thought I would have him always.

Now he is dead and I am the oldest, and I do not know how to be the oldest son. I am lost and broken in my heart.

I have not yet made even one tear for my brother. I do not know why. There is a thing wrong with me.

No tears.

Only rage.

The Samaritans were in a big shock to see a dead Galilean in their street. They gave up the evil man to their village elders. The village elders sent him to Jerusalem in the watch of soldiers of Samaria. The soldiers of Samaria gave him to the governor from Rome, a wicked man whose name is called Pilate. Governor Pilate heard the case this morning and gave order to flog the man and crucify him.

All the crowd shouted how that was a good justice.

That is not a justice, it is only a vengeance.

My stomach feels sour and my head hurts and my heart is numb. Vengeance will not give me back my brother.

I wish for HaShem to give me a justice.

But all I have are these soldiers of Rome, pushing the evil man toward this place where they have a stake fixed in the ground.

The evil man comes closer. Closer. Almost here.

He trips and falls on his face. He lies in the dirt, moaning.

The soldiers tear the ropes loose. They pull the crossbar off his shoulders and throw it on the ground. They rip the seams of his tunic at his shoulders and tear it off him.

The evil man lies naked on the ground. Bloody stripes cross his back from his neck to his waist where they flogged him.

The soldiers turn him on his back and drag him so his shoulders rest on the crossbar.

The evil man cries out in a big agony.

One of the boys of Jerusalem comes forward and raises his tunic and makes a piss on the evil man's face.

The soldiers grin on the boy and wait for him to be done.

I feel a heavy sickness in my heart. I hate the evil man who stole my brother from me. I should feel glad to see justice on him, but all I feel is sickness. There is a thing wrong with me. I know it is wrong not to feel glad on the matter, but all I feel is a wish to vomit.

One of the boys takes a stick and pokes at the evil man's underparts.

The evil man shouts and squirms.

That is not a justice. It is a big dishonor to have your nakedness exposed. I wish for the evil man to die quickly and make an end on the matter. But I know he will not, because the soldiers will not allow. The evil man will die slow.

One of the soldiers brings an iron spike and a wooden mallet.

The evil man sees him coming. He tries to roll away.

Four soldiers pin his arms and legs.

The one with the spike and mallet kneels beside him.

The evil man screams.

I feel a knife in my heart.

Two soldiers pull the prisoner's right arm onto the crossbar.

The evil man is an animal now—shrieking, kicking, biting, spitting, writhing.

The soldier sets the spike at the center of the prisoner's wrist.

The evil man screams like a woman.

The mallet swings down.

The spike bites deep.

The prisoner screams and screams and screams.

I feel as I will faint. There is a thing wrong in me. I should feel strong. I should feel glad. I should rejoice that HaShem is making a justice.

But I am in a deep sickness of my heart. I would run away if I could.

My father grips my arm with iron fingers. "Be strong, Shimon."

All the people shout curses on the evil man.

"Die, you Samaritan!"

"Murderer!"

"Dog!"

The soldier swings the mallet again and again.

The evil man's mouth hangs open, but no sound comes out. When a man's breath is taken away, that is a big agony.

The soldier takes another spike and goes to the left wrist.

He swings the mallet hard.

The evil man's body jerks like a fish on a gaff hook.

Black spots fill my eyes. I cannot see. I cannot think.

This is a justice HaShem is making on me. All the people say it is true. I know it is true. Only it does not feel like a justice.

I close my eyes and lean on my father. I feel my younger brother, Andre, on my right side, holding me up.

Andre says, "Shimon, are you well?"

I am not well. I am shamed, that I feel no joy in my justice.

The commander of the soldiers gives an order.

I hear the soldiers shift around.

The evil man screams more.

The soldiers all make a big grunt together.

The evil man's screams cut off.

I force my eyes open.

They have lifted the crossbar overhead.

The evil man hangs like a sack of stones. His mouth hangs open, but no sound comes out. All his body writhes in a big agony.

The soldiers carry the bar to the vertical stake and lift it up and drop it in a notch on top. One man goes around behind and lashes the bar tight to the stake.

The evil man's arms pop out of joint. His face turns red, then blue, then purple.

I hold my breath. They should let the evil man die quickly.

Two soldiers grab the prisoner's feet and push them up until his heels catch on a thin board nailed in the stake.

The evil man shoves himself up with his legs and takes a breath of air.

He screams. I thought I knew a bad screaming, but I was wrong. This is a mighty screaming.

The knife in my heart turns and turns.

My brother Andre says, "Are you strong, Shimon?"

I nod, but it is a lie.

The prisoner's upper legs seize in a big cramp. You can see the muscles tight like a board under his skin.

I have had a cramp in my lower leg, and that was a bad agony. I never had my upper leg cramp. I never had both legs cramp at the same time.

The evil man sags down until only his wrists hold him. Only the nails in his wrists. His face turns blue again.

Two soldiers twist his feet sideways against the stake. Another sets a spike at the middle of his left foot and swings the mallet.

The prisoner's head snaps up, but he has no breath to scream.

The mallet swings three more times. Each time, the stake shudders. Each time, the prisoner writhes like a snake in the fire.

When the soldier steps back, the prisoner pushes up and draws breath. He collapses before he can make a sound.

The soldiers spike the other foot.

The prisoner pushes up again. Draws breath. Screams.

This is justice.

This is not justice.

I do not know what this is.

The soldiers step back. The commander signals to the people to make a justice on the evil man.

The boys dig for more stones. They fling them on the evil man. One hits him full in the mouth. The boys shriek and jeer. "Yaw! Samaritan! Murderer!"

Two young men elbow the boys away. One swings a walking stick hard across the evil man's upper legs.

All his weight drops on his arms.

For an instant, I think the spikes will rip out, but the soldiers did their work well.

The young men back off.

The evil man pushes up again, sucking air.

The boys rush in and jab sharp sticks at his chest, his face, his armpits, his belly.

One boy smashes a fist-sized stone against the evil man's underparts.

I am angry now. I am angry on the evil man. I am angry on the soldiers. I am angry on the boys. I push forward and cuff two of them on the ears. "Stand back, children."

They spin on me, and there is a big anger in their eyes. When they see my face, they melt like wax and back away, staring on me and gibbering like monkeys.

Now is the time to make the spit of dishonor. Only I do not think I can do it.

My father and Andre come up beside me.

I feel the heat of Andre's rage. I turn to him. "You first."

Andre nods and steps forward, waiting, waiting.

The evil man hangs still for an age before pushing himself up. His eyes are wedged tight shut. His face is a skull. He breathes in little gasps, over and over. Slowly, the blue in his lips gets a little color.

Andre spits the prisoner's face.

The evil man's face snaps as he has been struck.

Andre steps back. "Now you, Shimon."

I have no breath in my chest. My throat feels dry as the Jericho Road. I reach for the waterskin at my hip and take a deep swallow of beer.

The people behind us mutter words I cannot hear.

But I know what they say. I am the kin, and here is the kinslayer, and now I should take my kin-vengeance on the kinslayer.

A hiss rises behind me.

I draw strength from them. I draw rage from them.

I step forward. I hawk my throat. I spit the evil man's face.

A great shout rises up behind me.

The boys shriek and run around the circle, hooting, scratching for more stones.

I step back, finished. I have no more spit in my mouth. Bile burns the back of my throat.

Our father steps forward and spits the Samaritan's face. He wears a grim smile.

I ask him, "Are you avenged, Abba?"

He grins on me.

I ask Andre, "Are you avenged?"

He grins on me. He looks hard on my face. His eyes turn bright as knifepoints. "Are you avenged?"

I do not know what to say.

His eyebrows rise. "Are you avenged, Shimon?"

I cannot look his eyes.

I spin away, wishing I will vomit.

They stole my brother from me. They stole my memory of the stealing of my brother.

A man cannot be avenged for a thing he does not remember.

That is why I can never be avenged.

CHAPTER SEVEN

Yaakov of Nazareth

"Yeshua!" Shlomi Dancefeet's voice shrieks from outside the house we have rented in Jerusalem. "Yeshua, I knew you would come!"

I rush outside, wondering if it can be true. We have heard nothing from Yeshua since he left Nazareth, and that was six weeks ago. We had to come to the feast without him. I knew he would find us, unless he was killed by some bandit.

Yeshua stands in the street. He is scorched by sun and wind, and he looks half-dead.

Shlomi Dancefeet wraps her arms around Yeshua and gives him many kisses.

I run to them and give Yeshua a kiss and a kiss and a kiss. "Yeshua! Are you well? Did you receive a word of HaShem from the prophet?"

"I ... heard a word of HaShem ... myself."

My mouth falls open and my heart stutters. "*You?* You heard a word of HaShem?"

He nods. Then his legs lose their strength.

Shlomi Dancefeet screams.

HaShem made me quick and strong. Before Yeshua's knees can touch the dirt, I lunge for him. I grip him in my arms. He is lighter than two sticks, and I wonder where he has been, but my heart leaps and I am full of joy. My brother is a prophet. He was always a *tsaddik*, and that is a big honor, but a prophet is more. Our family will have a great honor now, more than any family ever did. Yeshua is not fitted to be Mashiach, but he is well fitted to be a prophet. Moses was the greatest prophet that ever lived, and he had a brother to be his strong right arm and his sword.

From far up the street, Imma screams. "Yeshua!" She had gone to the market with our women to buy food for tomorrow's feast.

In an instant Imma is on us. She throws her arms around Yeshua, giving him a kiss and a kiss and a kiss.

My brothers come out of the house and crowd around us, Yosi and Thin Shimon and Yehuda Dreamhead. Our women stand back, but they are smiling. Tonight will be a night of rejoicing. We all feared Yeshua was dead.

I carry Yeshua into the house. There is a bench inside, and I sit, holding my brother in my arms.

Our brothers sit beside us. Imma and our women kneel on the floor before us.

"Yeshua heard a word from HaShem!" I feel my heart bursting in my pride. "Yeshua, tell us what HaShem told you."

Yeshua's eyes flicker open. "HaShem told me that … now I may eat bread."

I do not know how to make a sense on this. "Eat bread?"

He nods. "I fought a mighty battle with … the Accuser."

Ice surrounds my heart. That sounds like a big foolishness. Some say there is a mighty evil spirit, the prince of unclean spirits, who rules the nations. I do not know why they say so. The books of Moses say nothing on this Accuser. The prophets say nothing on this Accuser. The tale of Job tells of some accuser who is one of the sons of HaShem in the council of heaven. But the tale of Job does not say this accuser is an unclean spirit. And anyway, the tale of Job is only a tale.

"What happened when you fought the Accuser?" Shlomi Dance-feet's voice quivers, and her eyes are slits in her face.

"He told me to eat bread."

This is a very big foolishness. "The Accuser told you to eat bread? And HaShem also told you to eat bread?"

Yeshua nods. "I have not eaten bread in many weeks."

It is worse than I thought. My brother walks beside himself. His mind has a bad sickness. He must eat soon or he will die.

The women leap to their feet.

Imma shouts orders. "Break bread and dip it in wine. Give it to him in small pieces. Shlomi Dancefeet, take a *dinar* and run to buy kefir at the market. Hurry. Run, run, you goose! Run!"

My woman breaks off a piece from a round of bread.

Imma pours a bowl of good red wine.

I take the bread and dip it. "Yeshua. Take and eat."

Yeshua makes a weak grin. "Say the … blessing over bread."

I chant the words. "Blessed are you, Lord our God, King of the Universe, who brings forth bread from the earth."

His eyes are fixed on the bread. "And the blessing over wine."

Our brother Yosi chants the words. "Blessed are you, Lord our God, who creates the fruit of the vine."

I push the morsel in Yeshua's mouth.

He eats it like a wolf.

Imma hands me a stone cup of beer. "Make him drink, Little Yaakov."

I hold the cup to Yeshua's lips.

He sips.

It takes the fourth part of an hour to feed Yeshua a round of bread and half a cup of beer.

When Shlomi Dancefeet returns with the kefir, Yeshua drinks it all down in many small sips and gives her a kiss and a kiss and kiss.

"He should sleep," Imma says in that voice that says the matter is decided. "Take him upstairs."

Here in Jerusalem, houses have wooden rafters to support a second floor. I carry Yeshua up the stone stairway. Yosi takes Yeshua's cloak out of his pack, and I place Yeshua on it. Imma rolls up my cloak and puts it under Yeshua's head.

My heart burns to know more words that HaShem told Yeshua. I think HaShem should have explained the matter of who will be Mashiach.

I whisper in Yeshua's ear. "What else did HaShem tell you?"

Yeshua's eyes are closed. He makes a big smile. "HaShem said ... today I am his son and he is my father."

An iron fist squeezes my heart. Those are the words of a mighty psalm, the song of coronation of the king of Israel.

The son of HaShem is the anointed king of Israel. The son of HaShem is Mashiach.

Imma's eyes shine. "The man of HaShem said my son is to redeem Israel. Blessed be HaShem."

I am cold in all my parts. This is a wrong thing. Yeshua is a good man, a *tsaddik*, a kind man, and wise. All men love him. I love him with all that is in my heart.

And now Yeshua is a prophet, and he is well fitted to be a prophet.

But he is not fitted to be Mashiach.

He will never be fitted to be Mashiach.

This will not stand.

I will not accept.

CHAPTER EIGHT

Yoni of Capernaum

Iam going to meet my best friend in all the world, and my heart beats fast with a big gladness. Shimon does not know who is my best friend in all the world. If he did, he would call me a fool.

I tug on Shimon's hand to make him walk faster, but Shimon is lost in his grief, and he only walks slower. The Romans made a vengeance for him, but he does not seem to care.

Shimon's clan and my clan walked already from the west side of Jerusalem to the east and down into the Kidron Valley, and now we are walking up the Mount of Olives toward Bethany, the village where we are staying. I can feel the hot rage of Shimon, the same as I feel the heat of the sun.

Shimon is right to be in a rage on the matter. The Samaritan took his brother from him, and how can he have a justice? The murderer is dead, but that changes nothing. It is vengeance to trade a life for a life, but vengeance is not justice, and even Shimon knows it.

But there is a thing Shimon does not know. None of the others know. Only I know, and I will never tell. Not in many ten thousand years. All my family says I cannot keep a secret. They say I talk too much, and so I always tell what I know. It is not my fault that I talk so much. It is the way HaShem made me. But I should die before I tell this mighty secret.

I should put it out of my heart and never think on the matter, ever again.

I should think on something else.

I should think on the crucifixion.

That was a bad matter. I watched the first part, but then I went aside and vomited. A cross is a bad wickedness. Even when it makes a vengeance for us, it is a wickedness, because tomorrow it can make a vengeance on us. A cross is not justice. It is a weapon of the Great Satan.

I should think on something else.

I should think on my friend Shimon.

Shimon is a good man, but not clever. I like talking with him many hours in the night, when we fish on the Lake of Ginosar. I am the smallest man in our crew, and he is the largest, so our fathers partner us in one boat and we work. In the long hours of the night, I explain to Shimon the deep things of HaShem that I learned from the cantor in our synagogue—the village *hazzan*—who is a priest and knows Torah.

The village *hazzan* says I am a genius, and all the village says it is true, because I memorized the whole Torah already two years ago, but my father says they should not say it so much, or else I will get conceited.

I do not know why he says that. I do not know everything yet. There is a deep matter I do not understand, and that is the matter of knowing a woman.

I have asked Shimon on the matter many times. He has been a man twelve whole years and has a woman and two young sons who stayed home in Capernaum, and he knows more on the matter of women than I do, so that is why I ask him. I have been a man only a month, and my brother says I am no man yet, because I have still not got my man growth, but that is a lie. Torah says you are a man when you finish the thirteenth year of your age, and I did that, so I am a man.

But still I do not understand the matter of women, and that is why I ask Shimon about it, because he does not make a mock on me like my brother. I have five sisters, and I would die for my shame before I ever asked them. So I ask Shimon.

He knows the matter, and he explains it to the best of his power, but that is not so much. I cannot ask the village *hazzan*. He is an old man and his woman died many years ago, and I think he has forgotten what he ever knew on the matter of knowing a woman.

So I only ask the village *hazzan* about Torah. He says HaShem has given me a great gift, to be a genius in Torah, to see things in Torah that men three times my age do not see.

I think he is right, because I am clever in the matter of Torah, more clever even than the village *hazzan*. But I will never say so, because that would be a big dishonor on him, and I love him like my own father. The village *hazzan* taught me to read, and that is a mighty wonder, that small letters on a page can make thoughts in my mind. Most men of our village cannot read. My father is a priest and can read a little, but my brother cannot read at all. Shimon and his brother and father cannot read. HaShem gave me a gift, and I am glad on it.

Next year, my father will send me to Jerusalem to study Torah with one of the great sages of Israel. I hope to study with Rabbi Shammai, who is the greatest sage there ever was. We are a family of priests, and Torah is in our blood. My grandfather's brother was a sage.

All our village says I will be a great sage in Israel someday, and I think they are right. I want that more than anything. Sages are the keepers of Wisdom, and Wisdom is the Power of HaShem to mend the world. There are many broken things in the world. Torah is given to us for the healing of the world, and it is not yet healed, so there is a big room in the world for Wisdom.

The road at last levels out after our climb up the Mount of Olives.

We enter Bethany.

I look on Shimon's face again, and it is stone. Shimon is like a rock, and that is good when there is a need for strength. But it is bad when there is a need to bend. Now is a time to bend to the will of HaShem. We do not see the deep things of HaShem. We see things on the surface.

I know how Shimon's brother died, because I saw it happen, but that is a surface matter. I do not know why HaShem allowed it to happen. That is a deep thing of HaShem.

But I must not think on the matter, I must not think on the matter, I must not think on the matter.

I have been holding Shimon's hand the whole way, because he is my friend, and a friend holds your hand when you are in a big pain. It is a strong hand, rough from the fishing nets, burned by wind and sun. I wish Shimon's woman were here now. I think she would make a good comfort on him.

I look up on Shimon's hard face and squeeze his hand. "Shimon?"

He looks on me with dull eyes. "Yes, Yoni?"

"When Mashiach comes, he will make all things right, yes?"

Shimon sighs with a big sigh. "Yes."

"In the Resurrection, your brother will live again, yes?"

"Yes." Shimon's hand spasms.

I feel the pain rushing through his hand into my own. It is a hot pain, an angry pain, a deep pain. It burns my heart, but I do not let go of Shimon's hand. He is my friend, and a friend is for feeling a friend's pain.

Tears run out of Shimon's eyes.

It is good. Until now, Shimon has not made tears on the matter. Until the tears begin, a man's hurt festers inside. When the tears begin, that is when a man's hurt begins to heal.

We reach the large house of my mother's cousin, Uncle Elazar.

My clan goes inside, shouting greeting to Uncle Elazar.

Shimon's clan goes inside, shouting greeting to Uncle Elazar.

Shimon and I stand outside.

Tears run down his face now, many tears.

It is not a good time for him to be with people, and Uncle Elazar's house has all our people. I wrap Shimon's great hand in both of mine. "Shimon, walk with me a little and mourn the loss of Yehuda Stonefist."

Shimon shakes his head and bends down and gives me a kiss and a kiss and a kiss. "Better I should walk alone."

There is a strange look on his face. I never saw such a face on him.

I see a big grief. I see a big anger. I see something else, only I cannot read it.

A sick dreadness rises in my belly. I am afraid he knows more on the matter than he says. I do not know what to say. All my breath is stolen.

I must not think on the matter, but I cannot stop Shimon from thinking on the matter.

Shimon turns and walks away. There is a big weight in his steps, more than when we left the cross an hour ago under a heavy cloud of sorrow.

I beg HaShem that he will make Shimon forget the matter. I beg HaShem that Shimon will never know the truth of the matter.

I swear by The Name I will never tell. A friend does not tell a friend such a bad matter.

Shimon walks down the street to the bend and goes out of my sight.

I go in the house, shouting greeting to Uncle Elazar.

There is a receiving room just inside, but the room is empty. A door on the far side of the room leads into a large courtyard, and that is where our families are.

Uncle Elazar is a wealthy man who owns flocks and olive groves and a vineyard. His house is large, with many rooms that connect onto the courtyard. The courtyard has stone benches in the middle for sitting in the cool of the evening, and more benches in the shade for sitting in the heat of the day.

Our women stand together with the women of the house. Uncle Elazar's sisters are Aunt Marta and Aunt Miryam. They know the matter of death in this house, because of the summer fever that came through Bethany three years ago.

My heart springs up like a young lamb in the springtime, for I see my greatest friend in all the world.

She pretends not to see me.

I know she sees me, for she was not smiling when we came in, but now she smiles with a secret smile.

The men sit on the benches in the shade.

I run to sit with them.

Uncle Elazar calls to his sisters to bring us food.

Shortly, they bring it. Aunt Marta is a strong-faced woman who is a good worker and has three daughters, grown and married. Aunt Miryam is a soft-faced woman who is a good worker and has no sons or daughters.

The village calls Aunt Marta a blessed woman, because she has three daughters who lived to the age of marriage. The village calls Aunt Miryam a cursed woman, because she is barren.

I think on the matter differently. Aunt Miryam is my favorite person in all the world. She loved me with a mighty love since I was a baby. Since I was a small boy, she would answer any question I ever asked without lying, even hard questions that all the other adults made a dodge on. I call her Big Sister when we are alone. I do not know why HaShem made Aunt Miryam barren and Aunt Marta not. That is a deep thing, and the village *hazzan* has not explained the matter to me.

Aunt Marta serves us stone cups of water mixed with wine. Aunt Miryam serves us raisins and nuts and flat bread. When she gives me some, she strokes my hand and smiles on me.

I want to sing for my joy.

The women go back in the kitchen.

Already the men are talking of the weather and the harvest and the price of salted fish and the wickedness of the tax-farmers and how matters will change when Mashiach comes to throw off the Great Satan.

I stand and walk back into the receiving room and outside onto the street.

Nobody asks where I am going. Bethany sits on top of the Mount of Olives, which overlooks Jerusalem, and my family knows that I often go to look on the City of the Great King.

My heart thumps with happiness. I walk fifty paces down the street and wait.

In the heat of the day, the street of Bethany stands dusty and silent.

Shortly, Aunt Miryam slips out of the house. I knew she would. She runs toward me and throws her arms around me and kisses the top of my head. "Was it very horrible at the crucifixion, Little Brother? Are you well?"

"I am well." I always feel well with Aunt Miryam. Since I was a baby, whenever she held me on her lap, I felt that all the world was well.

She presses my face to her bosoms and kisses the top of my head again.

My face feels hot on a sudden, and my insides tingle. I do not understand what is happening. I never noticed before how large and soft Aunt Miryam's bosoms are.

"Little Brother, is something wrong?"

I do not know what to say. Nothing is wrong, but everything is different. I do not understand, but everything is different. I am finding it a hard matter to breathe.

Aunt Miryam takes my head in her hands and tilts my face up to look on her. There is a sad look in her soft eyes, but I am not thinking of the softness of her eyes.

I feel the heat of blood in my face.

"I am sorry, Little Brother." Aunt Miryam's voice is thick with a big sadness. "You are not a boy anymore. You are a man, and everything is different now, forever."

It breaks my heart to hear that. I do not wish things to be different. I wish Aunt Miryam will be my Big Sister forever. But I have entered the world of men, and she lives in the world of women, and those are worlds that do not meet.

Aunt Miryam takes my hand. "Come walk with me, Little Brother. We must talk."

My heart is stone and my throat is dry, but I squeeze her hand and walk with her.

CHAPTER NINE

Miryam of Bethany

I sit with my little Yoni on a stone terrace on the west face of the Mount of Olives. Across the valley is the City of HaShem. I come here often to admire the Temple. Tales tell that the Temple is the most beautiful building in the world, and I believe it. Tales tell that in days of old, the Presence of the living God—the Shekinah—rested in the Temple, and I believe it.

Yoni showed me a wonderful matter once. HaShem is a male, and yet Shekinah is a female word. Yoni calls this a paradox. I do not know what is a paradox, but this matter gives me a big gladness in my heart, for it means HaShem knows what it is to be a woman. If that is a paradox, I wish Yoni will show me more paradoxes.

I would give anything in the world to feel the Shekinah, to have HaShem wrap his arms around me. When I was a little girl, four or five, my father used to take me to the Temple for the afternoon sacrifices. He would put me on his shoulders, and we listened to the priests play harp and trumpet while the Levites sang psalms to the living God. I felt warm inside, safe and happy. All the world seemed good.

And sometimes I thought I felt the Shekinah. My father said it was not the Shekinah. He said only a prophet knows the Presence of HaShem. I think it was the edges of the Shekinah. I have not felt it in many years. My sister Marta would say it was only the warmth of the sun and the foolishness of a child. But I wish it was real. I wish I will feel it again.

Today, my heart is crushed, for I am losing something precious. My little Yoni has become a man, and I must explain to him why things must be different now, forever. I hate that it is so, but it is so. That is the way HaShem ordered the world. A woman cannot be a friend on a man. That will make a big scandal. It will make a shame on the woman and a dishonor on the man. Today, I must make an end on our friendship.

Yoni's eyes are deep pools of sadness. "Big Sister, why did HaShem make us this way, male and female?"

I have never lied to Yoni, and he has never lied to me. When he was in the fourth year of his age, he climbed in my lap and begged that I should always answer any question with truth. And I promised. How was I to know he would never stop asking questions? And such deep questions! I never saw such a clever boy. How can I answer him? How am I to know why HaShem made us different?

"I do not know, Little Brother. It is the way things are. HaShem commanded us to be fruitful and multiply. It is the first command-ment in Torah. He made us male and female so we could obey the commandment."

He sighs with a big sigh and stares across the Kidron Valley toward the Temple. He was always a sweet boy, and I love him. Everyone loves him, but I love him more than all the others. They see his great mind, and they love him for the mighty sage he will be someday. I see his great heart, and I love him for the kind boy he is already. But now he is a man, and no longer a boy. How can I give him up, the son I will never have?

The Temple is filled with life today. Many ten thousand men rush here and there in the outer courts, all doing the will of HaShem. Women go to the Temple, and they also do the will of HaShem, but the will of HaShem for women is different from the will of HaShem for men. I cannot fight the will of HaShem.

"Will you explain something to me, Big Sister?"

"You know I will."

"I … it is not permitted to ask."

My heart beats faster.

"But I have no one else I can ask."

Please, HaShem, let him not ask some wrong thing.

Yoni's cheeks are pink. "King Solomon said a proverb, that there is a thing he does not understand—the way of a man with a maiden."

The day is too hot and there is no breeze and I cannot breathe.

"Explain to me please what is the way of a man with a maiden."

"Little Brother, it is not fitting that I should explain the matter—"

He turns his head and looks on me with his huge brown eyes that pierce my heart.

I must be firm. I must. I shake my head. "Ask your father to explain the matter. Ask your brother. Ask Shimon. He is your good friend, yes?"

"I asked Shimon and he explained it, but he knows the matter as a man knows it. I asked him to explain it as a woman knows it, and he said that was a big foolishness, because a man is not a woman, so a man can never know it as a woman knows it. And anyway, he said there was never a man who wished to know it as a woman knows it. But that is not true, because I wish to know it."

That is why I love my little Yoni. He is not like other men. He does not think a woman is of small account. Someday he will be a great sage, maybe even a *tsaddik*. He has a great heart in him. But what am I to do? It is not fitting for a woman to speak on the matter to a man.

Yoni takes my hand in his. "In five years, or six, or seven, I will take a woman. Then I will know the matter as a man knows it. But I think my woman will be glad if I know the matter as a woman knows it, yes? I think it will give her a good happiness, yes? I wish to give my woman a good happiness, more than my own."

My heart is all in a big confusion.

Yoni looks on me, and I see his heart is pure and good.

Still he has put me in a box. If I explain the matter, then it is not fitting. If I do not explain the matter, then I have failed in my promise. *HaShem, why did you give me such a friend?*

Yoni's eyes fill with doubt. With pain.

My silence is crushing him.

I must explain the matter to him, even if it is not fitting. A promise is a promise, and I do not break a promise.

So I explain the matter as a woman knows it. If that is wrong, it is wrong, but I do not know what else I can do.

Yoni asks many questions, very naive and foolish. I do not laugh, though twice I smile and pinch his cheek. But I do not lie, and I do not leave out anything. That is part of my promise, to tell the truth, and all of it.

When I finish, Yoni's eyes shine. "Thank you, Big Sister. The matter is good, yes? HaShem made it good for a woman, and not only for a man."

"Yes, it is good. I remember many times when it was good." A gentle warmth wells up in my heart.

Then I remember the evil day, and my insides turn cold. On the day I had been married seven years, my lord told me that a woman who does not conceive by the age of twenty is barren. He said a barren woman is cursed by HaShem. He said a man must have sons, and I could not give him sons.

He said it was not a matter of his mislike, and it was not a matter of my wickedness. It was only a matter that HaShem made me barren. So he went to his writing room and wrote out a bill of divorce with his own hand and gave it to me and said I was divorced. He threw me off like an old tunic that is beyond mending. That was the most evil day that ever was.

Yoni looks across the valley to the Temple again. "Torah says Adam knew his woman and she conceived. I do not understand why you did not conceive."

All my skin is ice. He has put his finger on the boil in my heart. "It is because I am barren."

"Is it always the woman who is barren, and never the man?"

I want to run away somewhere and weep for a hundred years. But then Yoni would feel sad, and it is already a sad day. So I smile on his foolishness. He is twelve years younger than me, so of course he knows nothing on the matter. "A man cannot be barren. It is always the woman."

I do not add that some call a barren woman *zonah*. That is cruel, to call a woman *zonah* only because she is barren. I did not ask to be barren. HaShem made me barren. Why should I be called *zonah* when HaShem made me this way?

Yoni shakes his head. "I wish there were no male and female. It makes simple things hard, and it keeps friends apart who should not be apart. In the Age to Come, I do not think there will be male and female."

I do not know what to say. The Age to Come will be as HaShem says, not as Yoni says. HaShem does not follow the will of Yoni.

I lean close to Yoni and give him a kiss and a kiss and a kiss. I know it is the last time I will kiss him, forever. From now on, Yoni will live in the world of men and I will live in the world of women. It is the will of HaShem.

Blessed be HaShem.

Tears run out of my eyes.

Blessed be HaShem.

Yoni looks on me and his face is fierce. He clutches my hand. "Big Sister, you will promise me one thing, yes?"

I could never refuse anything to my little Yoni. "Yes."

"Promise me you will always be my friend, even now I am a man."

Fear squeezes my heart with a mighty squeeze. I do not know what to say. It is not done in Israel for a woman to be friend on a man. It is not done in Egypt. It is not done in Syria. It is not done in Rome. It is not done in any land in all the earth.

It is not done.

"Yes, Big Sister?"

I do not speak. Of course I cannot say yes. It is the most foolish thing in the world. Elazar and Marta would make a big scorn on me if they heard it. My lord who divorced me would call me a sinner and a shameless and a wicked. All the village would call me a seducing woman.

"Yes, Big Sister?"

Yoni's eyes shine with love. I remember when he was a little child and came to me, choosing me above all the adults. He stretched out his arms and walked past his own mother to come to me. I do not know why he chose me, but he did.

So I cannot say yes, but neither can I say no to my little Yoni.

I sigh with a big sigh. "If HaShem wills it, Little Brother."

Yoni smiles. "Then the Age to Come is upon us, yes?"

"I …" My heart wants that. My heart wants it very much.

But my mind knows it is a big wickedness, and a bad scandal will come on it.

CHAPTER TEN

Miryam of Nazareth

It is nearly four weeks since Yeshua came back to us. We had a big joy here in Jerusalem all that time. We made a great feast for Rosh HaShanah, but Yeshua did not make a move to redeem Israel. Then we made repentance during the Ten Days of Awe, but again he did not make a move. Then the high priest made atonement for Israel on Yom Kippur, but still my son delayed to make a move. Then we lived in booths on the roof of our rented house for the eight days of Sukkot, and all that time my son did not make a move. On the Shabbat after Sukkot, we rested, and of course Yeshua did not make a move on Shabbat. We have all asked him many times when he will make a move, but he says he will make a move when HaShem tells him to make a move.

Today we are leaving Jerusalem on the Jericho Road. The road is filled, for many thousand came to the feast, and they are all leaving today. My heart feels heavy with a big dread, for I cannot bear to return home.

For these four weeks, I was not once afraid on the cruel women of Nazareth. Nobody spat my feet or hissed *zonah* under her breath. It was good to feel free from the hate of our village, and now already we must go back? The time has been too short.

I walk with my son and he holds my hand tight, as I am a man and a friend. He makes a scandal by walking with a woman, but I do not care. When he is Mashiach, he can make a mighty scandal, and no one will say no.

I squeeze his hand. "Yeshua, we will go to Shlomi Dancefeet's wedding feast before you make a move, yes?"

His brothers move closer and bend their ears toward us. They are all wondering the same. Yeshua has not yet explained the matter of how he will make a move. A week and two days from today, my youngest daughter is to be married, and after that Yeshua can do all the things Mashiach must do.

Yeshua says nothing, but his face is troubled.

A cloud chills my heart, though the day is bright and the Jericho Road is hot.

Little Yaakov is the boldest of my sons, and he says, "We should raise up an army now. All these thousands are going to hear the prophet Yohanan at the Jordan on their way home from the feast. We should destroy the Great Satan at once. A wedding feast is a small thing next to that."

My heart thuds with hurt. A wedding feast is not small to the woman being wed. I do not know how Mashiach is to make a new kingdom, but if Yeshua has waited a whole month to make a move, he should wait another week until my daughter is married.

Yeshua says nothing, and his eyes turn inward.

I do not think he is hearing the voice of HaShem. But I think he is trying to hear the voice of HaShem. Trying and failing.

I clutch his hand tight, for I am desperate that HaShem will not take away all my sons to fight while my daughter is being married.

Shlomi Dancefeet seizes Yeshua's other hand. "Please, you will not make a big fight with the Great Satan before my wedding feast, yes?"

Little Yaakov scowls on Shlomi Dancefeet. "The war of HaShem is not to be delayed for a wedding feast."

All my other sons grumble their agreement.

My heart is stone inside me. I fear they are right, but I wish they are wrong.

Shlomi Dancefeet hops up and down for her anger. Tears run down her cheeks. "No! You are wrong! A wedding feast is not to be delayed for a war!"

All my insides are in a knot. I clutch Yeshua's hand so tight, I think my fingers will break.

Yeshua opens his eyes and they are troubled. "We will go to the wedding feast."

All my other sons make dark faces.

"Did HaShem tell you so, or are you afraid to make a move?" Little Yaakov asks.

"I … it is hard to hear the voice of HaShem. But I feel we should go to the wedding feast of our sister."

Little Yaakov scowls on Yeshua. "You *feel*? You will ask the prophet Yohanan on the matter, yes?"

Yeshua nods. "I will ask Yohanan for a word from HaShem."

"And if he tells you to make a move, will you make a move?"

I never saw Little Yaakov so angry. I think he will smite Yeshua right here in the Jericho Road, right now.

Yosi steps between them. He is my middle son and was always a peacemaker. We named him for my lord Yoseph, and he is well named, for there was never such a peaceable man as my lord Yoseph.

Little Yaakov puts a hand on Yosi's chest and pushes him away. "Stand aside, Yosi. This matter is between me and Yeshua."

Yosi makes a big grin on him. "With respect, this matter is between HaShem and Yeshua. We all agreed to go with Yeshua to speak with the prophet. If the prophet tells us to go to war, we will go to war, all of us. Did Yeshua ever say no to a commandment of HaShem?"

Little Yaakov swallows twice and says nothing. His face is red as a wood in a fire.

Yosi says, "And if the prophet tells us not to go to war yet, then we will not go to war, yes? Our fathers waited many hundred years for a prophet. Now we have a prophet, and we can wait a few more days until he tells us when we will smite the Great Satan."

Little Yaakov narrows his eyes. "You think the prophet will tell us not to go to war?"

Yosi shrugs. "I do not know what the prophet will say. If we knew what the prophet will say, we would not need the prophet, yes?"

I am more glad than I ever was that I have my Yosi. He is not a *tsaddik* like Yeshua. And he is not a fierce warrior like Little Yaakov. But he is not nothing, either. He is a quiet man like my lord Yoseph, and that is something.

Little Yaakov says, "What if the prophet does not say yes or no? Then what will we do? Will you hesitate like some woman, or—"

Yosi shrugs. "I never heard of a prophet who could not choose between yes and no, did you? If this prophet Yohanan will not say yes or no, then that will be a bad matter, but we should not climb that mountain unless we come to it, yes?"

Little Yaakov looks mispleased, but Thin Shimon and Yehuda Dreamhead nod their heads. Usually, they follow after anything Little Yaakov says, but it is hard to say no to Yosi when he makes a logic. That is what Yeshua calls it—a logic. I do not know why he calls it that, but I know Yosi has a good skill at making a logic.

Yosi grins on Little Yaakov.

He turns to look on Yeshua, and his grin runs away.

Yeshua stands a little apart from us all. His eyes are closed and his whole body shakes. His head tilts back, and a fierce light shines out from inside him.

Terror squeezes my heart. It is a fearful thing to see the Shekinah on a man.

My sons gather around Yeshua.

Little Yaakov's eyes bulge and his face is hard.

Yosi's mouth hangs down to his knees.

Thin Shimon wipes sweat from his forehead.

Yehuda Dreamhead seems ready to faint.

Shlomi Dancefeet puts a hand on Yeshua, then pulls back as she has touched fire. Her whole body trembles like a tree in a big storm.

We wait.

At last, the light fades from Yeshua's face. His eyelids flicker. He shakes his head and opens his eyes.

"What did HaShem say?" Shlomi Dancefeet cries out.

"I ... am not certain."

"But what do you think he said?"

Yeshua gives her a kiss and a kiss and a kiss, and his eyes shine with love. "I think HaShem will do a thing he never did before at your wedding feast."

"But you will not make a move at my feast, yes?"

"HaShem loves you."

She seizes his hands and kisses them. "You will *not* make a move at my feast, yes?"

"HaShem loves you more than even I love you."

"You are making a dodge on the matter! Did HaShem tell you to make a move?"

"HaShem's voice is faint, or else my ears are dull, but ... I think a mighty deed will be done at your feast."

Shlomi Dancefeet's face turns pale. That is any girl's worst nightmare, to be married on the day that begins the war of HaShem.

My veins are hot, and I am sweating. It is not right, but what can I say? I am only a woman, and what does a woman know of the war of HaShem? That is a matter for men to decide.

Even so, if Yeshua begins the war of HaShem on the day his sister is married, I will box his ears until he is deaf.

CHAPTER ELEVEN

Shimon of Capernaum

I stop and take a long drink of beer from my waterskin. "Yoni, slow down. Your brother is tired. My brother is tired."

Yoni looks back on the three of us. He hops up and down for his excitement, because we will see the prophet soon. "And you are tired also, yes, Shimon?"

"I did not say I was tired." I drink more beer and think how good it will be to cool my feet in the Jordan River. The day is hot and we have walked far and I am a big man, so I sweated a big sweat in the bright sun and now I need a drink of beer on account of the sweat. That is not the same as being tired.

Yoni wears a smirk. He is small and light of foot and does not sweat. Any fool can see he walks too fast for our brothers. I would slap his smug face if I could catch him.

In Jerusalem during the feast, all the talk was on this new prophet, this Yohanan the immerser. Today we will see if this man is a true prophet of HaShem. Our fathers think Yohanan is much smoke and little fire, but they agreed to let us young men come learn the truth on the matter.

I am desperate to know if Yohanan is a true prophet of HaShem. I am desperate for Mashiach to come. I am desperate for justice.

"I see them!" Yoni points toward a dull blot in the distance.

I shade my eyes and squint on the haze, but my eyes are not young as Yoni's.

We walk more, and after the fourth part of an hour, we arrive opposite the place. There is a camp on the other side of the river, just next to a dozen date palms. I see some acacia trees and many tamarisk trees and a little scrubby grass.

Many hundred men and their women and children have camped there. They all went up to Jerusalem for the feast of Sukkot, and today they all came down like we did to hear Yohanan the immerser.

This would be a good place to sell fish. I should tell the matter to Abba when we go home. We left Jerusalem this morning on the Jericho Road with our families. We walked slow on account of my mother's limp. Our families stopped next to Jericho to spend the night, and tomorrow they will take the Jordan Way north toward Capernaum. Our fathers said we young men could have two days to hear the prophet. Today and tomorrow only, and then we should go straight home.

I asked Abba what should we do if Mashiach comes.

Abba said if Mashiach comes, there will be a big war and a war needs an army and an army needs men and we are the men, so we must join Mashiach and fight the Great Satan. Otherwise, we should go home by the Jordan Way. He smirked when he said it. He does not think Mashiach will come today or tomorrow.

I wish Mashiach will come yesterday.

The river is fast and shallow at the fords, and we wade across in water that comes to our knees.

On the far side, Yoni runs a hundred paces to join a crowd of men sitting on the sandy ground under the acacia trees. There are many women too, and even children. That is a wrong thing. A prophet who tells judgment on the Great Satan will put fear even in a big man. It is no place for women and children.

Beside the river, a man sits on a large stone facing the people. He wears a tunic made of *saq*. It is the worst *saq* I ever saw. I think he wove it himself from camel's hair. The belt around his waist is the skin of some dead animal. His hair is long and ragged and hangs to his waist.

My heart thumps and my head spins. This prophet Yohanan looks like Elijah the prophet, who killed four hundred prophets of the *ba'al* in days of old. Here is a man I could follow into battle.

"When will HaShem return to Jerusalem and make a justice on the Great Satan?" shouts a man on the far side of the crowd.

I lean forward. That is the question that burns my own heart.

Yohanan has a big voice on him. "HaShem will come when HaShem will come. Now is the time for Israel to repent on her sins. A big judgment will come on Israel. You should put away idolatry. You should prepare your hearts. Judgment will come, and that means fire and destruction and death on the wicked. After that, HaShem will return and make a new covenant with the remnant of Israel, who will be saved from judgment. All Israel should repent and learn to do the works of HaShem."

My hands are damp and my face is hot. I thought this prophet came to tell judgment on the Great Satan. But he tells judgment on Israel instead.

"When will Mashiach come?" another man shouts. "Are you Mashiach?"

I wipe my hands on my tunic.

Yohanan shakes his head. "I am not Mashiach. I am the one who runs before Mashiach. I am the one who warns of judgment by the hand of the Great Satan at the end of the age. After judgment will come the age of Mashiach and the kingdom of HaShem. Then righteousness and justice will fill the earth. All the goyim and Samaritans will come to learn from Israel, as the prophets told long ago. But first comes judgment, and if you do not repent and do the works of HaShem, you will die in the fires of the Great Satan. So choose which you will have—judgment and death of this age, or repentance and life of the Age to Come."

My head aches on that. I do not wish to hear how the Great Satan will make a judgment on Israel. That is a bad news. I wish Mashiach will come and make a judgment on the Great Satan. That is a good news.

"What should we do to be saved from the judgment by the Great Satan?" shouts a man from the back.

"You should repent on your sins and do works of *zekhut*. You should take a good care on the widow and the orphan and the poor and the stranger."

I do not think that is a hard matter. My father taught me to give to the poor since I was a boy.

Beside me, Yoni jumps to his feet and shouts in his squeaky voice. "That is not a new thing! All the sons of Abraham know to give to the poor already."

I cannot breathe. Yoni is out of place. He is small for his age and looks like a boy of ten, and it is not done for a boy to challenge a man.

Yohanan's face turns dark and he scowls on Yoni. "Do not be a fool and think you are a son of Abraham and have no need to repent! If you have two tunics and see a man naked, give him one. If you have bread and see a man hungry, give him half. If you have beer and see a man thirsty, give him a drink."

That is not a good sense. I have two tunics so I can wear the one when my woman washes the other in the lake. If I give one to a naked man, what will I wear when my woman washes? Then I will go naked myself, and that is a bad sense. If I give half my bread to some hungry man, we will neither one have enough and both be hungry, and that is a bad sense. Doing *zekhut* is a good thing, but there is such a thing as too much righteousness.

"The ax is already set at the root of the tree," Yohanan shouts. "If you do not repent and do works of *zekhut*, the fire of HaShem's wrath awaits you!"

Yoni's breath hisses in his throat. Yohanan has touched his sore spot, for Yoni is terrified on the wrath of HaShem.

I do not know what Yoni ever did to fear the wrath of HaShem. I am not sure if he ever sinned. He has nothing to repent on.

Yoni falls forward on his face, gabbling in a big fear.

His brother Yaakov lays a rough hand on him and shakes him. "Yoni! Do not make a dishonor on yourself."

Yoni thinks on the prophets overmuch, that is his problem. All the village calls him the Genius of Capernaum, and that is his curse, to be a genius. When I hear the prophets read aloud, it puts a terror in my heart until the reading is over, and then I forget. But Yoni knows how to read for himself, and so he reads the prophets, and he remembers all he ever read, and then he thinks on the matter overmuch.

The prophets love to tell wrath and judgment on Israel. Jeremiah tells wrath and judgment more than all the others. In the days of Jeremiah, HaShem sent the armies of Babylon to burn our city with fire. That was the wrath of HaShem, but that is past. When HaShem comes again, his wrath will burn our enemies with fire, Babylon and Damascus and Alexandria and Rome. The smoke of their punishment will go up forever, as it did for Sodom. The wrath of HaShem is no more for us. In these last days, the wrath of HaShem should be for the Great Satan.

Yoni's voice rises higher and higher. All his body shakes with a big repentance.

I do not like the look of repentance. It makes a man look foolish. Every man has some little thing he could repent on, if he thinks hard enough. I do not think that is what HaShem wants. A man should look to the future, not the past.

The prophet Yohanan stands, and his face is like fire. "Enough talking. HaShem calls you to repent. And after you repent, you must immerse, and you will be clean for the life of the age. Who repented and wishes to immerse?"

I am a son of Israel. I do not tell lies or rob or murder or use *zonahs* for a pleasure. I did not sin. A man who did not sin does not need to make a repentance, but he still needs justice. I am desperate for justice. If I immerse, I will be clean for the day of justice that is coming.

All around us, men stand and move toward the river.

I stand. "Yoni, you have repented enough. Come immerse in the river."

Yoni stands slowly. There is still a big terror in his eyes.

Someday I should ask him why he is so afraid on the wrath of

HaShem. He is a good boy, better than I ever was. What does he have to repent on?

His brother Yaakov's cheeks glow red. When Yoni makes a big foolishness, his whole family feels the dishonor.

My brother Andre shakes his head and makes a grin behind Yoni's back. He looks as he wants to make a joke on the matter.

I give him a look like thunder. Andre always makes jokes on every kind of matter. Now is not a good time for making a joke. If he makes a joke on the matter now, I will box his ears until they come off.

Andre sees my face and hides his grin behind his hand.

We walk toward the river.

I take off the waterskin that hangs over my shoulder. I lay aside my pack that holds our food and money and my cloak. I take off my belt. I step out of my sandals.

I wait a little and watch how people immerse so I can learn how' they do it without showing their nakedness.

The prophet Yohanan chose a good place, close to the fords but deep enough so the water comes to the neck of a tall man if he goes to the center of the river. The river flows green and murky, but it is Jordan, and that counts for much.

When our fathers came out of Egypt to inherit the land, they crossed the Jordan River. To immerse in Jordan means the end of slavery. It means HaShem is with us, as in days of old, when he went before Israel in a pillar of fire.

Yoni grins. "When we come up from the water, all things will be changed, yes?"

"Yes." A big hope rises inside me. This is a new thing in Israel. It is the end of the old age and the beginning of the new. That is a fearful matter. And also the judgment to come, but I hope that is overspoken. Yohanan is a prophet, and prophets always overspeak the matter of judgment.

I step down into the river and wade out. My tunic clings to me. When I reach deep water, I fight with my tunic to pull it up over my head. I am a big man and I wear a big tunic. My face feels hot. I look down to see if my nakedness shows, but there is nothing but murky river. I hold my breath and plunge into the water, wondering what will happen.

When I come up, I do not feel any different.

I am sure I have done something wrong, so I immerse again.

When I come up, I still do not feel any different.

I immerse a third time and remain under until my lungs scream and my heart pounds and my head aches.

I burst up out of the water and suck in the sweetness of the air and the brightness of the sun.

Still I do not feel any different.

I brush the water out of my eyes and look for my friends.

Andre does not look any different.

Yaakov does not look any different.

Yoni's face is shining.

CHAPTER TWELVE

Yoni of Capernaum

I hold my breath and plunge beneath the surface. It is cold and burns like fire and shines like light. I stay under as long as I can, enjoying the cold and the fire and the light.

Heat wells up in my chest, a pillar of fire.

Fear grips my heart. What is this thing? I never saw such brightness nor felt such fire. Is it … the Shekinah? That is not possible. The Shekinah appeared to prophets of old, and to the kings of Israel, and to our fathers in the desert when HaShem gave them the covenant on Mount Sinai. But it has been many hundred years since ordinary men saw the Shekinah with their naked eyes.

If ordinary men now see and feel the Shekinah, then these are the last days, when prophets will return, and HaShem will be king of all the earth, and he will make a new covenant with Israel. All my breath is taken away. Today HaShem is returning to the land of Israel, calling his people to return from their long exile. *Today.*

My head bursts out of the water, and I shout for my joy. The Shekinah has come. Not in a visible cloud, but inside my heart. I know it is true and it is good.

It is very good.

I pull my tunic down over my body and scramble out of the river. I must talk to the others and hear what they saw.

Shimon comes up out of the water, rubbing his eyes and squinting on me.

I grin on him. "Did you feel the Shekinah?"

Shimon gives me a strange look. "Did you?"

"Yes, of course." I turn to look for the others.

My brother Yaakov comes out of the river. Yaakov is ten years older than I am—almost as old as Shimon—and he loves HaShem.

"Yaakov!" I shout. "Did you feel the Shekinah?"

Yaakov narrows his eyes on me and makes a big frown. He puts his feet in his sandals and his belt around his waist and his pack on his back and his waterskin on his shoulder.

I do not know the meaning of this.

Shimon's brother Andre has a dark look on his face, and that is strange. He wore a big grin when he went in the river. I thought he meant to make a joke on the matter.

I do not ask if he felt the Shekinah because I am sure he did not. My father says Andre makes too many jokes and HaShem is angry on him because of it.

I think Andre makes many jokes because he is the youngest and smallest son and that is his way of making a revenge on those who are bigger than him. I do not see why HaShem should be angry on him for that. Our father Jacob was also the youngest son, and he made a good joke on his brother Esau, but HaShem was not angry on him. Esau was angry on him, but that is not the same as HaShem being angry on him.

My eyes search up and down the bank of the river.

More men come out of the river. Some with happy faces. Some with puzzled faces. Some with faces that are merely wet.

I do not see any that glow with the Shekinah.

Some women come out of the river also. One of them has a face glowing with the light of the Shekinah. Her wet tunic clings to her body. She has large, round bosoms, almost as big as Aunt Miryam's.

I shake my head and turn away, but I know I will think on her bosoms for a week. I should think on something else. I should think on the matter of the Shekinah.

The prophet Yohanan comes up last out of the river. His face shines and his eyes burn with an inner fire and his great long ropes of tangled hair bristle with the Shekinah. The Shekinah is no surprise to him. He has done this many times.

I see now why people come here. Most people do not see or feel the Shekinah when they immerse. But they see the faint glow of the Shekinah on Yohanan when he immerses.

That is a wonderful sight, but it is not enough for me. I would not wish to be warmed at the embers of another man's fire. I wish to be scorched by the fire HaShem kindles in me.

I have felt the Shekinah, and that is good. But I think it is not enough. I do not wish to feel it only once and never more again. I wish to have the Shekinah with me always.

Now and forever, I want the fire of HaShem inside me.

❧

Yoni of Capernaum

In the evening, all the people bring out their food and spread their cloaks on the sandy ground and sit and eat.

We brought food in our packs, bread and cheese and olives and dates we bought in Jericho. We also have waterskins filled with beer.

The men next to us brought no food. I tell the matter to Shimon three times, and at last he says we must share with them, so we share. After we finish eating, Shimon grumbles that we will run out tomorrow, instead of having food for two days. I think that is good. Then someone will share with us.

In Capernaum, after people eat their evening meal, they gather in the village square to tell tales and sing songs and chant poems.

It is the same here. A man stands and tells the tale of how the prophet Daniel was thrown in the lions' den.

That is one of my favorite tales.

An old man stands and sings a psalm. It is a good psalm, but his voice is thin and cracked and he does not sing it well and he forgets some of the words.

I do not see how you can forget the words of a psalm.

Another man stands and tells the tale of how the sons of Israel came from Egypt and camped in this place and crossed the Jordan and burned Jericho and made a big war on the Canaanites and killed them all or chased them away.

It is a long tale, and I have heard it told better many times. Soon I am bored on it and forget to listen because I am thinking on the matter of the Shekinah.

There is a mystery here, a paradox, and I must solve it. The Shekinah was here, and yet not all men felt it. What is the meaning of that? When HaShem returns from his long exile, all men will know it. When he appears in his fullness, all men will feel the Shekinah. Why did only a few men feel it today?

That is one paradox, but there is another.

I think Aunt Miryam would have felt the Shekinah. She has told me all my life how she longs to feel the Shekinah. When she was a child, she used to feel the edges of the Shekinah. If she had come today, she would have felt it, like that woman I saw coming out of the river.

But that is a strange matter, that I saw the Shekinah on a woman. The men of my village say women are ignorant and gossips and lewd. How can someone who is ignorant and a gossip and lewd feel the Shekinah? That is not a good sense.

I think many women are ignorant, but so are many men.

I think many women are gossips, but so are many men.

I do not know if many women are lewd. I do not know any lewd women. I have seen *zonahs* in our village, but they do not look lewd to me, they look hungry. When I look on them, I feel as I am lewd. I have wrong thoughts, and then I must think on some other matter to forget them. I think when the men of our village say women are lewd, they mean that they think lewd thoughts when they look on the women. But that is not the same as the women being lewd.

Aunt Miryam is not ignorant nor a gossip nor lewd. She is good and kind and does *zekhut* all the time, even if nobody sees. Also, she is my best friend in all the world, only I cannot say so, because everyone says a man cannot be a friend on a woman.

People in my village say there is a world of men and a world of women, and women should not go in the world of men, they should stay in their own world. But that is not a good sense. If a woman does not belong in the world of men, then how can a woman be part of the world of HaShem?

In days of old, there were women who prophesied. Deborah was a prophet of HaShem who led the armies of Israel and made a big victory. Huldah was a prophet of HaShem, and we name the gates of the Temple after her.

There is a wrong thing here. The men do not see it is wrong. The women do not see it is wrong. Even Aunt Miryam does not see it is wrong. She thinks she is wicked because she is my friend. I do not think she is wicked.

That is a big paradox, that women can be part of the world of HaShem, but they cannot come in the world of men, and nobody says no to it. Why does nobody say no to it?

So now I have two paradoxes.

The evening passes and the tales end, and I do not solve my paradoxes.

All the people roll up in their cloaks and lie down on the ground and sleep.

I lie on the ground, rolled up in my cloak, staring on the sky and listening to the snores of Yaakov and Shimon and Andre, and trying to make a sense on my paradoxes.

I think HaShem is doing a new thing. HaShem never spoke to all men the same. In times past, he chose certain men and not others.

When Israel was young, HaShem spoke to men he chose, thick-tongued men like Moses, or wild men like Samson, or mighty warriors like Yiftakh, who was the son of a *zonah*. HaShem also spoke to women he chose, Deborah and Huldah and Miryam the sister of Moses.

When Israel grew old, HaShem spoke only to prophets and priests and kings and other men of a big renown.

When the new age comes, HaShem will do a new thing. When he brings Israel out of her long exile and makes her young again, all will see the Shekinah. All men and all women, the same. There will be no world of men and world of women. There will be only the world of HaShem. And I will not have to hide that my best friend is a woman.

But the kingdom of HaShem is not yet. Now, at the in-breaking of the kingdom, HaShem shows himself only to those with Wisdom. That is why he shows himself to Yohanan the immerser. That is why he shows himself to me, even though I am hardly more than a boy. That is why he shows himself to that woman I saw with the large bosoms. Also, in the kingdom of HaShem, I will look on women with large bosoms and not think lewd thoughts.

The kingdom is in-breaking, but it is not yet. That is why I can see the Shekinah, even if I sometimes think lewd thoughts.

That is the meaning of the paradox. Both paradoxes.

I feel glad in my heart that I solved two paradoxes in one day. That is why the village *hazzan* calls me the Genius of Capernaum.

I think HaShem will be pleased I have solved my paradoxes.

I think Mashiach will be glad of having my help to solve his paradoxes.

I think I will have a special place in the kingdom of HaShem when he comes in power.

CHAPTER THIRTEEN

Yeshua of Nazareth

"You will not really begin the war of HaShem at my wedding feast, will you?" My sister clutches my hand, and there are tears in her voice.

We stayed last night in Jericho and this morning we are walking toward the place where Yohanan the prophet immerses people. My brothers are in a fever to get there, but our women walk under a cloud of sadness.

I stop walking and turn to face Shlomi Dancefeet. "Do you think HaShem is concerned on your wedding feast more than rescuing his children who suffer?"

Tears well up in her eyes. "Do you think HaShem is concerned on killing evil men more than the joy of his children who love him?"

I hear my brothers muttering behind their hands. They think HaShem is eager on the matter of killing evil men, and they are glad on it.

Imma wears a hard look on her face. She fears my brothers are right, and she is angry on it.

There is nothing in me to love killing evil men, but I must not say so. My brothers already think I am a scandal, unfit to be Mashiach. I can read it in their eyes, and my ears are sharp to their grumbling words.

They are right. I am a scandal. I am unfit to be Mashiach. If HaShem wishes me to redeem Israel, he will have to make a miracle. He will have to give me a rage on evil men, more rage than he gave Little Yaakov. That will be a big rage.

I do not know what HaShem will do at the wedding feast of my sister, but I am sure he will do something. I have only just begun to hear the voice of HaShem, faint whispers in my mind. I do not know how to be Mashiach. The scriptures do not explain the matter. That is why I wish to speak with Yohanan the prophet—to ask for a word from HaShem, how I should be Mashiach when I have no wish to kill evil men.

HaShem does not call a man to do a thing without explaining the matter.

Here is the mighty question that has tormented me long. Every son of Israel knows Mashiach will destroy the Great Satan and bring a fiery judgment on earth and kill many evil men. Mashiach will be sent by HaShem to do these things. Yet I do not think HaShem takes a delight in killing evil men. How is it that HaShem will send a man to do a thing HaShem hates?

That question is a knife in my mind that I cannot shake loose. I am desperate to know the answer.

Shlomi Dancefeet clutches my hands to her lips and kisses them. "Promise me you will not make a big war on the day I am married."

I give Shlomi Dancefeet a kiss and a kiss and a kiss. "Trust in HaShem and see what he will do at your wedding feast. It may be that he will give you a great gift, and men will tell the tale of HaShem's kindness for a hundred years to come."

Shlomi's eyes shine with a big delight. "What … what will HaShem do at my wedding feast?"

I shrug my shoulders, because I do not know what HaShem will do.

But I trust HaShem to make a most wonderful scandal.

~

Miryam of Nazareth

"There is the prophet!" Little Yaakov points down the river.

I squint my eyes, but all I see is a blur of something on the other side, many hundred paces down the river.

Little Yaakov and Yosi and Thin Shimon and Yehuda Dreamhead all hurry ahead to see the great sight. Little Yaakov's concubine hurries after them. Yehuda Dreamhead's woman hurries after them. Shlomi Dancefeet hurries after them.

Yeshua does not hurry after them. He stays with me, walking at my pace, the pace of an old woman.

My throat feels tight and I think I will cry and I cannot walk even one more step.

"Imma." Yeshua wraps arms around me and gives me a kiss and a kiss and a kiss.

All my body shakes for my fear.

"Imma."

My knees give way beneath me.

"Imma." Yeshua scoops me up in his arms as I am a small child. He rocks me in his arms. He sighs deep.

Tears leak out of my eyes and run down my cheeks.

My son kisses each one.

At last all the tears in my head have come out.

"You are afraid," he says.

I nod my head.

"What do you fear?"

I do not know how to explain the matter. "The prophet will tell you how to make a big war. You will go away from me to fight the Great Satan. You will take away all my sons. You will take away Uncle Halfai. You will take away your cousin, Fat Shimon."

Yeshua says nothing. I feel the great thud of his heart in his chest.

"The village hates me. They will come to kill me, and no one will defend."

"What do you wish me to do?"

"I wish you will make a justice on me."

"How should I make a justice on you?"

"You should make HaShem punish the village."

"Punish them how?"

"In olden times, prophets called down fire from heaven to punish evil men. You should call down fire on them. You should burn their houses. You should burn their lips that make me an evil tale. You should burn their hands that throw evil on me. You should burn their feet that run to do evil on me."

Yeshua sighs long. "Imma, I do not know how to do any of those things."

"If you love me, you will make a justice."

"Imma, I love you."

"Then make a justice on me and take away my shame."

Yeshua says nothing.

His whole body shakes.

My son is crying for me. Crying, but nothing more.

My son will do nothing to make a justice on me.

Nothing.

~

Yeshua of Nazareth

My heart is heavy when we arrive at the camp where the prophet Yohanan tells repentance. Many hundred people are gathered around him, listening.

Shlomi Dancefeet holds tight to my hand. "There are women here listening to the prophet!"

Little Yaakov makes a big scowl. "It is men's work to hear the words of the prophet."

"You will not make a big war before my wedding feast, yes?" Shlomi Dancefeet wraps her arms around me.

I give her a kiss and a kiss and a kiss. "I will do what HaShem tells me."

Her body quivers. "What does HaShem tell you?"

I do not know what to say. The voice of HaShem is faint in my mind, like a shadow of a whisper of a thought. I am like a newborn babe in the ways of a prophet. "I will ask Yohanan what HaShem says."

Little Yaakov tugs on my elbow. "Send the women away to do their womanish things."

Imma's face turns dark, and I think she wishes to box Little Yaakov's ears. She tugs on the arms of my sister and the other women. "We should find a place where we will sleep tonight. I do not wish to hear talk of a big war."

Our women walk toward the far edge of the camp.

Little Yaakov and my brothers pull me toward the crowd of people. Many hundred sit in rows on the ground, listening to the prophet Yohanan.

We sit at the edge.

Yohanan tells repentance to Israel.

I wish he will tell me a word from HaShem. I am desperate to know how I am to redeem Israel. Everyone knows Mashiach must come and smite our enemies and make an end on this age and a beginning on the new age of the kingdom of HaShem. I want the kingdom of HaShem more than anything.

But I do not wish to smite our enemies. There is nothing in me to smite an enemy. If I must smite our enemies to redeem Israel ... I will be the worst Mashiach that ever was.

I feel the Shekinah all around me, a pillar of fire.

I am before the Throne.

HaShem smiles on me.

For a time, I know nothing but the joy of HaShem.

I do not know how long I rest before the Throne. It could be an instant. It could be many ten thousand years. There is no time in the Presence of HaShem.

I wait for HaShem to speak, but I hear nothing.

The vision fades. The sun hangs lower in the sky. I am sitting with my brothers among many hundred people.

Yohanan the prophet shouts and shouts.

I never heard such a great voice on a man, but my ears are dull from the vision of the Throne, and Yohanan's words thud on me like rocks on sand.

Men stand up all around us.

Little Yaakov stands. Yosi and Thin Shimon and Yehuda Dream-head stand.

I sit like a stone, immovable, wishing to return to the Throne.

"Yeshua, what do you wait for? The prophet Yohanan calls us to immerse." Little Yaakov extends his hand.

I take it, but my fingers feel like wood.

He pulls me to my feet.

My knees wobble for a moment, then hold. At last I feel fully returned, and the Throne is a cold memory. I am more lonely than I ever was.

We move toward the river. Toward Yohanan.

People throw off their packs, their belts, their sandals.

I continue toward Yohanan.

"Yeshua, you should immerse first, so you will be clean before you speak to the prophet." Little Yaakov seizes my elbow.

I continue toward Yohanan.

"Yeshua, you should wait for us to immerse, so we will be clean."

I push my way toward Yohanan. I need a word from HaShem now. A vision of the Throne is not enough. I must know the word of HaShem.

"Yeshua, the prophet is looking on you!"

Yohanan is doing more than looking on me. His eyes glow. The Shekinah is on him. I beg that HaShem will speak a clear word to him.

Yohanan moves toward me.

I move toward him.

He reaches me. "You! You came here many weeks ago. A *tsaddik* and a son of David. You asked for a word from HaShem. Then you immersed and went away. I have been much troubled since I saw you last."

"I have been much troubled also."

"You have been in the Shekinah."

"I have been learning to hear the word of HaShem."

He waits patiently, as he expects me to tell what I heard.

I say, "It is hard for me to hear a word of HaShem. I need a word of HaShem from you."

"What is your name?"

"My name is called Yeshua from Nazareth, and here are my brothers. Here is my strong right arm, Little Yaakov."

Yohanan grins on him, for Little Yaakov is a big man, and very strong.

"And here is Yosi, and here is Thin Shimon, and here is Yehuda Dreamhead."

Yohanan gives a strong right hand to each of them. "Five brothers, each a mighty hammer to smite the enemies of HaShem. Like the five Makkabi brothers."

My brothers grin on him. I never saw them so happy, that a prophet should call them after the Makkabi heroes who saved our nation.

Yohanan starts to speak, but then his eyes turn inward, and he tilts his head. His mouth hangs open for long, as he is frozen in his place.

When he is done listening, he stares on me with a strange, wild look in his eyes. "I have a word from HaShem for you."

My heart leaps within me. I need a word from HaShem. I am desperate for a word from HaShem. I am terrified of a word from HaShem, for I do not wish to smite our enemies, and I know that is what HaShem will demand.

"There are four Powers you must smite." Yohanan thumps his fist in his open palm four times. "You will smite them with the help of your four brothers maybe, yes?"

My knees are like water beneath me and I think I will fall over. "Who ... who are the four Powers?"

My brothers press in, and I feel their excitement all around me like the still before the storm.

Yohanan says nothing.

"Who are the four Powers?" I fear my heart will destroy itself in my chest for all its beating like a mighty hammer.

"The King of the South," Yehuda Dreamhead says.

"The King of the East," Yosi says.

"The King of the North," Thin Shimon says.

"The Great Satan," Little Yaakov says.

I shake my head. I do not wish to smite even one of these mighty enemies, much less all four of them. But Yohanan did not say the four Powers were Egypt and Babylon and Syria and Rome, and there is a look in his eye that says these enemies are nothing. I seize his arm. "Who are the four Powers?"

Yohanan shakes his head. "Do not be hasty to know the four Powers, Yeshua from Nazareth, son of David. HaShem will reveal them to you as you have strength. He will show you the first Power, and you must destroy it or be killed. He will show you the second Power, and you must destroy it or be killed. He will show you the third Power, and you must destroy it or be killed."

I wait.

"HaShem will show you the fourth Power, and you must destroy it."

A terrible silence falls all around us.

"Or be k-killed?" Yosi's voice squeaks.

The prophet Yohanan's face is a mask of stone. "Destroy the fourth Power, Yeshua from Nazareth, son of David. If you can."

CHAPTER FOURTEEN

Yoni of Capernaum

In the morning when I wake up, I wonder if I really felt the Shekinah. Yesterday seems like an ancient tale. I am afraid it was all a dream and nothing more.

We spend the morning listening to the prophet Yohanan.

Shimon and Yaakov and Andre all say Yohanan is a true prophet of HaShem.

I believe Yohanan is a true prophet of HaShem, but I wish for more than a prophet of HaShem.

I wish HaShem will return soon.

And before HaShem returns, he will send a man ahead of him to destroy our enemies. A son of David—Mashiach—who will rise up and make a big war on the Great Satan. Mashiach will lead the armies of Israel against the armies of Rome and throw down Caesar, and that will be the end of the age of the Great Satan and the beginning of the age of the kingdom of HaShem.

But there is a part of me that is afraid Mashiach will come too soon. I am a man now, but people sneer on me and say I am still a boy because I have not got my man growth yet. My brother Yaakov never got his man growth until he was seventeen. I am only thirteen. If I have to wait four years to get my man growth, Mashiach will come and fight the big war and throw off the Great Satan. Then all his armies will get a big glory, and I will not be part of it because I am too small to fight. That would be the worst thing in the world, to miss fighting in Mashiach's war because I was born a few years too late.

That is not fair.

I have complained on it to Shimon, and he says I should be patient, because HaShem will give me my man growth when HaShem decides to give me my man growth.

I have complained on it to Yaakov, and he says I should learn to wrestle, because that will make my muscles big and strong like a man's. Only he refuses to teach me to wrestle, because I am too small, and he is afraid he will break all my bones. But how will I learn if he will not teach?

I complained on it once to Andre, and he told me the secret to getting your man growth is to drink a whole skin of wine before going to the synagogue on Shabbat. I tried it, but I could drink only half the skin. Then I walked in the synagogue and threw up on the floor and fell down senseless in my own vomit.

All the village said Andre made a good joke on me.

I did not think it was a good joke.

Now I am wary on Andre and his jokes.

In early afternoon, the prophet Yohanan finishes speaking and goes away to his cave to eat food. I heard he eats nothing but wild honey and locusts. No wonder he looks angry all the time.

But we have no food, because we ate the last of it this morning.

"We should go back to Jericho and buy food," says Yaakov.

Shimon shakes his head. "I heard there is a small village on this side of the river, just north of here. We can get bread and cheese and beer. Yaakov, you and I will take empty packs to carry the food. Yoni and Andre, stay here and watch all our cloaks."

It makes me angry on him when he treats me like a small boy who is good for nothing except to watch the cloaks, but there is nothing I can do because Shimon is the oldest and so he should decide.

Shimon and Yaakov walk away toward the village.

I kick the dirt and scowl on them. They will buy food in the village and eat their fill, and Andre and I will have to wait.

Andre grins and sits by the cloaks under an acacia tree. "Tell me a tale while we wait, Yoni. You tell the best tales in all Capernaum."

"What tale should I tell?"

"Tell the tale of Samson and the *zonah* and the foxes."

I grin on him, for that is one of my best tales. But I want something for my efforts. "I will tell you that tale, but first you must teach me how to wrestle. Yaakov refuses to teach me."

Andre shrugs. "You are too small. See, your arms are so thin, they would break like twigs if I threw you down. Before you learn to wrestle, you should learn how to fall without being hurt."

"So teach me to fall."

He shrugs again. "Before you learn to fall, you should learn to make a bridge, so your neck will be strong. Your neck is thin as my finger."

"So teach me to make a bridge."

Andre narrows his eyes and studies me long. "I think you are too lazy to learn wrestling. It comes from being a genius. You read a passage of Torah once and you remember it forever, and you think everything should be so easy. Learning to wrestle is not so easy."

"Teach me!" I hate how he is making a dodge on the matter, and I will not stand for it. If Mashiach comes and I do not even know how to wrestle, I will be left home with the women.

"If I teach you the first lesson, how many times will you repeat?"

"Three times!"

He shakes his head. "That is a big foolishness. You are lazy, and why should I teach a slug?"

"Ten times!"

Andre scowls on me. "You think I am a fool and a simple? When my brothers taught me to wrestle, they made me repeat fifty times, until my whole body was bruised. Come back when you are ready to wear a few bruises. Until then, no."

"If you did it fifty times, I will do it a hundred! Now teach me!"

Andre looks on me as he does not believe me. "Do you swear you will repeat a hundred times? I do not wish to waste my time teaching a lazy boy. If the village sees you are a bad wrestler, they will make a blame on me for teaching you wrong."

"I will repeat a hundred times."

"Swear it by The Name."

I think for a moment. To swear by The Name is a fearful matter. If I swear by The Name and then fall short of the hundred …

Andre shakes his head and leans back and closes his eyes. "I wish to take a nap. Ask me again when you get your man growth."

"I swear by The Name I will repeat what you teach me a hundred times!"

Andre's eyes pop open. He grins on me for a moment. He stands and walks to a small patch of dried grass. "I will teach you to make a bridge. That is the first matter a wrestler must learn, so his neck will be strong."

He lies on his back on the grass and raises his knees so his feet are flat on the ground. Then he raises his lower back so only his head and shoulders and feet touch the ground. "See, Yoni, here is the start of the bridge. You can do this, yes?"

"That does not look so hard."

"I did not say it is hard. If you hold like this, your back will be strong, and that is good, but it is not enough. Your neck will still be nothing. Now here is how to make the whole bridge." Andre puts his hands beside his head and pushes back with his legs. His neck and shoulders rise up off the ground, and his whole body makes a backward arch. Only his feet and his head and his hands touch the ground.

"That still does not look so hard."

"We will see if it is hard when you do it yourself, instead of looking on me doing it." Andre brings his shoulders back to touch the ground. "There, that is once with the bridge. Now you do it once, and we will see if it is hard."

Andre stands, and I lie on the grass. I raise my lower back to the start of the bridge. Then I push back with my legs to make the backward arch. I feel the force of it in my neck.

"Hold there to the count of five," Andre says.

I hold to the count of five.

"Now back to the start of the bridge," Andre says.

I lower myself back to the start of the bridge.

"That is once on the bridge, and you did it well. Better than I thought you would. It is good you did it on the soft grass, because you are soft like a woman."

I scowl on Andre. "What do you mean, I am soft like a woman?"

"I mean you are soft like a woman. A real wrestler fights on bare dirt, but that will be for some other day. Today you should do it on grass until you are not so soft."

"Who said I am soft? I did not ask you to teach me to wrestle like a woman. I wish to wrestle like a man. When the war comes, Mashiach's men will not fight on soft grass. I should do it on bare dirt."

Andre shakes his head. "Do not make a blame on me that you are soft. I say you should do it only on the grass."

I leap up and kick the grass. "You said you would teach me! So teach me, and do not treat me like some woman."

Andre paces back and forth. "It will be a bad matter if you wear down your soft body on hard ground and cannot walk for three days for your soreness. Your brother will be angry on me. Shimon will make a blame—"

"I will do it on bare dirt like a real wrestler!" I shout on him. "I swore by The Name, and I will do it! If I am sore, then let Shimon make a blame on me."

Andre sighs and looks all around. "Over there is a good place. Help me bring the cloaks with us."

We walk a hundred paces away from the camp to a spot where there is no grass nor thorns nor bushes. The ground here has soft dirt, but also many stones.

Andre picks out all the small stones and sticks and stubble. "It is not a real arena, but it is enough to practice making a bridge. Yaakov will be jealous when he comes back and sees you already know the first lesson, even though he never taught you."

I lie in the dirt and make the start of the bridge. I push up and backward and hold myself in an arch to the count of five. Then I come back to the start.

Andre grins on me. "That was well done, Yoni! I think you do it better already than Yaakov ever did. His back is so thick he can hardly make an arch, but you make a big arch that a wild dog could run under."

I grin on him. Yaakov never says I do a thing well. Neither does my father. That is why I like Andre, because when I do a thing well, he says so.

Andre says, "That was one time. I will sit in the shade and make a count until you fill up the rest of the hundred. Only do not be lazy and make a cheat, because I will be watching."

I am more happy than I ever was.

I make a big arch and then come down to the dirt again. "Two!"

I make another arch and come down to the dirt again. "Three!"

After ten times, it is not so easy.

After twenty times, I see why Andre says it is hard.

After fifty times, my arms and back and neck are very tired, but I refuse to stop, because I swore by The Name.

After seventy times, I am more weary than I ever was, but I do not stop.

After eighty times, I think I will vomit, but I do not stop.

After ninety times, I am sweating with a big sweat and my tunic is wet all through, but I do not stop.

After I finish the hundredth time, Andre shouts with a big shout. "That was well done, Yoni! I never saw anyone make such a good bridge. If they had a competition on making bridges at Olympia, you would win the olive crown. Yaakov will be angry that you know so much already."

I grin on him and stand up slow. All my body feels weak and sore. My arms never hurt so much. My legs feel as they will make a big cramp. My neck feels as it is on fire. But I will make a big shock on Yaakov when he sees what I have learned already. Now he cannot make a dodge on me anymore. He will have to teach me the next lesson. Or else Andre will, or Shimon.

Andre stands and grins on me. "I did not think you would do it, Yoni. You are not a boy anymore. You are a man."

We take up the cloaks and walk back to the camp, grinning.

Shimon and Yaakov are not back yet, but there are still many hundred men of Israel sitting in the shade of the trees, and many women and some children.

As we get closer, a man sees us and makes a big grin.

He nudges his woman and juts his chin toward us, and his woman makes a big grin.

More men look on us and make a big grin and nudge their women.

Then more.

Then all the men look on us and make a big grin, and their women too, and their children.

Then all the people are laughing.

I do not see what is funny.

When we get close, one of the men shouts, "Did you catch the pig, boy?"

I do not know what they mean by a pig.

Then I see Andre laughing.

He falls to his knees, slapping the ground, roaring with a big laughter.

A drop of mud rolls down my face.

I touch my hair to see where it came from.

All my head is covered in mud.

All my hands are covered in mud.

The front of my tunic is covered in thin mud.

The back of my tunic is covered in thick mud.

And now I see the evil joke Andre played on me.

I sweated a big sweat in the hot sun. The sweat and the dust made mud. All my tunic is a big mud. My arms and feet and hair and face are a big mud. And I never noticed because all my thoughts were on completing the hundred. That is why they call me a genius, because I can put all my thoughts on one thing and forget all the rest of the world.

Andre shrieks and howls for his laughter.

All the men shriek and howl for their laughter. All the women shriek and howl. All the children.

When Shimon and Yaakov come back, they will shriek and howl for their laughter.

It is not a good joke.

While I stand there wishing I will shrink into a small ant and run away, I see Yohanan the immerser coming back.

He takes his seat and begins telling repentance to Israel.

All the men stop their laughing and listen to the prophet.

I make a big scowl on Andre and sit and think how I will make a revenge on him.

I keep looking toward the village where Shimon and Yaakov went, but they are taking long to return. I hope Yohanan will tell us to immerse before they get back. Then I can go in the river and immerse and wash off the mud and pretend I never made myself filthy as a pig.

Yohanan speaks long, and still Shimon and Yaakov have not returned.

My stomach complains on me for my hunger, but I hope Shimon and Yaakov will be slow.

More people come to hear the prophet Yohanan, and more and more. Yohanan talks and talks and talks and the afternoon wears away and still Shimon and Yaakov have not returned.

At last, Yohanan shouts all the men to make a repentance and then immerse in the river.

I already made a repentance yesterday, so I jump to my feet and walk fast toward the river.

Andre walks close behind me. "I thought you repented yesterday."

I walk faster. "It does no harm to repent a second time. You should try it the first time."

"I repented yesterday and I am clean," Andre says.

"Perhaps you have a new thing to repent on today."

We reach the river's edge.

Andre makes a big grin and does not go down in the river.

I go down in the river and immerse myself. The river is cold and dirty, but it washes off the mud from out of my face and my hair. I would take off my tunic, but my arms are too tired from the hundred times. My whole body aches. I feel heavy as a stone.

I try to scrub a small spot on the front of my tunic, but it will not get clean. And the back of my tunic must be worse. Now I have made a big trouble for myself. I do not know how to make a tunic clean.

That is women's work, and I never learned it. I am afraid the mud will never come out. Imma will make a big rage on me when she sees it. Abba will beat me for ruining a good tunic.

When I come out of the river, Andre grins on me. "You were not long in the water. That was a fast repentance."

He is a fool who does not even understand the matter of repentance and immersing. Immersing is not repentance. You repent first and purify your heart. Then you immerse after and purify your body. I understand the difference and Andre does not, but still I am the one with the muddy tunic. That is not fair.

My eyes fall on five men talking with Yohanan the immerser. One is a man with strong arms and a thin, pinched face and a deep wisdom in his eyes. I think he has been fasting much, to have such eyes. I think he is a *tsaddik*. I think I see the scorch marks of the Shekinah on him.

Yohanan is telling some matter to the five men. Their faces turn pale. Perhaps he is telling the wrath of HaShem on them.

I move closer to hear what they say.

"… or be k-killed?" says one of the men to Yohanan.

The look on Yohanan's face freezes my blood. He puts both hands on the shoulders of the *tsaddik*. "Destroy the fourth Power, Yeshua from Nazareth, son of David. If you can."

My knees are like water when I hear the fear in Yohanan's voice. What is this fourth Power he speaks on? It sounds more mighty than any army of men. I come closer and peer on the face of this man, Yeshua from Nazareth. The prophet called him son of David! My heart jumps to double speed. But Yeshua from Nazareth does not have the look of a warrior. If I passed him in the street and did not look on his face, I would think he was no different from any son of Adam. His shoulders are strong and his arms thick and his hands calloused.

But when I look on his face, I see the Shekinah glowing inside him.

Inside him.

I never saw the Shekinah inside a man before. I saw the Shekinah on people, but not inside them.

All my breath feels as it is stolen from me.

Yohanan the immerser sees me staring. He points to Yeshua. "See, here is a man who is a lamb of the very heart of HaShem!"

I think he underspeaks the matter. Yeshua from Nazareth looks quiet and peaceful. But it is not only lambs that are quiet and peaceful. Lions are also quiet and peaceful when they are not on the hunt. I think it will take a man who is a lion of the heart of HaShem to destroy this fourth Power, whatever that is.

All at once, I feel a burning in my heart to know what is the fourth Power, and the third, and the second, and the first. I am dying to know what sort of man should be sent to destroy these Powers.

And I want to know what sort of man is sent to do a thing that terrifies Yohanan the immerser, who is a mighty prophet of HaShem.

Who is this Yeshua from Nazareth? Why did the prophet call him son of David, unless he means ...

All my skin feels as it is poked with many ten thousand needles.

Yohanan looks all around at the many hundred people who are immersing, and his face shows that he had forgotten them. He spins in a big haste and goes down in the water.

I stare on Yeshua from Nazareth. I think there is a mighty thing here.

I step closer to the five men, for I wish to speak with Yeshua from Nazareth. His face is raw with sun and wind, and his tunic is torn and stained. I think he has been traveling long in the desert. When he looks on me, his eyes glow.

I feel my heart leap like a lamb in springtime. This man has been many days with the Shekinah. His skin is scorched by the sun, but his soul is scorched by HaShem.

He smiles a big smile on me. "My name is called Yeshua." He has a strong voice, and it warms me when I hear it.

"My name is called Yoni." I do not tell him I am the Genius of Capernaum. If I say so, he will think I am conceited. Anyway, he will find out soon enough.

I point to Andre. "My friend's name is called Andre."

Yeshua studies me and he studies Andre. "You have come here to meet HaShem, yes?"

I think he sees I have been in the Shekinah. I wish to know what it means to be the lamb of HaShem's heart. But I do not know how to say so.

I ask, "Where did you come from?" It is a foolish question, but this moment I do not feel like the Genius of Capernaum.

He grins on me. "Nazareth."

I already knew that, but I see in his eyes that he knows I ask where has he been traveling, to be so scorched by sun and wind and Shekinah. He makes a test on me, to see if I can read his eyes. I do not care where he was born and where he has lived. This man has been with HaShem. That is what I care about. He is a *tsaddik*, a holy man of Israel.

But he is more than a *tsaddik*. I think he is a teacher of men—a rabbi—for there is Wisdom in his eyes, and rabbis are the wisest of men. I wish to be a rabbi someday, if HaShem wills it. But first, I must find one to teach me, one who knows more than the village *hazzan*.

"Rabbi, where are you staying?" I think Shimon and Yaakov will wish to meet this man.

Rabbi Yeshua smiles again. "Come and see."

CHAPTER FIFTEEN

Yoni of Capernaum

The men with Rabbi Yeshua are his brothers. His whole family has a place at the far edge of the camp in the thin shade of a large tamarisk tree.

Rabbi Yeshua's mother is there, and three other women. The youngest wears a virgin's veil over her face. She has beautiful eyes. Her mother tells me proudly that she is to be married soon, for she has reached her thirteenth year.

I am glad men do not marry when they are thirteen, for I do not feel ready to take a woman. I do not understand why women marry when they are only thirteen, if it is true they are full of foolishness, as the village *hazzan* says. If men are wiser and more mature, why do they wait until they are eighteen or even twenty before they marry?

Andre and I sit on the ground with the family of Rabbi Yeshua. Nobody asks why my tunic is muddy like a boy who wrestles with a pig.

I ask Rabbi Yeshua on the matter of the four Powers.

His face turns hard. He tells me all the words Yohanan the immerser told him.

I ask if he is really a son of David.

His eyes are more fierce than I ever saw. He says he is son of Yoseph the *tsaddik*, son of Yaakov Mega, son of David.

I ask him when is the kingdom of HaShem to come in, and why Yohanan the immerser says there will be a judgment on Israel first by the hand of the Great Satan. He thinks long and says that is a hard matter to understand. Then I see Shimon and Yaakov returning with food at last.

Andre goes to fetch them.

I stay with Rabbi Yeshua. I do not wish to lose sight of him until I understand the matter of the Shekinah. I know in my heart that Rabbi Yeshua sees the deep things of HaShem. He has the eyes of a man who sees more than other men. Rabbi Yeshua looks on me now, measuring my wisdom. I do not need to tell him I hope to be a great sage in Israel. He sees it is so, and I see that he sees.

"You have felt the Shekinah?" Rabbi Yeshua says.

"When I immersed yesterday."

"Where do you come from?"

"Capernaum." I show him my rough hands. "We are fish-men. Next year I will live in Jerusalem and study Torah with a great sage of Israel. My family are priests, and my grandfather's brother was a sage, one of the Forty Heroes."

Rabbi Yeshua looks deep in my eyes. "I see you love Torah."

I think I never saw so much Torah as I see in his eyes. I do not understand how Torah can be in a man's eyes, but I know it is so. I think I like Rabbi Yeshua very much.

Andre returns with Shimon and Yaakov.

I shout on them, "Shimon! Yaakov! Come meet Rabbi Yeshua! He is a *tsaddik* and a prophet and a son of David, and Yohanan the immerser prophesied on him that he is to destroy the four Powers!"

Shimon's mouth hangs open like a fish mouth.

Rabbi Yeshua stands and goes to greet them. "My name is called Yeshua."

Sweat springs out on Shimon's forehead, and he looks as his knees should fail him. "My n-name is called Shimon."

I wonder why Shimon shakes like that.

Rabbi Yeshua measures him with his eyes. "My third brother is also named Shimon. We call him Thin Shimon, and I will call you Shimon the Rock, for you are a mighty tower."

I think Rabbi Yeshua has measured Shimon very well. That is a good name, and from now on, I will call him Shimon the Rock also.

My brother steps forward. "My name is called Yaakov."

Rabbi Yeshua gives him a strong right hand. "A good name. My first brother is called Little Yaakov, so I will call you Big Yaakov."

Little Yaakov comes to greet my brother. He is a tall man, and he grips my brother's hand with a thick hand that looks as it could crush stone. "It is good to meet you, Big Yaakov."

Big Yaakov is built like a stone jar, short and stout. He grins a mighty grin, for he is more than a head shorter than Little Yaakov, but he also has a thick hand that could crush stone. "An honor to know you, Little Yaakov."

Both of them seem very pleased on this joke. I think they will forge a mighty friendship, for they are cut from the same metal, bold and fierce.

We all sit on the ground.

Rabbi Yeshua sits next to his sister, holding her hand.

My breath catches in my throat. Rabbi Yeshua treats his sister in public as she is a man and a friend—the way I wish to treat Aunt Miryam. I never knew a man in Israel who had a woman for a friend. There is a deep thing here.

Shimon the Rock leans forward. "Rabbi Yeshua, how long have you followed after the prophet Yohanan?"

"I came down from Nazareth two months ago when I heard HaShem had raised up a new prophet in Israel."

"Two months!" Shimon's eyes go wide. "And you have been here with him all this time?"

Rabbi Yeshua shakes his head. "When I came and immersed with Yohanan in the Jordan, I saw the face of HaShem. Then I went out to the desert to learn to hear the voice of HaShem."

My heart pounds many times in my chest. Rabbi Yeshua has seen the face of HaShem! Yesterday, I saw the Shekinah and I thought that was a large matter, but it is a small matter next to the face of HaShem. And Rabbi Yeshua has spoken with HaShem! I never met a man who spoke with HaShem.

Shimon's eyes are round as pomegranates. "You … spoke with HaShem?"

A faint smile creeps across Rabbi Yeshua's lips. It is the smile of a man who has endured much pain and earned a great victory. "I called on the name of HaShem to hear a word from him, and I did at last, but I heard many words from the Accuser, and I fought a hard battle with it."

My heart quivers and all my body feels cold. Tales tell that there is a mighty prince of evil spirits called the Accuser. The scriptures do not tell of the Accuser, so I thought the Accuser was only an idle tale.

But I know there is great power for evil in the world, and I think that is the point of the tales. I think Yeshua is either very foolish or very mighty, to do battle with the Accuser. I think it is not only the scorching of the Shekinah I see on Yeshua's soul.

Shimon's face is pale and moist, and he licks his cracked lips. "And now you have returned to follow after Yohanan again?"

Rabbi Yeshua shakes his head. "I came to ask Yohanan for a word from HaShem, for I still hear The Voice only in whispers."

That was the very word I heard Yohanan telling. I bounce up and down for my excitement. "Explain the matter again. Who are these four Powers that Yohanan spoke of?"

A shiver passes through us all.

Rabbi Yeshua's face goes tight and hard. "No son of Adam knows who is the first Power, nor the second, nor the third, nor the fourth. When HaShem calls me to fight each Power, I will know it."

A muscle twitches in Little Yaakov's face.

Rabbi Yeshua's sister wraps her arms around him and kisses him. "You will not fight the first Power before my wedding feast, yes?"

I am astonished for her fearlessness. Most girls her age are quiet and shy, but she is bold as a prophet.

Rabbi Yeshua gives her a kiss and a kiss and a kiss. "Tomorrow we will leave for home. I do not think HaShem will tell me the name of the first Power before we arrive at your wedding feast."

My heart leaps to hear Rabbi Yeshua is going on the road to Galilee tomorrow, just as we are. That will give us three days on the road together, until we reach the fork at Bet Shan. In three days, I can ask him many ten thousand questions. But then he will veer northwest to Nazareth, and we will keep on straight north to Capernaum, and when will we ever see him again? Nazareth is more than a walk of one day from Capernaum. I wish to know when the kingdom of HaShem will begin. I wish to learn whatever wisdom Rabbi Yeshua can teach me. I measure him to be a wise man, deep in the ways of HaShem. I wish to be deep in the ways of HaShem. I wish to know what it means to be a lamb in the heart of HaShem. That is a very deep thing.

Rabbi Yeshua looks on me and my friends, and he tilts his head as he is listening to a voice only he can hear. At last, he says, "You men will come with us to the wedding feast of my sister, yes? It is in Cana, on the third day after Shabbat."

For a moment, I think all the universe has stopped.

He hardly knows us, and he asks us to the feast of his sister?

We hardly know him, and yet we should go to his sister's feast, when our fathers expect us home the day before Shabbat? We will be home five days late if we go to this feast.

If I had a choice in the matter, I would say yes, for there is a deep thing in Rabbi Yeshua and I wish to know it.

But I do not have a choice in the matter.

Shimon the Rock is the oldest, and it is his right to say yes or no. He will say no, for we should return to Capernaum as our fathers ordered. We have been gone long for Sukkot, and now it is time to go back to our lives. We have boats to oar and nets to mend and fish to catch. Our fathers need us. Shimon will say no.

Yeshua studies him as he thinks Shimon will say yes.

Shimon the Rock looks on me and Big Yaakov and Andre. There is a lost look in his eyes. I see he does not know what to say. We came to hear the prophet Yohanan. We came to immerse in the Jordan River. We came to see if the kingdom of HaShem is near, as men were saying in the streets of Jerusalem.

I think the kingdom of HaShem is near, but Yohanan is not the man to bring it in.

I think Yohanan the immerser is afraid on the four Powers.

I think Rabbi Yeshua is not afraid on the four Powers.

I think Rabbi Yeshua means to destroy the four Powers.

I think when a son of David destroys the four Powers, that will bring in the kingdom of HaShem.

But nobody cares what I think, for I am the youngest.

Our fathers need us, and Shimon will honor our fathers.

Shimon will say no.

Yeshua watches Shimon the Rock with keen eyes.

I think he measures Shimon to see if his heart goes after the deep things of HaShem.

Sweat stands out on Shimon's forehead.

Andre and Big Yaakov do not say anything. Shimon has not asked their opinion, and they will not dishonor him by offering it.

My fingernails bite my palms. Shimon will say no.

Rabbi Yeshua looks on Shimon the Rock and smiles as he knows a thing Shimon does not.

And that is the problem. Shimon the Rock is not a man who sees deep things. When the village *hazzan* explains a matter of Torah to me, I see it at once, and I understand it better than the village *hazzan*. Then I have to explain the matter many times to Shimon, and still he sees it as he walks in a fog. Shimon is not the Genius of Capernaum, and he does not know the deep things of HaShem.

Shimon will say no.

A muscle in Shimon's face flickers.

I am ready to shriek on him for my fury.

Shimon opens his mouth to speak, but no words fall out.

My heart leaps in my chest.

Shimon says, "Yes, we will go to the wedding feast with you, Rabbi Yeshua."

I cannot find my breath. Did I hear true? Can it be?

Andre's face tightens in a hard knot, for our fathers will be very angry on the matter.

Big Yaakov's eyes narrow, for he is almost as old as Shimon, and Shimon did not consult him.

But my spirit leaps within me, for Shimon said yes.

If Shimon had said no, I would have dishonored him and said yes.

But Shimon said yes.

I think Shimon the Rock knows more on the deep things of HaShem than I measured him for.

CHAPTER SIXTEEN

Shimon of Capernaum

I cannot believe I made such a big foolishness. We just met this man Yeshua from Nazareth, and yet I feel as I have known him long, so when he invited us to go to his sister's wedding feast, I thought I would like to go. I saw that Big Yaakov would like to go, but he was afraid. I saw that Andre would like to go, but he was afraid. And I saw that Yoni was dying to go, and he was not afraid.

So I said yes, because I will never let it be said that Yoni has more courage than me.

But how could I have said yes, when I promised my father to stay here two days only and then go straight home?

There is work to be done after being gone a whole month. Fish do not grow on bushes, my father says. Fish must be caught, and that is work, and work needs men, and we are the men.

And now I have agreed to go five days out of our way with Rabbi Yeshua. My father will make a rage on me if I go to this feast.

I should go home by the straight road, only I gave my word to Rabbi Yeshua, and I am a man of my word. But I also gave my word to my father, so now I am in a box. Whatever I do, I will go back on my word.

I try to think how it all happened.

Big Yaakov and I went to buy food this afternoon, but the village was farther than we were told. We bought food and beer and sat in the shade of a fig tree and ate and drank. Two young girls of the village came and made a flirt on us. They both wore the virgin's veil, so we knew they were of the age when they hope some man will make an offer to buy them from their fathers. They live in a small village of no account, and they saw us and made a flirt on us because they had nothing to lose.

We grinned on them, for they were young and foolish. One of them was a big-eyes girl, and I always had a liking for a big-eyes. It is not a sin to look on a big-eyes. If it is a sin to look, then HaShem would not have made big-eyes girls, but he made them, so how can it be a sin? Big Yaakov likes girls with slim waists and wide hips, but I like a big-eyes girl. Anyway, it was a fine afternoon and the girls smiled on us and made a flirt on us and we stayed too long, only out of a politeness, and then we had to hurry back.

I kept thinking of the big-eyes girl all the way back. It is not a sin, for I did nothing but smile on the girl. Still I will not speak on her to my woman, who stayed home in Capernaum all these weeks with my little sons. I do not think Yaakov will speak on the slim-waist girl to his woman either. It is a sore trial to be gone from your woman a whole month, and then have some big-eyes or slim-waist make a flirt on you in a strange village.

When we got back, Andre came running and said he and Yoni met a man who is held in a big honor by Yohanan the immerser. Andre said Yohanan prophesied that this man is to defeat the four Powers. I do not know what are the four Powers, but I know that a man who can defeat a Power is a man I should meet.

Then Yoni shouted on us that this man is a prophet and a *tsaddik* and a son of David. If Yoni says a man is a prophet and a *tsaddik* and a son of David, the man is something.

So I spoke to the man, and I knew for myself he is a prophet and a *tsaddik*, for he looked in my heart.

I never saw such a thing before. Rabbi Yeshua read my heart like a scribe reads a book.

I looked in his eyes, and I thought I saw the big-eyes girl. Only for a moment. Then I thought I saw my woman waiting at home for me. Only for a moment.

Then my body was all in a big sweat and my knees felt weak and I thought I would fall over.

I thought Rabbi Yeshua would ask me who is the big-eyes girl and call me a sinner. That is what a prophet would do. But Rabbi Yeshua is more than a prophet. He is also a *tsaddik*.

He smiled on me and said he wished to give me a nickname, Shimon the Rock. That is a good name. I mean to live up to it. That is what a *tsaddik* does, when he sees you could have done a wrong thing, but you did not. I never heard of a prophet who is also a *tsaddik*. Prophets are angry and *tsaddiks* are kind.

Rabbi Yeshua is a prophet and a *tsaddik,* and now he is my friend.

I never made a friend so fast.

Also, Yoni said Rabbi Yeshua is a son of David, and that is a mighty matter if it is true.

We talked more, and Rabbi Yeshua said he had seen the face of HaShem.

I thought I would stop breathing for the shock of it.

Even our prophet Moses never saw the face of HaShem. He saw the hind parts of HaShem and was in a big fear on the matter. But Rabbi Yeshua saw the face of HaShem and spoke on the matter like a thing you should expect. Then he said he fought long in the desert with the Accuser. I have heard tales of the Accuser, and those are bad tales. I do not know what it means to fight the Accuser. I think it is not like a wrestling fight between two men. I think it is too large a matter for a fish-man to understand.

I think it is a mighty thing to fight the Accuser.

I have known men who said mighty things on themselves and were liars. I know what is a liar and what is not a liar. Rabbi Yeshua is a man who can look in your heart and see what you are and grin on you and make a friend on you. That kind of man is not a liar.

So when he asked if we would go to his sister's wedding feast, all I could think was that here is a man who saw the face of HaShem and fought the Accuser, and he thinks so well on me that he wishes me to come celebrate in the joy of his sister. And I saw Yoni had courage to go, so I said yes.

And now I am in a box.

If we go to the feast, then I have lied to my own father, and that is a big sin.

But if we do not go to the feast, then I have lied to a mighty prophet and a *tsaddik,* and that is a bigger sin.

Yoni says, "Shimon, did you bring food with you from that village? Andre and I waited long, and you never came."

Andre makes a grin on us. "I think they ate it all and took a nap. Or else they chased some big-eyes girl around the village."

Yoni roars with a big laughter on us.

My neck feels hot on a sudden. I should teach Andre with my fist when is a good time to make a joke and when is not.

Big Yaakov scowls on Yoni and Andre. "The village was farther than we were told. We walked far and bought food and ate some and rested. Then a small-eyes girl and a big-waist girl came and asked if we needed to buy a woman. I said no, we both have women, but I have a brother who likes to roll in the mud like a pig and wishes to have a woman. So the girls ran away screaming for their fear. I think the small-eyes is halfway to Arabia, but if Yoni runs fast, he can catch the big-waist."

Rabbi Yeshua's brothers all roar with a big laughter on Yoni.

I reach behind Big Yaakov and pull out the packs we took to carry food. "Here are some rounds of bread and some cheese and some dried figs we bought. Also, I have beer in this skin. But before you eat it all like wolves, you should offer some to our friends."

Andre reaches for the bag. I see in his eyes that he does not think the food will go far if he and Yoni have to share with Rabbi Yeshua and his four brothers and their women.

Yoni looks as he will die of his hunger, which is a big foolishness because he ate only this morning, and now it is evening. That is not long to go hungry.

Rabbi Yeshua grins on us all. "We have food also that we bought in Jericho this morning and we can share it with you."

Rabbi Yeshua's mother and sister and their other women go to get their food.

Yoni grins.

Andre grins.

Big Yaakov grins.

I would grin, but I am still in a box and I do not know what to do. I like Rabbi Yeshua and his family, and I want to know more on this matter of the four Powers. But I told my father we would stay here two days only, and today is the second day. And my father grinned and said if Mashiach comes, we can join his army and fight the Great Satan, but otherwise we should come home by the straight road.

Rabbi Yeshua does not look like a man who means to fight the Great Satan.

And yet he says he means to destroy the four Powers. He does not even know what are the four Powers, but he means to destroy them. That is a bold man. I think it would take a son of David to be so bold. The four Powers must be four kings. But which four kings?

One could be the King of the South, which is Egypt. One could be the King of the North, which is Syria. One could be the King of the East, which is Babylon.

If those are the first three Powers, then the fourth must be the King of the West, which is Rome, which is the Great Satan, which my father gave me permission to fight.

My heart beats fast. Is there a way out of my box?

I do not *know* those are the four Powers. That is what my father will say when I come home five days late.

But I do not *know* they are not. That is what I will say. I will say Rabbi Yeshua is a prophet and a *tsaddik*, a man well spoken by Yohanan the immerser. And he is son of David. What if he means to be Mashiach? I will say we had to know for sure. I will say we had to look into the matter. I will say that if Mashiach is near, it is a bigger matter than taking fish out of the lake for five days.

My father will not agree, and he will call me a fool and a woman, but then I will put Yoni on him, and Yoni will tie him up with many clever words, and in the end my father will be so fuddled he will agree we were right to look into the matter. Nobody ever wins argument with Yoni.

It is a sore trial to have the Genius of Capernaum for a friend, but sometimes it is also a blessing from HaShem.

CHAPTER SEVENTEEN

Yeshua of Nazareth

I like these men who came to sit with us.

Four men, who came to me just after I heard the matter of the four Powers. I wonder if HaShem sent them to help me smite the four Powers.

Andre grins much and is cheerful and tells jokes and makes everyone laugh. He even makes Imma laugh, and that is a hard nut to crack. I am glad to have Andre with us.

Big Yaakov is already a big friend on Little Yaakov. I hope it is not only because of the joke on their names. I think they are alike in some ways, for they are both fierce.

Shimon the Rock has some secret in his heart. At first, I thought it was to do with a woman, but I think there is more to the matter than a woman. I think it is a thing he does not even know. I think he is a man drifting in a boat without an oar. But that is all I can see. I wish HaShem would explain the matter to me, but HaShem says nothing, and I am desperate to hear a word from him on the matter.

Yoni intrigues me. When I first looked on him, I saw a boy of the age of ten in a tunic covered with mud, and I wondered who brought some foolish child to a convocation of men. Then I looked in his eyes and saw a surprise.

Yoni has been in the Shekinah.

And there is more. Yoni comes from a family of sages and he speaks like a sage. He is thirteen years old, and he asks questions only a sage could ask.

I think Yoni is a deep lake.

I think he is a man I can teach.

I think he is a man I can learn from.

It was on account of Yoni that I asked them all to come to Shlomi's wedding feast. Tomorrow is the third day of the week. We will reach home before Shabbat, and then the feast comes on the third day after Shabbat, and that is a whole week.

That is enough time to learn what Yoni is made of. If I am to destroy the four Powers, I will need strong friends, and fierce, and men of good cheer. I think Shimon the Rock is strong and Big Yaakov is fierce and Andre is cheerful.

But I will also need a wise counselor who has been in the Shekinah, and I think Yoni is wise. I think it, but I do not know it. That is what I wish to learn in this week.

The women bring our food, and we recline on our cloaks and eat.

Andre tells the tale of the prophet Jonah who was eaten by a big fish. He tells the tale as the fish saw the matter, that Jonah had a foul taste, so the fish spit him out on the beach and then complained on the matter to HaShem, and HaShem said the fish had a point. Then Jonah complained that the inside of a fish smells worse than the outside, and HaShem said Jonah had a point. Then Jonah went to Nineveh and told repentance to them, and they repented and complained to HaShem that a prophet should not smell like the inside of a fish, and HaShem said they had a point.

I never heard the tale told with such a big foolishness, and yet I like the tale. Shlomi Dancefeet laughs so hard she falls on her back holding her sides. Imma laughs and laughs. It makes my heart glad to hear Imma laugh.

My brother Yehuda Dreamhead reclines next to Andre. They are both the youngest sons in their families and near in age, and I think they will be friends.

Thin Shimon sits with Yoni. Of all my brothers, Thin Shimon is the smallest. He was born small, for he was in Imma's belly only seven months. Then Yehuda Dreamhead was born after eleven more months. Imma gave all her sons milk to the age of three, except Thin Shimon, because Yehuda Dreamhead took all his share. He grew up wiry, and so the whole village called him Thin Shimon. They call our cousin Fat Shimon, even though he is not fat.

Of all of my brothers, Thin Shimon is the cleverest. When the men in the village square make a riddle, Thin Shimon knows the answer first, always. When we work in Tsipori and there is a question on how thick to make a wall, or how wide to make window slits, we ask Thin Shimon, and he explains the matter so we all agree he is right. Thin Shimon is the cleverest man in all Nazareth. That is why he sits with Yoni.

As I watch them talk, I think Thin Shimon is not the hundredth part as clever as Yoni. That is not a knock on Thin Shimon, for he is more clever than any man of my village. But in every village of Galilee, I think there is one man as clever as Thin Shimon.

I do not think any village of Galilee has a man as clever as Yoni.

All around us, other groups eat and drink and laugh. Many hundred men are here, and many have women, and some have boys down to the age of ten.

The sun is gone, and the air is pleasant after the heat of the day. The stars wink to life in the black sky, and it is peaceful.

When all have eaten, the tales begin for the night.

A man stands and tells the tale of Father Noah and the big rain. That is a mighty tale of judgment, and when it is done, everyone shouts on him that he told it well.

Another man stands and tells the tale of Gideon, who fought the Midianites and won a mighty victory. That is another tale of judgment.

At the end of this tale, I feel there is a wrong thing here. These tales of judgment are told with wrong hearts that look for vengeance, not justice.

Another man stands and tells the tale of Mordecai and his cousin Esther and how they defeated the evil Haman and hanged him and his ten sons on a mighty gallows.

The night air feels dense and hot, and I find it hard to breathe.

Another man stands and tells the tale of the prophet Daniel, how he broke the law of the Medes and Persians by praying to HaShem, and the king's evil counselors put him in the den with the lions. The Messenger of HaShem came and shut the lions' mouths, and Daniel came out alive in the morning, and then the king threw all his counselors in the den with their women and children. When this tale is done, there is a big shout for vengeance on our enemies.

Yohanan the immerser reclines with three of his men listening to the tales. I wish he would say a word on the matter of vengeance, that it is not a thing to rejoice on.

But Yohanan grins on these tales.

All my heart is in a big confusion.

Another man stands and tells the tale of the seven brothers who were killed by the King of the North in the time of the Makkabi heroes. It is a long tale and hard, for the seven brothers were killed only because they loved HaShem and kept Torah and refused to eat the flesh of a pig. By the end of the tale, the air feels like the moment before a lightning.

If I took iron to flint for a spark, all the rage in this place would burn up fast like pitch.

My body is in a big tension. I do not like what I feel, all this rage.

I catch Andre's eye. "Andre! Tell your tale of the fish!"

Andre makes a grin on me and jumps to his feet and tells the tale of Jonah the prophet and the big fish. He tells it the same as he told us earlier, but the crowd is not in a mood to make a laughter. They are in a mood to make a vengeance on goyim. They do not like this tale of how HaShem sent a man to make goyim repent.

Before Andre is the fourth part of the way through the tale, all the people make a grim silence on him.

He sees it and his face turns red and his knees quiver. He makes a quick work on the rest of the tale and sits down.

Nobody shouts that Andre told the tale well.

All around the camp, men avert their eyes. Some of them roll up in their cloaks and lie down to sleep. Others wander away to the big rock where men go to make a piss.

I make a big grin on Andre. "You told the tale well."

Andre's face burns.

Shimon the Rock looks like a man whose ox went in the synagogue and made *haryo* on the floor and all the people complained on the stink.

Big Yaakov yawns and says it is time to sleep. He stands and shakes out his cloak.

All my brothers do the same.

Shimon the Rock does the same.

Yoni looks as he is thinking hard on the matter.

I do not know what to say. I wish HaShem would show me what to say.

"Andre!" shouts a voice I do not know.

A man walks toward us, smiling, when all around the camp, people look away from us, scowling.

I wonder who is this man.

Andre jumps up and goes to meet the man. "Philip, are you well?"

This man Philip gives Andre a kiss and a kiss and a kiss. "That was a good tale, Andre. You should come tell it in our village square some night."

I think I like this man Philip.

Shimon the Rock jumps up and goes to meet the man. "Philip, are you well? Is your mother well? I heard you took a woman. Did you bring her here?"

Philip makes a big grin. "I took a woman last spring and already she is with child, so I had to leave her home for Sukkot. My mother and her mother and sister are with her. You would approve on her, Shimon—she is a big-eyes. Are all these your friends from Capernaum?"

Shimon the Rock brings Philip to meet us. "Here is my friend Philip the fish-man from Bethsaida, the village where I was born. We learned to swim together when we were boys. He saved me once from drowning, but I almost got him drowned for a reward."

Philip grins on us.

Shimon the Rock tells Philip that my brothers and I come from Nazareth and that I am a prophet and a *tsaddik*.

Philip greets us all with a strong right hand.

Shimon the Rock points to Big Yaakov and Yoni. "These are the sons of Zavdai, who is my father's partner in Capernaum. Big Yaakov works with Andre in his boat, and Yoni works with me in mine. Yoni is not usually so dirty, but today Andre made a bad trick on him."

Philip greets Big Yaakov with a strong right hand.

Yoni hides behind Shimon the Rock, scowling.

Philip goes around Shimon the Rock and greets Yoni with a strong right hand and a kind smile. "Friend, you should be wary on that Andre, or he will make a bad trick on you every day in the week. He made the same trick on me when we were boys, and my father gave me a beating for ruining my tunic. But let me tell you a secret on Andre Trickster."

Philip leans down and whispers something in Yoni's ear.

Yoni grins on him.

I am certain I like this man Philip.

"Who did you come with from Bethsaida?" Shimon the Rock asks.

Philip tells the names of six friends he came with. "We stayed last night in Jericho and came to hear Yohanan the prophet today."

"Why did you not bring them over here to greet us?" Shimon the Rock asks.

Philip looks as he does not know what to say.

I see what he is thinking. All Philip's friends saw that Andre was shamed, and they did not wish to be seen with him. But Philip was not afraid to be seen with Andre.

I look all around us and see the camp settled down for the night.

My family and I shake out our cloaks and roll ourselves up in them.

Philip goes back to his friends.

Shimon the Rock and Andre and Big Yaakov and Yoni shake out their cloaks and roll up and lie down.

Soon, all the camp is sleeping.

My heart is still in a big turmoil. Little Yaakov and my brothers think I should make a move here. They think I should call up a big army and lead it out to make a war on the Great Satan.

But I do not think that is what HaShem wants.

I do not know what HaShem wants, but I am listening every moment to hear his voice in case he tells me.

I think when HaShem wishes me to call up a big army, he will tell me.

I am dying to hear the voice of HaShem clear on the matter.

Right now, he speaks in whispers so faint I can hardly hear.

I need to hear his voice clear, if I am to smite the four Powers.

I like these new men. Shimon the Rock is a tower of strength. Big Yaakov is a barrel of fierceness. Andre is a man who will always keep us laughing. Yoni has a mind like no man I ever met anywhere, not even that *philosophos* I built a house for in Tsipori.

And Philip.

Philip is a man who is kind.

I think I will be in a big need of kindness.

Tomorrow, I will ask Philip if he also wishes to come to the wedding feast of my sister.

CHAPTER EIGHTEEN

Yoni of Capernaum

I wake up an hour before dawn, thinking I drank too much beer last night.

I unroll from my cloak and stand and look for the big rock where all the men go to make a piss. There is a little light in the east above the mountains of Moab, enough to see by.

My tunic feels as it is caked with mud. I think there is mud inside every strand of wool. It itches like sand fleas. I should put a scorpion in Andre's ear for this.

While I make a piss on the rock, I remember that man from Bethsaida we met last night. His name is called Philip, which is a Greek name that means he likes horses. I wonder why they would name a baby that. It makes no sense to say a baby likes horses. The only thing a baby likes is drinking milk.

Andre was also born in Bethsaida, and he also has a Greek name. It means he is manly, but it makes no sense to say a baby is manly. Greek names sound like a big foolishness to me. In Capernaum, we do not give our sons Greek names. Even if Bethsaida is only the walk of one hour from us, it is another world, for it lies across the border. I heard they have many Greeks there. Anyway, Philip told me—

"Yoni!" says a voice behind me.

I finish making my piss and drop my tunic and look back.

Philip stands there holding a plant in his hands. "I looked long for this and found some growing south of the fords."

I peer at it. "You are sure this will—"

"Come with me now. The others will be up soon."

I hurry after Philip toward the river.

When we reach the edge, he puts the plant on a large flat rock. He kneels beside the rock and takes out his fish knife and slices and slices and slices the plant. He mashes it with the flat of his blade. "Take off your tunic, Yoni."

I look all around in a big alarm. If I take off my tunic, I will expose my nakedness, and that is a dishonor on me.

Philip sees my face and gives me a kind smile. "Yoni, I cannot make your tunic clean while you wear it. Take it off."

Still I do not wish to take it off. There is nobody here except Philip, but it will be a big dishonor to expose my nakedness.

Philips sighs and takes off his own tunic and throws it on the ground. "There, see, I am naked too." His back is crisscrossed with old scars.

A shiver runs all through my blood. That is the back of a man who was beaten many times as a boy.

Philip does not look as he is ashamed to be naked. He holds out his hand. "Take off your tunic."

I take off my tunic and hand it to him and shiver in the cold air. "What is that plant called? I never saw it before."

"If you were a woman, you would know it is called *borit*."

"You are not a woman, so how do you know it is called *borit*?"

Philip dips my tunic in the river and pulls it out. "Here, lay it out on the stone."

I lay it out on the stone. "You are not a woman, so how do you know it is called *borit*?"

Philip takes a handful of *borit* and smears it on my tunic. He works it in hard with his hands, kneading it like a baker kneads dough to make rounds of bread. His hands are thick and tough like any fish-man's hands. But I never saw a fish-man knead *borit* into a tunic.

I never saw anyone knead *borit* into a tunic, for washing tunics is women's work. The women of Capernaum wash clothes in the lake in a closed-off place where the men are not allowed to come. I heard they work naked when the weather is hot.

Philip works and works. A thin layer of sweat springs up on his scarred back.

I still did not get an answer, so I ask again. "You are not a woman, so how do you know it is called *borit*? Also, who taught you where to find it in this wilderness? Did you walk far? Did you really save Shimon the Rock from drowning? Why did your father beat you when you were a boy? Why do the people of Bethsaida name Jewish boys with Greek names? Do you feel dishonored to have a goy name? How do you know how to wash a tunic when that is a woman's work? Also, why are you not ashamed to expose your nakedness?"

Philip grins on me and picks up the tunic and carries it down into the river. "Come help me, Yoni Many-Questions, and I will answer one or two thousand of your questions."

I step into the river.

I forgot how cold the water is. In the afternoons when the day is hot, the coldness feels good. In the morning, an hour before sunrise, it feels like a knife in my bones.

Philip dips the tunic once more in the water and then lifts it up and kneads it in his hands. "If you help with the scrubbing, the work will go faster."

"But that is women's work."

"How do you know it is women's work?"

"In Capernaum, only women do this work."

"In Bethsaida also, only women do this work."

"Therefore, it is women's work."

Philip grins on me. "How does that make it women's work? What if there were no women, and men had to do it? Would it still be women's work?"

I never thought on the matter that way. I knead the tunic in my hands. The *borit* feels slimy. The more I knead it, the more it foams. I knead and knead until my hands refuse to work.

Philip's hands seem to be made of iron. He kneads the tunic all over, front and back. When all the tunic is covered in foam, he puts it beneath the water. "Knead it again, Yoni. Knead out all the foam."

I seize it in my hands and knead.

We work and work on the tunic.

At last, Philip brings it out of the water.

I stare on it in amaze.

Philip has done a mighty wonder.

My tunic is clean.

Philip wrings out the tunic.

When I think there is no water left, he wrings again, and more water trickles out through his fingers.

Philip grins on me and hands me the tunic. "What do you think, Yoni Many-Questions? Even if there are no women here to make it clean, is it still clean?"

I ask, "Did your mother teach you that?"

"His sister taught him that," says a voice behind us.

I spin to look.

Rabbi Yeshua stands on the bank. There is a look on his face I cannot read, and I thought I was a good reader of faces.

I run up out of the water. "Rabbi Yeshua, in your village, who washes the clothes? In our village it is the women, and I say that makes it a woman's work. But Philip asks why that makes it a woman's work. What do you think? If only women do a work, is it women's work? Also, did you know that plant is called—"

"Friend, come up out of the water," Rabbi Yeshua says.

I turn to look on Philip.

He stands where I left him, waist-deep in the Jordan, staring on Rabbi Yeshua as he is a *phantasm*. "Who told you the matter of my sister?"

Rabbi Yeshua grins on him. "Friend, come up out of the water."

Philip wades toward us with his face in a big amaze. "Who told you?"

I think it is obvious who told him. "Rabbi Yeshua knows everything. He is a prophet, and HaShem tells him every secret thing you ever did."

Philip's mouth hangs open so far, I think he will step on his own teeth and fall in the river and drown.

Rabbi Yeshua helps me put on my tunic.

It is cold with river chill, but I know it will soon warm up. "Rabbi Yeshua, why did Philip's father beat him when he was a boy?"

Rabbi Yeshua narrows his eyes. "If you wish to know Philip's secrets, you should ask Philip."

Philip comes up out of the water and puts on his tunic. "Rabbi Yeshua, is it true you are a prophet? Shimon the son of Yonah said so, and now Yoni Many-Questions says so, but I wish to know if you say so."

Rabbi Yeshua grins on him and sits and pats his hand on the ground. "Sit with us and tell Yoni the tale of your sister Rivka."

I never saw a man with a face so white as Philip the fish-man of Bethsaida. All the strength goes out of his knees. He sits beside Rabbi Yeshua.

I sit beside Rabbi Yeshua.

Philip tells the tale of his sister Rivka.

Philip is the youngest of five brothers. After him, last of all, came his sister Rivka. As she grew to be a child, all the village said she was cursed. Her face was thick and round, with a flat nose, and her eyes were squint shaped. She was slow to learn to speak, and slow of wits. But she was kind and good, and Philip loved her.

When the boys of the village mocked her and called her Rivka Cursegirl and tried to piss her feet, Philip drove them away with his fists.

Philip's mother taught the girl to do women's work, to cook and weave and sew. Everything she did took long, but she did it with joy.

There came a day when Philip's mother could no longer wash clothes in the lake, on account of the big agony in her back. She sent Rivka to do the work, but the women of the village mocked her and spat her and called her Rivka Cursegirl and refused to let her wash with them, for fear they would bear a cursed child themselves. But a girl cannot wash clothes alone, on account of evil men who would do a wickedness on her.

So Philip went with her and helped with the work and took a good care on her until the day Rivka became a woman and her father sold her to some man who lived in a place called Kursi, a goy village on the east side of the lake.

I never heard such a thing, that a man of Israel would sell his daughter to be the woman of some goy.

Philip made a rage on his father and said he would not allow him to sell Rivka to a goy.

His father only grinned on him and said the matter was done.

Every day for the whole year of the betrothal, Philip made a rage on his father.

His father grinned on him and said the matter could not be changed.

At the end of the year, the goy came for Rivka.

Philip saw at last it was no use. He tried to run away with his sister to Capernaum, but he was only fourteen and had not thought the matter through. Before they got a mile from home, his father caught them and took the girl away and gave her to the goy, and Philip never saw her again.

Then his father tied Philip's hands to a tree in the village square. He tore off Philip's tunic, exposing his nakedness. He beat Philip with an old anchor rope from his boat. He beat him until the blood ran off his back in a river, and the men of the village came and said that was enough punishment for a disobedient son.

His father said Philip was not his son anymore.

The men of the village told him to stop beating Philip.

His father made a big rage on the matter. He shook the rope in their faces and beat Philip ten times more. Twenty times more. Thirty times. Fifty.

Then his father made a great gurgling sound in his throat and fell over and died.

All my body is in a sweat more cold than the Jordan River. That was a bad tale.

Rabbi Yeshua wears the face of a man hearing a tale the second time. "Friend, you are a kind man and brave."

Philip says nothing. His eyes are hollow, and he looks as he has just been beaten with a rope again.

Rabbi Yeshua says, "Friend, my sister's wedding feast is in a week from today in a village near Nazareth. Shimon the Rock and Big Yaakov and Andre and Yoni are coming to the feast, and I wish for you to come with us. I see you are a kind man and brave, and I have need of kind men who are brave."

Philip stares on Rabbi Yeshua with the wild eyes of a man who is drowning. He leaps up from the ground and runs away as fast as any man ever ran.

I am shocked that Philip ran away. "Rabbi Yeshua, what did you say that was wrong? I thought Philip would be amazed that you are a prophet who knew already all about his sister. Why does HaShem make cursed children? We had a cursed boy in our village, and he used to go in every house in the village as it was his own home. Some said he did not know better, and some said he did. One day he went in the house of Honi the woodcutter, and Honi beat him with his fists, and he died. Honi said the boy did a wickedness on his daughter, only the daughter said he did not. My father said it was a wrong thing to beat the boy, because he was slow in the wits and did not know what he was doing. The village *hazzan* said HaShem made the boy cursed and if Honi the woodcutter was angry on the matter, he should be angry on HaShem. What do you …"

Rabbi Yeshua's eyes are closed. He has the face of a man who listens to a quiet voice far away. Tears run down his face. When he speaks, his voice is cracked. "Do not call a child of HaShem cursed."

I feel as I am stabbed in my heart.

I think sometimes I ask too many questions.

I think sometimes I speak without thinking what I am saying.

I think sometimes I am the biggest fool there ever was.

CHAPTER NINETEEN

Yeshua of Nazareth

I do not understand what just happened, and I am desperate to know what it means.

I woke up and saw that Yoni was gone from our camp, and I went looking for him. He was not at the rock where all the men go to make a piss. I walked all around the camp and saw only one man awake, sitting under a fig tree praying to HaShem. Then I went to the river, and there was Yoni and this man Philip.

Philip was wringing out Yoni's tunic, and I could see it was all clean.

Philip said, "What do you think, Yoni Many-Questions? Even if there are no women here to make it clean, is it still clean?"

Yoni said, "Did your mother teach you that?"

And my mouth opened all on its own account and said, "His sister taught him that."

Also, I knew the whole tale of his sister and what befell her.

I do not know how I knew all that. I knew it faster than I had time to think the words. I knew in an instant all that Philip told us afterward in the fourth part of an hour.

I have been waiting weeks and weeks to hear from HaShem on the matter of how I am to go to war against the Great Satan, and I have heard only shards and whispers, and I am more confused than I ever was because HaShem says nothing.

And in one instant, HaShem told me more about a girl I was not asking on than he has told me in two months about the mighty thing I am desperate to know.

HaShem filled up my heart with the tale of a girl treated with a mighty cruelty.

We had a boy born in our village the same year Yosi was born, and all the people said he was cursed. Shimon the baker's daughter bore him. Some in the village muttered behind their hands that the woman sinned, to have a cursed child born. Shimon the baker scowled on them and asked what was the sin. Some said one thing, and some said another, and some said the child should be thrown off the precipice, whether anyone knew what was the sin or not.

People talked on the matter long, and after two years, the child crawled away when no one was looking and fell in the leather-man's piss-pool and drowned.

That was what I heard.

I was only a boy, and I believed the tale.

Now I wonder how the child got in the piss-pool, for there is a bank around it higher than the height of a child.

I think there is a dark secret in my village. I think it is a mighty wickedness, that some in a village can call an innocent child cursed. I think it is a mightier wickedness, that a whole village can believe a small child could drown himself, and nobody should ask even one question on the matter.

Yoni talks and talks.

I try to hear his words, but my own sorrow drowns all his words. Tears run down my face for the cruelty of my village.

Yoni says something about HaShem making a child cursed.

It takes all my strength to say, "Do not call a child of HaShem cursed."

Yoni sucks in his breath as I have slapped him.

I did not mean to hurt him.

Yoni stands to leave.

"Stay," I say.

Yoni sits.

I sit with my eyes closed trying to hear the voice of HaShem. In the fourth part of an hour, all the camp will be up. My brothers will ask what I mean to do. These men of Capernaum will ask what I mean to do.

I do not know what I should do, and it rips my heart not to know.

All I have heard from HaShem is that I should go to the wedding feast.

Something will happen there, but I do not know what.

I feel as I am a fool, to ask these new friends of mine to come to the feast, when I do not know why. I feel as I am a bigger fool, that these friends of mine think I am a prophet, when I hear nothing from HaShem but a few whispers.

"Rabbi Yeshua!" shouts a voice.

I open my eyes.

Philip walks toward us, holding the hand of the man I saw praying under the fig tree. I see they are good friends, for they move as one, like men who walk together much.

I stand to meet them.

Philip says, "Rabbi Yeshua, here is my friend Natanel. What do you know of him?"

I know nothing of him except I saw him sitting under the fig tree praying. I open my mouth to say so, but my voice makes words I never thought. "They say in your village that Natanel the hireling is too honest, and they mean he is a gullible and a fool. They call him Gullible Natanel, but I say HaShem loves an honest man."

Natanel stares on me for a moment in a big shock. Then he scowls on Philip. "What did you tell him on the matter? How does Rabbi Yeshua know what people say in our village?"

Philip shakes his head. "Ask Yoni Many-Questions if I told the rabbi one word on you."

Yoni grins. "How could a man be too honest? Are you a hired man? My father hires men to work in his fleet of boats, but he never said one of them is too honest. My father would be glad of having you work for him. Do you know Shimon and Andre, whose father is Yonah the fish-man? They used to live in Bethsaida and came to Capernaum six years ago on account of the border tax. Their father is partner with my father, whose name is Zavdai. You may have heard of him, for he is a big—"

"Yoni, just answer the one question!" Philip shouts on him. "What did I tell Rabbi Yeshua about Natanel?"

Yoni shrugs. "Nothing, of course. Rabbi Yeshua said you had a sister named Rivka, and you were amazed and came out of the river, and Rabbi Yeshua asked you to explain the matter to me, and you told the whole tale, and then Rabbi Yeshua said you should come with us to the wedding feast of his sister, and then you ran away. Why did you run—"

"Who told you our village calls me Gullible Natanel?" Natanel asks.

Nobody told me. HaShem told me. I do not know how.

Yoni says, "Rabbi Yeshua is a prophet and he knows everything. Also he is a *tsaddik* and a son of David. He saw HaShem, did you know? Our prophet Moses saw the hind parts of HaShem and lived, and that was a mighty wonder, but Rabbi Yeshua saw the face of HaShem and lived."

I make a grin on Natanel. "I saw you praying under the fig tree, and I thought you were a righteous man. And then when Philip brought you here, HaShem told me the rest, how they say in your village that Natanel the hireling is a gullible and a fool. And HaShem says an honest man is a thing he loves more than gold."

Natanel's eyes narrow. "If you are a prophet, then what was the matter I was praying on under the fig tree?"

I wonder why people think a prophet knows everything. I open my mouth to ask how should I know what he was praying, but my tongue makes words of its own accord. "Friend, why do the goyim make a rage, and why do the people think on a big foolishness?"

I do not know why I said that.

Natanel the hireling stares on me as I am a Messenger of HaShem. His mouth hangs open and his eyes grow large, and he looks as he has forgotten how to breathe. His knees buckle and he

collapses to the ground, chanting the words of a mighty psalm of
David the king.

> "Why do the goyim make a big rage?
> Why do the people make a big foolishness?
> The kings of all the lands stand up
> And the mighty make a counsel together
> On Yah and on his Mashiach:
> 'Let us tear off their bonds!
> Let us throw off their ropes that bind us!'
> But he who sits on the heavens laughs.
> The Lord makes a mock on them.
> So he will speak to them in wrath
> And terrify them in his rage:
> 'I set my king on Zion,
> On my mountain of righteousness.'
> I will tell the decree of Yah.
> He said to me,
> 'You are my son,
> Today I have become your father.
> Ask from me
> And I will give
> The goyim for your heritage,
> To the ends of the earth for your possession.
> You will beat them with a club of iron
> To shatter them like shards of clay.'
> Now be wise, you kings,
> And learn, you judges of the earth.
> Make a service to Yah with fear
> And make a joy with trembling.
> Make a kiss to his son
> Or he will be angry,
> And you will be destroyed in the road.
> His rage ignites in a moment,
> But happy are those who put their trust in him."

When Natanel the hireling finishes, I do not know what to say. He chanted the whole psalm of the coronation of the king of Israel, the son of Yah.

"Rabbi, you are a prophet of HaShem!" Natanel says. "I was praying that HaShem would send Mashiach, the son of David, the son of Yah. If you say you are the king of Israel, I wish to be first to join your army."

I did not say so. I said only a few words of a psalm. I see now why his village calls him Gullible Natanel.

Yoni says, "Rabbi Yeshua, what is it like to be a prophet? I always thought prophets were angry on everyone, but you are not angry on everyone. Is that because you are a *tsaddik*? The village *hazzan* said a prophet was for telling the wrath of HaShem, but you told the kindness of HaShem to Philip, and then you told what was in the heart of Natanel, and I think that was also a kindness. Does HaShem tell you kind things only about the people he loves like his own children? What does HaShem tell you about the Great Satan? When will you tell the wrath of HaShem? Also, who is the first Power you are to smite? Is it the King of the South? I think it is the King of the South."

Now it is me whose knees feel so weak they will not hold me.

Yoni said a thing just now that shocked me.

I have been waiting and waiting for HaShem to speak to me on his wrath.

And I hear nothing, only a few whispers.

Then I look on a man who needs kindness, and HaShem tells me more kindness on that man in a moment than a scribe could write in a month.

There is a thing wrong with me.

All my life I heard I am to redeem Israel.

To redeem Israel is to do battle with our enemies.

To do battle with our enemies is to smite the four Powers.

But how am I to smite the four Powers, if all I hear from HaShem is kindness?

If these men knew the truth of the matter, they would not call me a prophet.

They would call me a liar and a gullible and a fool.

CHAPTER TWENTY

Miryam of Nazareth

It is a walk of four days to reach Nazareth from the place where Yohanan the prophet tells repentance to Israel. For four whole days, I hear nothing but talk of who is the first Power. My sons love to argue. These new men love to argue—Shimon the Rock and Big Yaakov and Andre and little Yoni. There are two other men who joined us, Philip and Natanel, and they also love to argue.

My sons think the first Power is Syria or Egypt or Babylon. The new men think it is Egypt or Babylon or Syria.

My heart is like a lump of lead. I do not care what is the first Power or the second or the third or the fourth. I care that my son will leave me undefended. I know I should be brave, and I am shamed that I am not brave, but it is true. I am not brave. I am terrified. My son should make a justice on me first. Then he can go smite all the Powers he will find.

When we see Nazareth, it is the afternoon of the sixth day of the week. The village elders sit just inside the gate, looking west down the hill, watching us climb the steep, twisting path. They smile on my son Yeshua. They smile on my other sons and my daughter. They smile on the new men who joined us. They smile on Little Yaakov's concubine. They smile on Yehuda Dreamhead's woman.

They do not smile on me. Their lips curl and their noses rise as they smell the *haryo* of a dog.

I wish I can run away and hide. I wish HaShem will come and burn them down. I wish Yeshua will smite them.

He holds my hand, and that is good, but it is not enough.

We come in the gate and turn right and walk through the village square and down the short street to our house.

Yosi and Thin Shimon rush inside, shouting for their joy. Their women stayed home with small children all these weeks. Tonight, they will warm their men.

Little Yaakov shows the new men where they are to sleep. There are six of them and the weather is still fine, so they will sleep on the roof. I do not know where we would put them if the weather was foul.

The young women set to work making a feast. There will be lentils and chickpeas and broad beans and onions and spices from Babylon in the stew tonight. Dates from Jericho. Figs and raisins from Nazareth. Many rounds of bread. We will drink a whole amphora of wine that my brother-in-law made.

We will need water, but the young women are all working like bees.

I take a waterpot and call for Yeshua, and we walk.

When we pass the gate, the elders call out a greeting to Yeshua.

He grins on them and calls out a greeting to them. He is holding my hand. When he holds my hand, I feel brave of the village.

We walk past the ovens of Shimon the baker.

Still I feel brave of the village.

I see two small girls of the age of five playing in the dirt. They sing a song they are too young to understand. It is a song I have heard many ten thousand times. One girl sings a line and the other sings the next and then the first sings the next.

> "Once there was an evil tale
> An evil tale
> An evil tale.

Once there was an evil tale
And Miryam was her name.
Do not be an evil tale
An evil tale
An evil tale.
Do not be an evil tale
Like Miryam the *zonah*."

A woman shouts from inside her house.

The two girls see me and run away fast, shrieking.

Tears hide in my eyes, ready to run out again. I try so hard to be brave of the village, but always they find a way to put a knife in my heart.

Yeshua's hand is strong on mine all up the street.

We pass the leather-man's house and go out of the village. We were gone long from Nazareth, and I forgot the bad stink of his piss-pool.

Yoseph the leather-man wades at the far end, tanning his hides. Two new calfskins hang on a rack, dry from the strong sun.

Yoseph the leather-man makes a cruel grin on us.

I am an evil tale all over again.

Yeshua squeezes my hand to make me brave, but I will never be brave of Yoseph the leather-man.

We go through the narrows. We trudge up the path toward the spring.

My lips quiver. I cannot find my next breath.

Yeshua wraps his strong arms around me. "Imma."

I hold him tight for many thousand years until I stop my shaking.

We walk and walk until we reach the spring.

I dip my waterpot in the spring and set it on my head.

Yeshua takes my hand.

We walk back down the hill. We walk through the narrows.

At the far end, we stop.

Someone has thrown *haryo* in the path. Not the *haryo* of sheep or goats or cows. The *haryo* of men. Fresh from the day.

It is spread thick all across the narrows so we cannot walk around it. Yeshua could jump over it, for he is a strong man, but I cannot jump so far, even if I had no waterpot. I will have to walk on the *haryo*.

I am so angry I think I will drop my water.

All my body shakes.

Black spots dance in my eyes.

"Imma."

I have such a big rage on me, I shout on my son. "*Haryo* again! You should smite the Evil Boy. You should smite him so he dies. If my lord Yoseph were alive, he would curse the Evil Boy with Yaakov Mega's ring."

Yeshua says, "Imma, the Ring of Justice has no power to curse a man. The Ring is only a sign that the man who wears it makes a righteous justice. The man has the power, not the Ring. And anyway, the Ring is lost."

"Then find it! Find it and make a justice on me. If you love me, you will look in every place under heaven until you find it."

Yeshua says, "I love you, Imma."

"Not enough!" I scream.

Yeshua cringes as I have slapped him.

That is a worse knife in my heart than the song the girls sang.

"Wait here, Imma." Yeshua backs up a dozen paces and runs toward the *haryo*. He leaps over it and keeps running, straight and fast.

My heart pounds in my chest. He left me undefended.

A moment later, he runs back, carrying two calfskin hides.

Yoseph the leather-man chases after him, shouting and shaking his fist.

Yeshua throws the hides on top of the *haryo* and walks on them to my side. He takes my hand.

I walk on the hides together with him.

Yoseph the leather-man glares on us with hate in his eyes. "You ruined my hides!"

Yeshua releases my hand and strides toward him.

For a moment, I think he will smite the leather-man. I wish he will smite him so he dies.

Yoseph the leather-man takes a step back. "You ruined my hides!"

"You ruined your own hides," Yeshua says.

Yoseph the leather-man spits the dust. "Son of a *zonah*."

Yeshua takes a step toward him.

Yoseph the leather-man runs away fast.

Yeshua comes back for me. He takes my hand. His hand is hot and he is breathing hard and he reeks of sweat. A big anger shines in his eyes.

Today I love my son more than I ever did.

We walk together through the village, the whole long street. I am brave of the village all the way.

When we reach our house, Yeshua lifts the waterpot down from my head.

"Imma."

I feel as I might cry again.

"Imma, I swear by The Name that I *will* make a justice on you. How I will do it, I do not know. When I will do it, I do not know. But I will make a justice on your name."

I throw my arms around him and cry for my joy.

If my son says he will make a justice on me, he will make a justice on me.

Blessed be HaShem.

PART 2: THE EVIL BOY

Fall, AD 29

Do not be an evil tale
An evil tale
An evil tale.
Do not be an evil tale
Like Miryam the zonah.

CHAPTER TWENTY-ONE

Miryam of Nazareth

My heart is full today, for it is the wedding feast of my daughter Shlomi Dancefeet.

We made Shabbat in Nazareth, and I felt safe all the day long. Then we stayed one day more, and still I felt safe. My sons and the new men spent all that time arguing on who is the first Power. Little Yaakov asked Yeshua many times when he will make a move. Yeshua said he will make a move when HaShem tells him to make a move.

Today is the third day from Shabbat. If he makes a move today, I will scratch his eyes out.

Yeshua reclines on a dining couch with the father of the bridegroom. He is laughing and feasting and drinking wine. He does not look like a man who will make a move.

Yesterday we walked from Nazareth to the village of Cana. This morning, Thin Shimon read the wedding contract aloud and the witnesses signed it. The bridegroom is named Eliezer, a man of honor in his village. He is a peasant, so he will inherit land from his father, though not much, for he is the second son. His father owns a stone house with a large courtyard and many rooms, but he does not have much land, for he was the second son of his own father.

I wish one of my daughters had married a wealthy man, but Yeshua has done all he could do to find them men. Not all men are willing to marry the daughter of a *tekton*.

Today my daughter Shlomi Dancefeet is a married woman. I recline on a couch with her at a table with the other women. I am glad and I am sad, both at the same time. That is the way of a wedding feast. It has been a fine feast, but I think Eliezer spent many more *dinars* than he had. We drank wine and ate a fattened calf and drank more wine and ate spiced beans and chickpeas wrapped in bread and drank more wine and ate dates from Jericho. It has been long since I ate so well.

Eliezer hired women to make music. Three sisters play the flute, and their mother plays a harp, and three of their cousins stand behind and sing psalms of joy.

It is very good.

The steward of the feast approaches Eliezer and crooks his finger. He wears an angry face.

Eliezer rises from his couch and follows the steward out.

It is none of my business, but Eliezer is now my son-in-law, and I am curious. A mother-in-law has a right to be nosy on her daughter's wedding feast. I rise from my couch and follow them out of the courtyard into a large room.

At the far end, five manservants stand around a great puddle of red wine. Two large clay amphorae lie broken on the stone floor.

My heart thumps in my chest, and I think I will cry. The fools broke two vessels! One, I could understand, for everyone is clumsy sometimes. But two?

Eliezer points to the wine cellar and says something in a choked voice.

The steward shakes his head.

Eliezer asks another question and still I cannot hear him.

A manservant shakes his head. "It is the last of the wine, my lord."

Now I am crying. They are fools and simples. I would beat them with a stick if it would make any matter.

All the wine for the feast is lost, and there are still several hours before the going out of the day. The wedding feast is ruined, and my son-in-law is dishonored.

Now I cannot see for the tears running out of my eyes. A wedding feast happens once in a woman's life, and if it is ruined, there is no repairing it.

This is worse than if my son had made a move today.

Yeshua of Nazareth

"And when will you take a woman?" Eliezer's father asks.

We are reclining on the couch enjoying the music.

We were enjoying the music.

I do not know how to answer him. Every man wishes to take a good woman, but no man of my village will give me his daughter, on account of the smirch. Each one says he does not believe the smirch himself, only someone else in the village might, and then his grandsons would have the smirch, and so what can he do?

The smirch has been a big harm on me all my life, but now that I think on the matter, perhaps it is good I have no woman. I do not know the way ahead. I know it is dark. Yohanan's word from HaShem lies heavy on me. I must smite the four Powers, but I do not know what are the four Powers. I would have guessed that one is the Accuser, and perhaps it is true, but perhaps it is not. Are there Powers more mighty than the Accuser? The scriptures do not say. The scriptures do not even speak of the Accuser. They do not speak of any Powers. The scriptures tell how to live a good life filled with joy, but they do not tell how to bring in the kingdom of HaShem. I must find my own way through deep darkness, with the Shekinah as my only light.

The way forward will be a road of horrors, and no man would wish to walk it alone, but no man would wish to endanger a woman on such a road. I will go alone with Abba, and he will guide me.

Eliezer's father makes a big sigh. "My cousin took in a girl when she was an infant. She is *asufi* and soon she will come of age, only no man will take her. She is healthy and a good worker, and it is a big sadness on me. If you knew of some man who would take her, that would be a kindness on me."

He is being polite. An *asufi* child is a foundling. No man of Israel may take an *asufi* girl, for that is not fitting, to take a girl whose parents are unknown. It is not done. A convert may take her. Also a freed slave or a son of a *zonah* or an *asufi* man. Or a *mamzer*.

I smile on him. "I will make inquiries on the matter in Tsipori."

He means well, but I cannot take this healthy girl, not if she is the best worker that ever was. To take her would be to say yes to the smirch on my name. And to say no to redeeming Israel.

Imma calls my name from across the courtyard. Her face is tight, and there is a damp streak on her cheeks.

In an instant I am on my feet and rushing toward her. "Imma, are you well?"

She whispers in my ear. "They have run out of wine." She leads me into the house.

Two broken amphorae lie on the floor, and all the wine is spilled. The steward is shouting on the servants. They cringe before him like beaten donkeys.

For a moment, my mind is frozen and my hands feel damp. How has this happened? My sister's day is ruined, and there is nothing I can do. Nothing.

I look all around for the bridegroom, but he is not here. "Where is Eliezer?"

Imma tilts her head toward the village. "He went to see if the wine merchants will give him credit for two more amphorae."

That is useless. The merchants already gave him more credit than they should have. They will dishonor Eliezer now, and he will be angry when he returns.

Imma clutches my arm. "You must do something. You are a man of honor."

There is nothing I can do. I did not bring money, or I would give it all. I cannot get credit, for I come from a different village, and they do not know me here. I cannot make the merchants give Eliezer yet more credit when they already gave too much.

Imma weeps.

My heart is crushed, but there is nothing I can do. "Imma, please, my time has not yet come. I am no king, that I can take tribute."

She thinks I can snap my fingers and do anything because I am a *tsaddik*. I love her much, but she does not know how the world of men works.

Imma pokes her finger on my chest. "You will do something, please. Go to the village and get more wine." She points to the servants. "You men! Go with my son to get more wine. Do what he tells you." She turns and marches away.

I follow after her. "Where are you going?"

"To see what my son-in-law can do in the village. Bring the servants and follow me." Imma hurries toward the village.

I could never say no to Imma, but I do not know how to say yes.

The steward is still shouting on the servants.

Yoni pokes his head around the corner. "Rabbi Yeshua, what are you going to do?"

CHAPTER TWENTY-TWO

Yoni of Capernaum

I should not have spied on Rabbi Yeshua, but I was curious. I saw his mother beckon him out, and she had the look my mother wore when I was a small boy and ate all the Jericho dates before the evening meal.

So I followed them, and I saw and heard all. I think Rabbi Yeshua's mother expects much.

I wait for Rabbi Yeshua to answer my question.

But he does not speak. The Shekinah is on him.

When I first saw Yohanan the immerser, he had the Shekinah on him, and I thought it was strong. But the Shekinah is stronger on Rabbi Yeshua than on Yohanan, as the sun is stronger than the moon. Rabbi Yeshua is deep in the Presence of HaShem. There is a big wisdom here, and I wish to know this wisdom. I watch and I watch, but I do not see anything happen.

Then the Shekinah is gone, and Rabbi Yeshua smiles on me with a fierce smile. The danger in that smile makes my heart tingle, as Rabbi Yeshua is going to battle against some mighty warrior. I do not understand, for there is no mighty warrior here, and it is only a matter of some spilled wine.

Rabbi Yeshua laughs a great laugh.

The steward stops shouting on the manservants and stares on Rabbi Yeshua.

Rabbi Yeshua points to the puddle and tells the steward, "Friend, you will call some girls to clean up the wine."

The steward looks as he does not wish to obey, for he is the master of the feast and Rabbi Yeshua is not.

"Friend, you will do it now," Rabbi Yeshua says.

The steward goes away grumbling.

Rabbi Yeshua leads one manservant outside and points to a row of stone barrels as tall as my waist that stand along the back wall. "Are any of these empty?"

I think it is a foolish question. They are heavy, lathe-turned barrels for holding waters of purification. Stone is not susceptible to any impurity and it is good for holding water, but it is useless for carrying wine.

The manservant checks each of the barrels. "Rabbi, these four have water and these six are empty." He smirks behind his hand, because it would be foolish to go to the wine merchant carrying such heavy barrels. Even a strong man would stagger under such a big weight if it was filled with wine.

I think Rabbi Yeshua is making a joke. I think he will go out now to find a wine merchant. I do not think he will take these stone barrels.

Rabbi Yeshua smiles a big smile. "Bring some servant girls to me here with waterpots."

The manservant looks on Rabbi Yeshua with large eyes.

Rabbi Yeshua raises a fierce eyebrow.

The manservant runs to obey.

I wish to run and hide. This is a big foolishness. I do not see what joke Rabbi Yeshua is making. There is water enough in the other four barrels for any washing needed for the rest of the feast. But one does not drink water from purification barrels. There is no reason in what he asks. There is only foolishness.

I am alone with Rabbi Yeshua. "Rabbi, what are you doing?"

He gives me a terrifying smile. "I heard from Abba to fill the barrels. Therefore, I will fill the barrels."

"But it is foolishness." I do not like foolishness. I came to this village with Rabbi Yeshua to learn wisdom, when I could have gone home to Capernaum. If he is a man given to foolishness, I will go home and learn Torah with the village *hazzan* until my father sends me to Jerusalem to learn with a sage.

Rabbi Yeshua's eyes burn into mine.

Fear scalds my heart. I do not think Rabbi Yeshua likes me to call a word of HaShem foolishness, even if it is foolishness.

Soon a dozen servant girls come, each holding a waterpot.

Rabbi Yeshua greets them with kind words and asks them to fill the barrels of purification.

All of them walk out of the gate in a long line.

I step out into the dusty street and watch them. Cana has a good well, fed by a natural spring. The girls walk to the well and fill their jars and return. It is a thing I have seen every day of my life—girls carrying water. It is a thing I never saw in my life—great foolishness.

Each girl pours her water in the first of the stone barrels, until it is full, and then in the next. They walk to the well three times before all the barrels are full and covered again with their stone covers.

Rabbi Yeshua has been watching the whole time. The Shekinah is strong on him. He sends one girl to find the steward. The others return to their chores at the feast.

I am dying with my curiosity on this paradox. "Rabbi Yeshua, what are you doing?"

Rabbi Yeshua wears a cryptic smile. "I am doing what Abba tells me to do."

I like it when Rabbi Yeshua calls HaShem Abba. It has a good sound, and I feel warmed inside, but still I do not think Rabbi Yeshua knows what he is doing.

I lift the lid on the first stone barrel and dip my finger in the water. It is good water, fresh and clean, but it will not please guests who expect wine. And it will make them very angry to be served out of barrels made for washing hands. I cover the barrel and wait.

Rabbi Yeshua has the Shekinah on him still. I wish I could have the Shekinah like that.

Shortly, the steward arrives, along with the manservants and the bridegroom. The steward's face is red. I think the bridegroom has been shouting on him.

Rabbi Yeshua bows to the bridegroom, then points to one of the servants. "Fetch a pitcher and cup and draw from one of the stone barrels."

The servant's face is pale and moist. He knows Rabbi Yeshua is making a joke on him. He hurries away to fetch. He is gone long, and when he returns, he does not hurry.

I still do not know why HaShem told Rabbi Yeshua to make this joke. It is wasting time, to no gain.

"Draw from the barrel," Rabbi Yeshua says.

I back away to the far corner. The bridegroom will make a rage when he sees Rabbi Yeshua is making a joke on him. I wish I had not come to this feast. Rabbi Yeshua dishonors his brother-in-law, and he dishonors himself also.

The servant lifts the lid of the barrel.

He dips in a pitcher.

He draws it out.

Red wine drips down its sides and spatters on the ground.

Wine!

My heart thumps like the waves that beat on the hull of our boat in a storm. I do not think any prophet in Israel ever made such a mighty wonder, not even Elijah.

The servant's eyes are large as silver *dinars*. The other servants gabble among themselves like pigeons.

Anger draws the steward's face tight. "Fools! Why have you put wine in barrels of purification? It is not fitting."

The servant pours out a cup and hands it to him.

The steward tastes it. Delight rushes into his eyes. He turns to the bridegroom. "What foolishness is this? You kept the best for last, and put it in barrels not fitting!"

I think he is the fool, not to know a mighty wonder has taken place.

The bridegroom wears a look like a blank wax tablet. He does not know any more than the steward.

Rabbi Yeshua grins a big grin. There is a look on his face like a warrior who has won a great battle. I think King David wore such a face on the day he cut off the head of the giant. I think Elijah looked just so on the day he destroyed the false prophets of the *ba'al*. I do not understand why Rabbi Yeshua looks like this. There was no enemy he fought. It is a mighty wonder to turn water into wine, but we have farmers who can make wine already. We do not need more wine in the world. We need a man who will throw down the Great Satan.

Anyway, nobody saw the mighty wonder except me. The servant girls poured in water, but they did not see the wine. The manservants did not see the water, but now they see the wine. Only I saw both the water and the wine. It is foolishness to make a mighty wonder when only one sees it.

Rabbi Yeshua takes my hand and pulls me away. "Come, Yoni. The kingdom of HaShem is upon us." The sound of his voice makes me think of the roaring of lions.

I am afraid and I am delighted and I am astonished, all at the same time. I do not know what he means, that the kingdom of HaShem is upon us. That cannot be true. Rabbi Yeshua has made a paradox for me to solve. The sages tell that when the kingdom of HaShem comes, all Israel will be gathered to a great feast, together with Mashiach. But that will not happen until the wrath of HaShem throws down our enemies and HaShem returns from his long exile and the Shekinah shines in the Temple of the living God.

That has not happened, and therefore how can the kingdom of HaShem be upon us?

Still, it is a mighty wonder, and such a thing has not been seen in Israel for many hundred years.

I think I will not go to Jerusalem next year to learn Torah.

Yeshua of Nazareth

My face feels hotter than it ever did, and my heart pounds as I have run from Jerusalem to Nazareth.

HaShem has done a mighty wonder!

Only Yoni saw the mighty wonder, but soon everyone will know it, for Yoni talks more than any man or boy ever did. All will rejoice at the mighty wonder and give thanks to HaShem.

I give thanks for the mighty wonder, for it is good.

But there is a greater thing here that makes this mighty wonder seem like a small wonder.

I called on HaShem, and I heard his voice.

I heard, not like a man who strains to hear a faint whisper.

I heard, not like a man who listens with muffled ears.

I heard true and clear, like when I was a small boy sitting on Abba's lap and he told me tales of old. When he said I must go to bed, I tugged on his beard and begged for one more tale. And he laughed a great laugh and told another tale.

That is how clear I heard the words of HaShem.

The words of Abba.

I did not know the purpose of Abba's words, but I obeyed, and then Abba did a mighty wonder.

Some will say it is a small thing, to make wine to bring joy to the heart of one girl on her wedding day.

That is a lie.

It is not a small thing, it is a large thing.

A girl is born and grows to a woman. In the blink of an eye, she marries and gives birth and raises children. In two blinks of an eye, she is old, bent under the weight of years. In three blinks of an eye, she is dead and buried.

Of all the days of her life, there is one day most wonderful—her wedding day.

To give a girl joy on her wedding day is a thing precious to Abba.

My brothers will not understand that.

Shimon the Rock will not understand that.

Big Yaakov and Andre and Natanel will not understand that.

Philip might understand it a little.

Yoni will understand.

Abba has given me two gifts today. The gift of hearing his voice. And the gift of a friend who understands the deep things of HaShem. My heart is full, because—

"Yeshua!" Shlomi Dancefeet runs around the corner and throws herself in my arms. She laughs. She cries. She shouts my name.

I hold her close, for she is my last sister to be married. She is the one who loves me most, for she never knew our father Yoseph, who died before she was born.

Shlomi gives me a kiss and a kiss and a kiss. "You are the best brother who ever lived, and now you have my permission to go to war and smite the Great Satan. But you will be careful, yes?"

"Abba will go with me."

Her eyes shine. "Where will you go to begin the war?"

I do not know where I will go to begin the war, but my mouth opens of its own will and says, "Capernaum."

I did not know until this very moment that I was going to Capernaum, but now I know it with certainty.

Abba has given me new friends. Shimon the Rock and his brother Andre live in Capernaum. Yoni and Big Yaakov live in Capernaum. Philip lives in Bethsaida, which is just beyond Capernaum. Natanel was born in this village, but he works as a hireling in Bethsaida.

With my four brothers, that makes ten men for my army. I do not know what I will do with an army of ten, but Abba will show me.

We will go to Capernaum.

We will rest there a few days.

I will listen to HaShem until I know who is the first Power.

And then we will go to war.

~

Miryam of Nazareth

My son made a mighty wonder! I heard it from little Yoni, how the Shekinah rested on my Yeshua and he called for the servants of my son-in-law and gave them orders and they did them, and now see! Wine!

He would not have made this wonder except I asked him.

It is a sign from HaShem.

I asked my son, and he did a big thing.

My son loves me. HaShem loves me.

It is a sign Yeshua will make a justice on me.

He promised he will do it.

Now I know he will do it.

He will burn down our village.

He will close the lying lips of my accusers.

He will crush the fingers of those who put *haryo* in my path.

After he makes a justice on me, he can smite as many Powers as he wishes and throw down the Great Satan and redeem Israel and rule on David's throne.

CHAPTER TWENTY-THREE

Yaakov of Nazareth

"We will need swords to make a war on the Great Satan. Where can we get swords?" I am walking alongside Shimon the Rock, who is the leader of the men from Capernaum.

I like Shimon. He is a fish-man, and his father owns several boats. They have money, and we will need money to buy weapons. That must be why Yeshua chose him. Shimon looks almost as strong as me. He will make a mighty captain in my army.

Shimon the Rock looks back to where Yeshua walks with our women and children.

My face feels hot. The women and children slow us down.

Shimon says, "Why is Rabbi Yeshua walking with the women? He should be making a strategy with us."

I shrug. "He loves our mother overmuch."

Shimon sighs. "I thought he was eager to begin the war."

"The matter of swords. Are there iron-men in Capernaum skilled in making swords?"

"We can get sickles."

"A sickle is not a sword."

Shimon says, "We have iron-men in Capernaum who make sickles. We do not have iron-men who make swords. If the Romans heard we had iron-men who make swords, it would go hard on the iron-men."

"What about slings?" I ask.

"We have slings. Every boy from the age of three has a sling."

"And stones?"

Shimon's eyes burn hot. "We have more stones on one street of Capernaum than all the slingers in the world could sling if each had seven hands."

I smile on Shimon and pound his strong shoulder. "It is good. When our father David killed the giant, he did it with a sling. If we go out to kill the Great Satan with stones, HaShem will give the victory in our hands."

Shimon the Rock grins a big grin. "And if we go out with sickles, HaShem will also give the victory in our hands."

I like Shimon, but I will keep a watch on him, for he has some cleverness. Not so much as that little Yoni, but Yoni is a boy and Shimon is a man. One does not keep a watch on a boy.

Shimon's mouth is set tight. "The Romans have archers, yes? For those, we will need wooden shields."

"They do not have archers. They use javelins. For those, we need iron shields."

His face is dark. "We do not have men to make iron shields."

"Can your iron-men learn to make them?"

"They could learn, but they have no one to teach them. But Herod has a palace and a garrison in Tiberias. He must have men who can make shields. And swords."

I spit in the dust of the road. "We will have nothing to do with Herod. He is a finger in the hand of the Great Satan."

"We could break into Herod's armory and take what we need."

"Herod's men would make a big fight, so we would need more than ten men. How many men live in Capernaum?"

"Three hundreds, at least, maybe four. Many more if old men and boys are counted. But we are farmers and fish-men. Herod has twice that many trained soldiers."

My head spins. Three hundred strong men, or even four? Capernaum is bigger than I thought. Nazareth is only the tenth part of Capernaum. I know every man in Nazareth, every woman, every child. I do not think Shimon knows even all the fish-men in Capernaum.

Shimon the Rock turns to look on me. "Rabbi Yeshua must have a plan, yes?"

I do not know what to say. Yeshua has said nothing of his plan. Yesterday at the wedding feast he said we would go to Capernaum. At last he means to make a move. But he did not say how he will make a move. I do not think he knows how to make a move. I know how to make a move, and yet he is the one everyone expects to make a move. That is foolishness, but I will not say so. Not yet. Let him draw men. When it is seen that he cannot lead a fight, it will be seen that I can.

"We should ask him what is his plan." Shimon stops still in the road.

I do not wish to ask Yeshua, but I do not have a choice. I stop still in the road.

We wait for the women and children to catch up.

Yeshua holds the hand of my mother as they walk.

I have told him five hundred times, it is not done to walk and talk with a woman, nor less to hold her hand, but he pays no attention. If we lose these good men over his foolishness, I will break Yeshua's teeth with my fist.

Shimon the Rock is not stupid. His eyes are on Yeshua and my mother as they come nearer. He looks little pleased.

By the time Yeshua reaches us, my cheeks feel as they are on fire.

"It is a fine day, yes?" Yeshua says.

Shimon the Rock clears his throat. "Rabbi, you will make a move soon, yes?"

Imma's face turns pale.

Yeshua smiles. "I will make a move when HaShem tells me to make a move."

"And what move will you make?" Shimon asks.

All around us, Yeshua's men grow silent.

My brothers grow silent.

Imma's mouth is set in a hard, thin line. "You should go to Nazareth and punish our village for their wickedness."

Imma hates our village, but she thinks too small. Nazareth is not our enemy. The Great Satan is our enemy. After we destroy the Great Satan and rule on the throne of our father David, that will be a good time to make our village pay for the wrong they did on Imma. They did some of it on me, also. The leather-man will pay for what he did on me.

"I have been thinking on the matter," Yeshua says.

We wait.

Nobody speaks.

"I do not yet know what to do, but HaShem will tell me what to do. You saw what happened at the wedding feast."

My ears feel hot and my fists clench, for this is foolishness, to wait and wait and wait for HaShem to say a word. Anyway, I did not see anything at the wedding feast. Imma saw the wine lost, or says she did. Yoni saw the wine restored, or says he did. I drank wine, and it was a good wine, but that is all I saw. I think this tale of a mighty wonder is overspoken. For all I know, there was more wine in the cellar and the servants remembered and brought it up, and now they are grinning behind their hands on this gullible talk of a mighty wonder.

It drives me mad for Yeshua to keep waiting for some word from HaShem, while the Great Satan grinds its heel in our face every day. But it will go even worse if Yeshua makes some half-strength rising and then the Great Satan comes and destroys our nation.

Yeshua should let me make the move. I would raise up a mighty army and kick the Great Satan in its underparts. I would crush the Great Satan in a month, if Yeshua would say the word.

But I cannot say such things. I am not a speaker of smooth words. If Yeshua had any sense, he would see it without being told.

Yeshua looks past me toward the Lake of Ginosar. "Is that Tiberias ahead of us?"

"That is only Magdala," Yoni says. "Tiberias is south of it by a walk of one hour, but we do not go there because Herod built the city on a graveyard, so it is unclean. Capernaum is north of Magdala by a walk of two hours. That flat mountain just before Magdala is Mount Arbel, and from the top you can see the whole lake and every village and town. Would you like to climb it? It is not far, and the way is not steep if you go up by the back side, but I think Shimon the Rock is too tired to reach the top."

Shimon growls deep in his throat. "Hmmph! I climbed Mount Arbel when I was a boy, and it made a good adventure … for a boy. But men think on larger matters."

Imma tugs on Yeshua's sleeve. "I am too tired to climb some mountain. We will not walk all the way to Capernaum today, will we? The sun is low and we walked far today."

I think we have not walked far today. We started late in the morning, that is the problem. We brought all our women and children, against my advice. If we started early, we could have walked to Capernaum in a day.

Yeshua shakes his head. "Shimon the Rock, where can we make camp tonight?"

"Next to Magdala, by the shores of the lake." Shimon twists his hands and shifts his feet. "But Rabbi, on the matter of the move you are to make …"

His words hang heavy. Shimon does not wish to dishonor my brother by making blunt words, but we all wish to know what move Yeshua will make.

Yeshua says, "I will make a move when HaShem says to make a move."

It is the worst answer he could make.

Shimon's face turns to stone, and his eyes pull inward.

Andre scowls on the ground.

Big Yaakov rubs the back of his neck.

Philip and Natanel look on each other with wide eyes.

"You do not know how to make a move, do you?" says Yoni.

That boy is rude and impertinent, and I would smite him if he said such a thing to me. Only he says what we all think.

Yeshua does not know how to make a move.

Yeshua does not mean to make a move.

Yeshua is no Mashiach and will never be Mashiach. He has no *yetzer hara* to do great things, like our father David.

I am tired of Yeshua's womanish dithering. If he will not make a move soon, then I will.

CHAPTER TWENTY-FOUR

Yoni of Capernaum

Today is the third day after we left Cana, and today Rabbi Yeshua will make his move.

I will be the only one to see it, because I am the only one watching.

We arrived yesterday morning in Capernaum.

My father was angry we came home six days late. Shimon's father was angrier.

Shimon the Rock is the oldest, so they made a blame on him.

Shimon grinned on them and said they should hear me say a word on the matter.

So I told them how we found Rabbi Yeshua, who is a prophet and a *tsaddik*, and how it is prophesied he will smite the four Powers, only he needs our help on the matter, and also he is in the line of David the king, and he has four strong brothers with him like the Makkabi heroes of old, and we would have come straight home by the Jordan Way, only Rabbi Yeshua made a beg on us to join with him in the wedding feast of his sister, and also the prophet Daniel tells how in these last days will come Mashiach the king, the son of HaShem, and so we knew our fathers would give permission if they knew, but they did not know, so what could we do?

I made more words than that, more words than I ever made, and I wore them down, until at last they threw hands in the air and said we did well.

After that, Rabbi Yeshua talked long in private with my father and Shimon's father, all the afternoon. Last night, we all ate a good meal in the house of Shimon's father and told tales. I told the tale of the mighty wonder at the wedding feast. My father said it was a good tale and asked if I would go fishing in the night.

I begged off, because I saw Rabbi Yeshua's face while we were feasting, and I knew he would make his move today. I wish to be first to see it.

Shimon the Rock begged off because he said he was tired, only I think he wished to lie with his woman, who stayed here during the feast with her two young children. Shimon did not look tired. He looked eager.

Big Yaakov and Andre did not beg off, and they went fishing last night.

Philip and Natanel went fishing also. My father offered them a *dinar* each, and that is a good money.

Rabbi Yeshua's brothers and their women slept in the house of Shimon's father, for he has many rooms.

Rabbi Yeshua's mother slept in our house in my grandmother's room.

Rabbi Yeshua slept in my room.

I slept lightly, and now I am rewarded, because it is the hour before dawn, and I hear Rabbi Yeshua slipping outside.

I filled my waterskin with beer last night. I take it and follow after him at a distance of fifty paces.

He walks south on silent feet through the streets of Capernaum.

I follow on silent feet.

He passes the synagogue.

I pass the synagogue.

He goes out through the village gate.

I go out through the village gate.

He walks south along the road that runs beside the lake.

I walk south behind him. This road goes to Magdala by a walk of two hours and then turns west and goes to the Great Sea by a walk of three days and then turns south and goes to Egypt by a walk of three weeks. Rabbi Yeshua strides with strong purpose as he means to go all the way to Alexandria. Tales tell that a thousand thousands of Jews live there, and if he means to raise up an army—

Rabbi Yeshua stops and turns.

I freeze and try to make myself small in the darkness.

"Yoni, come walk with me." His voice sounds like laughter.

I do not think he is angry on me for spying on him, so I hurry to join him.

When I reach him, he makes a big grin on me. "You are out walking early. Where are you going?"

"To watch you make your move."

"What move do you think I will make?"

"If I knew, then the others would have wormed it out of me, and they would be here also."

"They would have to work hard to worm out your secrets, yes?"

I laugh on that, for everyone says I cannot keep a secret. My father says if I think a thing once, I say it three times. But everyone is wrong. I can keep a secret, if it is a mighty secret. The trick is not to think on the matter.

Rabbi Yeshua looks on me with sharp eyes. "What move would you make if you were me?"

I am pleased he asks my advice. Little Yaakov would not ask my advice. That man has a face of stone and arms of iron. When I look on him, I think of David our king. When I look on Rabbi Yeshua, I do not think of David our king.

Rabbi Yeshua raises his eyebrow. "You have no thoughts on how to make a war against the Great Satan?"

"I do."

Rabbi Yeshua takes my hand and begins walking. "I wish to hear what you think."

We are walking together and holding hands as we are friends! My heart pounds, for I had thought Rabbi Yeshua was going to be my master. A man is not friends with his master. A man washes his master's feet and serves him dinner and does whatever his master needs.

"Speak," Rabbi Yeshua says.

My thoughts come out in a rush. "We are eleven men, and the Great Satan is too mighty for eleven men to defeat in open battle. Therefore, we must build an army, but even an army of eleven thousands would be small next to the legions of the Great Satan. Therefore, we must attack with our strongest strength at the point of the Great Satan's weakest weakness."

Rabbi Yeshua nods. "And where is the Great Satan's weakest weakness?"

"The Great Satan has many mouths to feed in Rome, but not enough food grows in all Italy to feed those mouths."

"Man does not live only on bread."

"The Great Satan lives on bread, and bread comes from wheat, and wheat grows in Egypt. The Great Satan takes tribute from Egypt and eats for seven months in every year from the granaries of Egypt."

Rabbi Yeshua says nothing, but I see he is thinking.

"It does not take many ten thousand men to destroy a granary. It takes one hot coal of fire, and one man of determination, and one moment of opportunity."

"And that is your plan, to burn the granaries of Egypt?"

"I think it will go hard on the Great Satan if it loses the granaries of Egypt. Eleven men can burn many granaries. Eleven men cannot defeat the legions of Rome."

Rabbi Yeshua thinks on this for a few moments, but he says nothing.

I say, "Has HaShem shown you how to make a move?"

"HaShem told me to come this way and watch and see what I will see."

"But he did not tell you how to make a move?"

"Perhaps that is how I am to know how to make a move."

"What is it like to be a prophet? Were you always a prophet? When you were a nursing baby, did you hear the word of HaShem?

Does HaShem tell you things in your ear every moment of the day? Why are not all men prophets? Why are so few women prophets?"

"HaShem tells me things in my ear when there is no other way to hear things. But HaShem made the great world for us to see, and if we look with the eyes of HaShem, we do not need many words from HaShem."

"So HaShem prefers to show you his words more than tell you his words? Is that because a man remembers a thing better when he has lived it himself than when he has been told by another?"

Rabbi Yeshua's mouth drops open, and his eyebrows fly up. For a moment, he seems far away. Then he looks on me and smiles. "That was well said, Yoni."

My heart burns inside me. My father never says I said a thing well. Neither does Big Yaakov nor Shimon the Rock.

"Now walk with me, Yoni, and tell me what you see."

We walk south along the road. The light grows slowly until the red sun peers over the mountains on the east side of the lake.

We stop and begin the morning prayer, the Shema. "Hear, Israel, the Lord our God! The Lord is One!"

After we say the whole prayer, we begin walking again.

Rabbi Yeshua says, "What do you see?"

"The sun looks like the wrath of HaShem prepared for the wicked. When HaShem comes in his kingdom, he will burn their cities with a big fire as punishment for their sins. There will be weeping and gnashing of teeth when the wrath of HaShem falls on the Great Satan. There will be a bigger weeping and gnashing of teeth if the wrath of HaShem falls on us. The prophet Yohanan said the wrath will fall on us first, and the Great Satan next. What do you think?"

Rabbi Yeshua says nothing, and we walk on.

I saw the wrath of HaShem once when I was very young. It was only a taste, but it terrified me more than anything ever did. I am glad Rabbi Yeshua does not ask what I know on the matter, for it would horrify him. There are some tales that should not be told.

We reach the village of Ginosar, where the hills step back away from the lake to make a broad plain with many rich farms. Two jackals fight over the carcass of a dead sheep.

I say, "They fight over one carcass as they think there is too little for both. If they ate together in peace, they could each feast and be happy, but they will tear each other's eyes out because they hate peace and love fighting."

Rabbi Yeshua nods, and we walk on.

We reach the outskirts of Magdala. I do not like Magdala, for it is a large town. I think it might have five thousands in it, and maybe more. That is too many, and it makes me sad to think they cannot all know each other's business, as we do in Capernaum. I hear angry shouts and hurt cries.

We speed our steps.

When we come around the corner, I see a man beating his woman with a thick stick.

My father says when a man beats a man, that is injustice, but when a man beats his woman, it is not injustice because the woman was disobedient or burned his meal or made lewd eyes on some other man. I asked him once if he would think different if he were a woman. He gave me a beating for that, and said it is a good justice to beat a son who is conceited and arrogant. I do not think the person with the stick is the best judge of what is justice.

Rabbi Yeshua's hand clutches mine tight.

I smell the sweat of his anger. I think he will fight the man. I do not think Rabbi Yeshua is afraid on the man's stick.

The woman kneels with her face in the dirt, cringing and sobbing.

Rabbi Yeshua stops. He closes his eyes and cocks his head. The light of the Shekinah is on him.

The man smites his woman across the back with the stick.

She screams.

The man looks on Rabbi Yeshua. "What do you want, stranger?"

Rabbi Yeshua opens his eyes and makes a big smile. "Friend, I ask for a cup of cold water. We have walked far, and the sun is hot."

The man points at my waterskin. "You have water. Drink it and go your way." He smites his woman across the hips with the stick.

She screams.

"Friend, I ask for a round of bread. We have walked far, and we are hungry."

The man scowls on us. "Go see what the fig harvesters left." He smites the woman across the head.

She collapses and makes no sound.

"Friend, I ask for a walking stick. We are going on a long journey."

The man spits Rabbi Yeshua's feet. Then he draws back his stick and swings it fast in a flat circle at the level of our waists.

Rabbi Yeshua leaps inside his swing.

He catches the man's wrist.

He squeezes it with a mighty squeeze.

The stick falls from the man's hand.

Rabbi Yeshua twists hard on the man's wrist, forcing him to turn with his arm behind him.

The man shouts with a great shout. "Yehuda! Elazar!"

Rabbi Yeshua pushes the man down onto his face in the dirt. "Yoni, take the stick and run."

I take the stick. It is thick and heavy in my hand. "Shall I beat the man? I think he deserves a good beating. I think if he had a good beating, he would never beat his woman again. I think—"

Two men run around the corner of the house. Knives glint in their hands.

"Yoni, run now!"

I run.

Rabbi Yeshua's footsteps pound behind me.

He is fast, but I am faster, and shortly I am out of Magdala on the road to the Great Sea.

I run until I hear a shout from far behind me.

I turn to look.

Rabbi Yeshua has stopped and is bent over with his hands on his knees, breathing hard.

Three men stand at the gate of the town, shaking their fists and shouting. They are too far away to hear.

I walk back to Rabbi Yeshua. "That did not go so well."

Rabbi Yeshua stands again as he is listening. For a time, he says nothing. At last he looks on me with a twisted smile. "What did you see, Yoni?"

"I saw a man beating a woman."

"A good man or an evil man?"

"An evil man."

"And then what did you see?"

"I saw you speak words of peace."

"And words of peace made the evil man good?"

"They made him return evil words for good."

"Then what did you see?"

"You spoke more words of peace."

"And those made the evil man good?"

"They made him return more evil words for good."

"Then what did you see?"

"You spoke more words of peace."

"And this time they made the evil man good?"

"They made him return evil actions for good."

"Then what did you see?"

"You disarmed the man without harming him."

"And that made the evil man good?"

"It made him call for evil friends with knives."

"What if I killed the evil man?"

"Then we would still be running, with those evil friends behind us."

"What if we burned their granaries?"

"I do not think any road would be long enough for us to escape their vengeance."

Rabbi Yeshua takes my hand and begins walking along the road west toward Caesarea. "I wish to climb Mount Arbel. Show me the way."

We walk in silence along the road until the turning off. A dirt path on the left goes up the back side of the mountain like a long ramp. We walk the whole way in silence. I am thinking on what we saw. I wish we had a word from HaShem. There is more than one way to think on this matter. Suppose we had a hundred men in our army? Or a thousand? Or ten thousand?

When we reach the summit, there is a straight drop down, a hundred times the height of a man. Magdala looks small below us, and the people are like ants. The Lake of Ginosar lies before us. To the north, I see the village of Ginosar. Farther on, Capernaum. Beyond them, hazy in the distance at the north end of the lake, Bethsaida. South of us is Tiberias, an evil city, Herod's city. At the edge of sight at the south end of the lake, the Jordan River goes down toward the Salt Sea. On a clear day, I have seen the south end of the lake, but today is not a clear day, and my heart is in a big turmoil. I do not see why we have come here. I do not see how we are to fight the Great Satan. I am wondering if Rabbi Yeshua knows what he is doing. Sometimes I think Little Yaakov knows better how to make a move.

The sun is high in the sky now. I offer Rabbi Yeshua my waterskin.

He takes a long drink. "What did you see today, Yoni? What does HaShem show you?"

I do not know how to answer. "What did you see, Rabbi Yeshua?"

"I saw ... the name of the first Power."

I shiver, for when we were walking four days from Jericho to Nazareth, Rabbi Yeshua's brothers spent many words guessing who are the four Powers.

"Who is the first Power? What are you going to do? Are we going to raise up an army? What do you think of my plan to destroy the Great Satan? Will Little Yaakov lead your army? Do you think he is more mighty than Shimon the Rock? When are you going to make a move?"

Rabbi Yeshua smiles and says nothing.

I have not known him many days, but I have learned that when he does not wish to tell his mind, he does not tell his mind.

My whole body feels as it is filled with ants.

I am desperate to know what move Rabbi Yeshua will make.

I do not think it is a move Little Yaakov will like.

And when Little Yaakov learns I helped Rabbi Yeshua plan his move ...

I hope he will not get his hands on my walking stick.

CHAPTER TWENTY-FIVE

Yeshua of Nazareth

I sit with Yoni on the mountain, admiring the fine view. My hands sweat and my breath is stolen and my heart beats a rhythm like a galloping horse.

I know the name of the first Power.

My brothers think the first Power is one of the enemies who surround us—Egypt or Syria or Parthia or Arabia.

Any one of them would be a mighty foe to conquer. I do not know how I would smite Egypt or Syria or Parthia or Arabia.

But at least I would know what it means to smite them.

The first Power is not any of those powers. The first Power is not a nation that can be seen. The first Power has no army I can smite.

The first Power is the Power that lives inside every man, whether he is evil or whether he is good. Every man has a *yetzer hara*. Our prophet Moses had a *yetzer hara*. Our father David had a mighty *yetzer hara*. Our prophet Elijah had a great and powerful *yetzer hara*.

Little Yaakov says I have no *yetzer hara*. Men say I am a *tsaddik*. Men say a *tsaddik* has no evil inclination.

They are wrong.

In Tsipori, I have seen men training for the games. Jews do not train for such things, but Greeks and Syrians do. Every man who trains has a trainer—one who tells him what he must eat and when he must sleep and how he must run and lift weights and wrestle.

A weak athlete has a weak trainer who presses him weakly, for that is what he can endure. A middling athlete has a middling trainer who presses him middling hard, for that is what he can endure. A mighty athlete has a cruel and vicious trainer who beats him and robs him of sleep and shouts on him with rage every moment, for that is what a man must endure if he will win the crown.

Every man has a *yetzer hara*, given to him to tempt him to evil and so train him in the ways of HaShem. A weak man has a weak *yetzer hara*. A middling man has a middling *yetzer hara*. A *tsaddik* has a cruel and vicious *yetzer hara*.

I sometimes fear my *yetzer hara* is more cruel and vicious than I can endure. If men knew what it is to be a *tsaddik*, no man would ever wish to be a *tsaddik*.

I think before I can go to war against the Great Satan, I must have an army that is good and pure before HaShem. Men who are not over-come by their *yetzer hara*. I do not know how I will find such men. It seems a foolish quest.

It seems an impossible quest.

I do not know how to fight this battle against other men's *yetzer hara*. My own *yetzer hara* takes me to the limit of my strength. How am I to defeat the *yetzer hara* of a whole army?

Yoni studies me with large eyes. "Rabbi Yeshua, who is the first Power?"

I smile on him. "I prefer to show you what is the first Power, rather than tell you."

He laughs, for I have snared him in his own net. "Are you hungry? I am more hungry than I ever was. Did you notice the figs in the trees by the side of the road? They were as big as my head. I think two of them would fill my belly. Shall we go glean some of the leavings from the harvest? When are we going back to Capernaum? Will you make your brothers suffer as much as you make me suffer with your myste-rious ways? Do you think it will rain tonight? I think it looks like rain, even though it is too early in the year. Will you give me a hint on who is the first Power? I think it is Egypt. Will you tell me if it is *not* Egypt?"

I stand and take his hand and pull him to his feet. "I will answer the most pressing of your many ten thousand questions. Yes, I am hungry. I saw a few figs left, and I think you have overspoken them, but I am willing to eat them anyway, if they are no larger than the black of my eye."

We walk down the back slope of Mount Arbel. The sun is high in the sky now, and there is a fresh, damp wind blowing from the lake. It smells like rain.

By a walk of one hour we reach the road again and walk toward Magdala. We take care not to go by the way we came. Yoni still carries the stout walking stick, but the man we saw is armed with rage, and that is a mighty weapon. His *yetzer hara* controls him, and how am I to defeat that? It is a hard riddle.

We walk through the fig orchards of Magdala. The harvesters left a few figs, small ones. They are overripe. We eat all we can hold, until Yoni says fig juice oozes from our ears. My stomach is full, but my mind races.

How can a man defeat his *yetzer hara*? That would be a hard matter, for I never knew a man to defeat his *yetzer hara*, but that is not what HaShem calls me to do.

How can a man defeat another man's *yetzer hara*? That is impossible, but even that is not what HaShem calls me to do.

How can a man defeat the *yetzer hara* of a whole army? That is worse than impossible. That cannot be what HaShem calls me to do. And yet I fear it is what HaShem calls me to do. I have not heard a word from HaShem on the matter. But I think it is what I saw today, and so it weighs much with me. If I cannot solve the riddle, then surely HaShem will tell a word in my ear.

But if HaShem does not tell a word in my ear, it means I can solve the riddle.

We walk north on the road. It is a rough dirt road, thick with ruts, but if you follow it north by a walk of one day, you will reach a good Roman road paved with stone. That road goes to Damascus and divides there to go to Antioch and Babylon. Some say you can walk by Roman roads all the way to India in the east and Spain in the west.

The sun shines, but the wind blows harder, wet and cold. I pull my cloak up around my shoulders.

When we reach the farmland at Ginosar, Yoni points at the carcass of the sheep we saw this morning. The jackals are gone, and a wolf gnaws at the bones. "Two jackals are no match for one wolf, yes?"

I take his hand in mine, for Yoni is a friend. He thinks I am his master who can answer any question. And I am his master, but only because his questions make me see further than either of us could see before.

I feel a thought welling up inside me. There is a thing stronger than a man's *yetzer hara*. It is a thing I have known since I was the smallest boy, a thing that sticks closer than a brother. A thing I see in a man, rarely. A thing I see in Yoni, sometimes. A thing I feel in myself, always.

But it is not a thing I can command.

HaShem is showing me something new.

I do not understand it, not yet.

I do not see how this thing will defeat the Great Satan.

All I know is that the Shekinah in me is stronger than the *yetzer hara* in me.

I do not know how to give the Shekinah to another man, but I know that it must be possible. I know that HaShem will show me.

Rain begins falling on us, fine, cold drops.

I run, for I am mad with happiness. "Run, Yoni! Run with me!"

Yoni races after me, hooting with glee.

I do not think he knows why I am happy, but he feels it, and it makes his heart glad also.

I am more joyful than I ever was.

HaShem showed me more of my journey today. Not all. Not the whole long road to redeem Israel.

HaShem showed me the next step. He told me he would show it, and he did. If he told it all in one moment, perhaps I would collapse under the weight of it, as I would collapse if he told me I must run all the way to India.

But I know enough.
And I will know more soon.
I do not know all the long road to defeat the first Power.
I only know the next step on that road.
Each day, another step, and HaShem will take me all the way.

CHAPTER TWENTY-SIX

Miryam of Nazareth

I slept poorly last night. They put me in the room with the grandmother of the house, and she snores. At dawn, I give up trying to sleep and go see what work I can do to help the women of the house.

Yoni's mother is named Shlomzion. They do in Capernaum as we do in Nazareth—every person with a common name must have a nickname. Hers is Imma Shalom. She is well named, mother of peace, for she is broad and warm and kind.

I walk to the village well with Imma Shalom to fetch water.

She talks all the way, as fast as that boy Yoni. She has two sons and five daughters. The sons are the oldest and the youngest, Big Yaakov and Yoni. The five girls are in between, and all are married now. And these daughters live with their lords all in the House of Zavdai!

I am shocked on the matter. That must be a very great family, if a man marries a woman and comes to live in her father's house. In our village, a man marries a woman and brings her into his own father's house.

My son told me that the House of Zavdai is one of the mighty families of Capernaum, and now I think he underspoke the matter. Imma Shalom says they are a family of priests, and there have been sages in their clan.

Imma Shalom tells that Yoni is a man already, although I thought he was no more than ten. They call him the Genius of Capernaum. Next year, he is to go to Jerusalem to study with a great sage in Israel. They hope he will be taken by Rabbi Shammai or Rabbi Gamliel. Even I know those names, for they are the greatest sages of our age. My sons love to hear them expound Torah when we go to the feasts in Jerusalem.

When we return to the House of Zavdai, it is all in a roar.

The youngest daughter of the house is named Elisheva, and she tells that Yoni and Yeshua are gone. She was awake an hour before dawn and saw Yoni going outside and thought he went to look on the lake. But he never came back, and his room is empty, the room where Yeshua was sleeping.

My heart beats on my ribs for my fear. "What if they went to make a war on the Great Satan already?"

Elisheva takes my waterpot and smiles on me with kindness. "If they went to make a war, they will be back soon, for they took no men with them."

My mind says that is a good saying, but my heart does not know it, and it smites my chest.

Elisheva takes my hand. "Come down to the fishing pier with me. We can see if they went to help the men bring in the night catch."

I walk with her to the pier. The houses of Capernaum are made of some strange black stone I never saw before. It gives all the village a dark, angry look.

Elisheva is fourteen, and she loves her brother Yoni. She talks even more than he does, and before we have passed the synagogue, she tells how he came to have his nickname. His true name is Yohanan. When Elisheva was a small child, she could not say such a big name, so she called him Yoni, and it stuck. He is the baby of the family, and a kind boy, even if he is conceited. She says he should be conceited, for there never was such a mighty genius since King Solomon.

That is saying much, and I think it is oversaid. I will ask my son if Yoni is such a big genius as that.

When we reach the fishing pier, we find only the lord of the family, Zavdai, who is short and stout and fierce like Big Yaakov.

"Abba, where is Yoni?" Elisheva asks.

Zavdai scowls on her. "How should I know? Maybe fallen in the lake."

Zavdai frightens me. I clutch Elisheva's hand.

She swats at his arm. "Abba, do not make such a bad joke on him."

Zavdai raises his hand to shade his eyes and squints in the rising sun. "The boats are coming in. When you find Yoni, tell him to come give us a help with the fish, since he begged off going out last night. If he begs off again, I will let Big Yaakov throw him in the lake."

Elisheva kisses her father on the cheek. "When Yoni is a great sage in Israel, you will not make a joke on throwing him in the lake."

Zavdai growls something I cannot hear, but there is a look of pride in his eyes. I do not think Yoni will be thrown in the lake.

Elisheva takes my hand, and we walk along the beach. It is covered with stones the size of my fist. She points toward a small cove to the north. "Yoni likes to hide his clothes and swim there naked with his friends. Perhaps he took Rabbi Yeshua."

My whole body is in a big sweat. "My son does not know how to swim."

"Perhaps Yoni is teaching him."

I do not wish Yoni to teach my son to swim. My feet drag all the way to the cove.

It is empty.

I do not know which is worse—finding my son naked and dead in the water, or not finding him.

Elisheva points to a large house near the synagogue. "Perhaps they went to the House of Yonah to see Shimon the Rock. Your other sons are all staying there."

I like that better. Of course, my son went there. He can pray the morning prayers with Little Yaakov and the others.

My feet are light all the way to the House of Yonah.

Yeshua is not there. Yoni is not there. Nobody has seen them.

Elisheva and I walk all through Capernaum looking for my son and Yoni.

Capernaum is a big village, more than a hundred houses. Maybe two hundreds, but I never had to count so high. At last we go back to the House of Zavdai.

Yeshua and Yoni are still not there.

When the men come in from the fishing pier, we all eat the morning meal. My heart feels like a lump of lead.

The morning drags by, and then the afternoon. It is the sixth day of the week, and soon it will be time to make Shabbat. I do not feel like making Shabbat. I want to know where is my son. My other sons all gather in the House of Zavdai, waiting to know what is the news. Little Yaakov and Shimon the Rock sit in a corner talking and wearing grim faces.

I watch them and wonder which of them will be first in my son's army. Little Yaakov thinks it should be him, for he is Yeshua's brother and has a mighty *yetzer hara*.

But I think Shimon the Rock is as strong as Little Yaakov. I think he also has a mighty *yetzer hara*, and he comes from a big family with a good name in Capernaum. He thinks it should be him.

Yeshua will have to make a hard choice, and one of them will be angry. I had not thought on that.

Late in the afternoon, Elisheva shouts in the street. "Yoni! Rabbi Yeshua! Where have you been all day?"

I hurry out to see.

"We went to Magdala!" Yoni shouts. "On the way, we saw the sun rising like the wrath of HaShem. And we saw jackals fighting over a dead sheep. And we saw an evil man beating his woman with a stick, and Rabbi Yeshua fought the man and took away his stick and beat him soundly, but then his friends chased us with knives, and we were nearly killed, and Rabbi Yeshua fought them more powerfully than any man ever did, and they ran away terrified, and then we climbed Mount Arbel and HaShem spoke to us and told us who is the first Power, and now we are ready to make a big war on the Great Satan!"

My heart thumps again. My son fought with knife-men! I rush to Yeshua and wrap my arms around him. "Have pity on an old woman.

You were gone all the day without leaving word. And you were fighting knife-men."

My son gives me a kiss and a kiss and a kiss. "Yoni may have over-told the tale. I went out early to hear a word from HaShem, and Yoni followed, and I was glad of his help to make a strategy."

Big Yaakov scowls on Yoni. "What does a boy know on strategy?"

Shimon the Rock's eyes look like thunder. "Did you hear a word from HaShem?"

Little Yaakov wears a stone face. "Why did you leave no word with us?"

Andre and Philip and Natanel and my other sons stand back silent, but I see in their faces they think the same.

I think my son does not see his danger.

"Rabbi Yeshua heard who is the first Power, but he will not tell!" Yoni says. "I think it is Egypt. I think we should go there and burn the granaries and then raise up an army of many ten thousand men and fight the legions of the Great Satan."

Little Yaakov shakes his head. "Yeshua, the first Power cannot be Egypt, yes? It must be Syria. Why should we walk three weeks to Alexandria when we can walk four days to Damascus?"

Sweat stands out on Shimon the Rock's forehead. "Friends, this is not the way a man makes a strategy on the Great Satan. We need weapons first. We need an army. We need a man to command the army."

My stomach is all in a knot. Yeshua is a *tsaddik*. What does a *tsaddik* know on making a war?

Yeshua looks toward the sun, which hangs two hours above the horizon. "Shabbat will be here soon. Yoni and I are tired and dirty. I wish to find the public baths. I wish to welcome in the Shabbat. I wish to spend a day resting as HaShem commanded. Tomorrow night, after the going out of Shabbat, I wish to eat a good meal with all the friends HaShem has given me. When the meal is done, then will be a good time to speak on the matter of the first Power. Then I will tell you what I have decided."

He has decided.

I feel as my stomach is full of swarming locusts. My son has decided to go to war. He will leave me all alone.

And all his men are angry on him because he decided without them.

He decided with the help of the least of them, that little Yoni.

My son is a good and humble man, but that is his weakness, for he does not know what is ambition and what is envy.

He does not see the pit he is about to fall into, whichever way he may turn.

CHAPTER TWENTY-SEVEN

Yaakov of Nazareth

It has been a good Shabbat and we have eaten a good meal, and now I am ready to go to war. I am more impatient than I ever was. Yeshua should have made his move at the feast in Jerusalem, and now it is two weeks past and the winter rains will begin in a month. It rained a little yesterday, but the season of rain is not yet. We do not have much time to make a move.

We went to the synagogue this morning with the new men Yeshua has gathered. Shimon the Rock knows all Capernaum, and he introduced us. There are many men in Capernaum. Not all of them are fit for battle, but I think we could call up three hundreds. It is a start.

We have finished a large dinner at the family house of Shimon the Rock. His father's name is called Yonah, and he has a good name in these parts. He is old, almost fifty, and has some wisdom about him, and I could see at the synagogue that men hold him in honor. That will count for something.

That boy Yoni's family is also here—Big Yaakov and his father, Zavdai, and his mother and his five sisters and their lords and children.

Yonah raises his hand for silence.

Both clans quiet at once.

Yonah says, "Rabbi Yeshua, we have heard many words on you. My sons tell big tales on you. Your brothers tell big tales on you. But you do not tell big tales on yourself. You have been with us now three days. When will you make your move, and what will it be?"

Yeshua has that look on him now, as he is listening to a voice no other man can hear. The large courtyard of Yonah's house falls silent as Sheol. Even the children stare on Yeshua with a big awe in their eyes.

Yeshua stands.

For a moment I cannot take breath.

"Some say Egypt is the first Power, that we should make a war on it."

That boy Yoni grins like a monkey. I have heard him say Egypt fifty times.

"And some say Syria is the first Power, that we should make a war on it."

I feel all eyes hard on me. My hands feel hot and my neck feels cold.

"There is a thing to be said for each of these, for they are ancient *satans* of Israel, our enemies for many hundred years," Yeshua says. "I wish to hear the tale of each. Yoni, you will tell the tale of Egypt. Little Yaakov, you will tell the tale of Syria."

I do not like this matter. Yoni is a boy of many words. I am not a man of smooth words.

Yeshua reclines in his place.

Yoni leaps up and strides to the center of the courtyard.

I do not like that boy. He thinks he is something because he is clever.

Yoni stands as still as stone for a moment, and then he begins his tale.

"In the days of Joseph, our father Jacob went down to Egypt with all his clan, seventy men, plus women and children. And they settled in the land of Egypt, and time passed, and they had many sons and daughters."

I close my eyes and … I see the land of Egypt in my mind's eye. I see many hundred Hebrews working their lands and tending their flocks. A blink of an eye and a new generation arises, many thousand Hebrews working their lands and tending their flocks. Another blink of an eye and a new generation arises, many ten thousand Hebrews working their lands and tending their flocks. Another blink of an eye and a new generation arises, many hundred thousand Hebrews working their lands and tending their flocks.

I see the Pharaoh on his throne, shaking in a big terror to see so many Hebrews. I see him make orders to his officers. I see his officers make orders to his soldiers. I see his soldiers make slaves on our fathers.

I see our men beaten. I see our women used for a pleasure. I see our children thrown in the river.

I see our people cry out to HaShem to make a justice on Egypt.

But I do not see justice.

I see a child, born of a woman, hidden in a basket, floating on the river. I see the daughter of the Pharaoh find the child. I see her take the boy into her home. I see the boy grow into a man, a strong man, a bold man, a man of action.

I see the man Moses strike down an Egyptian who was beating one of our people. I see him flee to the desert, where he finds refuge, takes a woman, tends his flocks, grows old, turns timid. I see him waiting and waiting without ever making a move.

My fists clench. I want to shout on him to make a move.

I see the man Moses meet HaShem in the wilderness at last, after forty years. I see HaShem call him to make a move. I see him quivering, afraid to make a move.

I see HaShem bring his brother Aaron to join him, to be his strong right arm, to help him make a move.

I see Aaron and Moses speak to Pharaoh, demanding that he let our people go.

I see Pharaoh laugh in their faces, making a mock on them, asking who is HaShem, that Pharaoh should obey him.

I see Aaron the brother of Moses raise his rod and smite the great river and make it blood, and still Pharaoh makes a mock on him.

I see Aaron the brother of Moses smite the dust of Egypt and make it gnats, and still Pharaoh makes a mock on him.

I see Aaron the brother of Moses smite Egypt nine times with plagues, and still Pharaoh makes a mock on him.

I see Aaron the brother of Moses name Egypt with a new name, the Wicked Satan, the first enemy of our people.

I see HaShem send the Messenger of Death in the night to slay the firstborn of all the Wicked Satan, from the Pharaoh's palace to the rent-farmer's hut.

I see the Wicked Satan laid low.

I see our people set free.

I see them escape by a walk of three days to the shores of the Red Sea.

I see Pharaoh pursue with chariots and horses.

I see Aaron the brother of Moses raise his rod and make a path of dry land appear through the Red Sea and give the people escape.

I see the Wicked Satan pursue on the same path of dry land.

I see Aaron the brother of Moses drop his rod.

I see the waters return to their place.

I see the Wicked Satan drowned.

I weep for my joy.

The Wicked Satan is crushed.

Israel, the son of HaShem, is saved.

Saved at the hand of Aaron the brother of Moses.

The story ends, and I cannot speak. All that is within me says the Wicked Satan is the first Power. That boy Yoni has bewitched me.

When I open my eyes, I see it is the same for all the others. Every man in the room wishes to go make a big war on the Wicked Satan.

The Wicked Satan, Egypt, feeds the Great Satan, Rome.

To destroy Egypt is to starve Rome.

That boy Yoni is silent now, grinning on his victory, for he thinks he has defeated me.

But I will break his spell. Egypt was a mighty Power that slaved us many hundred years ago. But they are not the only Power in the world, nor the nearest.

Yeshua smiles. "That was well told, Yoni. I do not think any man could have told it better."

Yoni goes and reclines in his place. His father, Zavdai, rumples his hair. His brother, Big Yaakov, pounds his shoulder. His sisters smile on him with tears of pride in their eyes.

Yeshua turns to me. "But there is more to be told, and Little Yaakov is the best man to tell that tale. Please."

Yeshua leans back on his elbow.

My heart quivers in my chest.

I do not know how I am to best Yoni. That boy talks more than any man ever did. More than any woman. I will never be a man of smooth words. I am a man of mighty deeds. A man with a great *yetzer hara*.

Yeshua smiles on me as he knows me to be a mighty hammer, like Aaron the brother of Moses.

In the instant, I feel a big power in my veins, and I know I can do this thing.

Also, I know how to do this thing.

I will tell the Tale of Seven Brothers.

It is a tale every man of Israel knows well.

But I will tell the tale as it was never told before.

I leap to my feet and spring to the center of the courtyard.

I feel the weight of all their eyes on me.

I begin the tale.

~

The Tale of Seven Brothers

"Many hundred years ago, our fathers sinned a big sin. HaShem was in a big wrath and sent the king of Babylon to make a justice on us. Babylon killed our men in battle. They forced our women to spread legs in the streets. They broke down our city and burned our Temple and threw our dead bodies in the Hinnom Valley, where the worms never die. They slaved our children in a far country."

All the courtyard is silent. They have heard this evil tale many times.

"After seventy years, our people returned and rebuilt our city and our Temple, but HaShem did not return on account of our sins, and the king of Persia ruled us. After two hundreds of years, the king of Greece conquered the king of Persia and ruled us, but still HaShem did not return on account of our sins. The king of Greece died, and his kingdom was divided, but still HaShem did not return on account of our sins. The king of Egypt ruled us a hundred years, but still HaShem did not return on account of our sins. The king of Syria conquered the king of Egypt and ruled us, but still HaShem did not return on account of our sins."

I pause a moment and let the silence do its work, making a rage in all our hearts for the next king, the cruel king.

"A new king arose in Syria, more cruel than any king that ever was. So cruel, we named him the Cruel Satan. The Cruel Satan thought to unmake our laws, which HaShem gave us by our prophet Moses. The Cruel Satan sent his soldiers to our city and took it, but HaShem did nothing on account of our sins. The Cruel Satan sent men to our Temple to sacrifice a pig on the great altar, but HaShem did nothing on account of our sins. The Cruel Satan's men spread the legs of our women in the Temple courts, but HaShem did nothing on account of our sins. The Cruel Satan's men found mothers in Israel who had circumcised their sons, and killed them on the Temple Mount, but HaShem did nothing on account of our sins. The Cruel Satan looked through all the land of Israel and found seven brothers, righteous men who would not sin."

Until now, the tale is the same as it was always told. But now I will make a shock on them all.

I point to Shimon the Rock and beckon him to join me in the center.

Shimon's eyes pop open, but he does not come forward. He does not understand the matter.

I beckon him again to join me.

Shimon sits up, but still he does not come forward. He thinks this is my tale to tell, but he is wrong. Now it will be his tale, also.

I beckon a third time. "Come up here, First Brother."

At last Shimon understands the matter. A big grin spreads across his face. He comes forward, walking proud. The First Brother has a big honor in this tale.

I point to Yosi and Thin Shimon and Yehuda Dreamhead. I point to Big Yaakov. I point to Andre. "Come here, all of you, and fill up the count of the Seven Brothers."

All of them come forward to join me.

The whole courtyard is alive now. They have heard the Tale of Seven Brothers many times.

Now they will see it.

We lock arms together, seven heroes, seven soldiers of HaShem.

"The Seven Brothers had a mother, gray with years, who was more righteous than any woman." I point to Imma.

Imma beams. She springs forward on proud feet. A light like the sun is in her face.

"The Cruel Satan ordered the First Brother to eat the flesh of a pig." I pull Shimon the Rock out from our line.

He wears a fierce look, and proud.

He should be proud. If the First Brother had failed, the others would have too.

"The Cruel Satan cut out the tongue of the First Brother. The Cruel Satan cut off his hands. The Cruel Satan cut off his feet. The Cruel Satan ordered the First Brother to be fried alive in a great pan. The First Brother did not sin against HaShem, and he died in a big agony."

I push Shimon the Rock to the ground.

Shimon's father, Yonah, has a face more fierce than a lion. The light of pride shines in his eyes, for every man hopes his sons will be willing to die with the courage of the First Brother.

I choose out Big Yaakov next. "The Cruel Satan chose out the Second Brother and made a torture on him like the first. He tore out his hair and cut off his hands and his feet. When the Cruel Satan ordered the Second Brother to eat the flesh of a pig, he spit the Cruel Satan's face and cursed him, and then he was fried alive in a great pan. The Second Brother did not sin against HaShem, and he died in a big agony."

I push Big Yaakov to the ground.

His father, Zavdai, leans forward and smiles on his brave son.

I choose out Yosi. "The Cruel Satan did the same to the Third Brother, who held out his hands to be cut off and told the Cruel Satan, 'I got these hands from HaShem, and I will get them back again in the Last Day.' Then he cursed the Cruel Satan and was fried alive in the pan, and he died in a big agony."

I push Yosi to the ground.

Imma's eyes run over with tears, but there is a look of iron in her face.

"The Fourth Brother was tortured the same by the Cruel Satan. When he died, he told the Cruel Satan, 'I will be raised again by HaShem on the Last Day, but you will not!' Then he cursed the Cruel Satan, and he died in a big agony."

I push Thin Shimon to the ground.

"The Fifth Brother was tortured the same by the Cruel Satan. When he died, he told the Cruel Satan, 'HaShem will not forget that you tortured his people. HaShem will come again and torture you.' Then he cursed the Cruel Satan, and he died in a big agony."

I push Yehuda Dreamhead to the ground.

"The Sixth Brother was tortured the same by the Cruel Satan. When he died, he told the Cruel Satan, 'You are deceived to think you do this on your own account. HaShem uses you to punish us for our own sins. But HaShem will forgive us for our sins. HaShem will not forgive you for your sins.' Then he cursed the Cruel Satan, and he died in a big agony."

I push Andre to the ground.

Every face in the courtyard is pale. They feel the heat of the fires. They smell the stench of the roasting human flesh. They hear the death rattle of the Sixth Brother.

My mother shakes beside me, so fierce I think her knees will fail her. She knows the Seventh Brother will be tormented worst.

"The Cruel Satan begged the mother of the Seven Brothers to save her last son. He promised to give the Seventh Brother gold, to name him Friend of the King, to give him honor and power if only he would eat the flesh of a pig. The mother lied to the Cruel Satan and promised to speak favor to her son. But instead she told the Seventh Brother, 'I held you nine months in my belly and fed you three years at my bosoms. You shall remember that HaShem did not make the world from things that are, but from things that are not. Be a man like your brothers and trust in HaShem to make you again in the Age to Come on the Last Day.'"

My mother's face is hard as granite. I never saw her face so proud and strong. She has more mettle than I thought.

"The Seventh Brother laughed in the face of the Cruel Satan and mocked him to scorn. He told the Cruel Satan, 'You most vile of all men, you wretch, you *haryo*! We suffer now on account of our sins, but HaShem will raise us again on the Last Day on account of our right-eousness. HaShem will punish you on the Last Day for your sins.' Then the Seventh Brother cursed the Cruel Satan and spat his eye and mocked him. The Cruel Satan tortured him more terribly than all the other six together. The Seventh Brother cursed the Cruel Satan, and he died in a big agony."

My mother throws her arms around me, and I feel her great pride.

I look around the circle.

"When the Tale of the Seven Brothers was told through all Israel, HaShem raised up a righteous priest. All Israel called this man the Hammer, Yehuda Makkabi. He and his four brothers fought the Cruel Satan, and they took back the Temple and Jerusalem and the land of Israel, and they ruled in Jerusalem a hundred years, but HaShem still has not returned on account of our sins. And now the Great Satan rules in our land, and this is the final hour. HaShem wills that we take back our land and drive out the Great Satan and find a man to rule on the throne of our father David, and then HaShem will return and forgive us our sins. And HaShem will raise up new Makkabi heroes to do it, five brothers against the four Powers. The first Power is the one nearest us, and that is the Cruel Satan, Syria."

Yaakov of Nazareth

Every eye is weeping. The women hug their children close. The men grin with fierce grins.

Yeshua's face twists and his eyes clench tight. His face is in a big agony, more than the Seventh Brother when they fried him in the great pan.

I am sure I have won. Yoni told a great tale, but I told a greater, even though I am not a man of smooth words.

HaShem gave me the words for the tale. HaShem told me to show the tale, and not tell it only. HaShem will raise me up to be the mighty hammer that will destroy all the Powers, and last of all, the Great Satan.

Yeshua comes and gives me a kiss and a kiss and a kiss. He pulls up each of my brothers. He pulls up Shimon the Rock and Andre and Big Yaakov. He sends us all to our places.

It is only when I recline at my place that I see Yeshua has remained in the center.

There is a bold look on his face.

My stomach falls within me.

Yeshua also has a tale to tell.

CHAPTER TWENTY-EIGHT

Yoni of Capernaum

I thought my tale was well told, and all would see that the first Power is Egypt.

But Little Yaakov's tale was well told also, and I am afraid that now all think the first Power is Syria.

And now Rabbi Yeshua has a tale.

I do not wish for Rabbi Yeshua to tell a better tale than mine.

I am dying to hear him tell a better tale than Little Yaakov's.

Rabbi Yeshua begins his tale. "When HaShem led our people by the hand out of Egypt, he took us into the desert until we reached the Mountain of HaShem ..."

I close my eyes to listen and ... I see our people. I see many hundred thousand men and women and children. I see their flocks of sheep and goats and cattle. I smell the smoke of their cook-fires sharp in my nostrils. I taste the sweet manna from HaShem on my tongue. I see the Shekinah of HaShem, that guides us in a pillar of cloud by day, a pillar of fire by night.

And there is our prophet Moses and his servant Joshua.

I draw to within a stone's throw of our prophet Moses.

I draw to within an arm's length of our prophet Moses.
I draw to within a finger's width of our prophet Moses.
I step inside the skin of our prophet Moses.
I see with his eyes.
I breathe with his lungs.
I feel with his hands.
I am the prophet Moses.

~

The Tale of the Prophet Moses

I am Moshe, prophet of Yah, and here is the beginning of my tale.

I climb the mountain with my servant Yehoshua. There we spend forty days in the Presence of Yah, and it feels no more than forty blinks of an eye.

I am consumed by the love of Yah, who is like a shepherd who carries a lamb on his shoulders.

Yah writes his law on two tablets of stone with his own finger. I see him draw the letters. I read the glowing words. I feel his law written on my heart. His Torah tells us the way we should walk to have life, to have love, to have freedom.

I walk with my servant Yehoshua down the mountain, and my feet are light beneath me. I feel as I am the eagle who glides on the wings of the wind.

As we come near the foot of the mountain, I hear the sound of shouting. I smell the smoke of the feast-fires. I feel the mighty beat of the dance-drums.

We round the last bend, and there is all Israel, mired in sin.

They have built a golden image of Apis, the bull-god of Egypt. Its bull parts hang beneath it, huge and obscene.

Young virgins stand crowded around the image, forced together in a sweaty circle, naked, smeared with paint, their shocked faces twisted in a big terror.

Men crowd around them. They put rough hands on innocent skin. They seize one girl and pull her out from the others. They throw her to the ground. They fall on her and force her to spread legs. They use her for a pleasure. They seize another, and another, and another. The girls scream and scream.

Two strong men pin one young girl standing up between them, both using her for a pleasure, stealing her innocence, laughing on her fear, while she screams and screams with none to defend her.

My face feels hot as a smelter's furnace, and my fists become hammers. I crush the stone tablets of Yah in my fingers.

I run toward the abomination, shouting louder than the voice of Yah.

I reach the crowd of sweating men.

I smite one on the skull with my fist.

He falls to the ground senseless.

I tear another off a sobbing girl and fling him against the statue of the bull.

He lies there crumpled and still.

I see the two men taking their pleasure on the one girl, grinning on each other over the top of her head.

She screams and screams and screams in a big agony.

I fly at them in the rage of my fury. I seize their hair with my two hands. I slam their heads together, once, twice, three times.

The men fall senseless to the ground.

The girl's knees buckle.

I catch her before she can fall in the filth around us.

She is weeping, screaming, gurgling, gasping, choking.

I take off my own cloak and cover her nakedness. I hold her in my arms, this poor lamb of the heart of Yah, crushed by the sin of her own people.

I shout with a mighty shout.

All the wicked men fall to the ground, covering their ears.

The naked young women run shrieking away, covering their woman parts with their hands, crying tears of rage at the evil done on them.

My brother Aharon scuttles toward me, wringing his hands. "I … we thought you were dead. You were gone long on the mountain, and the people said Yah had abandoned us. They gave me the gold of their ears, and I made fire and heated the gold, and the bull sprang out, fully formed and—"

"Silence, fool."

Aharon stands with his mouth hanging open.

A woman approaches me, her face twisted with tears. She reaches for the girl in my arms. "My poor child!"

I give the girl a kiss and a kiss and a kiss and hand her over to her mother.

The two stagger away, crushed under the weight of the sins of Israel.

I turn to my servant Yehoshua. "Bring hammers and men not corrupted."

Aharon clutches on my arm. "What will you do? The people want—"

I smite his cheek with the back of my hand. "Fool! For every wicked man who wants this false god for a moment of pleasure, there is a woman shamed for a lifetime."

Yehoshua returns with many men. They bring hammers and iron bars.

"Destroy the bull-god." I take a hammer myself, and together we smite the image of the bull-god of Egypt.

Soon the abomination lies shattered on the ground.

Men bring flat stones, and we beat the gold into sheets.

More men bring round stones, and we grind the sin of Israel into dust.

More men bring baskets, and we heap the dust in baskets.

We carry the baskets to the water and pour out the sins of Israel.

We round up the evildoers and force them to drink their sin.

I am Moshe, prophet of Yah, and here is the ending of my tale.

～

Yoni of Capernaum

I am myself again, Yoni the son of Zavdai.

I fall forward on my face. Tears flood my eyes, and my belly aches with my sobbing. The sin of Israel weighs on me like a blanket of great stones. I cannot breathe for the horror of it.

I know what is the first Power.

But I do not know how to fight such a Power.

This Power has a hold on my own heart, for when I saw the women huddled around the bull-god, there was a thing in me that shouted to take a woman and use her for a pleasure. The first Power is inside me. The wrath of HaShem should fall on me, for I have a big wickedness in me.

All around me, I hear the sounds of weeping.

I wipe away my tears and open my eyes.

The children are huddled to their mothers.

The women are huddled to their men.

The men wear pale faces, tight with horror.

Rabbi Yeshua stands quietly watching us all. His face—I never saw such a face on a man. It is the face of our king David when he went to war. It is the face of our prophet Moses when he broke the tablets. It is the face of our father Abraham when HaShem told him to offer up his own son on the mountain.

"HaShem calls me to tell repentance to the sons of Israel," Rabbi Yeshua says. "Who will go with me?"

I am terrified to tell repentance to the sons of Israel. If I tell repentance to Israel, I must tell repentance to myself, for I am a son of Israel and the first Power is in me.

But if I do not tell repentance to myself, then the first Power will always have a hold on me and HaShem will never return as king and I will never enter the kingdom of HaShem until forever.

There is a loud silence.

"Who will go with me?" Rabbi Yeshua asks again.

Shimon's father, Yonah, clears his throat. "Rabbi Yeshua, you ask much. We have been gone many weeks to the feast in Jerusalem. Now is not a good time to tell repentance to Israel. Now is a good time to catch fish and earn money and wait for the rains to come and go.

When spring comes, then will be a good time to tell repentance to Israel."

Rabbi Yeshua flinches as he has been slapped, but he says nothing.

My father nods his head. "I cannot spare my sons to tell repentance to Israel. Not now. I need my sons for the winter. When spring comes, yes, I will send my sons to tell repentance with you."

Rabbi Yeshua says nothing.

Little Yaakov's face is red. "Our women and children cannot go to tell repentance to the sons of Israel. We must take them home before the rains begin. And we spent many *dinars* in Jerusalem. We live by the sweat of our labor. If we go now to tell repentance to the sons of Israel, our women and children will go hungry. Now is not a good time to tell repentance. When Pesach comes, we will go to Jerusalem and tell repentance."

Rabbi Yeshua's face is stone.

If he had asked them all to go to war against the Great Satan, they would not be begging off like this.

My heart lurches like a drunkard, and my back is cold with sweat. I cannot say yes to Rabbi Yeshua, for my father said no, and how would I face my father after such a mighty dishonor?

My eyes burn holes in Rabbi Yeshua, begging him to understand.

He sees.

He understands.

He goes to stand before my father. "Friend, do you need both your sons for the whole winter to catch fish?"

My father studies him with shrewd eyes. "Rabbi Yeshua, you ask much."

That is not yes, but it is not no, either.

"I ask you for one of your sons. HaShem asks you for one of your sons."

My father's face twitches. He drops gaze. He sighs deeply. "If HaShem asks for one of my sons, then HaShem must choose. Cast lots for my sons."

We do not have lots in our house. When we need to cast lots, we use finger-lots.

Rabbi Yeshua looks to Big Yaakov. "Are you ready to match lots with me?"

Big Yaakov nods.

My father counts the count to cast finger-lots. "Aleph… bet… gimmel!"

On the third letter, Rabbi Yeshua makes a number with his fingers behind his back. I cannot see his number, but most of the house can see it. Big Yaakov has also made a number behind his back, and I can see it because I am beside him. Big Yaakov made a five with his fingers. He brings his hands out and puts them on the table.

Rabbi Yeshua brings his hands out and puts them on the table. His fingers make a two.

The rule of finger-lots is that the numbers must match within two. Rabbi Yeshua's two is not a match for Big Yaakov's five.

My father breathes again.

I am sweating with a big sweat. Now it is my turn. I wish to go with Rabbi Yeshua. I am desperate to go with Rabbi Yeshua. But only the finger-lots will choose if I will go.

Rabbi Yeshua shifts to stand before me. "Are you ready to cast finger-lots with me, Yoni?"

"I … yes." My voice squeaks for my fear.

My father counts the count. "Aleph… bet… gimmel!"

I see Rabbi Yeshua's arms drop to make a number behind his back.

An instant later I make a number behind my back.

My father looks on my number. "Put your hands on the table, Yoni."

I put my hands forward. My fingers make an eight.

Those who can see Rabbi Yeshua's hands gasp.

Rabbi Yeshua brings his hands forward.

His fingers make a ten.

It is a match within two. I fight a smile that threatens to crack my face apart. I knew it would be a match.

My father's breath hisses between his teeth. "HaShem has spoken. You may take Yoni to tell repentance to the sons of Israel. In the spring, when it is time to go to war, you will have my other son. You will have my sons-in-law. You will have me. We will fight the Great Satan, and we will win."

Rabbi Yeshua's eyes are shining. He looks to Yonah. "Friend, I ask for one of your sons. HaShem asks for one of your sons."

Yonah cannot do less than my father did, for he would lose honor. He nods. "Cast lots for my sons."

Rabbi Yeshua casts lots with Shimon the Rock and loses. He casts lots with Andre and wins.

Now we have two.

Natanel the hireling says, "Rabbi, I will go to tell repentance with you."

Philip the fish-man says the same.

Now we have four.

Rabbi Yeshua goes to his mother. "Imma, HaShem asks for one of your sons."

She sighs deeply and nods. "Cast lots."

He casts lots with Little Yaakov and loses.

He casts lots with Yosi and loses.

He casts lots with Thin Shimon and loses.

He casts lots with Yehuda Dreamhead and wins.

Now we are five.

That is not much for an army, but we are not going to make a war on the Great Satan.

We are only going to tell repentance to Israel, and for that, five is as good as ten.

But there is a deep thing here, and I do not know what is the meaning.

In each family where Rabbi Yeshua cast lots, HaShem gave him the youngest son.

The least son in every family.

That means something.

When we go to tell repentance to Israel, I will ask Rabbi Yeshua what it means, for that is a deep secret of HaShem.

Also, I will tell him the only deep secret I know, which is how to cheat at finger-lots.

~

Miryam of Nazareth

I am more confused than I ever was. Yeshua makes a mighty disappointment on us all.

Little Yaakov begged him to make a big army and go to war and smite the first Power and defeat the Great Satan. I begged him to come to Nazareth and smite the evil people there and make a justice on my name.

But he means to do neither.

He means to tell repentance to Israel.

That is not a good sense.

All my heart is numb for the shock of it.

Yohanan the prophet has been telling repentance to Israel already. A man who means to redeem Israel should do more.

Much more.

Yeshua smiles on me with kindness. "Imma."

I sigh with a big sigh. "You should come to Nazareth and smite the Evil Boy and his house and the whole village."

"Imma, will you come with me to tell repentance?"

I remember the place we camped where the prophet Yohanan tells repentance. It is a place of scrubby bushes and thin trees and sandy ground. The nearest village has a hundred souls and is not close. Jericho is across the river and a walk of one hour. But winter is coming, and the rains will begin soon.

I slept outside once in my cloak in the rain. That was a bad sleep.

Our house in Nazareth is a good stone house with a dry roof. When it is cold, we make a fire and are warmed. We have food there, good food. If I go there, I will be warm and dry.

But the village hates me. They mock me to scorn. They have made a mock on me thirty years. If I go there, I will be scorned and shamed.

I do not know what to do. "Yeshua, you should come to Nazareth and tell repentance on them and smite them for their sins."

Yeshua opens his mouth to say something and then stops as he is frozen. He tilts his head and a light shines in his eyes, and I know the

Shekinah is on him. He stands like that for many ten thousand years. At last he looks on me. "Imma, I will come to Nazareth and tell them repentance on a day HaShem has chosen. But that day is not today. Will you come with me to tell repentance beyond Jordan now?"

I wish to say yes.

I wish to say no.

I do not know what I wish.

Little Yaakov comes to sit beside me. "Imma, the rains will come, and you will be cold and wet. Stay with us in Nazareth, and I will defend."

I smell his sweat, and I know he is angry on Yeshua for making a bad move. Little Yaakov wanted him to call out an army and name him commander and go make a big war on the Great Satan. If Yeshua had done that, Little Yaakov would not run away from a little rain and a little cold. He would not wish to return to Nazareth.

I close my eyes and think how it will be in my village if I return. When the small girls sing their songs, Little Yaakov will scowl on them and frighten them to silence. When the women spit my feet, Little Yaakov will call them *zonahs* and make a scorn on them. When the men put *haryo* in my path, Little Yaakov will fight them all. He will smite them with his rage. He will give me a big vengeance.

Little Yaakov will make a justice on me now.

I wish Yeshua will do it now, but he says he will do it only someday.

I have been waiting all my life for someday.

I wish for my justice now.

I take Little Yaakov's hand.

Yeshua's face flinches as I have slapped him.

I am sorry if he is sad, but he does not know how much the village hurts me. Every day, every hour, they stab me with their hate.

If he wishes me to choose him, he should make a justice on my name as he promised.

That is my decision, and blessed be HaShem that I have one son who will defend.

CHAPTER TWENTY-NINE

Yeshua of Nazareth

"There he is!" Yoni points far down the river.

I squint in the afternoon haze, but all I can see is a group of men beside the Jordan River.

Yoni shades his eyes with his hand. "Yohanan's hair has grown since we saw him last. I think it reaches his calves. I am glad I am not under a Nazarite vow. Yohanan's hair smells like dog *haryo*."

"That was not his hair you smelled," says Andre. "That was the *haryo* on your upper lip."

Yehuda Dreamhead laughs on Andre's joke.

Natanel the hireling laughs on his joke.

Philip does not laugh on his joke.

I do not laugh on his joke either. I remember a day I had to wash *haryo* from my face. Also from Imma's hair.

It was not dog *haryo*.

"Yohanan is telling repentance to the men of Israel," Yoni says. "There are not so many as two weeks ago. I think there are only fifty men."

Andre says, "Not so loud, Yoni. You will frighten every desert fox from here to Arabia."

"I am not so loud as Yohanan," Yoni says. "He shouts louder than any man ever did. My ears hurt for a week after I heard him. Yohanan will be glad on having us there to help him tell repentance. It will save his voice, and anyway, Rabbi Yeshua tells repentance better than he does."

"Yoni, hush!" Andre says. "Rabbi Yeshua, warn Yoni to be silent. He dishonors Yohanan the prophet."

Yoni looks on me. "But it is true! When Yohanan tells repentance, he frightens me so much I feel the fires of the wrath of HaShem."

"You should be frightened," says Andre. "If idle words were sins, you would have sinned more than any son of Adam ever did."

Yoni takes my hand. "It is not my fault I talk much. HaShem gives me many things to think on, and when I think on a good thing, I wish to say it. Anyway, I only told the truth. When Rabbi Yeshua tells repentance, I do not feel terrified of HaShem. I feel as HaShem has more mercy than wrath, and I wish to come to him, but I feel that first I must repent, and so I do it because I wish to do it, not because Yohanan shouted me to do it."

I clear my throat. "Yohanan is a prophet of HaShem. We will show honor to him. We will listen to him tell repentance. We will not speak until he speaks to us. We will not tell him how to tell repentance."

"You should *show* him how to tell repentance," Yoni says.

Andre scowls on him. "You should *show* us all how to honor a prophet of HaShem."

I stop in the road.

The others stop and look on me.

I wait a moment in silence until they are ready to hear. "I will show honor to Yohanan. I will not speak until he speaks to me. I will not tell repentance until he asks me to tell repentance. And you men also. A servant is not greater than his master. Therefore, you men will show honor to Yohanan more than I do. You will not speak until I have spoken. You will not say my way of telling repentance is better than Yohanan's. HaShem has given him to tell repentance in his way.

From this moment on, you will not say another word until Yohanan gives me leave to speak. Do you understand the matter?"

Andre nods.

Philip nods.

Natanel the hireling nods.

Yehuda Dreamhead nods.

Yoni opens his mouth. Then he makes a big grin and nods.

I begin walking in silence.

My men follow behind in silence.

I am glad of Yoni, for he said a thing I had not thought. Yohanan did not ask me to help him tell repentance to Israel. He may not wish for my help. I do not wish to make Yohanan angry on me. But I am called by HaShem to tell repentance to Israel.

I do not know what to do, but HaShem will show me what to do.

If I listen.

We walk in silence for the fourth part of an hour before we cross the fords and join the people gathered around Yohanan. Their eyes are wide, and sweat gleams on their foreheads.

Yohanan tells repentance in a great loud voice.

We sit quietly near the back of the crowd and listen.

Yohanan puts eyes on me once or twice, but his voice does not falter.

I listen to him tell repentance.

Yoni is right. Yohanan puts a big fear in my heart. He tells of the ax laid at the root of the tree. He tells of the generation of vipers who should fear the wrath of HaShem. He tells of the fiery destruction that will befall at the hand of the Great Satan.

He tells repentance well.

He tells repentance long.

When he is done telling repentance, all the people stand and go in the river and immerse.

It is a good message, but I do not feel a big need to immerse again in the river. I feel the Shekinah strong all around me. My men do not immerse in the river either.

It is the going out of the day, and the people are hungry. There are less than a hundred, mostly men, but some women and a few children. They all have food, and they sit in small circles and eat.

We brought food, some bread and dates and cheese and salted fish. We brought skins with wine and some with beer. We eat in silence. Yoni seems ready to burst with words, but he keeps his promise and says nothing. Andre grins on him like a wolf. The others hide their smirks behind their hands.

When everyone has eaten, someone calls for music or a tale.

A man stands and sings a psalm to HaShem. It is a good psalm, about sheltering under the wings of HaShem. About not fearing the terror by night or the arrow by day. About the Messengers of HaShem who guard us in the road, bearing us up so we do not strike our feet against a stone while we walk in the way of HaShem. About treading on the lion and the viper who stand in our way.

When it is done, all the crowd shouts approval, for it was well sung.

Another man stands and tells the tale of the prophet Daniel in the pit of lions. The tale is not told so well as it deserves, but it is a good tale, and when it is done, the crowd shouts approval.

Another man stands and tells the tale of the prophet Jonah and the big fish. The same tale Andre told two weeks ago, but so grim it seems almost a different tale. There are some who say the fish killed Jonah and ate him and his shade went down to Sheol and prayed to HaShem for mercy and HaShem heard his voice and made the fish vomit him out on dry land and then HaShem raised him to life again. This man tells it so, and at the end, Nineveh is shamed. He does not say Nineveh repents, only that it makes a big wailing.

Even if it is grim, the tale is well told, and there are shouts for another tale.

Another man stands and tells the tale of Elijah the prophet, who killed four hundred prophets of the *ba'al*.

Another tells the tale of David killing two hundred Philistine men for their foreskins as a bride-price for his woman.

The stars shine bright when the tale is told of Joshua destroying the city of Jericho. We can see the lights of Jericho from here, across the river by a walk of one hour.

Finally every group has told a tale or sung a song.

Every group except ours.

The man nearest us shouts, "Sing us a psalm, newcomers!"

My men look on me.

I shrug like a man who says no.

Yohanan the immerser looks on me with bright eyes.

Other men shout on us to recite an oracle from the prophets.

Again I shrug.

Yohanan the immerser studies me hard.

All the crowd begins calling me to tell a tale.

I look to Yohanan.

He makes a big grin on me. "Tell us a tale, Yeshua from Nazareth."

I raise my eyebrows like a man who asks what tale to tell.

"A tale of repentance," Yohanan says.

Yoni seems to be hopping up and down for his excitement. Andre grins. Philip leans back on one elbow. Natanel the hireling taps the side of his nose and smirks. Yehuda Dreamhead rubs his hands together for his glee.

I stand.

I tell the tale of Apis, the golden bull-god of Egypt.

As I speak, I watch the people. The men's eyes light up with a big rage. The women cover their mouths in dread. The children cry and cry for their terror.

I tell repentance to Israel.

When it is done, there is a long moment of silence.

Then all the men fall on their faces, repenting.

My men fall on their faces, repenting.

Yohanan the immerser falls on his face, repenting.

I sit in the sand and feel the Shekinah all around me.

A pillar of cloud.

A pillar of fire.

I look up in the night sky and wonder if Yohanan the immerser heard true from HaShem when he said I must destroy the first Power or be killed. I have made my first attack on the first Power, and see how easy it was. Everyone who heard my tale repents.

I do not see a hazard here. Yet Yohanan the prophet told that there is a big hazard.

That is what Yoni calls a paradox. He means the matter is deeper than it appears. The way ahead seems smooth, but hidden pits wait in the road for a man to fall in unawares.

I will trust in HaShem to protect me.

But I will discuss the matter with Yoni.

CHAPTER THIRTY

Yoni of Capernaum

"We are almost to Uncle Elazar's house." I point to the marker stone by the side of the road. "That is the third marker before Bethany. We will be there by the walk of one hour. The sun hangs one hour over the mountains, so we will get there at the going out of the day."

Rabbi Yeshua nods and says nothing. His lips are blue from the cold.

His brother Yehuda Dreamhead shuffles beside him. His eyes are half-closed, and I think that is ice on his eyelashes.

Andre and Philip and Natanel the hireling walk behind us. I hear their grumbling, and I do not blame them.

I think it is the coldest day of the year. Tomorrow begins Hanukkah, and we are walking up the Jericho Road to the home of Aunt Miryam and Aunt Marta and Uncle Elazar so we can celebrate with them. We went there two weeks ago for Shabbat, and they were all pleased to meet Rabbi Yeshua, for they had heard big tales on him already.

We have been helping Yohanan tell repentance to Israel now for five weeks, and it is good. Yohanan spends all but the hottest part of the day telling repentance. He still terrifies me, but I am getting used to him. When we first went to join him, I had evil dreams every night —Jerusalem burning in the fires of the wrath of HaShem. I have not had any evil dreams in a week. Yohanan seems angry all the time. I would be angry too if my hair ran with insects and smelled like *haryo*.

Every evening after we eat, the people sing psalms and tell tales. Now that they know Rabbi Yeshua, they demand two or three tales from him in a night. His tales are the best I ever heard.

I rub my hands together for the cold. It was warm and fine until yesterday, but the weather turned cold this morning. It rained all afternoon, a freezing rain mixed with ice. The Jericho Road is very steep, and now it is a big mud. All of us are wrapped in our cloaks, walking slow, careful not to step on a loose stick or a stumble-stone or a hole in the road.

There is nothing worse than walking all day uphill in a cold mud. But I know at the end of the road is Uncle Elazar's large house, and he will make a roaring fire, and Aunt Marta will serve us hot drinks, and Aunt Miryam will warm us with her smile.

Yehuda Dreamhead staggers sideways on a sudden. "Aughh!"

A fist-size stone runs out from under his feet. A roll-stone.

Yehuda falls hard on his right knee.

He collapses in the mud and clutches his left ankle.

My face feels hot and my neck is cold. I rolled my ankle once on a roll-stone, and I was lame for three weeks.

Rabbi Yeshua kneels beside his brother in the mud. "Yehuda! Can you walk?"

Yehuda Dreamhead shakes his head. His teeth grit against the pain.

My heart flutters. If Yehuda Dreamhead cannot walk, we must camp here and start a fire. But there is never any wood on the Jericho Road. A few twigs, maybe, but they will be wet and frozen.

We cannot stay here overnight. We must get to Bethany, to Uncle Elazar's house. But we cannot leave Yehuda Dreamhead here. He would freeze in an hour, lying on the icy ground.

I do not think we can carry him. Yehuda Dreamhead is a big man like Little Yaakov. He weighs more than any of us, even Andre.

My mind runs in circles like a three-legged dog with its tail on fire.

Rabbi Yeshua pulls up Yehuda Dreamhead's cloak and tunic to see the hurt.

His left ankle has a bad look on it. Also, blood streams from his right knee where he fell.

"Can you stand?" Rabbi Yeshua asks. "If we walk with one man on each side, can you hop on the right leg?"

Yehuda Dreamhead clenches his teeth. "Maybe."

All of us together lift him. Andre stands on his left side and Philip on his right.

Yehuda Dreamhead wraps his arms over their shoulders and puts his right foot to the ground. Slowly, slowly, he puts weight on it. His face twists in a big agony. "Aughh!"

Rabbi Yeshua shakes his head. "He cannot walk."

My belly burns and my nails bite my palms and my head hurts. If Yehuda Dreamhead cannot walk, even with help, he will die here. We cannot leave him to die. But if we stay with him, we will die too.

Rabbi Yeshua stands facing Natanel the hireling. "Put your right hand on my left arm, here."

Natanel the hireling clamps his right hand on Rabbi Yeshua's left arm, just below the elbow.

Rabbi Yeshua does the same with his own left hand on his own right arm. In a moment, their four arms lock together to make a square.

Rabbi Yeshua says, "We must test it. Yoni, sit on the throne." He and Natanel squat so their square is low enough to sit on.

I sit in the chair and put my arms around their shoulders.

Rabbi Yeshua and Natanel stand.

I grin on them. "It is very comfortable."

"Natanel, walk with me," Rabbi Yeshua says.

Together they walk. They are facing each other, so they must twist their backs a little. They are not fast, but they can walk.

"See? Not so hard," Rabbi Yeshua says.

Natanel the hireling shakes his head. "The boy is light as a sunbeam. Yehuda Dreamhead is twice the weight of the boy. Two men cannot carry one man so far."

Rabbi Yeshua shrugs. "When I was a boy, Little Yaakov and Yosi and I went to Mount Tabor to climb the mountain for an adventure. It is a walk of two hours, and Imma sent food with us. We climbed to the top and ate our food. Then Little Yaakov said we must run down the mountain like the army of Deborah the prophet attacking the army of Sisera the Canaanite. Yosi fell and hurt his ankle. Little Yaakov and I made a square and carried him all the way home. If two boys can carry one for a walk of two hours, then four men can carry one for a walk of one hour. Yoni, give place to Yehuda Dreamhead."

I jump out of the chair.

Andre and Philip help Yehuda Dreamhead sit in it.

Rabbi Yeshua and Natanel the hireling walk.

Every step is a grunt of hard work, but they are walking.

I hurry to walk alongside Rabbi Yeshua. "How did you think to make the square when you were a boy? That was a good cleverness."

"It was Little Yaakov's cleverness," Rabbi Yeshua says. "When we got home, all the village shouted what a clever boy I was. I said it was Little Yaakov's cleverness, but they did not believe me, and Little Yaakov made a rage on them."

I ask, "Is that why Little Yaakov is always so angry, because he is jealous on you?"

Yehuda Dreamhead moans with a big moan.

Rabbi Yeshua says, "Yehuda Dreamhead, are you well?"

"C-cold," Yehuda Dreamhead says. "Very cold."

Rabbi Yeshua says, "Yoni, run ahead to the village. Ask Elazar to bring us a donkey to carry Yehuda Dreamhead. Wait for Marta to warm a skin of water by the fire. And ask Miryam to find a cloak of goat hair woven tight. When you have both, bring them back to us as fast as you can run."

"Rabbi Yeshua, is that why Little Yaakov is always so angry—"

"Run!" Rabbi Yeshua shouts.

I run.

CHAPTER THIRTY-ONE

Miryam of Bethany

I hand Yoni the cloak and the waterskin. "Be careful and run slow!"

Yoni runs fast.

The sun is just disappearing over the hills behind Jerusalem. I shiver from the cold, for a terrible freezing rain has been falling all day. I think it might snow. We had snow once when I was six years old, and I thought it was a wonderful thing. Then we had snow again when I was twenty. I remember because it was the month after my lord divorced me. I wanted to go out and lie down in the snow and die. I would have too, if Marta had not stopped me.

"Miryam Big-Eyes!" Marta shouts on me. "Come in the house now!"

I hate my nickname. When I was the age of ten, the boys of the village named me Big-Eyes. They grinned when they said it, and I took it for a kindness. Then the men of the village called me Big-Eyes, and they grinned when they said it. Then the women of the village called me Big-Eyes, and they grinned when they said it. Last of all, the girls of the village called me Big-Eyes, but their grins were twisted by a thing I did not understand.

I asked Imma why all the village grinned when they called me Big-Eyes. I did not see why large eyes should be funny.

Imma would not explain the matter.

My sister Marta would not explain the matter.

My brother Elazar would only say it was not to do with my eyes. He said it was a joke.

I did not understand what was the joke.

Then one day one of the men of the village leered on me and called me Miryam Big-Eyes, only he was not looking on my eyes.

Then I understood the matter at last.

I did not think it was a good joke.

Imma said a big-eyes girl is blessed by HaShem, because her father can find many men who wish to buy her for their woman.

I thought that would make it right in the end.

It did not make it right in the end.

"Miryam Big-Eyes, come in now or your eyes will freeze off and fall down in the road and roll all the way to Jericho!"

I sigh and turn from squinting down the road after Yoni. He never calls me a big-eyes. He is a good boy, and I wish he will grow into a kind man and never make cruel jokes on a woman. That is the best a woman can hope, that a man will not be cruel on her.

Marta stands inside the door frowning on me. "We must throw more wood on the fire and make tea and put out food. Find basins to wash their feet—they will be filthy. Your tunic is too tight. Those fish-men will be staring on you. And do something about your hair—it is poking out again."

I scurry through the receiving room of our house.

The servants fly about. Shmuel the woodcutter lays more wood in the firepit while a boy blows air on the fire through a hollow reed. The servant girls run back and forth to the kitchen, preparing bread and cheese and olives and chickpeas and wine. Marta shouts directions on them all.

I reach the courtyard and slog through the wet slush to my room. The air there feels frozen, painful to breathe.

I inspect my tunic to see if it is too tight.

It is not too tight. I am cold, that is the only problem. If those fish-men never saw a big-eyes when she is cold, they will stare, but that is not my fault.

I touch the edges of my hair covering.

A few wisps poke out again.

I remove my hair covering and shake out its wrinkles. My hair falls to my waist. My hair is very thick and long. Marta's is thin and silky. When I was a small girl with thick hair, Marta praised it much. When I was a large girl with thick hair, she still praised it much. When I became a woman and a big-eyes, she said I had hair like a *zonah*. The day I was betrothed, I wrapped my hair in a covering, and no man has ever seen it since, except my lord. But my thick hair could not prevent me being barren, so Marta was avenged in the end.

The rabbi and his men will be here soon, and I will be shamed if even one strand of my hair shows. I am not a seducing woman, who lets little wisps of her hair hang out to be seen by strange men. There is a *zonah* in the next village who does that. I have seen it myself, and it is a big wickedness.

I wrap my hair in its covering and fold it as carefully as I ever did. I check it three times and then go back to prepare for our guests.

I am terrified on Rabbi Yeshua. Yoni told me the mighty wonder he did at his sister's wedding feast. Rabbi Yeshua is a prophet and a *tsaddik*—a very holy man. I am afraid he will know I am cursed by HaShem and he will make a big scorn on me.

He came with his men two weeks ago for Shabbat, and I was afraid to go in the same room with them. I was glad when they went to the Temple with Elazar most of the day. I do not need a *tsaddik* watching on me to catch me in a sin. I already have Marta.

Now they will be here for all of Hanukkah, eight whole days and maybe longer if the weather stays foul. I will have to hide away from Rabbi Yeshua all that time. I wish I can go somewhere with Yoni and talk, as we used to. But he is a man now, doing a man's work. Perhaps he will have no time for me.

If Yoni ignores me, that will be good, for then I will not make a scandal on him. But if Yoni ignores me, I will cry until all the tears in my eyes run out of my head.

I bring out foot basins from the storage room, twelve of them. We get them cheap from Gamliel the potter, whose foot is crippled. I lay out six basins in front of the benches in the receiving room and leave the rest as spares by the fire. I also bring out two large stone warming vessels and set them in their places in the firepit. I haul in three buckets of water from the cistern in the courtyard and fill the vessels so the rabbi and his men can wash in fire-warmed water.

When it is all done, I sit and wait.

After the fourth part of an hour, I hear shouts outside in the street.

Marta and the servants hurry to the door and go out to greet our guests.

I go to hide in the central courtyard, even though it is bitter cold. I will spy on them and see that Yoni is warmed and fed, and I will steal a look on the rabbi, and then I will run to my own room and hide.

Yoni comes in the receiving room first. His nose is blue, and his hair is caked with ice. He stands near the firepit and stretches hands toward the heat.

Elazar leads our donkey in, carrying the rabbi's brother. They all lift him off and set him down on the bench nearest the fire. Rabbi Yeshua peels up his brother's cloak and tunic to his knees. His legs are caked with mud and ice and blood.

Marta brings a basin and water and puts a servant girl to work washing his feet.

Rabbi Yeshua calls for his other men to sit and finds them all places on the benches.

Elazar leads the donkey out to the courtyard and back to the stables.

Marta runs around in a flurry, making sure that each of the men has a servant girl to wash his feet.

At last she turns and sees Rabbi Yeshua still standing, talking to Yoni.

"Rabbi Yeshua, what are you doing?" Marta says. "Sit! Sit! We should have seen to you first."

The rabbi smiles on her and says something in a quiet voice I cannot hear.

Marta pushes him to a bench and makes him sit. Her head spins around, and she sees what I have already seen.

All the servant girls are at work, washing the feet of the rabbi's men. There is none left for the rabbi.

Panic flashes in Marta's eyes. "Miryam Big-Eyes, where are you? Come serve the rabbi!"

I do not wish to go in the receiving room, but I will make a scandal on myself if I do not. It is my duty, for I am the youngest. I make myself small as a mouse and hurry in on my quietest feet.

Fear grips my belly in an iron knot. Rabbi Yeshua is a prophet. If he looks on me, HaShem will tell him I am barren and cursed and he will tell repentance on me. He will do it well, for he has been telling repentance to all Israel.

I pour warm water in the clay basin at the rabbi's feet. My head feels light and a great noise roars in my ears and I fear I will faint.

Rabbi Yeshua's sandals are thick with mud, ruined. I pull them off.

Marta takes them to dry by the fire.

I kneel before Rabbi Yeshua, looking only on his feet. Even a woman who is blessed by HaShem never looks a man in the eye. I am a woman cursed by HaShem, and I do not dare lift my eyes above his feet.

I immerse both feet in the warm water. They are stiff as wood and cold as snow and thick with mud. I massage them with my fingers.

The water turns black and cold.

Marta comes with another basin full of clean, warm water and takes away the first.

I work. It is a great thing to wash the feet of a mighty prophet of HaShem, but it is also a terror when you are a cursed woman. I wish I could go outside right now and run away and die.

The rabbi sits quietly, thinking the holy thoughts of a *tsaddik*. He surely takes no notice on me at all. I am only a woman.

After many basins, Rabbi Yeshua's feet begin to warm. The room is now hot, for Elazar and Shmuel the woodcutter have shown no mercy on the fire. Marta comes back from the kitchen with hot drinks and food and wine for the men. She brings first to Rabbi Yeshua.

He says, "Please, you will serve Yoni first."

I do not know why Rabbi Yeshua would say such a thing. Perhaps he loves Yoni much. Everyone loves Yoni much, so it is natural.

He says, "You will also serve Yehuda Dreamhead and Andre and Philip and Natanel."

Marta clucks her tongue. That means she does not agree. Marta is not used to being told what to do. Elazar is the man, so he should say how to order the house, but he is eight years younger than Marta and not strong of will, so Marta does as Marta wills. But even Marta obeys a mighty prophet of HaShem.

The room is hot and my face itches. I claw at it with my hand.

Marta stands above me with the drinks. She clucks her tongue again. "Miryam Big-Eyes!" she hisses in a hot whisper. "Your hair!"

In the instant, I know what has befallen. Shame rushes through my heart. When I scratched my face, I loosened my hair covering, and now a few strands of my hair peek out. I have made a scandal. Now Rabbi Yeshua will think I am a seducing woman. I reach up.

A hand is already there.

A man's hand, cold and rough and strong.

Rabbi Yeshua's hand.

"Please, you will allow me, little sister."

Shame and fear tremble inside me, but I do not move. It is not done in Israel for a man to touch a woman's hair, but what can I say? He is a *tsaddik*, and nobody accuses a *tsaddik* of lewdness.

Rabbi Yeshua tucks the loose strands of hair back inside my hair covering. His hand strokes my cheek with kindness.

Fire burns inside my soul.

It is a pillar of fire. Inside me. A pillar like the fire that guided our fathers in the desert when they came out of Egypt.

It is the Shekinah.

All my life I have longed to feel the Shekinah, and now it is here, when I least looked for it. Not the edges only. All of it.

My heart bursts with the joy of the Shekinah.

"Little sister." Rabbi Yeshua's voice is strong and low. "Look on me."

I do not dare look on Rabbi Yeshua.

"Look on me."

I lift my eyes to look on his chest.

"Look on me."

I raise my eyes to look on his face.

He is a mighty prophet of HaShem, but he has the face of an ordinary man. If you passed him in the street, you would see nothing unusual. His eyes peer into mine, and he reads my heart, and yet I do not feel shamed. I feel as I am a small girl again, safe in Abba's lap, surrounded by his strong arms of love.

"Little sister, have you ever heard the book of Isaiah read?"

"Y-yes." My voice is nothing, but at least I can whisper. I have heard the book of Isaiah read many times. Who has not?

"Abba spoke these words to the prophet Isaiah for you, little sister.

"Shout your joy
You barren woman,
You who never gave birth.
Break out in singing,
Shout it loud,
You who never had birth pangs.
For more are the sons of the rejected woman
Than her who has a lord."

My breath is stolen away. I have heard these words a hundred times. I have never heard these words. Tears fog my eyes. I am still a cursed woman in the eyes of the village, barren and rejected by my lord.

But I am not cursed in the eyes of HaShem.

I am blessed in the eyes of HaShem. I am blessed in the eyes of Rabbi Yeshua. I do not wish this moment to end. I wish the Age to Come will begin right now, with me kneeling before Rabbi Yeshua, washing his feet.

Marta clucks her tongue furiously above me. "Rabbi, you will take some wine, yes? Please forgive Miryam Big-Eyes—she is not herself tonight."

"Blessed be HaShem." Rabbi Yeshua takes a cup of wine. He says the blessing over wine and then sips from it. He smiles on Marta. "I thank you, Marta. You are a good woman, and you run a good house. You are blessed to have such a sister as Miryam, whether she is herself or whether she is not herself."

That is the sort of word Marta will treasure forever.

Rabbi Yeshua leans forward and looks in my eyes, so far in my eyes, I think he will fall in and drown. "You have a kind face," he says. "And beautiful eyes. And a big heart."

I feel as my head is filled with cotton.

He kisses my left cheek.

He kisses my right cheek.

He kisses my lips.

"I name you Miryam Big-Heart."

There is a great burning fire in my heart, in the place where it has been cold for many years.

I am not a big-eyes woman.

I am not a barren woman.

I am a blessed woman.

A woman whose heart sings for joy.

CHAPTER THIRTY-TWO

Miryam of Bethany

I am more excited than I ever was! We are going to hear the prophet Yohanan tell repentance to Israel.

Yesterday was the feast of Purim to celebrate the day when Mordecai, the cousin of Queen Esther, got the signet ring of the King of Persia and saved our people from Haman, the evil prince of Persia. Yoni and Rabbi Yeshua and his men came to feast with us.

Today, Elazar and I are going with them to the Jordan River to hear Yohanan. We will repent and immerse, and then we will not fear the wrath of HaShem and the judgment he will make on us. Already today, we have seen a hundred people on the road going the same direction. All Jerusalem is talking on Yohanan the mighty prophet.

Yoni walks beside me, talking and talking.

I do not understand all that he says. I am afraid he will forget himself and hold my hand as we walk. Then everyone will see he thinks on me as a friend, and they will call me a wickedness.

I do not see why it is wicked for a man to be friends on a woman. Yoni does not think it is wicked.

"There is the river!" Yoni hops up and down. "See, Aunt Miryam?

There is the camp where the people sleep. And there is Yohanan the immerser talking to three men—see his long hair? Did I tell you he is a Nazirite? He never cut his hair since he was born. He eats locusts and wild honey and he wears an old tunic of camel hair and I think it has never been washed, for it smells—"

"Yoni." Andre scowls on him and then juts his chin toward the man walking in front of us with Rabbi Yeshua.

That man. I do not like that man. His name is called Hananyah the nail maker. He has thick arms and a coarse beard and wild eyes. When he looks on my face, I think his eyes are angry. But when he looks on my bosoms, I think his eyes are hungry. He says he has followed Yohanan the immerser since last summer. Yoni says before that, he lived in Qumran with the Essenes, but there was a scandal and they threw him off. I do not know how Yoni knows such things.

Hananyah the nail maker came with Rabbi Yeshua and his men for Purim. I do not know why he came, for he ate little at the feast, and he drank no wine. Yoni drank so much he said he could not remember who is Haman and who is Mordecai, and then he threw up, and then I gave him water and let him lie with his head in my lap until he felt better. Hananyah the nail maker said Yoni should beware that a little nail should become a big nail. I do not wish to know what he means by that.

Hananyah is arguing with Rabbi Yeshua on some matter.

Rabbi Yeshua nods and smiles on him, but I do not think he agrees with Hananyah.

"We are in time to hear Yohanan tell repentance," Yoni says. "Then we will eat and drink and spend the evening telling tales. Rabbi Yeshua tells the best tales. You have not heard a tale until you have spent the evening under the stars hearing Rabbi Yeshua tell the tale of Daniel's friends in the fiery furnace."

"Does Yohanan the immerser tell tales?" I ask.

"Sometimes. Once he told the tale of Phineas the grandson of Aaron who killed the Israelite man who was lying with the Midianite *zonah* in his tent. Phineas ran them both through with one spear! That was a good tale, but I had a nightmare afterward. Yohanan's tales are not so good as Rabbi Yeshua's."

Hananyah the nail maker turns his head and scowls on Yoni.

He scowls on Yoni's hand.

On my hand.

How did I not notice Yoni had taken my hand while we were walking?

I begin coughing.

I stop in the road and cover my mouth with my hand.

I take a drink of beer from my waterskin.

After many beats of my heart, I begin walking again.

Yoni and Elazar are waiting for me.

We walk the rest of the way to the fords, and Yoni talks much, but I do not hear anything he says.

The Jordan River is smaller than I thought. I never came so far from home. I expected a mighty roaring river, but that is not what I see. The water is green and quiet, and it is only twenty or thirty paces across. The fords of the river are shallow and cold. When we reach the other side, we walk north to where people are gathered.

We all sit quietly to hear the words of the prophet Yohanan.

He has a big voice on him and speaks many ten thousand words, telling repentance. His voice is angry, and it hurts my stomach.

When Yohanan finishes, I feel small and tired. He makes me feel as I have done many big sins, only I cannot think what I did wrong, and I cannot see what to repent, and I do not wish to immerse. I came here to repent and immerse, and now I am in a big misery that I walked all this way for nothing.

I sit and wait while our men go to immerse. When they come back, Yoni's hair is dripping wet, and his face shines with the light of the Shekinah. Elazar's hair is dripping wet, and he is smiling. Hananyah the nail maker's hair is wet, and he is not smiling. Rabbi Yeshua's hair is not wet.

We brought too much food. Marta filled up our packs with food that twenty men could not eat. We do not need so much food. Elazar and I go back to Bethany tomorrow. But some people came with little food, so we share what we have.

Hananyah the nail maker eats with us, but he does not eat much, and he takes no wine. If he took some wine, maybe he would not have such a sour face.

After we eat, there are songs and tales until late. Andre sings a psalm. Yoni chants the poem of how HaShem made the world. Many people shout for Rabbi Yeshua to tell a tale. He tells the tale of Ruth the Moabite woman who found joy by joining herself to Israel.

Others tell tales and sing songs, and then people beg another tale from Rabbi Yeshua. He tells the tale of Rahab the *zonah*, who took in two spies of Israel and then was saved when our people burned Jericho.

I can hardly believe it is the same Jericho we see across the river. I wonder why the spies went to the house of a *zonah*. That should have made a big scandal on them.

After many people have told tales, last of all they shout for Rabbi Yeshua to tell the tale of Queen Esther.

I have heard this tale many times, but Rabbi Yeshua tells it better than anyone ever did. It makes me feel as I am Queen Esther myself, living in a big fear that I will be found out, a Jew in the harem of a foreign king. If I lived in some king's harem, I would feel like a *zonah*. In days of old, it was permitted. I do not know why.

When Rabbi Yeshua finishes the tale, all the people shout approval on him.

Yohanan the immerser has been sitting over to one side the whole time, talking with Hananyah the nail maker. Now he comes to sit with us. He smiles on Rabbi Yeshua and says he makes fine tales. He smiles on Andre and says he sang a fine psalm. He smiles on Yoni and says he chanted the creation poem well.

He looks on me and his eyes turn hard. "Yoni, this is your mother?"

Yoni shakes his head. "This is Aunt Miryam. And here is her brother, Uncle Elazar, who owns flocks and vineyards and olive groves in Bethany. Aunt Marta stayed home to tell the servants—"

"This Aunt Miryam is the sister of your father or the sister of your mother?"

I do not like the fierce lines in Yohanan's face. I do not see why he asks these questions.

Yoni shakes his head. "She is the cousin of my mother, who grew up in Bethany and married my father Zavdai, who is a priest and a mighty man in Capernaum and owns a fishing—"

"Your aunt is the woman of some man in your clan?"

"No, I told you already. She is my mother's cousin. She had a lord, but he divorced her."

I try to make myself small. I do not wish for Yoni to tell all the tale of my life to Yohanan the prophet.

"For what cause did he divorce her? Is she some lewd woman? Hananyah the nail maker says she is a lewd woman." Yohanan's voice is very loud.

People all around look on us. They look on me.

I wish to hide under a rock or a twig.

Yoni also speaks loudly. "Aunt Miryam is no lewd woman. Her lord divorced her because she was barren. That was not her fault—"

"Her village calls her Big-Eyes," says Hananyah the nail maker. "Look and see she has lewd eyes and she pushes out her bosoms to make them large. Also, she walks with brazen steps. I saw her once sitting with the boy's head in her lap. And she took his hand while they were walking in the way. She has no right to touch the boy. She is not the sister of his father or mother. I think her lord threw her off for lewdness."

I wish to run away and drown in the river.

Rabbi Yeshua leans forward. "Miryam Big-Heart is a good and righteous woman. HaShem smiles on her. I saw the Shekinah on her with these eyes."

"Then why did her lord divorce her?" Yohanan asks.

Tears run out of my eyes. My heart hurts, and my face is so hot I could fry a goose egg on it.

"Her lord divorced her because of his own sin," says Rabbi Yeshua. "Our prophet Moses made a law that a man can divorce his woman for any reason, and now see what evil things are done by that law. This righteous woman had no son. Was that a greater sin than our mother Sarah, who was barren many years? Or our mother Rebekah, who was barren many years? Or our mother Rachel, who was barren many years? Or your own mother Elisheva, a righteous woman, who was barren many years? HaShem might have given this woman a son in good time, but her lord threw her off."

"The law of Moses permits a man to write a bill of divorce for any reason," says Yohanan.

"To throw off a righteous woman for small cause is wicked," Rabbi Yeshua says. "Her lord threw her off. If he takes some other woman and lies with her while his first woman is alive, is that not adultery?"

Hananyah the nail maker leans forward. "You are saying a man who divorces his woman commits adultery?"

"You say so." Rabbi Yeshua crosses his arms on his chest.

"I did not say so. You say so." Hananyah the nail maker scowls on him.

Yohanan the immerser frowns on me.

Yoni leaps to his feet. "Rabbi, what of the matter of King Herod, who lives in Tiberias? He divorced his woman and married the woman of his brother, who is still alive. The law of Moses does not permit a man to marry his brother's woman unless the brother dies without an heir. And the law of Moses does not permit a woman to divorce her lord for any cause."

Rabbi Yeshua shrugs and looks on Yohanan and Hananyah. "What do you say on the matter? Did the woman of King Herod break the law of Moses by leaving her lord?"

Yohanan the immerser nods his head and frowns. "Yes."

"And did King Herod break the law of Moses by taking his brother's woman while his brother is alive?"

Hananyah the nail maker nods his head and smiles. "Yes."

I think Hananyah the nail maker takes a big delight in other people's sins.

Rabbi Yeshua comes to me and gives me a kiss and a kiss and a kiss. "This is my friend Miryam Big-Heart. Do not call my friend a lewd woman when she is a righteous woman."

All my body prickles like needles. I cannot think. Rabbi Yeshua called me friend. He gave me a kiss and a kiss and a kiss in front of Yohanan the immerser.

Hananyah the nail maker stands and storms away.

Yohanan the immerser gives Rabbi Yeshua hard eyes. "Yeshua of

Nazareth, you should spend more time telling repentance and less time telling foolish tales. Your tales are all honey and no meat. You tickle the people's ears, when you should tell the wrath of HaShem." He stalks away.

Rabbi Yeshua has the look of a man kicked in the underparts.

My heart is crushed to see him dishonored.

I am glad I will leave tomorrow with Elazar. I do not wish for Hananyah the nail maker to ask questions on me. I do not wish for Yohanan the prophet to look on me with his hard eyes. I wish to go away and make an end on this matter.

And I love the tales of Rabbi Yeshua. If that is honey and not meat, then I do not want meat. I am sick to my death of this talk of the wrath of HaShem.

CHAPTER THIRTY-THREE

Yoni of Capernaum

"Tell us a tale, Yoni!" says Yehuda Dreamhead. "Your tales are almost as good as my brother's. It will pass the time while we wait."

I am sitting under an acacia tree with Yehuda Dreamhead and Andre, in the place where Andre played that bad trick on me last fall. It is three days since Aunt Miryam and Uncle Elazar went back to Bethany, and now we need more food, so Rabbi Yeshua took Philip and Natanel the hireling to the village to buy more after our morning meal.

I make a grin on Yehuda Dreamhead. "If I tell you a tale, will you teach me another wrestling trick?"

He makes a grin back on me. "If you tell a good tale, I will answer one of your many hundred questions."

I think he offers a good bargain, only I will make a cheat on him and tell such a mighty tale, he will answer two questions. "What tale should I tell?"

"Tell the tale how Father Adam got a woman."

I tell the tale how HaShem planted a garden with four rivers all around it, and put Father Adam to work.

Father Adam was lonely and complained on the matter to HaShem.

HaShem made two animals and brought them to Father Adam.

Father Adam named them bull and cow and put them to work, but still he was lonely.

HaShem made two more animals and brought them to Father Adam.

Father Adam named them he-goat and she-goat and put them to work, but still he was lonely.

HaShem made two more animals and brought them to Father Adam.

Father Adam named them he-donkey and she-donkey and put them to work, but still he was lonely.

HaShem made a pair of every animal in the world and brought them to Father Adam.

Father Adam named each pair and put them to work, but still he was lonely.

When all the animals were made, Father Adam complained on the matter to HaShem.

HaShem gave Father Adam a great wineskin, filled with a strong wine.

Father Adam drank it all and fell in a deep sleep.

HaShem took out a rib from Father Adam and made a woman for him.

When Father Adam awoke, he saw the woman, and his flesh roused, and he took the woman and lay with her, and then he went in the river to immerse because he was unclean.

When I finish the tale, Andre grins on Yehuda Dreamhead. "You immersed in the river early this morning. Did you have a dream on your woman?"

Yehuda Dreamhead's face turns pink. "I have been gone long from my woman. Of course I dreamed on her and woke up unclean. Did you dream on your woman two nights ago? You got up early and went away and came back with wet hair and a wet tunic."

Andre shrugs. "My woman dreamed on me and came to me in the night and wore me out by making me lie with her many times."

Yehuda Dreamhead says, "That is a good thing, to have a lewd woman, yes?"

Andre smirks on me. "So Yoni, when did you last dream on a woman?"

I never yet dreamed on a woman. Shimon the Rock explained the matter to me once, how a man with no woman sometimes dreams on a woman, and his flesh is roused, and he lies with her, and his seed goes out of him, and he has to immerse afterward. But he said I will not dream on a woman until I get my man growth, and I am still waiting on that.

I do not wish to admit I never dreamed on a woman, so I make a dodge on the matter. "Yehuda Dreamhead, explain the matter why Rabbi Yeshua has no woman."

Yehuda Dreamhead makes a big scowl. "That is a matter not to speak on."

"Why is it a matter not to speak on? You promised you would answer a question if I told you a tale."

"You should ask some other question."

"You should answer the question I ask."

"You should ask Yeshua, if you wish to know."

"You are making a dodge on the matter. Every man takes a woman by the time he is twenty, but Rabbi Yeshua is already more than thirty. You and all your brothers have women, but Rabbi Yeshua does not. My father says when a man does not take a woman, there is a scandal in the matter. So I am afraid to ask Rabbi Yeshua, in case there is a scandal in the matter."

"We do not speak on the matter in our family."

I look on him with narrow eyes. Now I am sure there is a scandal in the matter.

Yehuda Dreamhead says, "Ask some other question."

I have many ten thousand other questions, but I ask only a few. "Why is Little Yaakov always so angry? He looks like a man who will explode for his rage, all the day long. Also, why does he act like he is the firstborn son, when Rabbi Yeshua is the firstborn son? He should give honor to Rabbi Yeshua, but he acts as Rabbi Yeshua should give honor to him. Also, when do you think Rabbi Yeshua will make his move? He does not seem like a man eager to fight, but if he is a son of David he should be a mighty man of war, and how can he be if he does not love battle? Also, who will he choose to be commander of his armies? Will it be Shimon the Rock or Little Yaakov? Both of them will be mighty men, but whichever man Rabbi Yeshua chooses, the other will be angry. How can Rabbi Yeshua solve this paradox? Also—"

Yehuda Dreamhead holds his head in his hands as he thinks it will come off his shoulders. "That is too many questions! I promised only one answer."

I grin on him. "Then you should make it a large answer. You are a good tales-man. Tell me a tale on Little Yaakov that will answer all my questions."

Yehuda Dreamhead sighs with a big sigh. He makes a guilty look behind him toward the village where Rabbi Yeshua went. He lowers his voice. "I will tell you a tale of Little Yaakov, but you must promise never to speak on the matter to anyone."

I smell a scandal coming. Now I will get answers to many questions. "I swear by The Name I will never speak on the matter."

Andre says, "I swear by The Name I will never speak on the matter."

Yehuda Dreamhead moves closer to me and Andre. "This is the Tale of Little Yaakov, which I heard with these ears, straight from his own mouth, on the day I asked him why our brother does not have a woman ..."

The Tale of Little Yaakov

My name is Little Yaakov, and I am the happiest boy in the village.

I have spent the whole morning running in and out of the house, fetching things for Imma, helping her with the food, holding Baby Yosi to make him sleep, and playing with the wooden ball Abba carved for me.

Baby Yosi cries out again.

Imma picks him up and rocks him for a moment and takes him inside her tunic to feed him. "Little Yaakov, run find Yeshua and tell him to come home and eat."

I am glad of a chance to help, so I run through the village looking for my brother. I love my brother more than anyone in the world. He is always kind to me. The whole village loves my brother. I see Shimon the baker making bread. I ask him where is my brother Yeshua. He tells that he saw Yeshua going toward the village spring with the other boys his age.

I run up the street to the end of the village. I pass the leather-man's piss-pool and run fast through the narrows and up the long hill to the spring.

The boys are a little way past the spring. They stand in a circle with Yeshua in the middle.

I run toward them shouting, "Yeshua! Imma says you are to come home and eat!"

But nobody hears me. The boys are shouting words on Yeshua.

Hard words.

Jeering words.

Words I do not know.

But I know they use cruel voices.

Yeshua has a look on his face as he has been kicked in the stomach. Tears fill his eyes, and his mouth hangs open as he does not know what to say.

"Son of a *zonah*! Who begat you, *mamzer*? You are nothing but donkey *haryo*. We should throw you off the precipice. Your mother should be thrown off the precipice. She lies with men for a *dinar*."

The biggest of the boys steps toward Yeshua. His name is called Yoseph, and he is son of the leather-man, and he always reeks of the piss-pool where his father tans hides.

Yoseph pushes hard on Yeshua's chest with both hands. "*Mamzer*!"

Yeshua stumbles backward.

Another boy punches him in the small of the back from behind.

I am more angry than I ever was. I run fast toward the boys, howling like a wolf. I leap on the back of Yoseph the leather-man's son.

He staggers forward.

I lock my arms around his neck. I kick on his legs.

He falls to the ground.

I punch him twice in the head.

Strong arms pull me off.

I jump backward and spin hard and tear myself free from some boy's grip. He is bigger than me, but I have rage on my side. I leap straight up at his face and smash his nose with my forehead.

He falls back. Blood runs out of his nose. He has the face of a dead fish. His mouth hangs open, and his eyes look shiny.

Another boy rushes at me.

I punch him in the stomach as hard as I can.

All the rest leap on me at once.

I scream and writhe and try to tear loose, but they are five boys of the age of seven, and I am one boy of the age of four.

Now they have me on the ground, holding me down.

Yoseph the leather-man's son scowls on me. "You are donkey *haryo,* Little Yaakov. Your mother is a *zonah.*"

I do not know what is a *zonah.*

He grins on me with a curled lip. "Ha! You do not know what is a *zonah,* do you?"

"Yeshua, hit them!" I shout.

Yeshua says in a quiet voice, "Let my brother go. He did nothing to you."

Yoseph the leather-man's son turns and kicks Yeshua in the stomach. He throws him on his face on the ground and sits on his back and pulls his arms back hard. "Your mother lies with men for a *dinar.*"

I do not know what it means for a woman to lie with men. I can think of nothing to say.

Yoseph laughs on me in a big happiness. "Little Yaakov is more a fool than I thought. He does not know the matter of a man lying with a woman!"

The other boys roar. "We should explain the matter."

They are boys of seven and they know nothing, but they are gleeful to tell what they know, using their fingers to make shapes to explain the matter as boys of seven know it.

I do not believe them. The matter makes no sense to me. I do not see the reason for this thing they tell me.

Yoseph the leather-man's son laughs on me again. "Your mother spreads her legs for any man for a *dinar*! That is what is a *zonah*. She enticed some man of the village, and he begat your brother. That is what is a *mamzer*."

I spit at him. "You stink like piss, and your breath smells like *haryo*."

His face makes a big rage on me. He flies off Yeshua's back.

The other boys still hold me pinned to the ground.

Yoseph steps toward me slow and grinning.

He kicks me hard in the underparts.

I scream like fire. I never felt such a big pain. Like a hammer smashing up inside my belly all the way to my heart.

The other boys leap up, laughing like jackals.

I cannot move for my big agony.

A second boy kicks me in the underparts.

The pain is ten times more, for my underparts were bruised already.

A third kicks me in the underparts.

The pain is ten times more again.

A fourth comes to kick me.

I scream so hard I cannot breathe. On a sudden, the world goes dark.

When I wake up, Yeshua is carrying me home.

My underparts feel as they are swollen to the size of my head. They scream with a big agony, more than I ever knew.

Tears leak out of Yeshua's eyes. "Little Yaakov, you showed a big courage."

The pain in my heart is more than the pain in my underparts. Yeshua should have fought the boys to defend me. I fought to defend him. Why did he not fight to defend me?

When we come to our house, Yeshua tells the matter to Imma.

I wait for Imma to say the boys are liars.

She cries and holds me, but she does not say the boys are liars.

I lie in the corner of our house all day in a big agony. My under-parts ache as the iron-man is beating them with a hammer on the anvil.

When Abba and our grandfather come home, Yeshua tells the matter to them.

I wait for them to say the boys are liars.

Our grandfather's face turns dark and he goes out in a rage.

Abba goes out after him.

Our grandfather shouts on him to stay in the house.

Abba comes back in with a face like a beaten dog.

An hour later, our grandfather comes back. "I told the matter to the leather-man, and he mocked me and said my son's woman is a *zonah* and my grandson has the smirch of a *mamzer*."

I wait for him to say Imma is not a *zonah* and Yeshua does not have the smirch of a *mamzer*.

Our grandfather says, "I showed the boy my Ring of Justice and gave him my judgment, that if he touches my grandsons again, I will drown him in his father's piss-pool."

Abba says, "That is not a righteous justice. That is a harsh justice. The prophet said—"

"Silence, fool." Our grandfather freezes Abba with a look. "Do not question the man who holds the Ring of Justice. You will wear the Ring yourself someday, if I judge you are worthy, and then you will know that justice must sometimes be harsh or else it is not a justice."

Abba's face turns hard and he dares to make an answer on our grandfather. "That boy is evil, but telling him a threat will not change his ways."

Our grandfather says, "You know nothing at all. That boy is evil, and after I drown him in his father's piss-pool, he will no longer be evil. That is my judgment, and you will not make a question on my judgment, until forever."

I do not understand this matter. Imma is the best woman in all the world. Why does the leather-man call her *zonah*? Why does he say Yeshua has the smirch of a *mamzer*?

I wait for them to explain the matter.

Our grandfather wears a look of rage all the evening, but he does not explain the matter.

Abba does not explain the matter.

Imma does not explain the matter.

They do not explain it that week.

They do not explain it that year.

They do not explain it ever.

But after that, I hear whispers in the village.

You can cage a secret, but you can never kill it, and the secret will out.

The village says Imma enticed a man before Abba took her in his house. Some say she enticed Abba. Some say she played the *zonah* and enticed another man, and so Yeshua is the son of adultery, a *mamzer*.

That is a riddle too deep for me.

I know Imma is good and she would never entice a man.

I know Abba was a *tsaddik* all his life, and he would never be enticed by a woman.

I know Abba claimed Yeshua for his son.

If that was all I knew, I would say the village is cruel and makes idle gossip.

Only I also know that Imma never once said Abba begat Yeshua.

Also, Abba never once said he begat Yeshua.

If Abba begat Yeshua, why will they not say it?

They could remove the smirch of the *mamzer* with a word. But they refuse to say it.

I tried once to ask on the matter, why they will not say Abba begat Yeshua.

My grandfather made a rage on me. He said in a hard voice we must never speak on the matter. He said one does not speak on a matter that shames a woman.

Then I knew that my grandfather thought Imma played the *zonah*.

That is a knife in my heart, a big agony more than any kick in the underparts ever was.

My name is Little Yaakov, and I am the angriest boy in the village.

CHAPTER THIRTY-FOUR

Yoni of Capernaum

When Yehuda Dreamhead finishes the Tale of Little Yaakov, all my heart is a big confusion. Rabbi Yeshua has a paradox, and how will he solve it?

The rabbis will say he is not a *mamzer*, that is what I know. The village *hazzan* explained the matter to me once. Torah does not tell what is a *mamzer*, exactly. Some say it is one thing. Some say it is another. But Torah means whatever the rabbis say it means.

The rabbis debated the matter and decided what is a *mamzer*. He is a child born to a woman who cannot make a Torah marriage with the man who begat him.

Also, the rabbis say the word of the father decides who is his son. So if a man claims a child for his son, then he is his son, because no man would claim a son he did not beget. And if a man ever did claim a son he did not beget, he would still be his son, because the claim of the father decides the matter, because that is what Torah means, because that is what the rabbis decided it means.

But now Rabbi Yeshua's father is dead and can no longer say what is his claim. So his father's claim is whatever the village decides his father claimed. If the village honors his father's memory, they will say he claimed Rabbi Yeshua for his son. But if the village decides to misremember the matter, they will say his father did not really claim Rabbi Yeshua for his son, and who will tell them no? Only his father's near-relatives, if they are strong of voice.

I say, "Yehuda Dreamhead, what does the village say on the matter of your brother?"

"All the village loves my brother and calls him son of Yoseph. Only there is a smirch on his name, because the leather-man and his father say Yeshua is a *mamzer*."

"And what does the village say of your mother?"

A dark look. "They call her *zonah*."

I think that is a bad matter. The village knows there is a paradox, and they do not know how to solve it, so they honor the man and shame the woman. That means their hearts are divided on the matter. "Is that why no man of the village will give Rabbi Yeshua their daughter to be his woman?"

Yehuda Dreamhead sighs with a big sigh. "They all say many words, how they do not believe the smirch themselves, only they fear that others might believe he is *mamzer*, and then their grandchildren would be *mamzer* to the tenth generation, so what can they do?"

"That is a mighty smirch, to last so long. A smirch should fade away."

Andre wears a big frown. "What will happen if Rabbi Yeshua makes a move? He says he is son of David—"

"He is son of David." Yehuda Dreamhead's voice is flat and cold.

"Only if he is accepted as son of Yoseph," I say. "What will happen if your village decides he is not son of Yoseph?"

"How can they decide he is not son of Yoseph?" Yehuda Dreamhead says. "My father claimed Yeshua for his son, so he is son of Yoseph, son of David."

Andre says, "But if your village ignores your father's claim, they will raise a stench on the matter. Other villages will not follow after Rabbi Yeshua if his home village says he is not son of David."

Yehuda Dreamhead says nothing. His fists clench tight and there is a big sweat on his forehead.

I say, "Your grandfather is dead, yes, Yehuda Dreamhead?"

"Yes, he died the year I was born, and I never knew him. My grandmother died the next year."

I ask, "But you have an uncle who lives in the village?"

"Yes, Uncle Halfai, the firstborn son, who inherited my grandfather's farm."

"Your uncle is an old man, and not strong of voice," Andre says.

Yehuda Dreamhead nods.

I say, "But your uncle must have inherited the Ring of Justice. I have heard tale on such things, and they are a sign of a big authority. Your uncle can enforce your father's claim by invoking the Ring of Justice, yes?"

Yehuda Dreamhead shakes his head. "When my grandfather died, he passed the Ring of Justice to my father, not my uncle. My father hid it in some secret place for a safety, only he died untimely, and now the Ring is lost."

I say, "That is a bad matter. Your father is dead. Your grandfather is dead. Your uncle is not strong of voice and has no Ring of Justice to enforce the matter. When your uncle dies, how many in the village will honor your father's claim?"

"Shimon the baker will honor my father's claim. He always loved Yeshua."

"And who else?" I ask.

Yehuda Dreamhead thinks hard on the matter. "Two or three others of the old generation."

"And what of the villagers of the age of Rabbi Yeshua?"

Yehuda Dreamhead's face goes tight. "The leather-man is just his age, and he is strong of voice in our village. He hates Yeshua. Once he came in the night and spread plaster on the wall of our house."

My chest has a big pain in it, just over my heart. I heard about that, how a village makes a dishonor on a *mamzer* by plastering his house with white plaster, to be a sign of shame that anyone can see from far away. I never saw it done, for we have no *mamzer* in Capernaum, but it is cruel.

"I did not see plaster on your house when we were there last fall," Andre says.

Yehuda Dreamhead nods. "It was long ago, soon after Abba died. The leather-man brought only one bucket, so he could not plaster the whole wall. But it made a big roar in the village, when they saw it. They came with hammers and broke the plaster and scraped it with chisels until it was all clean. Shimon the baker said they should throw the leather-man in his own piss-pool, but others said no, so they never punished him."

I do not know what to think on the matter. Rabbi Yeshua has the Shekinah all around him. He is a prophet and a rabbi and a son of David. But he has the smirch of the *mamzer* on him in his own village.

I think that is why he is slow to make his move. Anyone can make a move and raise up an army and lead them out against the Great Satan. But not anyone can be Mashiach and king of Israel, even if he is son of David.

When King David begat a son of adultery with another man's woman and then killed the man and took the woman, HaShem killed the son. If the son had lived, he could never have been king, because he was a son of adultery. But then King David begat another son with the woman, and that was Solomon, the greatest king that ever lived.

A son of adultery cannot be king.

A man with a smirch of *mamzer* cannot be king either.

But his brother can.

I think Rabbi Yeshua must find a way to make the village take away the smirch from his name.

Either that, or he must yield to Little Yaakov, and let him be Mashiach and king of Israel when HaShem makes his kingdom new.

I read Yehuda Dreamhead's face, that he thinks the same.

I read Andre's face, that he thinks the same.

Behind us, I hear a cough.

I leap up and spin to look.

Hananyah the nail maker hides behind the next acacia tree, grinning on us with a big happiness.

"Fool, what did you hear?" I shout on him.

Hananyah the nail maker jumps up and runs back toward the camp.

My chest thumps like a galloping horse.

I think Hananyah the nail maker heard all the matter of the smirch on Rabbi Yeshua.

~

Yeshua of Nazareth

When Philip and Natanel and I return to our camp with food, I see that something is wrong.

Yoni will not look my eye.

Andre will not look my eye.

Yehuda Dreamhead tries to look my eye, only for an instant.

In that instant, I read his heart. I do not know how I read it, but I read it.

He told them the matter of the smirch.

I do not know what to say. I do not know what to think. My father forbade to speak on the matter, because his father forbade to speak on the matter.

So the matter has festered thirty years.

I walk toward the river and sit on a rock and stare in the water, wishing HaShem will show me how to think on the matter. I must find a way to remove the smirch on my name, but I do not see my way clear. It is not in my power. Only the village can remove the smirch. I cannot force them to remove the smirch. I cannot even speak to them on the matter. My grandfather ate the sour grapes, but it is my teeth that are set on edge.

~

'*Your men are confused on the matter.*'

'*They should be confused. I am confused on the matter.*'

'*This matter will prevent you from taking up the sword, and that is your greatest wish.*'

'*You are a fool. I never would wish to take up the sword. There is no love in my heart for the blade.*'

'*Then what is your greatest wish?*'

'I wish to do the will of HaShem.'

'What is the will of HaShem? Is it not to destroy the Great Satan?'

'HaShem says I am to tell repentance to Israel.'

'To what gain?'

'So I may defeat the first Power.'

'To what gain?'

'So I may defeat the second Power, and the third, and the fourth.'

'To what gain?'

'To redeem Israel.'

'To be Mashiach?'

'You say so.'

'I do not say so!'

'The man of HaShem told Imma and Abba I should redeem Israel.'

'That is to be Mashiach, but a son of adultery cannot be Mashiach.'

'Abba claimed me for his son.'

'You cover yourself with a broken fig leaf. Your mother spread her legs for some man of the village, but then your father claimed you for his son for a kindness. You are still a son of adultery.'

'My father claimed me for his son, and the village voted long ago to honor his claim, and that is the end of the matter.'

'Your father lies dead in the ground, and his voice is silent, and a new generation is rising who hardly knew your father.'

'Uncle Halfai remembers the claim. And Shimon the baker and the elders.'

'The old leather-man denies the claim, and now he is an elder in the village. And his son is strong of voice. When you go to make your move, the village will deny the claim, and you will be shamed, and your move will come to nothing.'

'The village loves me.'

'The village hates your mother. Hate is stronger than love. When the matter comes to the point, they will deny your claim.'

'The village loved my father, and my father claimed me for his son. Almost all the village honors the claim.'

'Until every man of the village honors the claim, the matter will be in a doubt, and you cannot make a move, and you cannot be king of Israel. Do you defy my logic?'

'Here is a logic for you. HaShem called me his son. I heard it with these ears. And what is the son of HaShem? The scriptures say it is two things. First, the son of HaShem is our nation Israel. And second, the son of HaShem is the king of our nation Israel. Therefore, when HaShem calls me his son, he calls me king of Israel. That is my logic, and it is better than yours.'

'Your logic is a bad logic. The anointed king of Israel cannot be a son of adultery, even if he is son of David. If you make a move while there is a smirch on your name, your village will raise a stench on the matter. If your own village denies your claim, no other village will accept. They will say you are not the son of David, and you are not Mashiach, and you are not the king of Israel, and you are not the son of HaShem.'

I do not know what to say to that.

'And even if your own village accepts your claim, you know in your heart it is false. You know you are the son of adultery and not the son of Yoseph. Do you deny?'

'I deny.'

'How can you deny? Explain the matter.'

'I do not understand the matter. Only that my father claimed me for his son and he was a tsaddik.'

'Your father lived a lie and now you live a lie.'

'I do not live a lie. I live a question. It is a question I do not understand. I live a trust in HaShem. If I understood, I would not need to trust in HaShem, for I would have a certainty on the matter.'

'All your words are smoke. You choose to live a lie.'

'I choose to trust HaShem.'

'Your trust is a vain hope.'

'Leave me, you Accuser.'

'I will leave you, but you know I speak true, and my words will echo in your ears every hour of the day.'

'I demand in the power of The Name that you leave me.'

Silence.

I should speak to my men on the matter.

But what can I tell them that will not sound like a big foolishness?

I cannot speak to them on the matter until HaShem explains it to me.

HaShem, I beg on you, explain the matter.

I do not see how I can go back to my men and face the questions in their eyes. Only they will never dishonor me by asking. Even Yoni will be afraid to ask.

The questions fester in their hearts. The questions fester in mine.

HaShem, I beg on you, explain the matter.

Silence.

CHAPTER THIRTY-FIVE

Miryam of Nazareth

Little Yaakov stretches and stands. "We should go to the village square. There will be news tonight."

He does not mean I should go to the village square. He means his brothers. I have not been outside our house once since we came back to Nazareth. More than four months I have been in this house, safe from the village.

Yosi and Thin Shimon grin on Little Yaakov's words.

"We might hear news of Yeshua and Yehuda Dreamhead," Yosi says.

I do not think they will hear news of Yeshua and Yehuda Dreamhead. But they will hear news.

A traveler came to Nazareth today. The village elders gave Shimon the baker the honor of showing hospitality. Shimon the baker will hear the man's news first, but all the village wishes to hear the man. Tonight is the first warm night of spring, so all the village will be in the square hearing the news on the world.

I do not care to hear the news on the world. My Yeshua has been telling repentance to Israel all winter, but I am sure the traveler will know nothing on him. The traveler will tell what has passed in Caesarea or Tiberias or Jerusalem. I do not care what has passed there. If he had news on Yeshua, I would care what he has to say, but what is the chance he has news on Yeshua? Of course, none.

Yosi's woman nurses her new little son, who was born the last day of Hanukkah. Thin Shimon's woman helps Yehuda Dreamhead's woman clean the cook pot. They do not look like they wish to go hear the news in the square.

Little Yaakov's woman stands and sets her face to the door. She has a nickname now—Shlomzion Lewd. That is cruel, but she does not seem to mind. It would be more cruel if they called her Zonah. And most cruel of all if they called her the evil name. When a village calls a woman the evil name, they mean to kill her with shame.

So Shlomzion Lewd is not such a bad name. Anyway, the men of our village are quick to call any woman lewd if she enjoys lying with her lord. I think some of them have a big envy on Little Yaakov, to have a lewd woman. When they smirk on him and ask if she shouts loud in the night, he only grins and taps his ear as he is a deaf and asks them to repeat, and then they all laugh. I do not understand men.

Shlomzion Lewd looks on me with a kind smile. "Come with me to hear the news with the men." She does not like that I have prisoned myself in my own house. She does not understand why I fear the village. Why I hate it.

I shake my head. "No, never."

She takes my hand and tugs. "You should come, Imma Miryam."

"The villagers hate me."

"You will be safe with Little Yaakov and his brothers."

I cross my arms on my chest. She should know there are more ways to kill a woman than throwing stones on her. "Go without me. I do not wish to go."

She sighs and leaves with the men.

Not the tenth part of an hour later, she comes back, out of breath, grinning a big grin. "Imma Miryam! The traveler has seen Yeshua! I heard it from the baker's woman. She said the traveler went to hear Yohanan the immerser last week, and he heard Yeshua tell repentance! Come! You must hear him! They have not begun yet, so hurry!"

All my heart flutters.

Shlomzion Lewd seizes my hand and pulls. "Come now! If the villagers make a trouble on you, Little Yaakov will defend."

My heart screams for news on my son.

I go.

It is a fine evening, bright and clear. The stars are so large, I feel as I could reach up and pluck one, like a fig from a tree. I know that is a big foolishness. Little Yaakov says the stars are high up, higher even than the clouds, as high as the sun and moon. He says the stars are not things at all—they are holes in the hard bowl of the heavens that let through the light of the Messengers of HaShem. I never would have guessed it. I am glad to have a son who knows things.

All the men of the village sit quiet in the square. There are many women also. I creep up behind them on silent feet with Shlomzion Lewd and sit among my sons. I do not wish people to see me.

The traveler tells the news from Jerusalem. Rabbi Shammai is sick with a big sickness, and they fear he will die.

My sons gasp, for they love Rabbi Shammai.

I do not care a fig for Rabbi Shammai. I want to hear news on my son.

The traveler tells the news from Jericho. They are afraid on the king of Arabia, who is angry on King Herod for throwing off his daughter to marry another woman. If the king of Arabia makes a big war on Herod in the spring, he might cross the river at the fords near Jericho.

I do not care about the king of Arabia. I want to hear news on my son.

The traveler says he went to hear Yohanan the prophet telling repentance across the Jordan.

All my skin tingles.

The traveler says Yohanan the prophet spoke hard words on King Herod and his new woman. Yohanan the prophet says the king sins for marrying the woman of his own brother, while the brother is alive. That is against Torah. Yohanan the prophet says the woman sins for divorcing her lord to marry King Herod.

I never heard a woman could divorce her lord! That is not done in

Israel. That is a Greekish way, and a big sin.

The traveler says there was a man with Yohanan the prophet who told repentance better than the prophet.

My head feels all filled with lightness. I think it might come off my shoulders and float up as high as the stars.

"This man tells tales better than any man ever told," says the traveler. "His name is called Yeshua, and he said he is a *tekton* from Nazareth. Do you know the man?"

A hiss of excitement runs all around the village square.

Every hair on my neck stands up on its end. I am afraid to breathe.

"We know the man," says Shimon the baker. "He is a *tsaddik* and a man of honor. He has told tales here in this square from the age of nine, and they were good tales."

"There is talk that this Yeshua is also a prophet," says the traveler. "And some say he is a son of the House of David."

"He is no son of David," says another voice from the far side.

A sneering voice.

A voice I hate.

The Evil Boy stands. He is not a boy now. He is a man. Tonight, his lip curls as he smells *haryo*. "We know this Yeshua the *tekton*, and he is no son of David. He is a *mamzer*, the son of Miryam Spreadlegs, who is an evil tale."

Darkness closes in all around me. I hear a rushing sound between my ears. It is the sound of my rage. It is the sound of the worst day of my life …

⌇

The Tale of Miryam Spreadlegs

I shout, "Yeshua! Come walk with me to fetch water!"

My son comes running on his skinny legs. He is growing fast, and soon he will be eleven. His head comes to the level of my chin. Two more years and he will be a man.

I go in the house and find my waterpot and come out. "Little Yaakov, watch over the children."

Little Yaakov is playing chase in the street with Yosi and my oldest daughter, Miryam Beautiful. He says nothing, but I know he heard.

Yeshua and I walk together through the village. It is a fine summer day, still too early to be hot. The bright blue sky makes a high bowl above our heads. There is a beautiful breeze, and I hear the birds chirping. Yeshua holds my hand and greets the villagers as we walk.

They smile on him, but they say nothing to me. I am like the dust between their toes, but I have my Yeshua, and it is enough.

We walk through the narrows and up the long hill to the spring. I dip my pot in the water and lift it on my head.

Yeshua takes my hand, and we walk.

If all I had in the world was my Yeshua, that would be—

Something strikes me in the small of the back. About the weight of a stone, but softer than any stone.

I think some small bird flew into me. I turn slowly, on account of the waterpot on my head.

There is no bird.

Five boys creep out of hiding. They wear big grins. They hold something dark in their hands.

One of them draws back his arm and throws.

I am slow to move.

The thing hits me in the chest.

The stink fills my nose and stings my eyes.

Haryo.

All my body shakes with a bad shaking. My waterpot falls on the ground and shatters in many ten thousand shards. My hair covering comes loose. My hair flutters in the breeze. I feel naked and shamed.

"Zonah!" shouts one of the boys. "You should be thrown off the precipice and stoned!"

Another boy flings his *haryo.*

It hits the ground in front of me and spatters my feet.

Tears of rage jump out of my eyes.

Another boy draws back his arm.

I am frozen for my fear.

His arm moves forward.

I should make a dodge, but my feet will not move.

He throws a fistful of *haryo*.

I see it flying toward us.

All my body is a block of wood.

But the *haryo* is not flying at me.

It is flying at my son.

He starts to move, but he is too slow.

It hits Yeshua's face. It explodes in a thousand pieces.

He falls to the ground with a shout. He claws at his eyes, rolling, rolling, rolling away from me, blinded in a big agony.

The last boy walks toward me, grinning. The Evil Boy. He knows I cannot run away home, I cannot leave my Yeshua. He runs at me fast. He pulls back his arm. His teeth gleam like a dog's fangs.

When he is two paces from me, he throws.

The *haryo* smashes on my face.

My head snaps back.

Haryo goes up my nose. It goes in my eyes. It goes in my hair. It goes in my soul.

I fall down clutching my face.

I hear the hoots and shouts of the boys.

"Miryam Spreadlegs, if I give you a *dinar*, will you spread for me?" The Evil Boy squeezes my bosoms with his *haryo* hands.

I scream on him with a big scream. The stink of *haryo* fills my head.

The Evil Boy tugs on my tunic, but it will not come up. He tries to pull my feet apart. "Spread your legs, you *zonah*, you!"

I kick him in the face.

My son shouts.

Yeshua is on his feet at last, staggering like a drunkard, rubbing the *haryo* from his eyes, coming to my rescue.

The boys run away fast. I hear their footsteps like stones on my heart.

Now all I can hear is the sound of rushing in my ears, a mighty wind. The sound of my rage.

Kind hands pull me to my feet. "Imma, come with me."

Tears rush out of my eyes. I gag and retch from the stink of *haryo*.

My Yeshua pulls me up the path to the spring. He washes my face with his own hands. He washes my hair. He washes my tunic in the front and the back. He washes my feet.

But he cannot wash my heart.

Miryam of Nazareth

The rushing sound fills my ears and my heart and my soul. I will be avenged on that Evil Boy.

I will.

When I think on the Evil Boy now, I feel sick in my heart. It was his own *haryo* he threw on me, I am sure of it. And he was first in the village to call me Spreadlegs, that evil name he nailed to my heart. Now all the village calls me by it.

I hate that boy. Rage burns in my heart. I wish to kill the Evil Boy. I wish to roast his feet over a slow fire while his skin crackles and turns black. I wish to hear him scream and scream and scream in a big agony. I wish he will beg mercy for many ten thousand years.

But I will never give mercy. Never, ever, ever.

"Imma, come with us. Imma!" Little Yaakov's voice is strong in my ear.

I weep for my rage. I am blind with my tears and I gag as I will vomit. I smell *haryo* somewhere far away.

My sons help me stand. I feel their presence all around me.

"Yeshua will come back to Nazareth soon," Little Yaakov says. "He will come, and we will raise up a mighty army."

I do not care if he makes an army. I wish he will make a justice, only he does not know how. If Yaakov Mega were still alive, he would make a justice on me. He would use his Ring of Justice to avenge me. That Ring was a Power from HaShem to make justice in the world, only now it is lost. When Yeshua comes back, he should find the Ring. If he finds it, he will know how to use it.

He should come soon.

He should make a justice on my name.

He should come and burn the Evil Boy on a slow fire until forever.

CHAPTER THIRTY-SIX

Yoni of Capernaum

"**B**ig Yaakov! Shimon the Rock! We are home!" I jump up and down for my joy to see my brother and friend, now that Rabbi Yeshua and I have finished our work for the winter.

It is morning, and the boats of Capernaum are coming in after a long night of fishing. Shimon's boat has a hired man in it, and so does Big Yaakov's. I see they have many fish, and it is good, because it means they did not really need me and Andre.

Our fathers and Andre stand with me and Rabbi Yeshua on the stone pier, waiting.

When Shimon's boat comes alongside, he tosses me the rope.

I thread the end through a stone tie-hole in the pier and hitch it fast. "Shimon the Rock, you should have come with us! We did a great work with Yohanan the immerser. We told repentance to many thousand men looking for the kingdom of HaShem."

Shimon the Rock says nothing and does not look on me or Rabbi Yeshua.

I think he must be cold from the night of fishing, for spring is only just here.

Big Yaakov's boat comes in on the other side. He throws me the rope.

I make it fast to the pier. "I think more men were coming to hear Rabbi Yeshua than Yohanan. It is hard to know, because Yohanan moved north a week after Purim. He said there was more water in the north. I do not know why he said that, because it is the same river and the same water. Hananyah the nail maker went with him. I was glad, for he was rude on Aunt Miryam."

Big Yaakov grunts something in a low voice.

I think he must be very tired. His face is long and his mouth is set hard.

Rabbi Yeshua says, "Shimon the Rock, you did well with this catch. You are a loyal son to your father."

Shimon's face makes many expressions I cannot understand. But at the end of them, he is smiling.

Rabbi Yeshua hands me a leather bucket. "Here, Yoni, help Big Yaakov bring in the fish. He had a mighty catch. What do you think—does he have more fish even than Shimon the Rock?"

Big Yaakov climbs on the pier, and his mouth is no longer set hard. "Rabbi, it is good to see you. Did Yoni make a big trouble on you?"

"Yoni was a good help," Rabbi Yeshua says. "I thank you for giving him to me as helper. And you, Shimon the Rock, I thank for the help of Andre. He did well, and he told jokes that made us smile, only I think Yoni said many more words."

The men laugh.

I laugh too, for it is true I say many words, but they are wise words and not just many. Rabbi Yeshua told me so himself. I learned much from him this winter. I sometimes feel the Shekinah, but I will not tell Shimon the Rock or Big Yaakov. They will say I am getting conceited.

We brought many buckets to carry the catch. For the fourth part of an hour, we all work hard hauling buckets of fish. Most of the catch goes in an oxcart for the salting house. Some goes in the hand-cart of the boy from the fish market. We save the best for our morning meal.

When we are done unloading fish, Shimon the Rock gives me a kiss and a kiss and a kiss and says he has missed my foolish prattle these last months. Big Yaakov says I have grown much taller, at least the thickness of a rabbit's whisker.

We all go to the House of Yonah for a good meal.

Rabbi Yeshua and I and our men arrived in Capernaum last night just after the boats had gone out for the night. Imma hugged me many times and asked Rabbi Yeshua if I made a big trouble on him.

I do not know why everybody asks if I made a big trouble. Rabbi Yeshua asks my opinion often and says he is glad to have the Genius of Capernaum helping him. I am dying to understand the matter of the smirch on his name, but I would bite off my own tongue before I ask, for that is a matter Rabbi Yeshua should raise. Only I hope he raises it soon, or I will explode.

During the morning meal, Yonah asks the same question I have asked many times this week. "Rabbi Yeshua, why have you come back to Capernaum just now? We will all be going to Jerusalem in a week for Pesach. You walked four days to get here, and now you will walk four days back, to no gain."

Rabbi Yeshua shrugs. "Abba said to come back. Therefore, I have come back."

"But if you had stayed, you could have done a big work," my father says. "Just before Pesach, many thousand men will come down the Jordan Way from Galilee. You could have told repentance to them, but you cannot tell repentance if you are not there."

Rabbi Yeshua sips his wine. "Perhaps Abba has a new thing for me to do."

All my skin feels as it is on fire. I think Rabbi Yeshua should make a move soon. I have asked him many times when he will make a move, but he only smiles and says he will make a move when HaShem tells him to make a move. I think he delays on account of the smirch. But I cannot ask on the matter of the smirch, because I swore by The Name not to speak on the matter.

But now would be a good time to make a move. I heard from my uncle who lives in Jerusalem that all the city buzzes with talk on Yohanan the prophet. He says the chief priests in the Temple are talking on Yohanan the prophet. I do not think they will like Yohanan telling them repentance. I think they fear the Romans and do not wish

Mashiach to come because that will make a big confusion. I think they sent spies to hear Rabbi Yeshua and Yohanan tell repentance. I think that is part of the reason Yohanan the immerser went north.

I feel happy after a good night of sleep in my own house and a good meal. "Rabbi Yeshua, will your brothers come here before Pesach? We need Little Yaakov if you are to make a move. I never saw such a mighty man. Little Yaakov will be your strong right arm when we go to make a big war on the Great Satan, yes?"

For a moment, it feels as the room has no air.

Shimon the Rock's smile runs away.

Big Yaakov frowns on me.

"Yoni, eat your fish and do not talk so much," my father says.

I do not understand what I said wrong. Rabbi Yeshua's brothers are strong men and will be fierce to fight. Also, they are sons of David. Even if Rabbi Yeshua has a smirch forever, he can make a move if he lets Little Yaakov be Mashiach. And he needs me. I am not big and strong like Little Yaakov and Shimon the Rock. But the advice of a genius is worth more than many strong men.

"I am going to Nazareth today," Rabbi Yeshua says.

"But we just got here!" I do not like to complain, but it is long since I slept in Capernaum, and it is hard news that I must leave again so soon.

"I will go alone with Yehuda Dreamhead."

For a moment, I think my ears bring me a lying report. "But … you need me, Rabbi!"

My father gives me a hard look. "Yoni, you have said enough words for one day."

Shimon the Rock whispers something to Big Yaakov behind his hand, and they both scowl on me.

I think they are just sorry they did not come with us for the winter. They should be sorry, for we did a big work, and they were left out. But they should not worry. Rabbi Yeshua will find a place for them when he comes into his power. Little Yaakov will need them as captains in his army.

Rabbi Yeshua smiles on me. "Yoni, I thank you, but I wish to see my family. You have been away from your family long. Eat and sleep and allow your mother and sisters to hug you a few days. I will be glad of your help when we reach Jerusalem. You will not forget me before Pesach, will you, Yoni?"

I feel warmed inside at his words. "Rabbi, we will all be there at Pesach when you make your move."

My mother makes a shushing noise on me and gives me a look that says it is not my place to say what we will all do.

My father clears his throat and looks on Shimon the Rock and on Big Yaakov. "Rabbi Yeshua, you have been gone long. We wish to know if ... if you will still be glad of *all* of our help when you make your move."

Rabbi Yeshua's eyebrows jump up and his mouth falls open and he stares on my father. Then he looks on Big Yaakov and Shimon the Rock.

They have their arms crossed and they wear frowns.

I see the matter now. They wish to know who will command Rabbi Yeshua's armies. They are afraid Rabbi Yeshua will favor Little Yaakov over them. If they knew of the smirch, they would be more afraid.

Rabbi Yeshua smiles on them. "Shimon the Rock. Big Yaakov. Andre the cheerful. You men are like my own brothers. Zavdai and Yonah, you are like fathers to me. HaShem has great things for you to do. When HaShem calls me to make a move, I will need each one of you. But you spoke true, that I have been gone long. Perhaps you have other things you wish to do."

Shimon's father leans forward. "Rabbi, we know you are the son of David."

I choke on my wine.

Andre gives me a hard look from across the table. He and I are the only ones who know the truth. Yes, Rabbi Yeshua is a son of David. But that is not enough, on account of the smirch.

Andre will not speak on the matter. I will not speak on it either. It is Rabbi Yeshua's place to speak on it.

Only it is a hard thing for me not to speak on a matter when it burns like fire in my heart.

"Will you make a move at Pesach?" Shimon's father asks.

Rabbi Yeshua tilts his head as he is listening. An uncertain smile comes across his face. "HaShem says I will make a move at Pesach. HaShem asks if you will stand by me when I make my move."

All the room goes quiet.

I think I might faint for my excitement. I have been waiting long to hear him say he is ready to make a move.

"I will stand with you," says my father. "Even if the mountains shake and the heavens fall, I will stand with you."

"And I also," says Shimon's father.

Shimon the Rock and Big Yaakov and Andre all say the same.

I do not say anything, because I already gave my word earlier, and they shushed me. Now they will not shush me. Now they are following in my steps like sheep.

I see that Shimon the Rock wants Rabbi Yeshua to tell him he will have first place in his army, ahead of Little Yaakov. I do not know if Rabbi Yeshua sees it. I should explain the matter to Rabbi Yeshua and give him my advice. I think he would be glad on it.

A fierce grin slides across my father's face. "The chief priests in Jerusalem will tremble for their fear when we make our move."

He is right, for the chief priests in Jerusalem are fat and rich on the money they have cheated from our people. My father hates them, for they used to cheat him of his tithes when he went to serve his week in the Temple. Now he is too old to serve, but he has not forgotten.

When Rabbi Yeshua makes his move, he will throw out the chief priests who make a cheat on our people.

If I were one of the chief priests in Jerusalem, I would not wait for Rabbi Yeshua to make a move.

If I were a chief priest, I would make my own move first.

CHAPTER THIRTY-SEVEN

Hanan ben Hanan

"There are more of them than we were told." My brother Fat Yonatan stops and stares north up the river. It is near the going out of the day, and we at last are coming near the place where the false prophet spreads his poison.

I count with my eyes. We were told there were a hundred fools here, perhaps two. I know the look of a hundred men. This is more. "A thousand sheep. Strike the shepherd and they will run." I tug on Fat Yonatan's sleeve and stride forward.

He follows with a big reluctance. Fat Yonatan is captain of the Temple guard and should be bold, but he is fifteen years older than me and overcautious. That is the reason our father sent me also. Of the five sons of my father, I am the youngest, but men say our father's blood runs truest in me—the blood of a tiger.

Our father told us to question the false prophet to see if he leads Israel astray.

If he leads Israel astray, we are to bring him to Jerusalem to answer to my father.

If he refuses, we are to flog him.

If he resists, we are to kill him.

That would be easy if we had been told the true tale of things. We were told the man had a hundred followers. We were told he was camped across the Jordan east of Jericho by a walk of one hour. Both tales were false. This lying prophet is camped on this side of Jordan, north of Jericho by a walk of two days. And the number of his followers is many hundreds, almost a thousand.

Now we have walked three days from Jerusalem, sleeping in our cloaks on the ground every night. And we must scatter these sheep and take the shepherd.

A hundred sheep would be nothing. A thousand sheep are not nothing. But a thousand sheep are still sheep.

Now is the time to make our move, while many of the men are in the river. A man waist-deep in water wearing a wet tunic will think twice on fighting two Temple guards with iron swords.

We stride quickly toward the false prophet. I keep my eyes on the men in the river. They make a mock on true immersion. Torah does not say you should immerse in public, wearing a tunic. Torah says you should immerse in private, naked. I have an immersion pool, a *mikveh*, in my palace. I immerse there as Torah says.

Not in some vile river.

Not in a tunic.

This is abomination. No man of the chief priests would immerse here. This immersion is against Torah. This man is a false prophet, and HaShem has not spoken to him. HaShem only spoke to one man ever, and that was our prophet Moses. Chief priests accept only Torah. We are not fools like the Pharisees, who accept many false prophets— Isaiah and Jeremiah and Daniel. Liars, all of them.

"Hurry, Fat Yonatan." I do not wait for my brother. He has more than forty years and is a thick man and a slow-foot. I am enough to frighten a thousand sheep if I move with speed.

Many men are in the river, but more are not yet in the water, or already came out.

The false prophet stands in water to his waist. He points a bony finger on me. "Who warned you to repent, you viper, you?"

I rest my hand loose on my sword. "I am sent by my father, Hanan ben Set, and by Yoseph Qayaph, high priest of the living God. Who sent you?"

"HaShem sent me. HaShem calls men to repent. HaShem says judgment is coming on Israel at the hand of the Great Satan."

"You are ordered by my father to come to Jerusalem."

"You think you are sons of Abraham and have no need to repent, but HaShem says you must repent and immerse and do acts of *zekhut*."

Fat Yonatan comes up beside me, stinking of sweat and fear. He shouts, "They say you speak against the Temple. What is the truth of the matter?"

The false prophet's long wet hair hangs in wretched tangles to his waist. His face is rough as leather, scored by wind and sun. "You hide in your Temple of stone and think you are safe from the wrath to come. You are wrong! When the Great Satan comes to make a judgment on you, it will burn your den of thieves with fire. All you rich, who abuse the poor. You priests, who oppress the people with a second tithe and many thousand offerings. You landowners, who turn out peasants for profit. The fire of the Great Satan will destroy you!"

I do not have time for foolishness. "If you have grievances, bring them to the courts and let the judges make a justice on you."

"The courts! Bah!" The false prophet spits in the river. "The courts are owned by those who abuse the poor. There is no justice from the courts. HaShem will make a justice on the poor. HaShem will turn out the rich. HaShem will cast judgment on the earth, and then he will make his kingdom new."

My insides turn to springs of coiled iron. "If you need a king, there is one not far from here who will hear your appeals for justice."

The false prophet's eyes burn. "Herod? That son of an Edomite? He stole his own brother's woman and married her. He is adulterer and she is adulteress. There is no justice from Herod. There is no justice from the Temple. The only justice is from HaShem, and it is coming soon. The ax is already laid at the root of the tree."

My fists curl in knots. The tree he speaks of is the olive tree of HaShem, which is Israel. Our nation is a well-watered tree, planted by

HaShem long ago. This false prophet leads Israel astray. "My father orders you to come to Jerusalem to answer to him."

The false prophet remains in the river. "Your father will be cut down and thrown in the fire. You will be cut down and thrown in the fire."

My brother is not quick to anger, but now he draws his sword. "Hanan, go in the river and bring him out."

I draw my sword and run down into the water.

The false prophet steps back, but he is slow, for he is in deep water.

I splash forward fast. Speed is my friend, and the water comes only to my knees.

The false prophet shouts with a great shout and turns to flee.

I lunge forward.

The false prophet has a big terror on his face.

I step in a deep hole and go down. Water closes over my head.

I hear Fat Yonatan shouting, but he is muffled.

I flail about and find my feet. When I break the surface, I am in water to my chest.

The false prophet has moved upstream.

And many hundred men are on the banks of the river, waving sticks.

I look for my brother.

He is running backward faster than he ever did, jabbing his sword at a dozen men who pursue him with sticks.

Stones fall in the water all around me, small but many. One hits me in the face.

I press backward, away from my enemies, keeping my sword up.

They are fools and less than fools, but they are not so foolish as to come within reach of my sword.

I misjudged the matter. I was foolish to misjudge, and that was a big error, but I will learn from my error. I thought they were sheep, and it is true, but they are angry sheep, and sheep have teeth. I cannot fight many hundred sheep when I am in the middle of a river.

The false prophet scrambles up on the shore, and now I am wrong-footed. He can run and I cannot.

More men throw stones at me.

I back toward the far shore at my best speed. The water never comes higher than my neck.

Nobody pursues, for there is no gain in it. They throw small stones, but none large enough to make a hurt on me. The stones are a warning, nothing more.

When I reach the far bank, my heart has stopped its pounding. Cold rage runs in my veins.

My brother is still across the river on the western side, but south of me. I walk south for many hundred paces until I find a place that looks more shallow. It is not a proper ford, but neither was the place where I crossed. The Jordan is not deep. I stride into the river and cross, wary of holes. Soon I come up out of the river.

Fat Yonatan stands waiting for me. His face is gray and sweat shines on his forehead and he still gasps for breath. "There were more of them than we were told."

That should not have mattered. We were foolish and underthought their rage because they are sheep. I will never underthink a sheep's rage again.

I stare up the river at the sheep gathered around the false prophet.

They shake their fists and shout curses.

The false prophet smiles.

Let him smile while he has teeth.

He is a dead man, or I am no son of my father.

Hanan ben Hanan

"You will tell the king exactly what the false prophet told you." Father's face shows nothing, but his voice tells me his temper runs hot today.

It should run hot. Pesach will begin in a week and four days, and soon many ten thousand pilgrims will fill the city, sleeping in their cloaks in the Kidron Valley and up the Mount of Olives. Those pilgrims are dry wood, and the words of the false prophet are a torch. We must remove the torch.

King Herod Antipas is not really a king. He is a tetrarch over Galilee and Perea and he wishes to be king like his father, who died long ago, Herod called Magnificent. When Father wants a favor, he calls Herod king. When Father does not want a favor, he still calls Herod king, because the day will come when he wants a favor.

There are four of us going to see the king. My brother-in-law, Yoseph Qayaph, is high priest. My brother Fat Yonatan is captain of the Temple guard. Father has no office, but he is head of the great and mighty House of Hanan, and all Jerusalem quivers before him.

We stride all together across the bridge from the Temple outer courts to the stone square in front of the Hasmonean Palace. In better times, a century and two ago, the Hasmonean kings were priests, men of good Makkabi blood who loved the Temple. Herod Antipas is no priest and has not one drop of Makkabi blood. Perhaps he loves the Temple, but he does not love chief priests, so we must walk a thin line today.

We come to the great iron gate before the palace. Father steps to the wooden door beside it and puts his mouth to the small grate. "Hanan ben Set to see my lord King Herod."

The door swings inward. Herod is expecting us.

Father leads the way across the courtyard and up the steps into the palace. Large men with pale skin and yellow hair stand guard on either side—uncircumcised Germans from the barbaric north.

Such men make me shiver for a disgust. It says much on the Herod family that they use vile foreigners for their personal guard.

Inside, we cross the marble floor of the receiving room and enter the Hasmonean throne room.

At the far end of the room, Herod Antipas sits. His woman stands behind him.

It is not fitting that this woman should be queen. A man may not marry the woman of his brother. Torah forbids. Even the foolish Pharisees agree on the matter.

Herod's marriage to this woman is no Torah marriage.

But better the false prophet said it than me.

"My lord the king." Father gives the smallest possible bow to

Herod and then points a finger on me. "Tell what the false prophet said."

Herod's face is hard and flat. He does not trust Father and never did.

I waste no time on small matters. "The false prophet threatened you, my lord the king. He said you will face judgment. He said you and all your house will burn. He said the ax is already laid at the root of the tree."

Herod's eyes narrow to fine points. "And that would make you lose a big sleep, yes, Hanan ben Hanan? Did he make a mock on the Temple, also?"

"He called it a den of thieves, my lord the king."

Herod makes a big grin. "The man sounds like a true prophet of HaShem."

I knew Herod would sneer on us, but I also know what he is afraid on. I say nothing. I put on the face of a man who knows a secret.

Herod stares on me long, and his face turns uneasy. "Is the man gathering an army?"

"He has nearly two thousand men with him, my lord the king."

"What does he tell these men?"

"He tells repentance to them."

Herod grins on me again. "Repentance is no crime. I would pay many talents to get more of it. Did he tell repentance to you?"

"He called me a viper and asked who called me to repentance."

Herod laughs out loud.

I flinch, even though I was expecting it. This vile man mocks chief priests for sport. If he were not the client of Rome, I would put a knife in his grin and laugh on him while he bled out.

Behind me, Father sucks in his breath. That is the signal to complete the business.

I wait for silence and allow it to hang until it is full ripe. "He also called you to repentance, my lord the king. He spoke hard words on your woman."

Herod's eyes turn cold.

Behind him, the queen leans forward. Her name is called Herodias, and she is known to take offense. "Say more on that." The eyes of Herodias are the eyes of a viper.

My belly burns like fire, for I know there is gold here. "The false prophet said my lord the king is adulterer. He said my lord the king stole his brother's woman and married her against Torah. He said she left her lord without a divorce, so she is adulteress. He said there is no justice with Herod."

Herod's face is stone.

His woman's is ice.

"You have witnesses?" Herod says.

Father snaps his fingers at Fat Yonatan.

Fat Yonatan steps forward.

I smell the sweat of his terror.

Father points a finger on him. "Fat Yonatan, did you hear the same? Swear by The Name you heard the same, or else swear by The Name you did not hear the same."

Fat Yonatan swears by The Name that he heard it just as I said.

Fury lights Herod's eyes.

My heart shivers when I look on his hard eyes.

But the eyes of his woman …

The eyes of Herodias stop my heart cold.

CHAPTER THIRTY-EIGHT

Yoni of Capernaum

Rabbi Yeshua's secret is burning a hole in my heart. I thought he would explain the matter of the smirch when we went to Capernaum. Instead, he went to Nazareth without saying a word. I am terrified Andre will tell the matter in a loose word. I am more terrified I will tell the matter.

We will see Rabbi Yeshua in Jerusalem tomorrow, and if he does not explain the matter then, I will die from holding his secret inside me. I must never think on the matter. Never, ever, ever.

"How much farther to Bethany?" my sister Elisheva asks.

"It is a walk of one hour."

"You have been quiet today. Are you well?" Elisheva puts a hand on my forehead. She is kind like Aunt Miryam and never teases me like my other sisters and Big Yaakov.

"I am thinking on a matter."

"It must be a small matter," says Big Yaakov. "I never saw the Genius of Capernaum thinking and not talking."

My family laughs, except Elisheva. Shimon's family laughs.

I do not think Big Yaakov's joke is funny. I am desperate to understand the paradox of the smirch. I have wished many times to ask Rabbi Yeshua how he will answer his village on the smirch, but his eyes have been haunted lately.

He must make an answer on them, or he will never be Mashiach.

I think he does not know himself how he will answer them.

I thought a prophet always knew the answer.

I thought a prophet never doubted himself.

Rabbi Yeshua is not what I thought a prophet would be. He is less fierce and more kind. I remember when we met him last fall. The first thing I noticed was the light of the Shekinah shining out from his eyes. I can remember every word he ever told me. I listen again in my mind's ear to each thing he said.

He never said he means to be Mashiach.

So why do I think he means to be Mashiach?

I think it is because his family acts as that is what he means to be. But Mashiach must be accepted as the son of David.

Rabbi Yeshua's village thinks his mother played the *zonah*. That is not such a bad matter. The mother of King Solomon also played the *zonah*.

What mattered in the end is that King David claimed Solomon for his son, and all Israel accepted. The people knew his woman played the *zonah* before, so they would never trust her to say who begat Solomon. But they trusted King David to say who was his son.

I think the matter is like Yiftakh, a mighty warrior whose mother was a *zonah*. The man who begat him was Gilead, a great man in the village. Yiftakh would have been nothing, a *mamzer*, only Gilead claimed him for his son. Gilead's other sons hated him for being the son of a strange woman, but they never denied he was son of Gilead.

Because Gilead claimed Yiftakh for his son.

I do not know how he knew the boy was his own, since a *zonah* lies with many men.

The tales do not tell how he knew it. The tales only say Gilead begat Yiftakh, so he must have claimed him. And the village accepted.

Rabbi Yeshua's mother made a big trouble by enticing a man before the time. Some in the village think it was not her own lord she enticed, and that is why there is a smirch. But her own lord was a *tsaddik* and claimed Rabbi Yeshua for his son. That should be the end of the matter. She enticed her own lord before the time, and Rabbi Yeshua is son of Yoseph, son of David.

It is a wrong thing that there is a smirch on Rabbi Yeshua. The village makes a trouble on the matter only because they are cruel. Rabbi Yeshua's mother should not have enticed her lord before the time, but if she had not enticed, Rabbi Yeshua would not have been born, and then who would we follow after? It makes my head hurt to think on the matter.

I think Little Yaakov thinks he should be Mashiach instead. Little Yaakov is also son of David, and he is a man with a strong *yetzer hara*. I can see him in my eye taking a sword to smite the Great Satan.

It is harder to see in my eye Rabbi Yeshua taking a sword to smite the Great Satan. He is a *tsaddik* and a mighty teller of tales and a prophet of HaShem. He has the Shekinah all around him, but he does not have the rage to power.

Little Yaakov has the rage to power, but he does not have the Shekinah all around him. I think none of us would follow after Little Yaakov, even though he has the rage to power. I think we follow after Rabbi Yeshua because we see the Shekinah in him. A man who has the Shekinah does not need the rage to power to smite the Great Satan.

A man who has the Shekinah has all that he needs to be Mashiach, because the Shekinah is more than the rage to power.

That is what I think. That is not a deep thing. Even my family knows it. And Shimon's family also.

But if they knew Rabbi Yeshua has a smirch, they would make a hesitation, because a man's own village should believe in him first, before another village.

I should tell them he has a smirch.

I am dying to say he has a smirch.

But it is not my place to tell it. It is Rabbi Yeshua's place to tell it.

It is a sore trial to know a mighty secret and not be able to tell it.

I have been watching Andre. He is disturbed also, but he knows it is Rabbi Yeshua's place to tell the matter to our families.

"Tell us a tale, Yoni!" Elisheva says. "It makes the road go faster when you tell a tale."

I do not wish to tell a tale.

"Yes, a tale, Yoni!" says my mother. "Perhaps the tale of how Ruth the Moabite got a man. Only if you tell her with large bosoms again, I will box your ears."

My face turns hot. I did not know I ever told Ruth with large bosoms.

"You had better tell her with bosoms twice as large as Miryam Big-Eyes, or else I will box your ears," says Big Yaakov.

All my family roars. Shimon's family roars.

If they knew how much I think on bosoms, they would not laugh so loud. They would tell repentance on me harder than Yohanan the immerser.

I tell the tale of Ruth, the Moabite woman who married a man from Bethlehem. Then she became a widow, but she still took a good care on her mother-in-law, Naomi. At last she married her kinsman redeemer and bore a son who begat a son who begat David the king.

"Tell us another!" says Elisheva. "Only this time, tell the tale of some young girl, for you gave Ruth such small bosoms she might as well have been a child."

I did not know I told Ruth with small bosoms.

I think for a moment and decide to tell the tale of Yiftakh the mighty warrior. When Yiftakh went to war, he swore by The Name that if Yah gave him the victory, he would sacrifice the first living thing that came out of his house when he returned. He thought it would be a sheep or goat, and he would make a burnt offering to Yah.

Instead it was his only child, his little daughter, who came out to greet him, for she loved him more than any daughter ever did.

Yiftakh wept great tears when he saw it, for his daughter was the apple in his eye for beauty.

He gave the daughter leave to go two months to mourn, for she was virgin. Then she came home, and he offered her as a burnt offering to Yah on account of his vow.

When I finish the tale, all the women are weeping.

Big Yaakov blinks many times and complains on the dust stirred up in the road.

My father looks on me with strange eyes.

Shimon the Rock looks on me with strange eyes.

Andre clears his throat and looks on me and taps the side of his nose.

I do not understand the meaning of this.

Elisheva takes my hand and squeezes it. Her eyes are red from weeping. "That was well told, Yoni. Only …"

I know I have done something very wrong.

"Yoni, why did you change Yiftakh's name in the middle of the tale?"

I did not know I changed his name. Yiftakh is no common name. It is not done to name a boy Yiftakh, on account of the horror he made in Israel. "What name did I change it to?"

Elisheva says nothing.

And then I know.

My heart seizes inside my chest.

I should stuff a millstone in my mouth to keep from telling more secrets.

I told the tale of Yeshua, the mighty warrior of HaShem, the son of a *zonah*.

CHAPTER THIRTY-NINE

Shimon of Capernaum

We are all eating the morning meal in Elazar's courtyard when I hear a stranger shouting outside in the street and beating on the door.

"Yoni! Andre! Give help! Are you there?"

Yoni chokes on the dried fig he was eating. He coughs a big cough and spits out the fig on the floor and makes no move to go greet the stranger.

We arrived last night at the home of Elazar in Bethany, where we always stay for Pesach. I ask, "Yoni, who could know we are here already?"

Yoni's lip curls as he smells *haryo*. "It is that terrible man."

Andre frowns. "We should not answer. He will go away and be rude to some other family."

"Yoni! Andre! I beg you, give help!"

The face of Miryam Big-Eyes is completely white.

Marta strides out of the courtyard to greet the stranger.

She brings back a man with thick arms and wild eyes.

He staggers as he is exhausted. He looks as he has been running all night. The sweat of fear is on his face. His tunic is filthy, as he has fallen in the road many times.

Yoni scowls on him. "What brings you here, Hananyah the nail maker?"

This man Hananyah the nail maker falls at Yoni's feet. "I came to warn you. I have been running two nights and a day. They took Yohanan the prophet. They will come here also."

My heart hammers in my chest. "Who took Yohanan the prophet?"

"Soldiers from Herod." Hananyah's eyes are hungry on the bread I am eating. "I ran as fast as I could. They will come here soon."

"Come here? Why?" Marta asks.

"They said Yohanan the prophet spoke evil on Herod on the matter of his woman. They asked who else spoke evil on the matter of his woman. Could I beg some bread from you? I have not eaten since Yohanan was taken."

I do not like this Hananyah the nail maker. "Why did you come here?"

Yoni scowls. "His family lives in Joppa. That is another day's walk, but he is hungry now. That is the only reason he came here."

"But I also wished to warn you and your friend, Yeshua from Nazareth." Hananyah stands to his feet.

I think it is more a matter of hunger than concern for Rabbi Yeshua.

Yoni shakes his head. "Rabbi Yeshua is not here yet. He is coming to Pesach with his brothers and mother by the Samaritan Road. We came by the Jordan Way and are to meet him here."

"You should warn him away," Hananyah says. "And you should run too, Yoni. You spoke ill on Herod's woman first, and then Yeshua did. Yohanan the prophet only spoke ill on Herod's woman after the both of you. Herod's men will come for you."

My father paces back and forth. "Yoni, you spoke ill on Herod's woman?"

Yoni says, "I told the truth, how Herod took his brother's woman, against Torah. And the woman divorced her lord, against Torah."

I do not understand why they were so foolish as to speak on this matter.

"You should run," Hananyah says. "Run for your lives. Do not take the Jericho Road. Herod's soldiers will come back by that way. If Yohanan the prophet tells them what Yeshua said—"

"He will not tell," Yoni says. "Yohanan the prophet will spit their eye and call them wicked and fools. And anyway, Rabbi Yeshua is to make his move at Pesach."

Hananyah scowls on Yoni. "You know he cannot make a move. That is a big foolishness."

I cross my arms on my chest. "Why can he not make a move? He is son of David."

Hananyah shakes his head as I know nothing. "Yes, he says he is son of David, but what of the smirch on his name?"

I think he is more arrogant than any man ever was. "Leave us, you filth. Take bread and cheese and go. You are not fit to tie Rabbi Yeshua's sandals. What smirch do you think he has on his name?"

Hananyah the nail maker's eyes fill with a big scorn. "Yeshua from Nazareth has the smirch of *mamzer* on him."

I slap his vile face with the back of my right hand. "Leave now, you lying *haryo*. And do not take bread and cheese. Go!"

"All of us heard it from his own brother, how some in his village say he is *mamzer*," says Hananyah the nail maker. "Yoni, Andre, tell what you heard."

I look on Yoni and Andre, and my heart misses a beat. "Yoni? Andre? Why does he insult Rabbi Yeshua? What do you know on the matter?"

Yoni looks guilty as the thief we caught once in our house in the middle of the night. "I thought Rabbi Yeshua would explain the matter himself. He should have explained the matter when he came to Capernaum, only he left for Nazareth. I think he meant to explain the matter—"

"What matter?" I shout. "Say it and be done with it, without so many ten thousand words."

"Rabbi Yeshua has a smirch on his name in his village," Andre says.

"Some say his mother played the *zonah*, and so some other man of the village begat him."

I do not believe them. This must be one of Andre's jokes, only it is a bad joke and a wickedness. Rabbi Yeshua cannot be a son of adultery. Rabbi Yeshua is to be Mashiach.

Yoni clutches my arm. "The rabbis say the word of the father decides the matter. We know his father was a righteous man, Yoseph the *tsaddik*, and he claimed Rabbi Yeshua for his son. Therefore, he is his son. That should be the end on the matter."

Hananyah the nail maker makes a happy grin. "But his own brother says there is a smirch on his name. He says not all in the village accept. He says no father of the village will give his daughter to Yeshua. I say Yeshua would never dare to make some foolish move. If his own village does not accept, they will raise a stench on the matter. You will make a fool on yourself if you follow after a man with a smirch. And anyway, Herod will kill him because Yeshua spoke ill on Herod's woman."

My father seizes Yoni and spins him around. "You admit you spoke ill on Herod's woman?"

Yoni nods.

"And Rabbi Yeshua spoke ill on Herod's woman?"

Yoni nods again.

"And Rabbi Yeshua has a smirch on his name?"

Yoni stares on the ground.

My father has always been quick to decide. He turns on his heel and begins shouting. "Quickly, everyone, we are leaving. Pack your cloaks. Take food. We will be gone in the fourth part of an hour."

"Abba." My heart hammers in my chest. "Tomorrow is Shabbat. Also, we will have to take the Samaritan Road."

"Then we will travel on Shabbat, and we will take the Samaritan Road!" he roars.

It is a wrong thing to travel on Shabbat. And I do not wish to take the Samaritan Road. I am afraid on what I will do if I walk through the village that killed my brother.

Yoni's father stands. "We also are leaving. Prepare your packs. Call the women. Give this man some bread and cheese and send him on his way. Quickly!"

Yoni stamps his foot. "What are you doing? We promised Rabbi Yeshua we would wait for him here. That we would join him when he makes his move! That—"

"Hush, Yoni," Zavdai says. "You should have told us this man has a smirch. Nobody will follow a man with a smirch when he makes a move. Elazar, tell the *mamzer* that Capernaum is closed to him. If he comes there, we do not know the man."

"I told you, he is not a *mamzer!*" Yoni shouts.

My whole body trembles and my hands feel moist. We should stay. There may be a big fight, and we should stand with Rabbi Yeshua. But we cannot stay. We have women here with us. And Rabbi Yeshua has no great army. He has four brothers and a few of us friends.

We are dead men if we stay.

We are cowards if we run.

"Quickly!" my father shouts. He strides around the edges of the courtyard, bellowing orders to our women to prepare to leave.

I am balanced on the edge of a knife. I wish to honor my father. But I wish to stay and fight. But I wish to protect our women. But I wish to—

Yoni hops up and down for his anger. "We do not know Herod's men will come for us. We do not know they will come for Rabbi Yeshua."

All my skin is cold. "We do not know they will not. You should not have spoken ill on Herod's woman."

"But it was true!" Yoni shouts. "Torah forbids a man to take the woman of his own brother, when the brother is alive."

"Hush, Yoni." He is a fool if he does not know when to leave a true thing unsaid.

Yoni jabs a finger at my chest. "Shimon the Rock, you will not run like a woman, will you? It is foolish for us to leave now. Rabbi Yeshua is about to make his move."

I scowl on him. "He cannot be Mashiach if he has a smirch."

Yoni shakes his head. "Rabbi Yeshua never said he is to be Mashiach! What if he means for Little Yaakov to be Mashiach? Rabbi

Yeshua can be the prophet of Mashiach, whether he has a smirch or no. When they come into their power, they will throw off Herod. Speak to our fathers and tell them there is nothing to fear. HaShem will protect us!"

I cannot look on Yoni. Yoni is young and not wise in the ways of things. If HaShem will protect us, why did he not protect the prophet Yohanan? Yohanan is a true prophet and Rabbi Yeshua is a true prophet, but true prophets can be arrested and killed by evil kings. It has happened many hundred times. And anyway, I do not wish to follow after Little Yaakov.

"Shimon the Rock!" Yoni pushes his face in front of mine. "Think on what you are doing! Tell no to your father. We must stay and fight for Rabbi Yeshua!"

I hate that Yoni says what I dare only to think. Yoni is not more brave than me, he is more rash. He does not think out all paths. A man should think before he makes a move.

"You promised to fight for him!" Yoni's lip curls as I am pig *haryo*.

I glare on him. "Yoni, there is a time to fight and a time to protect our women. It is foolish to wait idly for Herod's men to come and kill us."

Yoni says, "Coward! You have a fish knife, and Andre also. I have a blade. With HaShem on our side, why should we be afraid?"

I seize Yoni's tunic in one fist and pull him close to my face. "You will never call me coward again. You will show honor to those who are older and wiser than you. You will fill your pack and be ready to leave in the fourth part of an hour. Yes?"

Yoni's eyes gleam large and white.

I shake him. "Yes?"

Big Yaakov comes up beside me and pulls him away. "Yoni, we are leaving. All of us. Do not dishonor our father by disobeying. Yes?"

"I will not run like a woman." Yoni's words hiss out through clenched teeth.

Big Yaakov gives him the back of his hand.

Yoni's face goes red. "Shimon the Rock! Speak sense to him. Do not run like a woman."

I am so angry, I wish to break his teeth. I turn and stride out of the courtyard to find my pack.

Yoni is young and does not know what a Herod can do.

A Herod crucifies his enemies for cause of an insult.

A Herod kills his favorite woman for cause of jealousy.

A Herod executes his own son for cause of rivalry.

We have seen Herods do such things.

Any man who does not fear a Herod is a fool.

Even a mighty prophet of HaShem.

Rabbi Yeshua should have made his move before. Now it is too late. Now he must run. Now we must run also.

If we are lucky, we will never see Rabbi Yeshua again.

CHAPTER FORTY

Yeshua of Nazareth

When we reach the village of Bethany, I point down the street. "The man of the house is called Elazar, and he loves HaShem. He is cousin to Yoni's mother. If you like Yoni, you will like Elazar."

My family and I came to Jerusalem by the Samaritan Road and arrived last night and rented the same house we always do. This morning we all slept long, for we were tired from our journey. Now my brothers and I are going to meet with Shimon the Rock and Andre and Big Yaakov and Yoni and their families.

My stomach is so tight, I think I might vomit. I do not know what to tell my men and my brothers. They think I know how to make a move. I told them I would make a move. But still I do not know how to make a move.

Yet I am certain HaShem will show me a great thing here during Pesach.

I know it. I do not know how I know it, but I do.

HaShem will show me how to smite the first Power. He must show me. I spent all winter telling repentance to Israel, and it was a good work. We saw many men repent. But I think there is more to smiting the first Power than telling repentance. That is a good work, but it is not enough. I am burning to know what to do next.

When we reach the house, I call at the door. "Elazar, friend! Are you well?"

Footsteps.

The door cracks open.

A frightened pair of eyes peep out.

"Miryam Big-Heart, are you well?" I ask.

She looks up and down the empty street and then pulls the door open. She whispers, "Come in and be quick. Did anyone in the village see you?"

My heart flutters. That is a strange welcome. We walk into the receiving room.

Miryam Big-Heart shuts the door. "Elazar!" Her voice cracks. "We have some men to see you!"

Some men. I feel as I am slapped with the backhand of dishonor. I am a friend of this house. I am not *some men.*

Elazar comes in from the central courtyard. His face is pale, and sweat shines on his forehead. "Rabbi Yeshua, you are in a big danger! King Herod has taken Yohanan the prophet. Your friends are gone back to Galilee."

Taken! My heart explodes in my chest. Dark spots appear before my eyes. My knees feel weak. I put a hand on Little Yaakov's shoulder.

He is a rock of strength.

I look to my other brothers.

Thin Shimon's mouth hangs open. Yosi and Yehuda Dreamhead stare on each other.

Marta appears. Her mouth is set in a thin line. "Elazar, what are you thinking? We have guests! Bring them in. We must give them food and drink. No matter that King Herod may arrive at any moment and take us all away, we have our duty as hosts. Miryam Big-Eyes, run, run, and fetch food!"

Marta is not subtle, and I love her for it. I shake my head. "We will not stay. I will not put you in danger. Only explain the matter to me, for we have not heard this news."

Elazar explains what has befallen. This morning, word came that Yohanan the prophet has been taken by King Herod's men. Hananyah the nail maker came to tell it. He ran all the way here in a terror to warn them. Elazar gave him food, and he has gone to Joppa to hide. Yoni's father and Shimon the Rock's father were terrified and fled back to Galilee with their families by the Samaritan Road. Little Yoni wanted to stay and fight, but the others forced him to leave. His father and Shimon's father left word for me—that Capernaum is closed to me, that the House of Yonah and the House of Zavdai do not know me.

When he finishes, Elazar cannot look my eye.

I think he has something more to say.

Little Yaakov's fists are clenched tight. "These false friends are cowards. We are not afraid. Now is the time for us to make a move."

My other brothers all nod.

I step closer to Elazar. "And there is more? I do not think you have said all."

"It is … no, Rabbi Yeshua, there is—"

"Do not be foolish, Elazar," Marta says. "Hananyah the nail maker said a strange thing on you, Rabbi Yeshua. And Yoni would not say no to it, that … you have a smirch on your name. Mashiach is to be son of David, yes?"

I feel as I am kicked in the underparts. The question I have been running from these last three weeks has caught up with me, and still I do not know the answer.

Elazar looks on me with sharp eyes.

"My father claimed me for his son," I say. "He was Yoseph the *tsaddik*, son of Yaakov Mega, son of David. When I was a baby, a man of HaShem prophesied over me, how HaShem calls me to redeem Israel."

Little Yaakov sucks in his breath.

Marta says, "But Andre also says there is a smirch on your name."

I do not know what to say to that. There is a smirch on my name.

Elazar gives me a stony silence.

Marta bites her lip and will not look on me.

Miryam Big-Heart says, "There is food and beer in the courtyard. Please, you will eat?"

Marta clucks her tongue.

Elazar's face is closed like an iron door, and his eyes dart toward the street.

I bow to Elazar and then to Marta. "Elazar, we will not put your house in a big danger. Marta, we thank you for your hospitality. Miryam Big-Heart, please, you will look in the street to be sure there is nobody to see us leave."

Miryam Big-Heart creeps to the door and slips out. A moment later, she is back. "The street is empty. Must you leave so soon? Can you not eat and drink?"

"Perhaps another time." I give her a smile, for she looks like a frightened rabbit.

She blushes and looks only on the floor.

A moment later, we are all outside in the street and the door is shut behind us.

My brothers scowl on the house.

Thin Shimon says, "Herod will not come here. This Hananyah the nail maker sounds like a liar. He is a liar, yes? Who told him the matter of the smirch?"

Yehuda Dreamhead nods. "A liar and a coward and always grinning on other people's troubles."

Thin Shimon scowls. "I think he ran like a woman when his master was taken and then told Elazar a fearful tale so he could have excuse to beg food on his way."

Now that I think on the matter, that is a good logic. That is why Yoni refused to run.

"We are not afraid." Little Yaakov fingers the short blade he keeps hidden in the cloth belt around his waist. "Now is the time for us to make a move."

Yosi nods. "We will not run like women. Shimon the Rock ran like a woman. Andre and Big Yaakov and Yoni ran like women. We do not need cowards. We came here to make a move with our brother. Yeshua, we will stand with you."

Thin Shimon says, "But who told them the matter of the smirch?"

Yehuda Dreamhead says, "When will we make a move, Yeshua? You said we would make a move at Pesach. Where will we do it and when?"

I open my mouth to say I do not know when we will make a move.

But when I speak, my words are not the words I meant to say.

The words are the words of HaShem, speaking through me. "We will celebrate Pesach here next week. On Shabbat after Pesach, we will go to the Temple. And while we are there, HaShem will make a move more mighty than any we ever imagined."

Yehuda Dreamhead grins a big grin.

Thin Shimon grins a big grin.

Yosi grins a big grin.

Little Yaakov's mouth is set tight. He does not believe I will make a move.

I do not know what move I will make, but I know HaShem will show me.

But before Shabbat, there is a thing I must know. It is the thing that has burned in my heart all my life. It is a thing only Imma can answer. It is a thing she has never told me.

She must tell me the truth of the matter, who begat me, who is my blood father. All my life, nobody would speak on the matter. Now we must speak on the matter.

And then I must ask HaShem how to remove the smirch on my name.

I can never redeem Israel while I have a smirch.

CHAPTER FORTY-ONE

Miryam of Nazareth

My heart weeps within me, for my son is so sad. He went out with joy this morning with his brothers to find his friends. When he came back, he was crushed more than any man ever was.

Little Yaakov's eyes burned with fury, but he would not tell what is the matter. Yosi would not tell. Yehuda Dreamhead would not tell.

Thin Shimon told me all. Yohanan the prophet is taken. And Yeshua's men know the matter of the smirch on his name.

Only they do not know the matter. Even Yeshua does not know the matter. No living person knows the matter, because I never told. Yaakov Mega shut my mouth on the matter. But even if he had not, I would not have told, because who would believe?

After Thin Shimon told me the matter, Yeshua asked me to come walk with him, and now we are walking. He will ask who begat him. I will not tell, for then he would call me a fool and a simple.

I never told one pair of ears.

I tried to tell once and learned a hard lesson.

I will never tell one word again.

Never, never, never.

"My friend Elazar owns this place," Yeshua says. "It is good, yes?"

I look all around me. We are in the valley between Jerusalem and the Mount of Olives. To our left, the Temple Mount rises above us, a hard stone fortress, angry on me for my sins. To our right, the Mount of Olives. We are in the middle of an olive grove. Ahead of us, I see an olive press and a cave. Beside the cave is a stone bench. It is a peaceful place. You would never know that a hundred paces behind us is the road that comes down the Mount of Olives and leads into the city, with many thousand people tramping down it each day. Here, all is quiet and calm.

Yeshua leads me to the stone bench, and we sit. He holds my hand. Now he will try to worm out my secret.

I will not tell. I will eat *haryo* before I tell. He will make a scorn on me if I tell.

Yeshua's voice cracks when he speaks. "What did your father say when you told him you were with child?"

My eyes flood with tears. That was the worst day that ever was. It was four months or five after the day I went to the village spring and saw the Messenger.

I remember how surprised I was to see a man there at the spring. I did not know at once he was a Messenger. How was I to know? People in olden times saw Messengers, but people in these times do not. I do not know why.

So I thought the Messenger was just some young man, a beautiful man, more beautiful than any man I ever saw. All my thoughts ran away. I dropped my waterpot and stared.

He smiled on me and greeted me and told me my name. In those days, my name was Miryam Beautiful.

I wished to run away, for I was not in the custom of speaking to strange men, but my legs had no strength.

The Messenger said I was favored by HaShem.

I could not think what it meant to be favored by HaShem. I was only a girl of twelve, the daughter of a village farmer, and I never thought I was anything. Here is what I knew of favor—two men asked to buy me from my father. Some girls had no man ask to buy them, and I had two! That was what I thought it meant to be favored.

I did not like the way the Messenger looked on me, for I could not look away from his face. His eyes saw inside my heart, and I was terrified.

The Messenger said I should not be afraid. He said HaShem promised I should have a son.

I was glad, for every girl wishes to give her lord a son.

The Messenger said my son would be the son of HaShem.

I was more than glad. My son will be king of Israel!

The Messenger said my son would take the throne of his father David.

I thought how glad my lord Yoseph will be, for he was of the House of David, and now his son was to be Mashiach.

The Messenger said my son would rule over Israel, and there would be no end to his kingdom.

I asked the Messenger why he told me, and not my betrothed lord Yoseph, for this was a mighty honor on him.

The Messenger said my lord Yoseph would not beget my son. He said no man would beget my son.

I told the Messenger that was a big foolishness. I was only a girl of twelve, but my father owned sheep and goats, and I knew how lambs and kids are begotten. I knew a son is not born unless a man begets him.

The Messenger said the power of HaShem would overshadow me, and the son to be born would be a gift from HaShem.

I could not think what to say. My mind was all a big confusion, and my heart filled my chest with a mighty hammering.

The Messenger came toward me, and his eyes burned bright.

All my body was cold for my terror.

The Messenger said HaShem did not command. He said HaShem asked permission. He said HaShem would not give me a son unless I said yes.

I did not think what that would mean.

I was a foolish young girl, as simple as a stick.

I never thought how I would tell the matter to my lord Yoseph.

So I said yes.

The Messenger came nearer and looked in my eyes and smiled on me with kindness.

I think I fainted.

I do not remember what happened next. When I came to myself, the Messenger was gone, and my body was warm with the heat of the Shekinah, and my heart was full with a big gladness. I would have thought it was all a dream, only my waterpot was beside me, broken in shards.

All the way home, I tried to think how to tell the matter to my mother. When I reached our house, I still did not know how to tell the matter.

Before I could open my mouth, my mother asked where was my waterpot.

I told her I had broken it.

She made a big rage on me and shouted me for a fool and a simple.

I could not think how to tell the matter of the Messenger, for Messengers are not seen in these days, and I knew my tale would sound foolish. I thought I would tell her tomorrow, but the next day, I could not think how to tell the matter. Days passed, and still I could not think how to tell the matter. Weeks passed. Months. The matter burned a hole in my heart, but still I could not think how to tell it.

But the matter did not stay hidden. There came a day when my mother saw the roundness of my belly and asked hard questions. Had my monthly blood come lately? When had it stopped? Had some man forced me to spread my legs?

I tried to explain the matter of the Messenger. I said I met a beautiful young man by the spring.

Imma cried out for her fear.

I said the man told me I should have a son if I said yes.

Imma cried out for her shock.

I said I told the man yes.

Imma cried out for her rage. She screamed on me that I was a fool and a simple and a wicked *zonah*. She would not listen to my tale.

My heart felt as it was burned. That was the day I knew no one would ever listen. They would say I told some idle tale. They would never believe.

That was the day I clamped my mouth shut with my tale inside. I vowed a vow to HaShem that I would never tell it, and I never have, and I never will. Never, never, never. The village says I am a wicked *zonah*. If I tell my tale, they will say I am a wicked liar also.

When my father came home, my mother took him aside and made pained whispers with a dark face.

I never saw him so angry, his face so hard, like stone. He would not look on me for his rage. He did not ask how it befell. I would not have told if he asked, but he did not even ask.

He went to my betrothed lord Yoseph to ask after the matter, for he thought my lord Yoseph took me into the chamber before the time.

My betrothed lord Yoseph came to our house, and his anger was hotter than my father's, for he knew he was righteous in the matter. His words bruised my heart as stones crush a flower. He said he would go to Tsipori and find a letter-man to write me a bill of divorce quietly. As if the matter could be kept quiet.

I cried and cried, but there was nothing I could say that he would believe, so I said nothing.

If I had known how it would be, I would have told the Messenger no. I should have told the Messenger no. That was a burden more terrible than any girl of the age of twelve should ever bear.

But the next day, my betrothed lord Yoseph came back and said he had changed his mind, and now he would take me as his woman as soon as might be. A Messenger had come to him in a dream in the night and explained the matter. But he did not tell my parents that, for he knew they would not believe.

My father thought Yoseph begat the child, and said at least he was an honorable man, if not righteous. My mother called my father a fool, for she remembered my lord Yoseph's face when he heard the news, and she knew my lord Yoseph did not beget my son. But she never learned why he chose to take me, so she thought he was a fool and a simple until the day she died. My father thought him an unrighteous man all his life.

Some in the village believed my father, that I enticed my lord Yoseph before the time.

Some in the village believed my mother, that I enticed some other man of the village.

All the village hounded after me to tell who I enticed, but what could I say? Farmers know a child is not begotten without a man to beget it.

My lord Yoseph claimed Yeshua for his son. But my lord Yoseph was a *tsaddik*. He would not make a lie, to say he begat Yeshua. And now my lord Yoseph is dead many years. Every year, the village hounds after me more, to tell who I enticed.

If I tell the truth, they would shout to stone me for a liar. But I tell them nothing, so they shout to stone me for a *zonah*.

"Imma, what did your father say when you told him you were with child?"

I wipe my eyes and try to look on Yeshua, but he is blurred. "My father said my lord Yoseph was not a *tsaddik*."

"My father was a *tsaddik*, yes?"

"He was righteous in the matter." My voice is thick in my throat.

"The man who redeems Israel must be son of David."

I seize his hands. "Your father is Yoseph the *tsaddik*, son of Yaakov Mega, son of David."

"The man who redeems Israel must have no smirch on his name."

"The smirch is unjust."

"I would still love you if—"

"There is no smirch in the eyes of HaShem. We will not speak more on the matter."

Yeshua kisses my tears away. He kneels before me, looking in my eyes.

He has bright, shining eyes.

I never saw such bright eyes on a man.

He has eyes like the Messenger.

He leans in close and looks deep in my eyes.

He sees all the way into my heart.

He reads my tale like a man reads words on a page.

I cannot turn my head. I cannot blink my eyes.

He reads my tale all to the end.

He looks on me in wonder for many ten thousand years.

"Imma?"

I cannot breathe. I cannot speak.

"Imma, you did well to say yes."

I do not think I did well to say yes. But if I said no, I would not have my Yeshua.

"Imma, I believe your tale."

My eyes are nothing but tears. My body is nothing but heat. My mind is all a big confusion.

I never thought anyone would believe my tale.

My son Yeshua believes my tale.

I love him more than I ever did.

CHAPTER FORTY-TWO

Yeshua of Nazareth

'So the village is right, you son of a zonah.'

'The village is wrong.'

'Do not be a fool and a simple like your mother. She met some stranger at the spring. She saw he was beautiful. What can that mean, but that she desired for him? And so she spread—'

'You lie. Imma is innocent.'

'She desired for him, and she spread her legs, and he begat you.'

'Liar!'

'Some fine-faced stranger is your blood father, fool.'

'Imma says I am the gift of HaShem.'

'That is a bad gift, if it is true, for see how much sorrow it caused. But you do not believe this foolishness, yes? No more than you believe the ancient tales of wicked spirits who came to earth and lay with the daughters of men and begat the Nephilim, yes?'

'Those are idle tales.'

'And you do not believe the tales the Greeks tell, how their gods came to earth and lay with women and begat heroes, yes?'

'Those are idle tales.'

'And you cannot believe this idle tale, that HaShem came to earth and lay with your mother and—'

'That is not her tale. HaShem has no body, that he can lie with a woman.'

'Then what is your mother's tale?'

'The Shekinah came upon her—'

'She spread her legs for the Shekinah?'

'That is not her tale. The Shekinah has no body. The Shekinah does not lie with a woman. Her tale is that HaShem did a mighty wonder.'

'A woman does not beget a son on her own.'

'I did not say she begat a son on her own. That is not the way of things. If that was the way of things, I would not call the matter a mighty wonder.'

'How did it come about then? Explain the matter.'

'One does not explain a mighty wonder.'

'Why should you believe there was a mighty wonder? Why not rather believe some stranger begat you? You have only the word of your mother, and why should she not lie to save herself?'

'She did not lie to save herself. She never told this tale. Never once. She held it in her heart.'

'She was afraid to tell it, for it is foolishness.'

'Now you change your accusation. First you said she lied to save herself. Now you say she did not, for she knew it was foolishness. These cannot both be true. What is your accusation?'

'You are a fool if you believe this tale.'

'I am not a fool.'

'Do you believe this tale?'

'I must think on the matter. Leave me.'

∾

Silence.

My body is all a big sweat. The Accuser tells lies, always sweetened with truth. This is a matter hard to understand. I do not understand the matter. I do not think I will ever understand. If I were a *philosophos*, perhaps I might understand. I built a house once for a *philosophos* in Tsipori, and I spoke with him often, for I know a little Greek. He said that for any matter, there is a logic to understand it.

I do not see a logic to understand this matter.

The village asks what man begat me. Who did Imma entice to sin? Was it Yoseph the *tsaddik* or some other man? They hate Imma because she will not tell the name of the man. Some whisper they can guess the man, for there were two men who asked to buy Imma. Her father accepted Yoseph the *tsaddik* and rejected Yonatan the leather-man.

Some say Yoseph the *tsaddik* begat me. Therefore, my mother was wicked to entice a righteous man before the time. That would be a good logic, only I do not look like Yoseph the *tsaddik*.

Some say Yonatan the leather-man begat me. Therefore, my mother was wicked to entice a man when she was betrothed to another. That would be a good logic, only I do not look like Yonatan the leather-man.

Some say some other man of the village begat me. Every woman of the village gives her man sideways eyes, wondering if Miryam Beautiful enticed him. Only I do not look like any man of our village.

The Accuser says this Messenger was some stranger from another village who begat me. If the villagers had ever heard of this stranger, they would say it is a good logic, for it explains the matter.

But the tale I read in Imma's eyes is a tale of a mighty wonder, a tale that HaShem did a new thing. That is a strange tale and it sounds like a bad logic. Imma believes this tale, but that does not prove the tale, for she does not know a good logic from a bad logic.

I told Imma I believed her tale, but now the Accuser has put hard questions in my heart. When the Messenger came near Imma, she fainted. An evil man might do a wicked thing on a girl who fainted, and she would never know. There were no others to see. There is nobody to say what the Messenger did while Imma lay in a faint. If the Messenger was some wicked stranger with a fine face, he could have begat me. Then Torah says Imma would be innocent, for she was taken by force in a lonely place.

If that were all I knew, I would say Imma's tale is a bad logic and the Accuser's tale is a good logic. Also, I would say my blood father is some wicked man, and I am born from some cruel sin on Imma.

I do not have a logic to say no to the Accuser's tale.

But there is another matter to consider. All my life, I have known the Shekinah. When I was a small boy, I thought everyone felt the Presence at all times in all places. Then I learned my brothers do not. Imma does not. Abba did not. Yaakov Mega did not. My friends do not. The villagers do not. Galileans do not. Judeans do not. Even the prophet Yohanan does not.

I never met anyone who walks in the Shekinah as I do. I have done no good work to merit the Presence. Yet even in my earliest memory— the day Little Yaakov was born—the Shekinah was with me, on me, in me.

If I am begotten by some wicked stranger, how would I know the Shekinah as I do?

If I am made by HaShem, how would I *not* know the Shekinah as I do?

I am not a *philosophos*, but I think that is a point in favor of Imma's tale. I do not think a *philosophos* would call it a good logic. But he would not call it a bad logic either. It is not a logic at all. It is only a point. I think it is a strong point, but it is not a logic.

I do not believe there is a logic to settle every matter. When you see the sky is blue, you do not need a logic to know it, for seeing a thing is a matter outside logic. Also, when you hear a logic, you know in your heart the logic is true, for seeing the truth of a logic is also a matter outside logic. Otherwise, you would need a second logic to prove you saw the truth of the first logic, and a third logic to prove the second, and a fourth to prove the third, and the matter would never end.

HaShem knows if Imma's tale is true, and if he chooses to tell me, then I will know the matter. If he chooses not to tell me, it is because my heart already knows the matter.

My heart says Imma's tale is true. If it is false, then it is false, and the Accuser told true.

But I think Imma is true and the Accuser is a liar.

I believe Imma's tale, because it explains why I am not like other men in the matter of the Shekinah. The Accuser's tale cannot explain this.

If Imma's tale is true, then no man begat me. That is why my father refused to say he begat me. That is why it is a lie that some man of the village begat me. I am no son of adultery, and the smirch is false. I can never prove to the village that the smirch is false. But I can walk light on my feet. I can stop my longing to know my blood father. I know my true father, and that is HaShem.

But still I have a smirch on my name, and how will I remove? That is what Yoni calls a paradox, but I cannot ask Yoni's help in the matter. Yoni would not believe Imma's tale any more than the village would believe. He would mock it to scorn, and he would be right to mock it to scorn. I myself would mock it to scorn, only I have the matter of the Shekinah inside me that makes a mock on all mockery and scorn.

But I cannot show the Shekinah to the village. I cannot make a logic on the matter of the Shekinah to the village.

I must find a way to remove the smirch, when there is no way.

Unless I remove the smirch, I will never redeem Israel, for the village will raise a stench if I try.

And that is another matter I must think on. What does it mean to redeem Israel?

All my life, I was told that to redeem Israel means to take up the sword and destroy the Great Satan. I thought there was a thing wrong with me, because I do not wish to take up the sword. But all my life, I was also told there is a smirch on my name, that Imma played the *zonah*. I thought there was a thing wrong with me, on account of the smirch.

Now I am sure the smirch is a house built on sand. Is this tale of redeeming Israel also built on sand? Am I truly to take up the sword? Am I truly to be Mashiach? Am I truly to defeat the Great Satan? Am I truly to rule on the throne of my father David?

Tomorrow is Shabbat.

Pesach comes on the fifth day of next week.

I told my brothers I would make a move on the Shabbat after

Pesach. That was HaShem speaking through me, so it was a true word. I will make a move a week from tomorrow. I do not know what move I will make, but I will make a move.

I have one week to rethink all I ever knew in my life so I will know how to make a move.

PART 3: THE MAMZER BOY

Spring, AD 30

Once there was a mamzer boy
A mamzer boy
A mamzer boy.
Once there was a mamzer boy
Yeshua was his name.

CHAPTER FORTY-THREE

Miryam of Nazareth

"Yeshua, will you make a move tomorrow?" Little Yaakov asks.

My stomach feels tight when I hear his voice, for he sounds angry on Yeshua. When he looks on me, I think he is angry on me. I do not know what I have done.

It is the going out of the sixth day of the week. We had Pesach yesterday, and it was a good Pesach. But Yeshua disappeared this morning very early. When we all awoke, he was gone. Little Yaakov and Yosi and Thin Shimon and Yehuda Dreamhead went to the Temple to hear Rabbi Shammai. When they came home, they all wore angry faces.

Yeshua ate his evening meal as he is in a daze. He has walked all this week as he is in a daze. I do not know what he is thinking. He does not tell what he has been doing, but I think he has been praying to HaShem. I think he goes every day to that cave of his friend Elazar, but I did not ask, and Yeshua has not told. There are new lines of grief and worry around his eyes.

"Yeshua, what move will you make tomorrow?" Little Yaakov asks.

Yeshua's eyebrows crowd against each other. "I ... we will go to the Temple tomorrow, and HaShem will make a move."

I do not know what that means.

"You do not know what you will do." Little Yaakov scowls on him.

Yeshua sighs with a big sigh.

I am afraid on what will happen tomorrow. Yeshua promised he would make a move tomorrow, but he still does not know what he will do. He has told us all week that HaShem will show him, but it is plain as his nose that HaShem has not shown him. If Yeshua does nothing, I am afraid Little Yaakov will make a move.

Yosi takes a long sip of wine. "Rabbi Shammai says the time is now to destroy the Great Satan. He says now is the time told by the prophet Daniel, that Mashiach should come and make an end on our sins and reconcile us to HaShem and restore Jerusalem. Rabbi Shammai says he is an old man and before he dies, he demands to see HaShem redeem Israel."

Thin Shimon and Yehuda Dreamhead begin chanting. "We want Mashiach now! We want Mashiach now!"

My stomach makes a cramp when I hear that. When Mashiach rises and makes a big war on the Great Satan, all my sons will go fight in his army and leave me alone. Who will defend me?

"Imma." Yeshua puts a hand on my shoulder. "Before there is a war, I will make a justice on you."

Little Yaakov hisses. His face is dark, and he scowls on Yeshua.

"You have a thing to say?" Yeshua says.

Little Yaakov shakes his head.

"Say what you have to say," Yeshua says.

Little Yaakov says nothing.

Yosi looks as he will burst for his impatience.

"Yosi, you have a thing to say?"

Yosi looks on Yeshua. He looks on me. He looks on Yeshua again. He clamps his lips tight.

Thin Shimon picks at a callus on his right thumb.

"Thin Shimon, you have a thing to say?"

Thin Shimon looks only on his fingers. He says nothing.

Yehuda Dreamhead's eyes are shut tight. He is a bad liar and can never keep a secret.

"Yehuda Dreamhead, you have a thing to say?"

Yehuda shakes his head.

"Yehuda Dreamhead, look on me."

Yehuda's eyes crack open to the width of a hair.

"Yehuda Dreamhead, look on me in full."

Yehuda's eyes open all the way. His face is red as a *zonah's* lips.

Yeshua looks in his eyes. I think he is reading Yehuda's heart. He reads long, and as he reads, his face turns pale. "You think Imma should make a justice on her own name."

I feel as I am stabbed in the face.

"You think Imma should confess her sin and the village will forgive."

Yehuda Dreamhead closes his eyes again.

Thin Shimon tears off the callus on his thumb.

Yosi's lips make a thin line in his face.

Little Yaakov scowls on Yehuda Dreamhead.

I want to run away somewhere and hide. My sons think I sinned. I always thought the worst thing in the world was that my mother and father thought I sinned. Now I know there is a thing worse. The sons I nursed at my own bosoms think I sinned.

"Imma did not sin," Yeshua says.

Little Yaakov stands and takes the hand of his woman and leaves the room.

Yosi leaves.

Thin Shimon leaves.

Yehuda Dreamhead looks on me and he looks on Yeshua and he looks on his woman. Then he takes his woman's hand and leaves the room.

Yeshua sighs deeply. There are only him and me left.

"What move will you make tomorrow?" I ask.

"HaShem will show me."

"When will you make a justice on me?"

"Imma, HaShem does not hate our village."

I cannot breathe. I feel as the room is closing in on me. HaShem does too hate the village, more than any village that ever was. "You should call down fire from heaven on the village."

"I will not call down fire on my friends."

That is a viper bite in my heart, that he calls them friends. "You should make a curse on the village."

"I will not make a curse on my friends."

That is another pair of fangs in my heart. "Then what? You will grin on them and make jokes with them and never tell them their sin?"

Yeshua winces as I have slapped him. "I … you ask a hard thing."

"What is a hard thing?"

"To tell my friends their sin."

"They did an evil thing on me. All my life they did evil on me. They would stone me tomorrow and make a joy on it. Why will you not tell them their sin?"

"They think you are a sinner, and they tell you your sin, and it makes you cry. You think they are sinners, and you wish me to tell them their sin and make them cry."

I hate when he makes a logic on me. "I want you to make a justice on me. I want you to punish them for what they did."

"I do not know how to make a justice."

"I will tell you how to make a justice. You should find the secret place where Abba hid the Ring of Justice. If you have the Ring of Justice, you can judge the village. Whatever you command them, they must do it. If you curse them, HaShem will bring it to pass."

"Imma, that is not the way of the Ring. The prophet told how in the last days, HaShem will raise up a righteous Branch of David, to make justice and righteousness on the earth. The Ring of Justice is only a sign of the Branch of David. The Ring is not a Power, to force my will on men."

I shake my head on his foolishness. "The Ring of Justice is too a Power! Yaakov Mega used it for a Power, and who could say no to him?"

"No, Imma, that is an evil Power, to force men to obey. I will not do it."

"Find the Ring of Justice and make a justice on me."

"I will make a justice, Imma. On the day HaShem shows me how, I will make a justice on you. But HaShem does not hate the village."

I am sick to my death of him saying so. HaShem hates the village. HaShem makes a scorn on the village. HaShem looks on the village as it is *haryo*.

I stand and go out of the room.

I do not look back.

Yeshua is kind, and I always loved him for it.

But there is such a thing as too much kindness. He shows too much kindness on the village.

I think he will never make a justice on me.

I think he will never make a move.

I think he will be the worst Mashiach that ever was.

CHAPTER FORTY-FOUR

Yaakov of Nazareth

I hate my brother now more than I ever did. "Yeshua, you must make a move today."

Yeshua's forehead wrinkles with small lines. "HaShem will make a move today. I told you he would make a move on Shabbat in the Temple. It is Shabbat, and here we are in the Temple. HaShem will make a move."

I despise this womanish indecision. Yeshua refuses to stand and fight like a man. When we were small children, I fought to defend him, but he did not fight to defend me. He let those evil boys kick me in the underparts, and he did nothing. If he means to be Mashiach, he should raise up an army and take up the sword and make a big war on the Great Satan.

But he does not do any of those things. He waits and he waits, hoping HaShem will make him Mashiach. HaShem will not make him Mashiach if he does not act like Mashiach.

Yeshua will only dither and delay. Perhaps he will make some small move against the Great Satan. Even though it is only a small move, the Great Satan will rise up in wrath and hold down our nation and kick us in the underparts many hundred times. The Great Satan will crush us, and we will be worse off than before. Half a move is worse than none.

There was never a better day than today to make a move. All the city heard how Herod put the prophet Yohanan in prison. All the city is angry on Herod. All the city is angry on the chief priests. When all the city is angry, that is a good time to make a move.

The Temple is filled with angry men. When we came this morning, Yeshua led us here to the southwest corner of the outer courts. This is the place called the pinnacle, which looks out over the city. He did not say why, but I can guess. The Temple Mount at this corner is very high. I think if I dropped a stone over the parapet, it would take three beats of my heart to hit the ground. From here, a man with a big voice can be heard by many thousand men. The people below us on the street are small as ants.

I peer down on them, and my stomach rises into my throat. Today is the day of HaShem. Today Yeshua should make his move, or else he should stand aside so a better man can make a move.

I jab my finger at Yeshua's face. "Your friends ran like women. They are no friends, and it is good they left."

"They are good friends."

"Good friends do not run for fear of a trouble when there is no trouble. King Herod trembles in his palace and does nothing." I see his palace from here, close enough to count the German guards in the courtyard. There are only five. I see many ten thousand sons of Israel in the streets. Many more ten thousand in the Temple courts behind us.

"HaShem says my friends are good friends."

"When will HaShem tell you to make a move?"

"When he decides I should make a move."

"What if HaShem waits for you to make a move? When a viper rises up in your path, you do not wait for HaShem to tell you to crush its head. You pick up a stone and crush its head. Or else it bites you in the leg and you die."

"HaShem says I am to wait."

"And so you wait and you wait and you wait! What if he spoke already and you failed to hear? What if he waits for you to do what he said?"

"HaShem says I am to wait."

"What if HaShem speaks to you through other men? You are not the only prophet. Yohanan the prophet said the ax is laid at the root of the tree. What does that mean? It means now is the time, yes?"

"HaShem says I am to wait for him."

"That is a big foolishness! I do not wish to wait for you to wait. HaShem tells me it is time to make a move."

"I will wait on HaShem."

"Then I will make a move myself." In an instant, I see how to force Yeshua to make a move. I put my hands flat on the stone parapet, which comes to the level of my waist.

"What … move will you make?" Yeshua's voice cracks for his fear.

I climb on the parapet, which is flat and broad. I stand to my full height, looking down on the city below me.

"Little Yaakov! Do not be foolish!"

My heart drums fast in my chest. The wind blows in my hair. I feel more alive than I ever did. I know that now is the time to make a move.

"Little Yaakov! Come off the parapet!"

In a big voice, I begin chanting the psalm of David the king.

"The man who lives
In the secret place of El,
He will rest in the shadow of Shaddai.
I will say to Yah
That he is my shelter,
That he is my fortress.
He is my God,
And my trust is all in him."

Yeshua's face is pale. "Little Yaakov, I command you to come down."

I shake my head. "I will not come down."

"You will be blown off by the wind and be killed."

"I will not be killed if you come up and stand with me."

"Never."

"Then I will be killed. I will leap down and be smashed on the street."

"Come down now. Men are looking on you."

"They should look on me. They should look on you. Come up here with me. We should show them a sign."

"What sign?"

"We will leap off together. HaShem will not allow you to be killed."

"Who told you such foolishness?"

I continue chanting the psalm.

> "For he will rescue you
> From the snare of the trapper,
> The plague of ruin.
> In his feathers he will cover you,
> And under his wings you will trust."

Men far down below look up on me. They point on me. They call to friends.

Yeshua steps toward me stretching out his hand. "Little Yaakov, HaShem says to come down."

"I will not come down to you. I will *leap* down to the streets below. If you do not leap with me, I will die and my blood will be on you. But if you leap with me, HaShem will save both you and me. You know he will."

My brother loves me. That is his weakness. I have put him in a box. If he does not make a move, I will die. Therefore, he must make a move.

Yeshua seems frozen like a stone. His eyes say that I speak true. His eyes say that he knows HaShem will not allow him to die. His eyes say that I have won.

All around the Temple court behind Yeshua, men look on me. Down below, men look up on me, shading their eyes against the sun.

"Jump!" shouts some boy down in the street.

But I will not jump without Yeshua. In my biggest voice, I chant the rest of the psalm.

Soon, all the crowd chants with me, for all men know this psalm.

Yeshua's eyes show that his resolve grows weaker. He longs to come up with me. He knows that all Jerusalem would stand with him if he made a move. All Jerusalem would stand with us.

> "For his Messengers
> He will command
> To watch over you
> On every road.
> In their hands
> They will carry you
> So you will not smash
> Your feet on the stone."

All the crowd of men shout. "Jump! HaShem will bear you up!"

Yeshua's love for me is a fire in his eyes.

"Come up with me, Yeshua! Is HaShem with us, or is HaShem not with us?"

His face tells that he knows HaShem would not allow him to die. Yeshua will join me now. Here is our chance to make a move that will light fire to this city.

I turn my back on Yeshua and face the city. Far below me, many ten thousand men watch me and shout, "Jump! Jump! Jump!"

I wait.

Down in the streets, many ten thousand men point fingers on me. But behind me, a sudden silence.

I wait.

More silence.

I wait.

Silence like Sheol.

I cannot bear not knowing what Yeshua is doing to make this silence.

I turn to look.

Yeshua is gone.

No, there he is, fifty paces away. He turned his back on me! He left me!

The light of the Shekinah is on him like a pillar of fire.

All the men in the courts behind us who were watching me have drawn off to look on him. That is a wicked trick.

I come down off the parapet and take a step toward him. But no, I made a crowd down below in the streets. What of them?

I am frozen in a big indecision. I think long on the matter, but I cannot see what to do.

Yeshua is ahead of me, shining with the light of the Shekinah.

The streets are behind me, far below, throbbing with rage.

I take another step toward Yeshua. But that is a wrong move. I do not shine with the Shekinah, so what use to stand beside Yeshua?

I turn back to the parapet and look down on the street below.

I have lost my moment.

The men below have stopped shouting. They have stopped pointing. They have stopped looking.

I have become like one who is not.

Even my brothers went away with Yeshua.

They all left me when I meant to make a move.

A rage rises in me, bigger than any rage I ever knew. My heart feels as it is molten iron.

I stride toward my brother, hating him more than I ever did. "Yeshua!"

As I walk, I see the Shekinah fade on him.

I walk more and it fades more. "Yeshua!"

By the time I reach him, the Shekinah is gone.

"Yeshua!" I seize his shoulder and spin him around.

His eyes are very weary. Sweat covers his face, as he has fought some mighty battle.

The blood runs hot in my body, and my fists are strong as stones. "Why did you leave me? Do you not love me?"

Yeshua's voice is a croak in his throat. "In the days of our fathers, they tested Moses in the wilderness at the testing place, asking him to prove whether HaShem was with them or not with them."

Every son of Israel knows this story. The sons of Israel tested Moses and he struck the rock to make water. HaShem made water come out of the rock, and the people drank.

Yeshua sighs deeply. "Torah forbids to test HaShem again, as our fathers tested him at the testing place. When they tested Moses the second time, he failed the test, and HaShem forbade him to enter the land of Canaan. HaShem says I will make a move when he tells me to make a move, not when the Accuser tells me to make a move."

Yeshua calls me the Accuser! My rage is like a flame in my stomach. I can stand this fool no longer.

There is a stone on the pavement twice the size of my fist.

I stoop to seize it.

I stand to kill.

I pull back my arm.

All the world is red with the heat of my rage.

I hammer the stone forward with all my strength at Yeshua's face.

I hate my brother now more than I ever did.

CHAPTER FORTY-FIVE

Yeshua of Nazareth

I was never quick to act in a hazard. If a hornet flies at Little Yaakov's face, he can catch it in one hand and crush it and throw it aside, all in the blink of an eye. Yosi and Yehuda Dreamhead are quicker. Thin Shimon is quickest of all.

But I am slow. If a hornet flies at my face, I stare at it in a frozen terror, and I see every beat of its wings as each instant is a thousand years, but I cannot move, and it stings me.

I see Little Yaakov's hand holding the stone. It is coming at my face. It has been coming at my face for many ten thousand years. I see it and I am paralyzed. It will crush my face. I should move. I wish to move. I cannot move.

There is a blur to my left. A man-shape flying toward me.

I cannot see it, but I know what it is.

My brother Thin Shimon, throwing himself in front of me. Thin Shimon, whom I love. Thin Shimon, whom I should protect, is protecting me instead.

He arrives just before the stone.

It smites him in the forehead.

There is a hollow thump, like a ripe melon being hit with a hammer.

Thin Shimon's body slams against me.

I stagger back.

I catch Thin Shimon.

We fall to the pavement.

Horror washes across Little Yaakov's face. "Thin Shimon!" he screams.

The stone falls from his nerveless hand.

I kneel beside Thin Shimon.

Blood leaks out from a gash in his forehead.

His sightless eyes stare up at the sky.

I feel for his heart.

It quivers beneath my touch.

I put my hand above his mouth.

There is the faintest puff of air.

He is alive.

For the moment.

Little Yaakov falls on his face, weeping. He loves Thin Shimon. He loves me also. Some fit of rage drove him to this thing.

And now Thin Shimon is dying.

I should do something.

I do not know what to do.

There is nothing any man can do.

My brother has killed my brother.

Yaakov of Nazareth

My whole body is on fire. "Shimon!" I scream.

Thin Shimon lies unmoving on the pavement.

Black spots appear in my eyes. My head feels as it is spinning. My knees collapse beneath me.

I fall on my face, weeping.

I have killed my own brother.

Some wicked spirit must have seized me. I am not the kind of man who kills his own brother. And yet I have killed my own brother.

I hear voices all around me.

"Look, he crushed his head with a stone."

"Call for the Temple guards."

"He should be killed himself."

It is true. I should be killed. I am a murderer. I had rage in my heart, only not on Thin Shimon. I had rage on Yeshua. I wished him dead. But I love Yeshua. He is good and kind, and it would be him lying sightless on the ground, except Thin Shimon prevented.

But it should be neither of them. It should be me.

Tears burn in my eyes. I clutch the stones of the pavement, tearing at them with my fingers. I would do anything to undo the thing I have done.

I am evil. More evil than any man ever was. I should die now.

But I will not die. Instead, Thin Shimon will die. We will carry him outside the city and bury him in some pit.

Imma will die from the shock of it. She always said my *yetzer hara* was too strong. I always said Yeshua's was too weak.

It is not Yeshua's fault. It is the way he was born. I would not care, if this matter of Mashiach had not come up. If they did not tell him all his life he would redeem Israel. It is a lie. He cannot redeem Israel. He is weak. He stands in my way. If he would stand aside, I would not hate him. That is the thing I can never forgive, that he will not stand aside.

And now because of it, I have killed Thin Shimon, our smallest brother.

If I could unmake that wound on his head, I would do anything.

I hear Yeshua's voice. "Abba, forgive him. Forgive our brother. He did not know what he was doing."

It is not true. I knew. I was filled with rage, but I knew. I wished to kill Yeshua. Instead, I killed an innocent man.

"Abba, forgive!"

HaShem cannot forgive. I am more wicked than Cain, who killed his brother Abel.

"Abba, I beg you, forgive."

The pain of his words stabs my heart. It is not possible that HaShem should forgive.

I will never forgive myself.

I meant to kill.

I did.

Yeshua says more words to HaShem.

I cannot hear his words. Black despair falls on me. It crushes me. I am not fit to live. *HaShem, kill me now. Take me and kill me. It will not give us back our brother, but kill me, for I am a wicked—*

A shout goes up all around.

The sound of it pierces my head like hot iron.

More shouting.

Men pressing forward.

Laughing.

They should not laugh at such a bad time. I clutch my ears with both hands. *HaShem, kill me—*

"Yeshua, what have you done?" Yehuda Dreamhead laughs for joy.

Yosi laughs for joy.

Yeshua laughs for joy.

Thin Shimon laughs for joy.

What?

Thin Shimon cannot laugh for joy. Thin Shimon lies dead on the pavement.

Someone puts a hand on my back.

Leans close to my ear.

Whispers into my heart.

"Little Yaakov, HaShem says this, that what you did for harm, he has undone for good. HaShem says he loves you like his own son. HaShem says he made you to be great in the kingdom. HaShem says he forgives."

❧

Yeshua of Nazareth

Thin Shimon sits up and shakes his head and blinks his eyes and smiles.

My heart runs faster than a rabbit and my face burns hot as the sun and my head feels as it weighs no more than a feather.

I healed my brother.

I did not know I could heal. Scripture does not tell that Mashiach is to be a healer. And yet I heard the voice of HaShem, to lay hands on my brother and tell him to be healed.

I did it, and now he is healed.

I cannot believe what I have seen. What I have done. What HaShem has done in me.

Little Yaakov is still on his face weeping, repenting. He does not need me to tell him repentance. If ever a man repented, it is Little Yaakov. But repentance is not enough.

And now I see a new thing.

All the repentance in the world cannot change that a man lies dead on the pavement. Unless HaShem had restored him, Thin Shimon would be in Sheol now, sleeping the long sleep with our fathers.

When HaShem restores, the time for telling repentance is over.

The time to tell forgiveness has begun.

I put a hand on Little Yaakov's back and lean close. "Little Yaakov, HaShem says this, that what you did for harm, he has undone for good. HaShem says he loves you like his own son. HaShem says he made you to be great in the kingdom. HaShem says he forgives."

Little Yaakov lifts his face off the pavement. Dirt and loose stones are buried in his face.

He looks on me.

He looks on Thin Shimon.

His eyebrows leap up and his mouth falls open. "Thin Shimon?"

Thin Shimon stands. He gives Little Yaakov a strong right hand and pulls him to his feet. "Little Yaakov!"

Then they both seize me in their arms. They give me a kiss and a kiss and a kiss.

"HaShem made a mighty move," Little Yaakov says. "You said he would make a move today, and he did."

I feel as some great stone is lifted off my shoulders.

It is true.

HaShem made a move today.

It is not the move I expected. I do not know what it means.

But HaShem made a move, and my life will not be the same again, forever.

CHAPTER FORTY-SIX

Miryam of Nazareth

"I mma! Come walk with me."

I am afraid to walk with Yeshua, for I fear he means to tell me what I do not wish to hear.

We are back home in Nazareth after Pesach. Little Yaakov has changed. He is kinder now to his woman. He does not look on me as I am a sinner. He no longer seems ready to explode for his rage. I do not know how to think on the matter, but I am glad Little Yaakov is changed.

Yeshua is changed also. He seems more confident. He goes away each morning to speak with HaShem. I think HaShem tells him big plans on how to make a war on the Great Satan. I wish HaShem also will tell him how to make a justice on my name.

I wish Yeshua had made a war on the Great Satan while we were still in Jerusalem. Instead, we came home to the scorn of the village. They do not scorn Yeshua. They love Yeshua, for he is a *tsaddik*. Almost all love him.

But all the village scorns me. The heat of their scorn is like the heat of the sun, which I feel on my face even with my eyes closed. I hate the village, and I will always hate it.

Yeshua takes my hand and smiles on me.

We walk up the street.

The children playing in the dirt call out a greeting to Yeshua, but they look on me as I am an evil tale and run away.

We walk through the village square.

The village elders sitting in the village gate call out a greeting to Yeshua, but they look on me as I am *haryo* and spit the dust.

We pass the ovens of Shimon the baker.

Shimon the baker calls out a greeting on Yeshua, but he looks past me as I am not.

My hand squeezes Yeshua harder than it ever did.

My son stops and looks on me. He looks on Shimon the baker. He turns around. "We will go another way today, Imma."

We walk back through the village square toward our house. We pass our house and take the path that leads south from the village. The path is far, more than a mile, but it will lead us to a mighty place I love, the lookout at the precipice. From there, you can see the whole Jezreel Valley, spreading south toward Samaria, west toward the Great Sea, and east toward the Jordan.

We walk in silence. Yeshua is thinking hard on some matter.

I do not wish to break his thoughts. It is enough to feel the strength of his hand in mine and the warmth of the sun and the cool spring breeze and to know I am safe from the scorn of the village. This way is downhill from our house, and so it is easy. When we come back, it will go harder, but I will not think on that now.

When we reach the precipice, we sit on large stones and look out over the valley.

Yeshua smiles on me. "You looked happy just now."

"This is a happy place."

He lifts an eyebrow. "You were happy here once?"

That is a knife in my heart. I nod, for I do not trust myself to speak.

"Tell me."

"You will say it is a big foolishness."

"Tell me."

"When I was small, my father and mother brought us here some-times for picnics. My younger sister would play chase with me, and my older sister would tell me tales. And my father would run with me in circles."

"In circles?"

"He would take my hand and turn and turn and turn in place while I ran around him in circles. I ran and ran until the whole world was spinning. Then he took both my hands and swung me around and around, high in the air, as high as an eagle. I felt as I was flying."

Tears run down my cheeks. I remember how I felt as I was free. I felt as I was happy. I felt as I was innocent. After the Messenger came, I never felt free or happy or innocent again.

Yeshua sighs deeply and looks out over the valley before us.

I look to the east. There is Mount Tabor, standing like a bowl turned upside down on a table, only a walk of two hours from here. My sons went there once as boys. They came back as men.

Yeshua sighs again and looks on me. "Imma, you are more beau-tiful than yesterday. How is it possible?"

My heart breaks in shards. Tears run out of my eyes. "When are you leaving?"

"HaShem says I am to go tomorrow."

I fight for my breath. My face is hot and my belly is cold and I want to leap for joy and weep for sadness. "Where will you go?"

"I do not know. HaShem will show me where I should go."

"What will you do? You were to defeat the first Power, but I do not understand what is the first Power. You spent all winter telling repen-tance to Israel, and see what happened—Yohanan the prophet is taken. What more can you do?"

"Telling repentance is good, but it is not enough. The first Power is the lying words of the Accuser. I will do battle with the lying words of the Accuser."

A shiver seizes me. He speaks as the Accuser is real, and not some idle tale. "I do not see—"

Yeshua leans close and gives me a kiss and a kiss and a kiss.

All my confusion runs away like smoke.

"Imma, when HaShem commands to do a hard thing, he gives understanding to do it. I do not know what I am to do, nor how I am to do battle. But I trust HaShem to show me. That is what I learned this winter, that I can trust HaShem to guide me. That is what I learned again at Pesach. HaShem says that now is the appointed time. The kingdom of HaShem is upon us. Tomorrow I will go."

I seize his hand and hold it to my heart. I cannot see for my tears. "Take me with you! I cannot bear to stay here without you. Have mercy on an old woman and take me with you wherever you go."

~

Yeshua of Nazareth

Imma's crying rips at my heart. I do not wish to leave her here. The village hates her. Little Yaakov and the others can protect her from the village's stones, but never from its scorn.

Abba, can I not take Imma with me? Show me how I should answer her. She would be safer with me on the field of battle than here in Nazareth.

I close my eyes and wait.

The Shekinah draws near.

Nearer.

Nearest.

~

I stand before the Throne. *HaShem's brightness is greater than it ever was. My eyes are destroyed for its brightness.*

'Abba, may I take Imma with me?'

'My son, first you should ask where you will go.'

'Where am I to do battle first?'

'Capernaum.'

My hands turn hot and my breath comes in gasps. 'I am not … welcome in Capernaum. My friends threw me off. That is the last place I thought to go.'

'You will forgive your friends.'

'I … of course, I have forgiven my friends. But the heart of the matter is that they have thrown me off.'

'You have forgiven them, but they have not received forgiveness.'

'How am I to make them receive forgiveness?'

'You will do battle with the Accuser.'

'Yes, I know I will do battle with the Accuser. How long until I win?'

HaShem does not answer.

'Please, Abba, you must tell me. I will win, yes?'

HaShem does not answer.

'Is the Accuser … stronger than me?'

HaShem does not answer.

My heart quivers within me.

The Throne disappears.

In my mind's eye, I see a long and dusty road.

I must walk that road for many hundred miles.

I must go hungry and thirsty, naked and cold.

I must battle the Accuser at every step.

I see the Accuser like a great bird of war, swooping on me, crying with loud screams, picking at my flesh to destroy me.

I see Imma with me.

I see the Accuser slashing at her soul with its claws.

I smell the sweat of her fear.

I hear the rage of her screams.

I see her fall.

I see the Accuser diving on her.

I throw myself between her and the Accuser.

I feel the claws of the Accuser tearing my body, tearing my mind, tearing my soul.

If I take Imma with me, the Accuser will destroy us both.

If I do not take her with me, the Accuser will destroy her alone.

The vision fades.

∼

I am sitting with Imma, looking out over the precipice.

Imma is crying.

It twists my heart to hear her weep. I give her a kiss and a kiss and a kiss.

"Yeshua, please, you will take me with you."

"Imma, you will never be free until you release the village."

"I will never be free until you confront the village."

I cannot confront the village. Not for myself. Not for Imma. If I confront the village, I am terrified I will crush it. But I love the village. Rather I should tear out my own eyes than confront the village. Yet if I do not confront the village, I am terrified they will crush Imma.

"Will you take me with you, or will you leave me to die?"

She does not know what she asks, and I do not know how to explain the matter. I bury both her hands in mine. "I will walk many hundred miles on dusty roads. I will sleep in the rain and the cold and the wind. I will be pursued by evil men. I will do battle with the Accuser. How can I take you with me on such a—"

She throws her arms around me. "Take me anyway!"

My heart is crushed within me. I have not said it right. There is no way to say it right. I open my mouth to say I cannot take her with me.

I hear myself saying words I did not think. "HaShem says I should take you with me, Imma. So I will take you with me."

I never said such a foolish thing in all my life.

I am going to war with Imma.

Miryam of Nazareth

When we come back to the house, Yeshua tells his brothers what he has decided.

"Take me with you," says Little Yaakov.

"And me also," says Yosi.

Yehuda Dreamhead takes out his invisible sword and waves it in the air. "We will go to war!"

Thin Shimon looks on his woman, who sits nursing their little son on the bench. He sits beside her and says nothing.

Yeshua looks on them all and shakes his head. "I will go with Imma only."

Little Yaakov and Yosi and Yehuda Dreamhead begin shouting on him, all together.

I do not wish to hear such a big roar. I take a waterpot and crook my finger on Thin Shimon. "Come walk with me to the spring one last time before I go away. I may be gone long."

Thin Shimon stands to join me.

We walk out in the street together.

We walk to the village square and pass by the village gate.

We walk up the street to the end of the village.

All that long way, the people of the village shout a greeting on Thin Shimon and throw looks of scorn on me.

Thin Shimon is not brave of face, but I do not care. There is a thing I want, and only Thin Shimon can give it.

We walk out of the village and past the leather-man's piss-pool.

He throws such a look of scorn on me as should kill a lion.

I do not care. I piss on his scorn.

We walk through the narrows and up the hill to the spring.

I sit on a large rock and put down my waterpot and spit the path that leads back to the village.

Thin Shimon wears a big scowl. "Yeshua should make a justice on you."

I shake my head. "He will never make a justice on me until he is brave of speech."

Thin Shimon raises an eyebrow. "Yeshua will never be brave of speech."

I say, "Your grandfather was brave of speech, more than any man of the village ever was."

Thin Shimon says, "Yeshua is not Yaakov Mega."

"But he could be like Yaakov Mega."

"I have heard tales on Yaakov Mega, how he was fierce and bold. Yeshua will never be fierce and bold."

"Yaakov Mega had a thing that made him fierce and bold, and he passed it to your father."

Thin Shimon's eyes narrow. "The Ring of Justice? That did not make Abba fierce and bold. How will it make Yeshua fierce and bold?"

"Your father never wore it. He hid it away for a safety, for fear of the bandits on the Tsipori Road. If he had worn it himself, he would have been fierce and bold. If he had passed it to Yeshua, your brother would be fierce and bold."

"The Ring of Justice is lost."

I seize Thin Shimon's shoulders. "So find it!"

Thin Shimon stares on me. "How should I find it? Abba was clever and hid it well. After we put him in the tomb, we searched all the house, and it was not there."

"You are the cleverest man I ever knew, more than your brothers, more than your father, more than the whole village. If any man is clever to find the Ring, it is you!"

Thin Shimon shakes his head. "How should I find it? Abba must have hid it somewhere near the village. Not more than a thousand steps from our house, but it could be north or south or east or west. That is a thousand thousands of places to search, and I am one man. It cannot be done."

My fingers bite into his shoulders. "Do not tell me it cannot be done! Yaakov Mega never said a thing could not be done. When Yaakov Mega set his mind on a thing, he did it. You are a clever man, more even than your father. Think like your father. Suppose you have a gold ring, a ring of great price. You must hide it for a safety, only not in your house. Where will you hide it?"

Thin Shimon sighs with a big sigh.

He will not do it unless I force him.

I stand and dip my waterpot in the spring and set it on my head. "Tomorrow, Yeshua and I go to Capernaum. I made a beg on him to give me a justice, but he will never make a justice on me, and I will die in my shame. Only I refuse to die in my shame. I demand a justice, and Yeshua will not give it unless he wears the Ring of Justice. So here is my oath before HaShem. I swear by The Name that I will not return home to this village until you find the Ring of Justice. Only you are clever enough to find it. I demand that you find it."

Thin Shimon stares on me in a big shock.

I never talked to him that way before.

But I have no choice.

I will not live with my shame in this village one more day.

Thin Shimon's eyes turn inward.

I have seen that look on a man's face before.

That is the face Yaakov Mega wore when he set his mind on a thing.

Thin Shimon is clever. He will think on the matter and think and think and think until he knows where my lord Yoseph hid the Ring of Justice.

When he finds it, he will give it to Yeshua.

Yeshua will become fierce and bold when he wears the Ring of Justice. He will curse the Evil Boy.

That is the only way I will ever have my justice.

That is the will of HaShem, and I will not rest until his will is done.

CHAPTER FORTY-SEVEN

Shimon of Capernaum

I shake my head again. "Yoni, none of us wish to discuss the matter." He is so impudent today, I could strangle him.

"You should admit you were wrong! King Herod made no trouble at Pesach. Rabbi Yeshua was not taken. We would have heard if he was taken, but we have not heard. Therefore, he was not taken, and we ran like fearful women."

My neck feels hot. I am no fearful woman. I am a wronged man. I will have vengeance against the goyim someday, but when the time is right, not when the time is wrong. "Zavdai, please tell your son to silence himself."

"Yoni, be silent." Zavdai's voice is weary. It is a sore trial to have a genius for a son. More than a sore trial to have an impudent one.

We are mending nets in our boats, which are tied fast at the stone pier at Capernaum. We will not go fishing tonight, for Shabbat begins at the going out of the day. The late afternoon before Shabbat is a good time to mend nets. It is not a good time to talk of foolishness.

We are all tired of Yoni telling that we ran like women. We did not run like women. We ran like men who have sense. A few fish-men are no match for many soldiers of Herod.

Yoni says, "If Yeshua comes here, he will ask why we were not at Pesach, and we will all be shamed."

"Yoni!" Zavdai roars.

Yeshua will not come here. I am certain he hates us, for we threw him off. If he came here, he would be a fool.

Anyway, Zavdai told Elazar to tell Yeshua he is not welcome in Capernaum, on account of the smirch. If he came here, he would be twice a fool.

Anyway, we are only a walk of three hours from King Herod's palace in Tiberias. I see Tiberias from where I sit. If Yeshua came here, he would be three times a fool.

I should forget I ever knew Yeshua, for he will forget he ever knew me.

"Rabbi Yeshua, what are you doing here?" Yoni shouts.

I refuse to listen to Yoni make a bad joke on us, worse than Andre ever made.

Footsteps crunch on the gravel on top of the pier.

I do not know who could be coming here, but it is not—

"My friends, have you caught anything today?"

My heart leaps in my chest. It is a cheerful voice.

A teasing voice, for no man can catch fish while he is mending nets.

Yeshua's voice.

All my skin goes cold. I am shamed he is here. I will not look on Yeshua. We dishonored him by running. We dishonored ourselves.

Yoni springs out of the other boat and runs up the pier. "Rabbi Yeshua!"

His words are daggers in my heart. I lost the right to call Yeshua Rabbi. I ran when I smelled danger. I made Yoni run too.

"Yoni, it is good to see you!" Yeshua's voice is warm as a mother's touch.

"Rabbi Yeshua, have you come here to live?"

I wish Yoni would silence himself. Yeshua cannot come here to live.

"No, I have come with Imma to rejoice in Shabbat with my good friends, the ones I love."

Friends. The word stings my ears like a nettle. I did not behave like a friend.

More footsteps.

I keep my head down, minding my mending.

Footsteps stop above me. A shadow appears in the boat at my feet.

Still I refuse to raise my head. How would I look his eye? How would I explain why we ran like … like men who abandoned a friend? Shame wells up in my heart, and sweat runs down my sides.

Yeshua steps into my boat and kneels in the bottom and peers up into my face. "Shimon the Rock! I think I am even more glad to see you than you are to see me!"

My heart lurches within me like a boat in a storm. That was well said. Yeshua did not shame me. Yeshua is glad to see me. Hot joy rushes through my soul.

I put down my net.

I raise my head to look on him.

He sits on the other bench and smiles on me.

I fall on my knees before him and my eyes blur and my voice cracks. "I … beg forgiveness. I sinned against you and—"

"Shimon the Rock." Yeshua's voice rumbles over me, quiet and strong.

"Y-yes?" I do not dare call him Rabbi.

He grips me by the shoulders. He raises me up. He gives me a kiss and a kiss and a kiss. "It is good to see you, friend." His eyes show no sign of anger.

Only joy.

My heart fills up with lightness. I never felt such a big freedom. Such a big joy. "It is good to see you … Rabbi Yeshua."

"Your woman and your sons are well?"

"They are well."

"And you are well?"

I do not know if I am well. There is still a bad matter that makes me sick in my heart. I do not see how to think on the smirch on Rabbi Yeshua's name. "Rabbi, there is a matter Yoni told that I wish to—"

"Imma says I am the son of David."

I think the word of a woman will not stand against his own village.

"Abba said I am the son of David."

I think the word of a dead man will not stand against his own village.

"HaShem says I am the son of David."

Now I am in a box. I know Rabbi Yeshua is a true prophet of HaShem. If he says HaShem calls him son of David, I will follow after him with a sword in my hand.

But if we mean to throw off the Great Satan, all Galilee must follow after Rabbi Yeshua with a sword in their hands. But Galilee will not if his village will not. And his village will not because they say he has a smirch on his name.

I do not see how that makes a good sense, to follow after a man with a smirch.

The scriptures do not tell that Mashiach will have a smirch on his name.

Here is what I know on the matter of Mashiach.

The scriptures tell that Mashiach is to be the anointed king who sits on the throne of David.

But the scriptures also tell that the throne of David is never to stand empty.

And yet it stands empty.

Now that I think on the matter, I do not see how that makes a good sense, that the throne of David stands empty when the scriptures say it will never stand empty.

That is what Yoni calls a paradox. I hate paradoxes. I think a thing should be plain and simple. The matter of David's throne is not plain and simple. The matter of the smirch on Rabbi Yeshua is not plain and simple either.

Here is what I know on the matter of Rabbi Yeshua. He is a *tsaddik*. He is a prophet of HaShem. He did a mighty wonder in Cana. He told a tale of repentance that shook my bones. He came and found me and told me forgiveness when I ran like a woman.

I love this man. I trust this man. It may be I am a fool to love and trust him, but I do.

But Yoni is not a fool, and he loves Rabbi Yeshua also and trusts him.

I know that does not answer the paradox. But Yoni has many hundred paradoxes that are also not answered, and still the world goes on. A man can live all his life without answering one of Yoni's paradoxes.

I study Rabbi Yeshua's face.

There are new lines of sorrow under his eyes. He is more scorched by the Accuser than before.

"Rabbi, has HaShem spoken to you on the matter of the smirch?"

He shakes his head. "HaShem has spoken to me on the matter of the kingdom of HaShem. I am sent to tell the kingdom of HaShem. And HaShem has spoken to me on the matter of you. I am sent to ask you men to follow after me. Shimon the Rock and Andre and Yoni and Big Yaakov, I ask you to become fish-men who will draw in your nets and bring many in Israel into the kingdom of HaShem."

My knees wobble beneath me, and I do not know what to say. With all my heart, I wish to follow after Rabbi Yeshua. I wish for HaShem to make a justice on the land. Make a justice on murderers and Samaritans and all the goyim. I wish for HaShem to rescue his people, who cry out for justice. I wish for HaShem to avenge the blood of my brother.

But I am afraid I will run like a woman again. All my life, I thought I feared nothing. At Pesach, I saw I was wrong. I am not the rock of courage I thought I was. If I say yes, I fear to dishonor myself again by running. To say yes now is to say yes forever.

Andre's face shows that he longs to follow Yeshua, and yet he too holds back. Big Yaakov also.

Yoni's face shines.

Yoni is young and foolish and naive. He would say yes at once, but he holds back so as not to dishonor those who are older and wiser.

Andre and Big Yaakov look on me.

If I say yes, they will say yes also. That is a heavy weight.

I lean against the side of my boat, more weary than I ever was. I love the lake, the wind, the rain, the work. It is a good life and a good living.

But I love Rabbi Yeshua more, who forgives his friends for running like women and comes looking for them in love and does not shame them. For a man like Rabbi Yeshua, I should do anything and follow anywhere. Even if he has a smirch on his name.

If HaShem wishes for Rabbi Yeshua to redeem Israel, HaShem will take the smirch off his name. That is not a hard thing for HaShem.

My father in the next boat seems to be holding his breath. He taught me to love Torah and say the prayers and follow after HaShem. He would not wish for his sons to go, but he would wish for his sons to please HaShem.

I step up onto the pier. I step down into my father's boat. I wrap my arms around him and kiss him. A deep sigh rises within me. Perhaps this is foolish and perhaps it is not, but it is what HaShem calls me to do.

I breathe the lake air deep, a free man for one breath longer. "Rabbi Yeshua, I will follow you wherever you go, forever."

"And I also," Yoni and Andre and Big Yaakov say, all in one voice.

I feel as our anchor is lifted and our line loosed and our oars set in place.

My father frowns on Rabbi Yeshua. "Where are you taking my sons?"

"Yes, where?" Zavdai asks.

Rabbi Yeshua wears the face of a man who has received a precious thing in trust and will guard it with all his might and strength and soul. "Wherever Abba sends me. Wherever I am, there is the kingdom of HaShem."

My heart leaps within me, but my mind can make no sense on this saying. It is another paradox. When the kingdom of HaShem comes, it will crush the kingdom of this world. If the kingdom of HaShem were truly here, Rome would lie in dust and ashes, and HaShem would reign in Jerusalem, the city of the Great King. The thing is a mighty paradox, and therefore it must have some mighty explanation.

Rabbi Yeshua himself is a paradox.

Now I will be part of that paradox too, until forever.

CHAPTER FORTY-EIGHT

Yoni of Capernaum

I sit in the synagogue with my mantle enfolding my head and joy enfolding my heart. It is Shabbat, and the village *hazzan* has finished reading from Torah and the prophets.

Today is the day I have longed for all my life. Today, Rabbi Yeshua will make a move. Today he will announce the kingdom of HaShem. Today will begin the Day of Vengeance.

I know because Rabbi Yeshua explained the matter last night, mostly. He and his mother are staying in my father's house. He sleeps in my room, and his mother sleeps in my grandmother's room. We talked late on how we will defeat the four Powers. Rabbi Yeshua told me what happened in the Temple at Pesach with his brothers. He said he understands better now what is the first Power. He said HaShem says we are to begin a new thing today, only he did not tell what it will be.

I am sure it will be the Day of Vengeance. I am ready to fight. We spent all winter telling repentance to Israel, and I am sick to my death of it. I would be happy if I never told repentance to anyone again. I wish to attack the Great Satan. I still think we should burn the granaries of Egypt, but Rabbi Yeshua only smiled when I told him. He said HaShem has another plan. I promised to obey Rabbi Yeshua, so I will wait. Only I am very impatient.

I think now is the time. I think here is the place. I feel the Shekinah. I see it on the face of Rabbi Yeshua.

I think the president of the synagogue sees it also. His name is called Yair, and he owns the village salting house. He has a daughter two years younger than me, who used to tease me when I was a boy, only not lately, now I am a man. Imma tells me every week how Sara the daughter of Yair is a good worker. I do not see why Imma says so every week. I heard it the first time.

Yair is a big friend on our family. My father spent all winter telling Yair about Rabbi Yeshua and boasting how I was gone with him to tell repentance to Israel. Also, how we will call up an army to fight the Great Satan in the spring. And now it is spring and Rabbi Yeshua is here and today is the day.

Yair looks on Rabbi Yeshua and makes a big smile. "Rabbi Yeshua, Zavdai the fish-man says you are a prophet. If you wish to expound on Torah or the prophets, please, you will speak a word to us."

Rabbi Yeshua nods and strides to the *bema* and sits in the Seat of Moses, the chair where a man sits to expound Torah and the prophets.

All the synagogue holds its breath to hear him speak. They all must have heard by now that Rabbi Yeshua is a mighty prophet of HaShem who will smite the Great Satan. They expect much from Rabbi Yeshua, and they honor him with their silence. And they know Rabbi Yeshua stays at the House of Zavdai, so our family has a big honor also.

Rabbi Yeshua's eyes smile, and he seems to look only on me. "The kingdom of HaShem is like a lump of leaven, which a woman hides in three measures of flour."

He raises his eyebrows to ask if we have understood the matter.

I do not understand the matter at all. How is the kingdom of HaShem like leaven? Why would a woman hide it in flour? That is a foolish place to hide leaven, for it will grow and grow and not stay hidden. And why three measures? One measure of flour is three times the size of my head. Three measures is enough to feed a hundred men. When Father Abraham entertained HaShem unawares, he made cakes from three measures of flour.

That was a mighty meal. Is Rabbi Yeshua saying we are to entertain HaShem unawares? Is he saying the kingdom of HaShem is to be a great feast? I thought the kingdom of HaShem was to do with smiting the Great Satan. I do not understand the matter. Rabbi Yeshua has made a paradox.

I look all around and see that nobody understands the paradox. Now I do not feel so foolish. For a moment, I thought the Genius of Capernaum had lost his wits.

But my stomach has become a big knot. I never heard a rabbi teach like this. A rabbi should begin with Torah or the prophets and then expound the matter according to the sayings of the fathers. A rabbi should not begin with a paradox about some woman. That is a bad beginning. Tonight in my room, I will explain the matter to Rabbi Yeshua.

Rabbi Yeshua stands.

Is he finished already? A rabbi never stands while teaching.

Rabbi Yeshua tugs at his beard, and again he looks only on me.

I feel a great warmth in my belly.

He spreads his hands like a fish-man casting a net. "The kingdom of HaShem is like a net cast in the lake. They pull it up and find many fish. The good fish, they keep. The bad fish, they throw away. That is what the kingdom of HaShem is like."

I like this saying better. It is to do with the judgment on the last day. That will be a fearful day, for the wrath of HaShem will fall on the earth. I am terrified of the wrath of HaShem. I saw it once when I was a small boy. If it falls on me, that will be a bad matter. But I repented already, so it will not fall on me. It will fall on the goyim, and that is a good matter.

I think I know the meaning of Rabbi Yeshua's tale. The bad fish are the goyim, and the good fish are the sons of Israel. The net is those of us called by Rabbi Yeshua to fish for men. I like that Rabbi Yeshua put me in his tale. I like that he did not make a paradox.

Rabbi Yeshua waits for a moment. He has the look of a craftsman, only he crafts words, not stone or metal or wood.

The men in the synagogue whisper to each other behind their hands.

I think they are still confused by the paradox. I am still confused by the paradox.

When it becomes quiet, Rabbi Yeshua speaks out again.

"The kingdom of HaShem is like an oil lamp, set on a stand. The light shines out, and those who live in darkness see its light. If the lamp is covered, who will see its light? That is what the kingdom of HaShem is like."

I like this tale very much. Israel is the oil lamp, a light given to the nations. HaShem gave Israel Torah and the prophets so that those who live in darkness will see a mighty light and repent. But the goyim do not repent, because they are evil and dogs. When the kingdom of HaShem comes, the goyim will be cast into Outer Darkness, for they have refused the light, and Israel will become the kingdom of HaShem.

"The kingdom of HaShem is like—"

"Leave us alone, Yeshua from Nazareth!" It is a loud voice and angry, and it comes from the door behind Rabbi Yeshua, at the head of the synagogue.

I know that voice. My heart stutters, for the man who owns the voice is a big trouble on the village.

The voice belongs to Yoseph ben Yoseph, only the village calls him Yoseph the Rage, for he has a spirit of rage. Twenty years ago, his woman died in childbed, leaving him with five daughters. A man does not need daughters. A man needs sons. But Yoseph cannot get sons, because no woman will have him on account of his rage.

"Have you come to destroy us, Yeshua from Nazareth? Have you come to mock us before the time? We know who you are. You are the *tsaddik* sent from HaShem. Leave us, for—"

"Silence." Rabbi Yeshua's voice is so strong it makes my bones quake. So kind, all my fears run away.

I did not know any man could speak like that.

The Shekinah burns in Rabbi Yeshua's eyes.

Yoseph the Rage has his mouth open as he will scream, only no sound comes out.

All the synagogue is silent for terror.

Rabbi Yeshua speaks in a calm and quiet voice. "Come here, friend."

Yoseph the Rage snarls and takes small, cunning steps toward Rabbi Yeshua, like a lion stalking prey.

I want to run to save Rabbi Yeshua, but my feet have forgotten how to move. My hands are hot, and sweat runs down my back. I think I will vomit.

Yoseph the Rage stops. His mouth hangs open, and spit dangles from his lip. He looks as he is preparing to pounce.

I want to shout Rabbi Yeshua to run away now to save his life. My throat is so dry I cannot speak. Anyway, if Rabbi Yeshua runs away, I am afraid Yoseph the Rage will pounce on me.

Rabbi Yeshua smiles on him and does not look afraid.

I think Rabbi Yeshua does not know the matter of evil spirits.

An old man from Bethsaida came once to drive out the evil spirit. He brought new ropes for tying up Yoseph the Rage. He brought herbs that smelled foul as the *haryo* of many ten thousand dogs. He brought an iron pot for burning the herbs. He said he would shout the evil spirit away.

But his ropes were useless. Before the men of the village could tie up Yoseph the Rage, he attacked and scattered them. He beat the old man many times in the face until blood ran out of his nose. He bit off the old man's ear and ate it, and then he ran away to the hills for two days. When he came back, he did not remember anything. The village elders did not even try to punish him, because it was the evil spirit that did it. Also, they feared for their ears.

Yoseph the Rage is only ten paces from Rabbi Yeshua now. He glowers and snarls and waits for his moment to spring.

"You spirit of rage, come out of him."

Yoseph the Rage springs at Rabbi Yeshua.

Rabbi Yeshua springs at Yoseph the Rage.

They meet in the air.

Rabbi Yeshua catches Yoseph's arms in his two hands. He lands light on his feet, holding Yoseph out at the length of his arms. "Spirit of rage, come out of him!"

Yoseph the Rage snarls for his fury and spits Rabbi Yeshua's eye and tries to kick him in the underparts.

Rabbi Yeshua twists aside. "Come out of him now and do no harm!"

Yoseph the Rage screams a big scream.

I never heard such a scream. There is a bad rage in that scream.

Yoseph the Rage rips loose from Rabbi Yeshua and staggers back.

"HaShem says to come out now!"

Yoseph the Rage writhes in a big agony, like a wild dog I saw once that some boys crippled with clubs and threw in the fire alive. He screams many ten thousand screams. He falls to the stone floor holding his head as it is coming off. He gives a shriek more mighty than he ever did.

His head flails around and around like a loose sail in a high wind.

It smites the floor so hard I think it cracks the stones.

All his writhing stops. He lies on his back, unmoving. His body is twisted and his eyes are closed.

Yair shouts, "Water! Bring water! He is knocked senseless."

Rabbi Yeshua steps toward Yoseph the Rage.

I think it is a trick. I think he is luring Rabbi Yeshua in. I try to shout a warning that he should beware on his ears, only the words stick in my throat.

Rabbi Yeshua kneels beside him. "Friend, HaShem says you are free."

Men crowd forward to see.

I cannot breathe, and my heart beats so hard it aches in my chest. I push through the crowd to pull Rabbi Yeshua away.

Rabbi Yeshua touches the face of Yoseph the Rage.

Yoseph the Rage opens his eyes.

Rabbi Yeshua gives him a kiss and a kiss and a kiss.

Yoseph the Rage smiles.

I never saw him smile.

Yoseph the Rage laughs for joy.

I never heard him laugh.

My head feels light, and I cannot draw breath. Sending away an evil spirit is a heavy thing, but Rabbi Yeshua made it seem a light thing.

All the synagogue shouts for amaze at this mighty wonder.

They think it is a great thing, but they are fools. It is a bad thing.

Rabbi Yeshua was in the middle of telling the kingdom of HaShem. Then Yoseph the Rage broke in on him.

Now everyone has forgotten the matter of the kingdom of HaShem.

I am so angry I think I will swallow my tongue for my fury.

Rabbi Yeshua sent away the evil spirit, but the evil spirit outfoxed him. People will be talking on the evil spirit for three weeks and a day. They are not talking on the kingdom of HaShem.

Today will not be the Day of Vengeance after all.

Rabbi Yeshua knows the matter of evil spirits, but he does not know the matter of strategy.

This evening in our room, I will explain it to him.

Yeshua of Nazareth

I am more confused than I ever was. HaShem said today I would make a move. That he would show me what move to make. He gave me some tales and I told them. I do not think anyone understood them. I am not sure I understood them.

I was waiting to see if HaShem would give me a tale of repentance to tell Capernaum, but he did not. Then the man with the evil spirit came in, and I knew what to do.

I do not know how I knew. I have seen men with evil spirits in the past and never knew what to do. But today I knew and I did it and the evil spirit fought me, but I was not afraid and I won.

I do not know what this has to do with the kingdom of HaShem.

Everyone thinks I have a plan.

Yoni asked me last night what is my plan.

I do not have a plan.

My only plan is to do what HaShem tells me, and that is not a plan.

I wish I knew the whole mind of HaShem on this matter. I wish—

I am standing before the Throne.

The Messengers of HaShem shout with a great shout. They dance all around me. Their joy pulses through me.

I feel my own joy welling up inside me.

I dance before the Throne.

HaShem comes off the Throne.

HaShem begins dancing.

I am undone. HaShem is dancing.

'You did well, my son.' HaShem gives me a kiss and a kiss and a kiss.

I am twice undone.

For a time, there is only joy.

I do not know how long the joy lasts. It feels like many ten thousand years. All heaven rejoices over this one man, who was a slave and now is free.

Free.

In an instant, I see a new thing.

The kingdom of HaShem is freedom.

When a man is set free from an evil spirit, he has a share in the kingdom of HaShem.

That is a new thought to me. It should not be a new thought. I feel as I have walked in my sleep all my life and have suddenly wakened.

The kingdom of HaShem is freedom.

HaShem smiles on me and dances for all his might.

The Messengers make a circle around me, shouting for joy, dancing for freedom.

Joy grows in my heart, greater and greater, like a roaring fire. I am sent to make my people free. Every man I make free is a victory for the kingdom of HaShem.

I no longer feel confused. I still do not know the whole matter. I think *there is more to be said on the matter. But I understand enough to fight the next battle. At last I have a plan.*

The vision fades.

I am back in the synagogue.

No time has passed.

All is still a big confusion.

Yoni tugs on my sleeve. His face tells that he thinks I made a mistake in the matter. Yoni sees further than my other men, but he does not see far enough.

Not yet.

But he will.

CHAPTER FORTY-NINE

Shimon of Capernaum

"No, no, no! Rabbi Yeshua will eat at our home today!" I am sick to my death of shouting on these fools who wish to take the honor of feeding Rabbi Yeshua the Shabbat meal. The honor is ours and we will keep it.

We are walking back to my father's house from the synagogue. My heart is all in a big confusion. Rabbi Yeshua meant to make a move today, but he was prevented, on account of Yoseph the Rage. He puts a good face on it, but the truth is that the moment was ruined.

The only good that came is that Rabbi Yeshua gained honor. Before now, Capernaum had only our word that Rabbi Yeshua is a mighty man of HaShem. Now their own eyes saw an evil spirit run from Rabbi Yeshua.

But that is not what we looked for. HaShem is not concerned on one man with a spirit of rage. HaShem is concerned to raise up an army and throw off the Great Satan and make a new kingdom. Today, Rabbi Yeshua was to raise up that army, and he was prevented.

Yoni walks together with Rabbi Yeshua, holding his hand as he is a friend. Yoni is impudent. Zavdai should speak to him on the matter.

"Rabbi Yeshua, when will you raise up an army?" Yoni asks.

We all grow silent, for that is the question we are all thinking, but none of us would dishonor Rabbi Yeshua by asking. Yoni needs a good beating, that is what I think. But still I am glad he asked.

My woman Yohana comes running up the path from my father's house, waving her hands at us. "No! Stop! Go back the way you came! There is summer fever in the house!"

I feel hot all over, and my chest aches.

The summer fever is a killing fever. We had it here ten years ago, and it took the tenth part of the village. It is caused by an evil spirit that lives in the north marshes. I hate those marshes, for they also have mosquitoes. They are bad mosquitoes, but the evil spirit is worse.

My father's face is white. "Who has the summer fever?"

Tears leak out of my woman's eyes. "My mother! She woke up this morning with a great ache in her head. Now her whole body is hot and she is sweating a big sweat. Do not bring the rabbi near the place."

We should none of us go near the place.

"Take me to the woman," Rabbi Yeshua says.

My woman shakes her head. "Rabbi, with respect, no. It is a fearful—"

"Take me to the woman."

I push forward. "Rabbi, you do not see the summer fever in your village, but in Capernaum we do. My woman knows it well, for her father died of the summer fever. If she says her mother has—"

"Take me to the woman."

Now everyone shouts all at once, for Rabbi Yeshua wades in water beyond his depth. A rabbi knows about Torah and the prophets and the writings. A rabbi does not know about fevers. It is a woman's work to know about fevers.

Rabbi Yeshua begins walking toward our house.

Now I am angry on him, for he will risk his life, to no gain.

We all stand staring after him.

He turns and smiles on me. "Shimon the Rock, please, you will come with me."

My tongue sticks to the roof of my mouth, and my hands are sweating.

"Shimon the Rock, please, you will come with me."

I do not wish to go into a house of fever. But I promised yesterday to follow Rabbi Yeshua wherever he goes.

"Shimon the Rock."

I follow.

"Shimon!" my father calls after me. "You will not go with the rabbi. This is foolishness."

It is foolishness, yes. But I made a promise.

Footsteps clatter behind me. Yoni catches me and takes my hand.

I scowl on him. "The rabbi did not ask you to come."

"If the rabbi is not afraid, then I am not afraid."

Rabbi Yeshua walks like a man who is not afraid. He goes in through the gate into our courtyard.

Yoni and I hurry to catch him.

"Where does she sleep?" Rabbi Yeshua asks.

I point across the courtyard to the guest room at the back of the house. "When people are sick, we keep them in there."

Rabbi Yeshua strides across the courtyard like a soldier going to battle. I never saw such an eager man.

I hurry after him. "Rabbi, the woman's name is Fat Miryam."

"I know her name." He pushes open the door.

Two maidservants kneel beside the bed. One wrings out a wet cloth into a stone basin. The other applies a cloth to Fat Miryam's forehead.

The woman moans and struggles softly, but her eyes are shut.

I do not think she knows we are here.

Rabbi Yeshua kneels beside the bed and puts a hand on the shoulder of the maidservant. "Please, you will allow me to send away the fever."

The girl stands and backs away. Her mouth twists and her eyes narrow in a way that says Rabbi Yeshua is a fool and worse than a fool.

Rabbi Yeshua takes Fat Miryam's hand. "You will leave her now, you fever."

Something shivers in my belly. I never saw such foolishness, to speak to a fever.

"Leave her now, fever!"

The servant girls both hiss their scorn.

"Now!"

Fat Miryam's eyes flicker.

They open.

They look on Rabbi Yeshua.

Fat Miryam smiles.

A cold wind races down my spine.

The servant girls make little gasps.

"Rabbi Yeshua!" Fat Miryam's voice booms in the small room, for she is a big woman with a big voice. "Are you … well?" She looks all around, and she grasps at her hair, for it lies uncovered in damp coils around her head. Shame floods her face.

I wish to turn my head away, for it is dishonor for a man to look on a woman's hair, and it is shame to the woman.

Rabbi Yeshua reaches for a hair covering and slips it under Fat Miryam's head. "Shalom, Mother Miryam. Do not be ashamed. I have a mother and sisters, and I have seen a woman's hair. It is a gift of HaShem, yes?" He wraps her hair and knots the covering as swift as any woman, and then gives me a smile that says a woman's hair is not a matter of scandal.

It may not be a matter of scandal for a *tsaddik*, but it is a matter of scandal for me.

Rabbi Yeshua takes Fat Miryam's hand again. "Come, stand up. You are whole."

That is more foolishness. To wake from a fever is one thing. To be strong after a fever is another. The summer fever leaves you weak for many hours.

Fat Miryam sits up in bed. She flings off the damp sheet that covers her. She stinks of sweat. Her tunic clings wet to her body like skin.

I turn my head away, for I do not wish to shame her.

Yoni's face is more red than it ever was. He is not married and never saw a woman's body.

Rabbi Yeshua speaks to the serving girls. "My daughters, you will give her a clean tunic, please, and bring her out to enjoy the Shabbat meal when she is ready." His voice turns stern. "And you will tell no one what you have seen today."

The girls' eyes are bright moons of astonishment, but they nod meekly. "Yes, Rabbi."

I do not believe them. They are both gossips, more than most women.

Rabbi Yeshua must be teasing the girls, for why should he not wish anyone to know the matter? In days of old, mighty prophets like Elijah and Elisha could heal the sick, but that was many hundred years ago. This is a mighty work of HaShem, and it is proof Rabbi Yeshua is a prophet of HaShem. It is a bigger proof than sending away a spirit of rage. People do not die of a spirit of rage, but people die of the summer fever. Rabbi Yeshua should ask the girls to tell the whole village. They will do it anyway, or I am a tax-farmer.

Rabbi Yeshua takes me and Yoni out of the room and back through the house and outside.

Our families wait in the path. Their mouths hang open and their eyes are tight. "Rabbi Yeshua, are you well?" my father calls out.

Rabbi Yeshua smiles on them. "I am well. The woman Miryam is well. The kingdom of HaShem is upon us. Come, let us eat the Shabbat meal!"

My woman runs to meet us. "Is she truly well, Rabbi?"

"She is truly well, and she will be truly hungry soon. Please, you will go bring out the Shabbat meal, for all of us are hungry."

My woman makes a little shriek and runs toward the house.

The men come to join us, and we all move toward the house. My father's eyes are narrow and his face is tight.

Andre tugs on the sleeve of my tunic. "What happened?"

I explain the matter of how Rabbi Yeshua told the fever to go and how he took Fat Miryam's hand and spoke strength into her body. I do not tell the matter of the hair covering or the wet tunic, for that is not fitting.

As I finish my tale, I see the older serving girl slip out of the gate.

All Capernaum will know the matter within the hour. Tonight, at the going out of Shabbat, it will not be only a few folk with evil spirits who come to this house. Many hundred people will bring their sick.

My head feels dizzy, and my legs are weak as water.

Now I see why Rabbi Yeshua did not wish the girls to spread the tale. That will make it sure that Rabbi Yeshua will have no peace for many days.

Now how will he raise up an army?

Rabbi Yeshua is not wise if he lets himself be turned aside by foolishness such as evil spirits and fevers, when he should be bringing in the kingdom of HaShem.

~

Yeshua of Nazareth

'You call yourself a prophet, so do the work of a prophet. Tell these people their sins.'

I am more weary than I ever was. This evening, after the going out of the Shabbat, all the village came to the House of Yonah, the father of Shimon the Rock. They called my name, begging me to heal them or send away evil spirits.

That was hours ago. Now it is very late and there are still a hundred people here, all desperate to speak to me.

The woman standing before me is the age of my own mother and has a blistered hand that has festered. Pus oozes out of the sores, and there is a red streak running up her arm.

My stomach clenches inside me, and I think I might vomit. "Imma, what happened?"

"I … splashed boiling oil on it last week."

'She did it last Shabbat, when it is not permitted to cook. She is a lawbreaker, and this is her just punishment. You should tell her the wrath of HaShem.'

"Imma, how many days ago?"

Her face reddens and she cannot look my eye. "It was two days before Shabbat."

'Now she lies. That is no repentance. HaShem will not forgive her. HaShem will not heal her. You should tell her a liar and send her away.'

"Imma."

Tears run out of her eyes.

'False tears of false repentance! Tell her away. She is not worthy of healing.'

I lean close to give her a kiss and a kiss and a kiss.

She twists her head away, for she hears the lies of the Accuser. She is shamed by them. "Rabbi, no, I should not have come. I … did a wrong thing, and HaShem is punishing me."

"No, Imma."

'Evildoer! Lawbreaker! Liar! She should die in her sins.'

She turns and pulls away from me.

I wrap my arms around her.

She struggles in my arms. "No, Rabbi, leave me."

I bend down to whisper in her ear. "HaShem loves you."

She is weeping now.

"HaShem loves you, Imma."

Loud cries of anguish.

Angry muttering in the crowd.

"See how he hurts the woman."

"That is lewdness, to clutch at her."

"Somebody should break his teeth."

I whisper a secret word in her ear.

She spins in my arms and clutches me, wailing her grief.

I hold her close, kissing the top of her head.

'What are you doing? You are wicked. You are full of lewdness. What was that word you spoke in her ear?'

I feel strength going out of me.

I think my knees might buckle beneath me.

At last she ends her weeping.

She pulls back from me.

She holds up her hand.

The redness is gone.

The pus is gone.

The blisters are gone.

Her eyes light up. "Blessed be HaShem! The rabbi healed me!"

All around us, a hiss of excitement.

She moves away from me through the crowd, holding her hand above her head, shouting for joy.

'You should have told her repentance. She will go and sin again.'

I am more weary than I ever was.

A dozen people press closer.

"Rabbi, a moment!"

"Rabbi, I have been waiting long!"

"Rabbi, just one word, please!"

'You see what foolishness this is? They will wear you out, to no gain. You should raise up an army and leave these sick to die in their sins.'

My feet are numb. A dark cloud dances before my eyes. I feel myself falling from a great height into blackness.

'You are no prophet. You are no son of David. You are not doing the work of HaShem. You are not ...'

CHAPTER FIFTY

Yoni of Capernaum

An hour before dawn, I wake.

Something is wrong.

Rabbi Yeshua is just slipping out into the courtyard.

I throw on my cloak and run to see where he is going.

Already he is in the street. Last fall when I followed him, he went south on the road along the lake. Today he walks west into the hills above the lake. There are vineyards that way and olive groves and many ten thousand fig trees.

I follow him at a great distance, beyond the edge of hearing.

He climbs uphill for the fourth part of an hour. It is quiet here. A pink glow in the east tells that day will come soon.

Rabbi Yeshua sits under an olive tree with his back against the trunk.

I hide in a vineyard and watch him.

He is not moving. He is speaking to someone. I cannot hear the words, but I think he is speaking to HaShem. I think HaShem is also speaking to him.

His face looks tired. He should be tired. Last night he healed many people, but it took long, because he spent too much time with each person. He also sent away many evil spirits. I thought he would wear himself out, and I was right. When he finally collapsed, it was me who caught him and shouted for Shimon the Rock and Big Yaakov to help. We carried him to my room so he could sleep. But I did not get a chance to ask him questions or explain the matter of strategy to him.

I am desperate to know what he says to HaShem. I am desperate to hear what HaShem speaks in his ear.

I push through the vines to the next row. I still cannot hear him, so I push through to the next row, and the next, and the next, and the next.

At last I can hear.

"Yoni, come out from your hiding."

My face feels as it is on fire.

"Yoni, I wish to speak with you."

Sweat is all down my back.

"Yoni, I will answer one of your questions if you come out."

Rabbi Yeshua knows my weakness. I hurry to join him.

He pats the ground beside him.

I sit there and lean against the trunk of the olive tree.

"You are up early, Yoni."

"Rabbi, where did you learn to heal people? Why do you not use foul herbs to drive away evil spirits? Why did you not bring your brothers when you came to Capernaum? Is it true there is a prince of evil spirits called the Accuser? What did you tell that woman last night to make her cry? Does a *tsaddik* feel desire to lie with women? How long until we destroy the Great Satan? Is it true that before That Day, HaShem will send his wrath to punish us for our sins? Why did HaShem create—"

Rabbi Yeshua laughs long. "I offer you a drink and you want the whole well! Which of your many ten thousand questions shall I answer?"

I like it when Rabbi Yeshua teases me. He does not do it with cruelty like Big Yaakov or my sisters. But I cannot decide which question he should answer. I want them all.

Rabbi Yeshua's eyes narrow. "Explain your question on the matter of the wrath of HaShem."

I think he is teasing me, for who does not know about the wrath of HaShem? I study his face.

He raises an eyebrow at me. "Explain the matter, and I will tell you what I told the woman last night to make her cry."

So I explain the matter. In ancient times, our fathers went after other gods, idols that our prophet Moses warned against. HaShem sent many prophets to tell our fathers repentance. Sometimes, they repented, and sometimes they did not. Finally, HaShem sent the prophet Jeremiah. Our fathers punished him and mocked him and refused to listen.

Whenever our fathers did a wickedness, HaShem raised up his wrath to punish them. Sometimes the wrath of HaShem was an earthquake. Sometimes it was a big storm. Sometimes a fire or a flood or a plague. Sometimes a wicked king. In the time of Jeremiah, the king of Babylon became angry on us and came to make war, and HaShem gave us into his hand.

The king of Babylon broke down the walls of Jerusalem. He burned the Temple with fire. He leveled the city. He killed our mighty warriors. He used our women for a pleasure and also our girls to the age of three. He cut off the man parts of our young men. He took our people as slaves to Babylon. That was a bad wrath.

Rabbi Yeshua has been studying his hands while I explain the matter. When I finish, he says, "All that was long ago. What is the wrath of HaShem that you fear now, today?"

I am astonished that he should ask such a question. "The king of Rome is a mighty king. What if he becomes angry on us and comes here to punish us for our sins? What if he burns our city and our Temple? Yohanan the immerser said the ax is laid at the root of the tree. He says the wrath of HaShem is coming to punish us. The prophet Malachi says HaShem will send his messenger before the great and terrible day of HaShem, when he destroys the wicked, root and branch."

Rabbi Yeshua's eyes are thin slits in his face. That is the way a man looks when he hears a thing he does not believe.

He should believe. I have seen the wrath of HaShem, and it is a terrifying thing.

"HaShem loves you," Rabbi Yeshua says. "I told the woman last night that HaShem loves her more than she loves her own children, and the proof is that her hand was healed."

I do not know what to say to that. I think Rabbi Yeshua should read the scriptures more. The wrath of HaShem is real. The wrath of HaShem is coming. The wrath of HaShem will punish evildoers.

"HaShem says I am to go through all Galilee and tell the good news of the kingdom of HaShem."

My heart races. That means I will go with him. And Shimon the Rock and Big Yaakov and Andre. "When will we leave? Are we going to make a big army? Will you take your mother? Will we go to Nazareth for Little Yaakov and your other brothers? Is it time to smite the first Power? Are you going to do more mighty wonders? What will we eat?"

Rabbi Yeshua makes a big grin and stands up. He gives me a strong right hand and pulls me to my feet. "We are going to your father's house, where we will eat as much as we can hold. Then your mother and your sisters will kiss you many times until you are sick to your death of being kissed. Then we will walk to Bethsaida to find Philip and Natanel the hireling. After that, HaShem will tell us what to do."

I jump up and down for my excitement. All of that sounds wonderful except for the matter of being kissed. The kingdom of HaShem is about to begin.

But I will have to keep explaining the wrath of HaShem to Rabbi Yeshua until he understands it.

Shimon of Capernaum

My woman shakes me awake before it is dawn. "Shimon, there is some man at the gate asking for Rabbi Yeshua. He says strange things, and I do not know what to say to him."

I do not wish to speak to some strange man. I wish to sleep another hour. "You should send him away."

"He refuses to be sent away by a woman. He says he is a friend of yours, but I never heard you speak on him."

"What is his name?"

"He says he built a boat for your father. He says it was the best boat ever made in the whole world."

My head fills with a mighty pounding, and my stomach raises a sour taste in the back of my throat. I leap out of bed and throw on my cloak. "That can only be Toma Trouble."

"Why do you call him Toma Trouble?"

I wrap my cloth belt around my waist twice and tuck it under itself. I push my feet into my sandals.

"Why do you call him Toma Trouble?"

"I will send him away. Rabbi Yeshua does not wish to speak with him."

"Why do you call him Toma Trouble?"

I hurry out of my room into the main courtyard of my father's house. My mother and the servant girls are cooking the morning meal.

I reach the gate to the street and go out.

Toma Trouble paces back and forth, muttering to himself.

I scowl on him. "What do you want?"

Toma Trouble makes a big grin on me. "I saw Rabbi Yeshua send away the evil spirit from Yoseph the Rage yesterday with a word. That is a sign of the *logos*, yes?"

I do not know what is a *logos*. I think it is some Greekish foolishness. I do not care what it means, but I want Toma Trouble gone before Rabbi Yeshua comes here. "You should go home. Rabbi Yeshua is not here."

"I heard he came here. I heard your woman's mother had the summer fever. I heard Rabbi Yeshua sent the fever away with a word. Did you see? Is it true? I did not see it, and therefore I think I should not believe it. Only I saw Rabbi Yeshua send away the evil spirit yesterday with a word, and that is reason to think he could send away a fever with a word. What did you see, and what do you know on the matter?"

Toma Trouble always talks about what a man can know and what he can believe. I am sick to my death of him. All that he says is a babbling in my ears. "Go home. Rabbi Yeshua is not here."

"Do you know where he is? I heard he was staying here. If he is not here, then I should go to the House of Zavdai. What do you think, is he there? I heard that Yohanan the son of Zavdai is a friend on Rabbi Yeshua. Do you know? Is it true? If there is one man in the whole village who is not a complete fool, it is that Yohanan, only he talks too much."

Toma Trouble is the only person in the village who calls Yoni by his whole name, which is Yohanan. I think it is a matter of the sow calling the boar fat for Toma Trouble to say Yoni talks too much. It is true Yoni talks too much, but he is the Genius of Capernaum. Toma Trouble is not. If he is anything, he is the Fool of Capernaum, only I would be guilty of the Evil Tongue to say it, so I will not say it, even if it is true.

Anyway, I know Toma Trouble is easy to turn aside by asking him about boats. "I heard you are making a new boat for Yair the synagogue president. Is it true?"

Toma Trouble nods. "It will be the best boat ever made in the whole world, even better than the one I made for your—"

"Shimon the Rock!" Yoni shouts from far up the street. "Do you know what we are going to do today? First, we are going to my house to eat as much as we can hold. Then my mother and sisters will kiss me many times until I am sick to my death of being kissed. Then we are going to Bethsaida to find Philip and Natanel the hireling. Then HaShem will tell us what to do. Rabbi Yeshua is about to make his move!"

I would shush Yoni's shouting if I could, but nobody ever shushed Yoni.

Toma Trouble turns to look up the street.

Yoni walks toward us.

Holding Rabbi Yeshua's hand.

Toma Trouble grins and strides toward them. "Rabbi Yeshua, I wish to ask you a riddle."

I hurry after him. I should warn Rabbi Yeshua away, or Toma Trouble will tie him in a big knot.

Rabbi Yeshua comes forward and makes a grin on Toma Trouble. "Shalom, friend. My name is called Yeshua from Nazareth."

Toma Trouble extends a hand to him. "My name is called Toma the boat maker."

Rabbi Yeshua greets him with a strong right hand.

"What do you want, Toma Trouble?" says Yoni.

"I want Yohanan Talk-Talk to not talk while I discuss a matter with the rabbi."

Yoni scowls on him. "Did you come to ask Rabbi Yeshua a riddle about a logic? He will make a piss on your logic."

Rabbi Yeshua shrugs and makes a grin on Yoni. "That is a matter you should teach me sometime, Yoni, how to make a piss on a logic. What is your riddle, Toma the boat maker?"

"If there are two men, and each has two fish, that is four fish."

"That is not a riddle."

"I am not done yet. If there are four men, and each has four fish, that is ten fish and six."

"That is still not a riddle."

"I am still not done. If there are ten men and six, and each has ten fish and six, how many fish is that?"

Rabbi Yeshua stands thinking hard on the matter.

That is why all Capernaum hates Toma Trouble. He makes riddles that are not riddles. They are only matters of counting. Toma makes a large matter on the number two. Yoni says it is because Toma is a twin. I do not think that is a reason. There are other twins in Capernaum, and they do not make foolish riddles on the matter of two and four and eight. Toma Trouble can tell you what is two of two of two of two taken many times. I do not see why anyone should care on the matter.

At last Rabbi Yeshua says, "Toma the boat maker, that is a good riddle, but it is too hard for me."

"It is two hundreds and fifty and six fish," Yoni says.

Toma Trouble nods. "I already knew you could answer the riddle, Yohanan. I came to see if the rabbi could answer it."

I spit in the dirt. "It is a foolish riddle. The rabbi is concerned on the kingdom of HaShem—"

"It is not a foolish riddle," says Toma Trouble. "There is a deep matter in the number two and in the numbers that come from two. How do you think HaShem made the world, if he did not know this deep matter?"

That is such a foolish thing, I do not know how to answer.

Rabbi Yeshua puts a hand on Toma Trouble's shoulder. "Friend, you should come eat with us at the House of Zavdai and explain to me why the matter of the number two is a deep thing of HaShem. I knew a *philosophos* in Tsipori who—"

"You knew a *philosophos*?" Toma Trouble stares on him like a starving man who hears there is free bread in the market square.

"I built a house for him, and he explained a matter called *logic* to me," Rabbi Yeshua says.

Sometimes I think I should beat my head with a stick until it cracks open. Saying the word *logic* to Toma Trouble is like slitting open a sheep at dusk when the wild jackals come out to hunt. I do not know what this thing *logic* is, but it is some Greekish matter and I am sure it is a wickedness and a lie.

Now we will not be rid of Toma Trouble for a week.

CHAPTER FIFTY-ONE

Yaakov of Nazareth

I stand and stretch my back, which aches from the hard work of the day. "We should go to the village square."

My brothers all nod.

"The stranger must have heard news of Yeshua," Yosi says.

Yehuda Dreamhead and Thin Shimon draw invisible swords and begin dueling.

My woman makes the *tsk* sound she always makes. "Grown men should know swords are not a game."

My woman does not understand matters of war.

We had a traveler come to the village today. I asked the elders for the honor of giving hospitality, but they gave it to Shmuel the iron-man. So we have to wait to hear the news with the rest of the village.

I am desperate to hear it. Our brother Yeshua has been gone more than five weeks. We have heard nothing since then. I do not think it was wise for him to go to Capernaum. His friends threw him off, so why should he go there? And it was foolish to take Imma with him. Most foolish of all was that he refused to take me. I am still angry on the matter.

Yosi's woman nurses her younger son. Thin Shimon's woman and Yehuda Dreamhead's woman are cleaning the cook pot. My woman looks on me with desire burning in her eyes.

I feel a big heat in my belly. After I hear the traveler's news, there will be time enough to warm my hands at my woman's fire. I will make her shout louder than she ever did, enough to wake the whole house.

My brothers and I walk to the village square with Uncle Halfai and our cousin, Fat Shimon. My woman and Uncle Halfai's woman follow behind us.

Most of the village is already there.

We sit in a comfortable place and wait.

Shmuel the iron-man stands with the elders and the traveler, making a big grin while he tells some jest. When he finishes, the elders and the traveler laugh.

When all is silent, Shmuel the iron-man turns to the villagers and tells the traveler's name, which is Elazar. He is a man from Banias in the far north, at the place where the waters from the Jordan River spring out of the great rock. Shmuel the iron-man says Elazar has news of a man from Nazareth.

All my body feels hot.

Elazar tells how he was in Yodefat two weeks ago. Yodefat is a village north of here by a walk of half a day. He tells how one of the men of the village had a daughter with an evil spirit that sometimes threw her on the ground and made her foam in the mouth. The girl was of an age to be married, but no man would take her on account of the evil spirit.

The same day Elazar came to Yodefat, eight other men came also, along with one old woman. They asked in the village square if there were sick people in the village or any with evil spirits. They said these were the last days, and the kingdom of HaShem was at hand, and HaShem would heal all who were sick and would send away all evil spirits.

The people of Yodefat brought out many sick, and they were healed.

They brought a man with a shriveled arm, and he was made whole.

They brought the girl with the evil spirit, and there was a mighty battle. The leader of the men tried all night to send away the evil spirit, but it would not go. He tried all the next day, but it would not go. He spent the whole next night praying to HaShem. In the morning, he went back to the house of the girl and sent away the evil spirit with one word.

Elazar stops talking for a moment. There is a look of wonder on his face. "I saw the thing with these eyes. I heard it with these ears. The man who did these mighty deeds is named Yeshua. He said he comes from Nazareth. What do you know of him?"

"We know Yeshua the *tekton*," says Shmuel the iron-man. "He is a *tsaddik*, but we never heard he could send away evil spirits."

"And he heals people," says Elazar. "I saw it. The man with the shriveled arm—"

"Yeshua never healed anyone," says Shimon the baker.

"Yes, he did," Yehuda Dreamhead says.

Old Yonatan the leather-man shakes his head. "He never did. If he heals people, why does he do it in other villages, and not here? He should heal people here first, and not dishonor us by healing other villages."

I stand up. "Yeshua healed Thin Shimon at Pesach in Jerusalem. He was as good as dead, and Yeshua healed him. It was a mighty wonder. I saw it with these—"

"We never saw it," says another voice.

My underparts ache when I hear that voice.

Yoseph the leather-man grins. "Yeshua the *tekton* is the son of the spreadlegs."

Red spots fill my eyes. All in one instant, my temples pound with hate and my fists harden to stones and I lunge forward.

The arms of my brothers are quicker than snakes to catch me, holding me back.

All I can see is the sneer on the face of Yoseph the leather-man.

All I can smell is the *haryo* on Imma's clothes on the day she came back from the spring.

All I can feel is the mighty pain in my underparts.

I throw myself forward with all my strength, desperate to get loose.

Yoseph the leather-man's voice rises on the night air, singing his evil song.

"Once there was a *mamzer* boy
A *mamzer* boy
A *mamzer* boy.
Once there was a *mamzer* boy
Yeshua was his name."

I break free of my brothers' grip.

I rush at Yoseph the leather-man, hot with my rage.

He rushes at me, his eyes glowing with hate.

I smash into him with a mighty smash. I claw at his throat to squeeze the breath out of him.

He twists to one side and staggers free, gasping for air.

I leap at him again, forcing my advantage.

He tries to back away but trips and falls flat on his back.

I dive forward.

He raises one knee.

I impale myself on his knee.

Pain knifes up through my underparts.

All the strength goes out of my body.

The world turns dark and cold.

I hear men shouting.

My brothers pull me away.

The pain is like an ax blow between my legs.

Yoseph's voice sounds very far away. "Your mother spreads her legs for a *dinar*. I had her myself when I was a boy and made her shout louder than your woman ever did."

I weep for my rage. Tears blur my eyes, and I gag as I will vomit.

"Yoseph the leather-man, your breath smells like piss," says Yosi. "Little Yaakov, come home with us."

Strong hands help me stand.

I feel as I will die from the pain in my underparts. I wish I will die, to make the pain stop.

"Yeshua will come back to Nazareth soon," Yehuda Dreamhead says. "He will come back with an army."

He should come soon.

He should come and kill Yoseph the leather-man.

Only I know Yeshua, and he is weak-minded.

He will not kill Yoseph the leather-man.

He will not kill anyone.

So I will.

CHAPTER FIFTY-TWO

Miryam of Nazareth

Sometimes I wish I had not begged to come with my son. Every day we walk to a new village. The villagers are eager to give hospitality and hear the news, so we always have food to eat and a place to stay. In the evening, my son tells tales and heals sick people and sends away evil spirits. Sometimes we stay a second day or even a third, but then we go to a new village. I do not know why we are doing this. I thought my son meant to raise up an army and make a big war, but he has only seven men, and that is not an army.

I am walking with my son. He holds my hand, and I love him for it. I know his men mutter about me, that it is foolishness to bring an old woman who is slow, but I do not care what they say. Yeshua does not complain that I am slow. That boy Yoni also walks with us, and he asks many hundred questions. Sometimes Yeshua answers one of them.

We have walked through Galilee now for six weeks. Most weeks, we go back to Capernaum for Shabbat, and that is good, but then the next day we walk another road. I never knew there were so many roads in Galilee, so many villages. Yoni says there are more than a hundred.

The new man, Toma the boat maker, says there are two hundreds and fifty and six. I do not know which of them is right.

The heat of the summer is on us, and it would be a hard thing if we walked far each day. But Galilee is thick with villages. If you walk any way on any road, you will come to a new village by a walk of one hour. The wheat harvest is just in, so if we are hungry on the road, we glean a few stalks and rub them in our hands and eat.

Yoni talks more than any boy I ever knew. I would have grown tired of his questions long ago, only he is kind to an old woman, and that counts much.

We come to a crossroads and stop. My son shades his eyes with his hand. He looks straight ahead. He looks to the right. He looks to the left.

"Rabbi Yeshua, where are we going today?" Yoni asks.

My son tilts his head to one side like a man who is listening. That means HaShem is speaking to him.

"If we go straight, that is the way to Bethlehem of Galilee." Yoni makes a big grin. "When I was small, I thought it was the same as Bethlehem near Jerusalem. I thought we could go to Bethlehem of Galilee by a walk of two days and save four days' walking to get to Pesach."

Big Yaakov snorts. "One year I told Abba to send him that way. It would have saved us six days' talking."

I do not know why Big Yaakov is so cruel on Yoni.

"We will go this way." Yeshua points to the right.

"Rabbi Yeshua, are we going back to Yodefat?" Yoni asks.

"We are going to Bethlehem of Galilee."

"But then we should go straight—"

"HaShem says we will go to the right." My son takes my hand and begins walking north.

Yoni hurries to catch up. "Rabbi Yeshua, I do not understand what is your plan. When are we going to raise up an army? Why have we not yet gone to Nazareth? We passed by it on the road three times, and you never turned to go up the hill. Is Little Yaakov going to be your commander? I think he would command your armies well, what do you think? Did HaShem tell you what we will eat tonight? How often do you hear HaShem speaking to you? When I was small, I thought a prophet heard HaShem speaking in his ear fifty times in an hour, but that is not the way of it with you. Sometimes you do not hear a word for a whole week, and you look as you will break from the torture of waiting. Why does HaShem—"

"HaShem is teaching me obedience," my son says. "When you long for a word from HaShem many days and at last you hear it, you treasure that word more than many ten thousand words from one who speaks every moment."

"What did HaShem tell you just—"

"Yoni, hush!" Big Yaakov says. "Can you not tell when the rabbi is making a joke on you?"

I did not think my son was making a joke on Yoni.

"Rabbi Yeshua, were you making a joke on me?"

My son stops and looks at the hillside we are passing. Two caves stare down on us like the eyeholes in a skull. My son looks like a man trying to remember something. "Yoni, have you read in Torah about *tsaraat*?"

Yoni grins on him. "Who has not read many times of *tsaraat*?"

"My memory is dim on *tsaraat*. Remind me what Torah says on the matter."

I shiver to hear him speak of it. *Tsaraat* is a punishment for a big sin. HaShem makes a man's skin have a rash or scaliness or white patches for a time. A man who has *tsaraat* is unclean until he repents. Then HaShem makes it go away, and he is clean again. *Tsaraat* is what we call "little leprosy," and Torah tells how to know when it is unclean and when it is clean again. I do not know those things. A priest knows them.

Yoni closes his eyes and begins reciting Torah. He sways as he speaks, the way a man does when he reads a scroll.

I think I see why they call Yoni a genius, for he recites many words without stopping. Torah says much about *tsaraat*, and Yoni recites long. I do not know how anyone can know so much.

When Yoni stops, my son says, "You told the matter well. What do you men say? Did Yoni tell the whole matter?"

Shimon the Rock says he thinks Yoni told it all.

Toma the boat maker says he doubts Yoni told it all.

Yoni says he knows he told it all.

Big Yaakov scowls on Yoni as he always does when he thinks Yoni is being conceited.

I do not think Yoni is being conceited. My son asked him to tell the matter, and he told the matter. I do not know why brothers cannot get along.

I do not know why my son wants to hear about *tsaraat* now. I am hungry and wish to go to the next village and eat a good meal. Eating a few kernels of wheat by the road is not a good meal.

My son begins climbing the rocky hillside. "All of you, stay back."

He climbs the steep hill until he stands before one of the caves. He shouts a greeting.

A man comes out of the cave. I think it is a man. His face is thick with bumps and folds and horrible scabs. His fingers ooze with sores, worn down to half their length. He is thin as a wild dog that digs in the garbage pits. I never saw such an ugly man.

This man does not have *tsaraat*.

This man has something worse. People call it "the mighty leprosy," and it is caused by a terrible evil spirit. A man can be cured of the little leprosy, but there was never any man cured of the mighty leprosy. A man who has the mighty leprosy will die of it.

The leper steps away from Yeshua. "Stand back! I am unclean!"

Yeshua takes a step toward him. "Friend, do you know who I am?"

"You are a fool if you do not stand back."

Yeshua takes another step. "Do you wish to be clean?"

"Fool, the mighty leprosy cannot be made clean." The leper holds up his hands as he means to push Yeshua back.

Yeshua reaches for him.

I feel as I will faint. If you touch a man with *tsaraat*, you will be unclean for a time, but the *tsaraat* will not go in you, because *tsaraat* is not a thing that goes in you, it only goes on you. But if you touch a man with the mighty leprosy, the evil spirit will go in you, and you will have the mighty leprosy in you until you die.

The leper turns as he wishes to run into his cave. He trips on his own feet. He falls. "Stand back! Back!"

Yeshua squats beside him. He reaches toward the leper.

The leper cringes away. "No!"

Yeshua touches the leper's hands.

My head feels as it is spinning. I think I will fall over.

Yeshua touches the leper's face.

I see black spots before my eyes.

Yeshua gives him a kiss and a kiss and a kiss.

I bend down and retch in the grass.

The leper's eyes flood with tears. I think he has forgotten what it was to be touched.

All my skin is on fire. My mind is numb. Yeshua has touched a mighty leper.

"Be clean, my friend," Yeshua says.

I cannot breathe. Now where will we go tonight? No village will have us. If Yeshua gets the mighty leprosy inside him, he will never raise up an army. He will never make a justice on my name.

The leper shouts a great shout, like a man with his hand in the fire.

He shouts again.

Again.

But it is not a shout of pain.

It is a shout of surprise. "Blessed be HaShem! Blessed be HaShem!"

The scabs on the man's hands fill up and become whole. The fingers on his hands grow out to their full length. The huge bumps on his face smooth out and disappear.

I shiver and shiver all over. My body shakes and my knees lose their strength and my heart skips and dances in my ribs. It is not possible. I see it, but I do not believe it. Such a thing was never done in Israel. It was never done anywhere. Tomorrow, I will think it was some dream and wonder if it happened. But for this one moment, I think it might be true.

Shimon the Rock gasps for air like a man who has run many miles.

Andre says, "Blessed be HaShem," over and over.

Yoni says, "That was a mighty wonder, Rabbi Yeshua!"

Toma the boat maker says, "I will not believe it unless I inspect the man." He climbs up the hill toward the leper.

The leper stands.

Toma the boat maker leaps back with a big leap. He stumbles on his own feet. He comes tumbling down the slope.

The leper looks on his hands in wonder. He touches his toes. He hops up and down like a man with new feet.

Yeshua smiles on him. "Friend, you are clean."

The man puts his hands to his face. He smiles so wide, it must break his cheeks. He laughs out loud. He shouts. He lies back on the ground, pounding it with his hands. "Blessed be HaShem!"

Yeshua takes his hand and helps him down the slope. He points in the direction we came. "There is a crossroads not far that way. Go west from there, and you will come to Bethlehem of Galilee. They have a family of priests. Ask the village elders at the gate to find a priest, and show him your skin. The priest will tell you what to do."

The man stares on Yeshua. "Who … who *are* you?"

"My name is called Yeshua from Nazareth, and I am sent to tell the kingdom of HaShem."

"The kingdom of HaShem is coming?"

"The kingdom of HaShem is breaking in on us."

I do not know why he said so. That is not true. Yeshua oversaid the matter. The kingdom of HaShem cannot be breaking in. The kingdom of HaShem—

"Blessed be Yeshua from Nazareth!" The man runs away toward the crossroads. He does not look back to see if we follow.

Yeshua's eyes smile on me. He leads us back the way we came.

I follow behind him. I am afraid to touch my son. He touched a man with the mighty leprosy. I never heard such a thing. Even Elisha the prophet never healed a man with the mighty leprosy. He healed some Syrian with *tsaraat*, and that was a great work of HaShem.

Yoni hurries ahead to join my son. He takes my son's hand.

I think Yoni has lost his wits.

"Rabbi Yeshua, did you come this way only for the leper?"

My son says nothing.

"It is a mighty work to heal the mighty leprosy, yes?"

My son says nothing.

"It is a mightier work to touch a man with the mighty leprosy, yes?"

My son says nothing.

"But it is the mightiest work of all to know you will heal a man with the mighty leprosy."

My son turns his head and smiles on me. "Imma, come walk with me."

I am terrified to walk with my son. He touched a man with the mighty leprosy. Now he will hold my hand, and I am afraid the mighty leprosy will come in me and I will die of it.

"Imma, if I can heal a man with the mighty leprosy, then the mighty leprosy has no power anymore, forever. Now walk with me."

I hurry to walk with him.

A thing has occurred to me, and it makes my heart glad.

My son has power over the mighty leprosy. I saw it with these eyes.

If Yeshua can heal a man with the mighty leprosy, then he can curse a man to have the mighty leprosy.

That is what I want. He should curse the Evil Boy. Curse him with the mighty leprosy. Curse him with a living death. Curse him to suffer as I have suffered.

The Evil Boy will not sing his wicked song when his lips fall off from the mighty leprosy.

CHAPTER FIFTY-THREE

Shimon of Capernaum

We returned last night to Capernaum, and I was glad, for I had been away from my woman two whole weeks and that is a sore trial. Usually, we come back every Shabbat, but this time we went to the ends of Galilee in the far north. That is a walk of two days each way, and we stopped in many villages on the road, so we were gone long and missed being home for Shabbat twice. I feel sorry for Rabbi Yeshua, for he has no woman. But he is a *tsaddik*, and perhaps *tsaddiks* do not have such a strong *yetzer hara* as other men.

Today, we are in the House of Zavdai. Two scribes from Magdala came to ask after Rabbi Yeshua, and many men of Capernaum came to listen, for Rabbi Yeshua has a big name now. All Galilee buzzes with the mighty wonders Rabbi Yeshua has done. The house is so full there is not room for one more man.

Rabbi Yeshua tells the tale of Daniel the prophet, who had a vision from HaShem on the matter of the kingdoms of the world. First there was the kingdom of Babylon. Then the kingdom of Persia. Then the kingdom of Greece. Then the kingdom of Rome. Last will come the kingdom of HaShem, and that will be the kingdom of the Age to Come.

One of the scribes from Magdala asks, "Rabbi, when will the kingdom of HaShem begin? You say it is coming, but why are you not raising an army to bring in the Age to Come?"

That is the question I have asked myself many times. When Rabbi Yeshua called me to follow him two months ago, I thought we would make a big army and take up the sword and throw off the Great Satan.

But so far, nothing. It is a sore trial to talk and talk on the kingdom of HaShem, when we should be making the kingdom of HaShem.

I hope Rabbi Yeshua will make a good answer.

Rabbi Yeshua stands as he is listening to a voice only he hears. "The kingdom of HaShem is all around you. It is breaking in on you. He who has ears to hear will hear it. He who has eyes to see will see it. The kingdom of HaShem is like a lump of leaven, which a woman hid in three measures of wheat."

I do not like this answer, which is no answer at all. I have had enough of idle talk. I wish for action. The blood of my brother keeps crying out from the ground to make a justice on him.

Footsteps overhead. Shouts.

I turn my eyes to the ceiling. Some fool outside has climbed the steps to the roof. Several fools, by the sound of it. Zavdai will be angry if—

A sharp thud on the roof.

My heart leaps within me.

Another thud.

It sounds as the fools brought a pick!

More thuds, and then the sound of breaking through.

Clay trickles onto my face.

A small hole appears in the roof between two of the wooden rafters. It is a good strong roof made of reeds laid across the rafters, with clay packed on top. And they are destroying it, for no cause.

My stomach boils with rage. That is a big evil, to break a roof.

Everybody is talking now, shouting.

A heavy iron bar pokes through the roof.

I try to seize it, but they pull it back fast.

Zavdai's face is pink, and he hops up and down for his anger. "Stop this, fools!"

If I could move through this crowd, I would push outside and run up the steps and throw them off the roof.

"Rabbi Yeshua!" Yoni shouts. "Make them stop!"

Rabbi Yeshua wears a crooked smile. "The kingdom of HaShem is breaking in on us, yes?"

The bar pokes through again. The hole is larger now.

I try again to seize the bar, but they are too quick for me.

More strikes with the pick. A handful of roof falls on my head, broken reeds and dried clay. More handfuls. More.

I cough and shake my head and feel the blood pounding in my temples.

The hole in the roof grows and grows. Four faces grin down on me.

I will go up there and break their teeth and see if they still grin.

All around me, men press back from the hole, complaining on the mess.

Rabbi Yeshua pushes through the crowd and joins me and Yoni. "It is good, yes?"

My head throbs for my anger. "No, it is not good." I do not see why Rabbi Yeshua thinks it is good. The hole will cost five *dinars* to repair, maybe six. Zavdai will need three men or four and a whole day to mend the damage. These fools will pay the cost.

Another section of roof falls between the rafters. Another. The hole is so big I could climb up through it.

I should go up and give the fools a lesson with my fists.

Something comes down through the hole.

A bed, lowered by ropes. With a cripple-man lying on it.

I should smite his face, only it is not done, to smite a cripple-man.

The bed reaches the floor. The cripple-man's face twists in a big agony.

I am sorry he has a big agony, but that is no good reason for breaking a roof, when there is a door already. Rabbi Yeshua should tell them all fools.

Rabbi Yeshua kneels by the man and kisses him. "My son, your sins are forgiven you."

A sick lump fills up all my belly. That was not well said. That is what we call a blasphemy. It means to make a scorn on HaShem. Rabbi Yeshua has no right to tell forgiveness. Only HaShem can forgive sins. Rabbi Yeshua can tell repentance every day in the year, but telling forgiveness makes a scorn on HaShem. All my body feels hot. Sweat runs down my sides, and my head feels light. I think I will vomit.

"Some of you ask if the son of Adam has authority to tell forgiveness for a man's sins." Rabbi Yeshua reaches down to the man. "My son, if your sins are truly forgiven, then stand up and walk. If your sins are not truly forgiven, then do not stand up and walk."

I cannot breathe for Rabbi Yeshua's boldness. That was overbold. A man cannot tell forgiveness for sins. HaShem will be angry on Rabbi Yeshua for that.

The man reaches up a feeble hand.

Rabbi Yeshua gives him a strong right hand. "Stand and walk."

Nothing happens.

The air in the room seems stolen away.

"Stand and walk!" Rabbi Yeshua says.

A big shaking runs all through the man's body.

Dark spots fill up the inside of my eyes. I taste bile in the back of my throat.

"Stand and walk by the power of HaShem!"

The man shakes and shakes all over. His arms gain strength. His neck gains strength. His body gains strength. He sits up in his bed. He pushes himself to his feet.

He throws his arms around Rabbi Yeshua and kisses him many times.

My head feels as it is swimming in water. It is not possible that I have seen what I have seen. I would not believe it if seven honest men swore by The Name that they saw it.

All the men in the house grumble on the matter. They stand back and scowl on Rabbi Yeshua and mutter behind their hands.

I cannot remember when Rabbi Yeshua ever looked so happy.

Yoni tugs on my sleeve. "Shimon the Rock, my eyes are lying to me. Did you see what I saw?"

I scowl him to silence. It is not the thing I saw that disturbs me. I have seen Rabbi Yeshua heal many men.

It is the thing I heard that disturbs me. Rabbi Yeshua told forgiveness to the man, which he had no right to do. That made a scorn on HaShem. Then he begged HaShem to show him righteous in the matter.

And HaShem showed him righteous in the matter. HaShem showed him righteous in making a scorn on HaShem. That is not a good sense.

Up has become down. Black has become white. Wisdom has become foolishness.

I do not know what to think.

Rabbi Yeshua has no right to tell forgiveness for sins.

And yet he told forgiveness for sins.

Rabbi Yeshua had a good name, and now he has lost it.

That will make a mighty scandal.

It is worse than the broken roof.

I know how to mend a roof that is broken.

I do not know how to mend a good name that is broken.

Yoni of Capernaum

I am so shocked I cannot stand. My hands and my feet feel numb.

I thought Rabbi Yeshua was making a paradox when he told forgiveness to the cripple-man.

I did not think he meant it. But he meant it, and he proved he meant it by telling healing to the man.

And the man was healed.

Everyone is leaving.

I would leave too, except I cannot feel my feet to walk out the door.

My father paces back and forth. His face is red and he is breathing hard.

Rabbi Yeshua's face is calm, but his hands clench tight, and sweat shines on his forehead. He puts on a strong face, but he knows he did a wrong thing, making a scorn on HaShem.

Shimon the Rock and Andre and Big Yaakov all went outside already. I never saw Shimon so angry, not even last year when we went fishing and Andre put pitch on his oar handle. I thought that was a good joke, but Shimon did not think so.

Toma Trouble sits in the corner with his head in his hands, muttering something. Philip and Natanel the hireling talk in quiet voices and throw angry looks on Rabbi Yeshua.

"Rabbi Yeshua, you should go back to Nazareth," my father says. "You made a big scandal on yourself. You made a big scandal on us."

I saw a fight once between two drunkards. The first drunkard was loud and foolish and called the second drunkard's mother a spreadlegs. The second drunkard put his fish knife in the first drunkard's belly and pierced his guts. The first drunkard's face turned white, and he fell on the ground and clutched at the blood oozing out of his belly. It took him three days to die, but he knew he was dead from the moment his guts were pierced.

That is how Rabbi Yeshua looks right now, like a man whose guts are pierced. His face is so white I think he will faint.

"What do you have to say?" my father says. "Why did you tell forgiveness to the man, when only HaShem can forgive sins? That makes a scorn on HaShem."

"Because ..." Rabbi Yeshua's cheek twitches, and he takes many breaths, long and slow. "Because that is what HaShem told me to say."

I close my eyes and try to make a sense on the matter. Rabbi Yeshua is a man. A man cannot forgive sins. Only HaShem can forgive sins. HaShem always forgives a man when he repents. All the scriptures say so. When a man repents, he goes to the Temple and makes a sacrifice, but the sacrifice is not the reason HaShem forgives his sins. Repentance is the reason. HaShem forgives any man who repents, whether he makes a sacrifice or no. The sacrifice is only a sign of the repentance. Then the priest tells the man his sins are forgiven, on account of his repentance, because Torah says it is so.

None of us saw the cripple-man repent, but Rabbi Yeshua is a prophet. I think he heard from HaShem that the man repented, even without seeing. I think he heard in his ear that HaShem forgave the man's sins. I think that is why he told forgiveness to the man.

I do not know that is what happened, but I think that is what happened.

Still, Rabbi Yeshua made a big scandal. He made it sound as he forgave the man himself, when what he meant is that HaShem forgave the man, and then HaShem told forgiveness to Rabbi Yeshua, and then Rabbi Yeshua told it to the man.

Rabbi Yeshua should have told the matter more clearly. I think he knows it now, but still I should explain it to him to make sure on it.

I open my eyes.

Rabbi Yeshua is gone. My father is gone. Everyone is gone except Toma Trouble, who sits in the corner. He looks as he was hammered on the head with the thighbone of a pig.

"Where did Rabbi Yeshua go?" I ask.

Toma Trouble gives me a blank stare like a sheep. "He went out. Your father shouted him all the way out to the street."

I tell Toma Trouble what I think is the explanation of the matter.

He tugs on his beard and narrows his eyes. "I doubt that is a right explanation."

I scowl on him. "It could be right."

"That is not a good logic, to say it could be right."

I do not care if Toma Trouble misbelieves me. He always wants a logic on any matter. I do not have a logic on this matter. I have a guess. It is a good guess, but it is not a logic.

We go outside and find Shimon the Rock and Andre and Big Yaakov talking to my father.

I tell them what I think is the explanation of the matter.

It takes the fourth part of an hour, for they are not quick of wit, but I finally convince Shimon and Andre and my father that I could be right.

Toma Trouble and Philip and Natanel the hireling come to listen, and I explain the matter to them all over again.

At last they say yes, most of them. Toma Trouble still says it is not a good logic. Big Yaakov only scowls on me.

"We should ask Rabbi Yeshua if that is how it was," says Toma Trouble. "Until I hear it from him, it will be only the boy's opinion on the matter."

I do not like his tone.

"Where is Rabbi Yeshua?" Toma Trouble asks.

Rabbi Yeshua's mother stands nearby, wringing her hands. "He ran away up toward the hills. I do not know where."

I say, "I know where. He went up there to speak to HaShem once, and I followed him."

"Go find him and ask him on the matter," Toma Trouble says. "If a man asks him hard questions, it is a big dishonor, but a boy can ask as many questions as he likes and it is only foolish questions."

I should remember to put a scorpion in Toma's cloak some night while he is sleeping.

The others all nod their heads.

"Go, Yoni," my father says. "The rabbi does not mind your foolish questions."

I do not wish to go. I am afraid I am wrong. If I am wrong, then Rabbi Yeshua made a scorn on HaShem and I will have to throw him off.

Rabbi Yeshua's mother takes my hand. "Please, you will find my son." Tears stand in her eyes, and she looks as she will start wailing.

So I go. I am afraid of what I will find, but I am more afraid of having a wailing woman. That would make another scandal.

One scandal is already a heavy load. I do not think even the Genius of Capernaum can carry two.

CHAPTER FIFTY-FOUR

Yeshua of Nazareth

'You think you can forgive sins? You are a fool. Only HaShem can forgive sins.'

'I ... I did what HaShem said to do.' I hurry up the path that leads to an olive grove where I can be alone. I need to speak with HaShem. I do not need to speak with the Accuser.

'Only HaShem can forgive sins. If you think to forgive sins, then you make a scorn on HaShem and you have left the path of truth.'

'I did what Abba told me.'

'Why do you call him Abba? You are not the son of HaShem. Israel is the son of HaShem, but you are not Israel. The anointed king of Israel is the son of HaShem, but you are not the anointed king of Israel.'

'I am the son of Adam, and Adam is the image of HaShem.'

'There will be a big scandal on account of what you did.'

'I did what HaShem told me. If it is wrong, then you accuse HaShem, not me.'

'You do not have the power to forgive sins.'

'I told forgiveness on behalf of HaShem.'

'You do not speak for HaShem. Who told you that you speak for HaShem?'

'HaShem told me I speak for him.'

'You are a liar and the son of a liar.'

'Let us see if I speak for HaShem. HaShem commands you to be silent. Now what do you say to that? If you are not silenced, then I do not speak for HaShem.'

∼

S ilence.

Cold sweat covers my back. HaShem keeps showing me new things. Today, he showed me forgiveness of sins is part of the kingdom of HaShem. When a man's sins are forgiven, the kingdom of HaShem grows and the kingdom of the Accuser shrinks. But I do not understand why HaShem told me to tell forgiveness first. If he had said to tell healing first, I would have done it, and then I could have told forgiveness later and it might not have made such a big scandal.

As it is, I made a mighty scandal, and now all my men are angry. The scribes from Magdala called me a liar before they left. I am sick in my heart. I did what HaShem told me. Why did he tell me such a hard thing?

I reach the olive grove. The day is hot and the air feels steamy and I wish I will sleep and never wake up.

I sit and lean against the trunk of a tree and close my eyes.

I am before the Throne.

The Messengers shout with great shouts. HaShem is dancing again. I have seen it now many times, and always it fills me with a big joy.

The Accuser is angry because I set a man free. Free from sickness and free from the guilt the Accuser speaks in his ear. The battle took strength from me. It gives me strength to see HaShem dancing.

For a time, I know nothing but the joy of HaShem.

I am at peace.

The Accuser is far from me.

"Rabbi Yeshua? Rabbi Yeshua!"

It is a woman's voice. I do not know this voice. I wish to be with HaShem. I am worn down by the battle. I do not have strength for another battle so soon.

"Rabbi Yeshua, help me!"

Slowly, I open my eyes. It is a hard thing to be torn from the Throne.

A young woman stands before me, clutching her hands and weeping. She is very beautiful. A few wisps of hair peek out from under her hair covering.

"What is it, my sister?" I stand and step toward her.

I never saw such a beautiful woman. She wears a thin tunic, too tight for her body. Her hands reach up to cover her face, and great sobs wrack her soul.

"Rabbi … I heard you can heal."

"HaShem heals. He is the one who gives me power to heal."

"I have a swollen part in my bosom, and I am afraid. My mother had it, and she died of the wasting disease."

I ask, "Which bosom has the swollen part?"

'*S*top *looking on the woman's bosoms. You have no right to look on them.*'

'*HaShem says I must look on them to know how to heal her.*'

'*Liar. You wish to lie with the woman. That is why you look on her bosoms.*'

'*I …*'

'*You have nothing to say? You wish to lie with her. That is half the loaf already. Why do you not lie with her? She is beautiful and you are far from the village and nobody sees. You could take her by force. She is some zonah who is nothing. She is not even from Capernaum. Nobody knows her. You could lie with her now, and who would know?*'

'*I …*'

'*What? Are you not a man?*'

'*I am a man.*'

'*Does your yetzer hara not burn within you to lie with this woman?*'

'My yetzer hara is strong.'
'Then take the woman. She will not say no. She lies with fifty men in a month.'

~

A thick fog clouds all my mind. Little Yaakov always says he has a mighty *yetzer hara* and I have none. He is wrong. HaShem gave me a mighty *yetzer hara*. I think it is more mighty than any man ever had. It burns strong inside me now. I am a man, and here is a beautiful woman. I would not be a man if there were no urge in me to have her.

But I have the Shekinah inside me also, burning fierce. It burns and it burns.

Bit by bit, the fog lifts from me.

"Rabbi, can you heal me?"

I look on the woman and think on my mother. I think on my sisters. I think what they would do if they were starving and had no family, no man to feed them.

I take the woman's hand. "Sit with me and tell your tale."

We sit with our backs to the olive tree.

The woman's name is Hana, and she comes from Magdala. Her father worked in a salting house, packing fish to be sent to Tiberias and Damascus and Caesarea and Rome. Hana had two sisters and no brothers. Then her mother died of the wasting disease. Then her father sliced his hand on a fish knife at the salting house, and the wound festered. A spirit of death came in through the wound. His hand turned red. His arm turned red. The spirit of death grew and grew, and his arm swelled up with it. After two weeks or three, the spirit of death took him.

Hana and her sisters had no brothers or uncles or cousins to take care of them.

After two days going hungry, they made a pact. One of them would become a *zonah* to earn money to feed them all. It was a hard choice, but otherwise they would all die. They drew finger-lots and Hana lost and she became a *zonah*. That was five years ago. Hana's

SON OF MARY 379

sisters are married now and give her money to eat, so she is a *zonah* no more, but she is ruined, and no man will ever take her for his woman. And now she has this curse from HaShem.

"HaShem hates me on account of my sin." Hana buries her face in her hands.

I do not know what to say, so I hold her hand and weep with her. She reminds me of my own sister Shlomi Dancefeet, who was born after our father Yoseph died. Shlomi was fortunate, for she had five brothers and an uncle and a cousin to watch over her. But what if she had not?

What if my little Shlomi Dancefeet grew up in a family with no man to earn bread? She is not crippled, so she cannot beg. She could sell herself as a slave, but there are evil men who buy girls as slaves so they can lie with them. She could live free and be a *zonah*.

I would still love Shlomi Dancefeet if she were a *zonah*. She is my sister. Being a *zonah* would not change that.

I kiss Hana's hand. "HaShem loves you."

Hana wails. "HaShem hates me."

I kiss her hand again. "HaShem loves you."

She shakes with great wracking sobs. "HaShem does not remember me. I am like a lost coin."

I kiss her hand again. "Two years before I became a man, my father went to Sukkot alone and left us ten *dinars* to live on until he came back. My mother kept the coins in her belt. On the second day, she counted and saw there were only nine, and her heart was crushed. A lost *dinar* meant we would all go hungry three days. The lost coin filled all her mind. She could think of nothing but that one lost coin.

"My mother was large with child, so she made me and my brothers and my sister take all the mats and pots out of our house. She gave me a broom and made me sweep the dirt floor, but I could not find the coin. She made Little Yaakov sweep. She made Yosi sweep. She made Little Miryam sweep. None of us could find the coin. She beat the floor with a stick until a great cloud of dust filled the house, but still we could not find the coin. She made us sweep and sweep and sweep in every corner. The cloud of dust went out in the street and filled all the village. All the people came to look, and they scowled on her and said she lost the coin on account of her sin.

"Then at last Yosi found the coin. It was black, covered with dirt. Yosi gave it to Imma, and she shouted with a great shout. She took the coin and washed it. She polished it with her own sleeve until it gleamed. At last it was the brightest coin of the ten. She kissed it and shouted for her joy and showed it to all the village, and she was glad, for her lost coin was found. And she loved it more than all the others, because she had to make a big search to find it."

Hana's hand grips mine so tight I think she will break my bones. "But ... HaShem did not lose me. I lost him. I went away far from him. HaShem is angry on me."

I kiss her hand again, for I hear cracks in her voice. "There is a man in our village whose name is called Yehuda the sheep-man, for he has many sheep. I heard he has a hundred sheep, and he knows every one by name. He loves his sheep more than any sheep-man ever did. Every morning he takes them out to the meadow to graze. He watches over them all the day. In the evening, he brings them back to the village and counts them into the pen.

"One night he brought them home early, ahead of a big storm. He counted them into the pen, and his heart nearly failed him to see one was missing.

"Yehuda the sheep-man locked up the ninety and nine and lit an oil lamp and took his staff and went looking for the one. The village called him mad, for it was only one sheep, one little ewe lamb. But he knew that ewe lamb by name, and he went out calling her.

"He searched in the meadow, but she was not there. The rains began.

"He searched on the stony path that leads down to the road, but she was not there. The wind howled its fury.

"He walked on the road while the rain and wind beat his face. He walked until his cloak was soaked through, and at last he saw a fire among some trees.

"He crept through the trees to see who makes a big fire on a stormy night. It was a gang of bandits. They had stolen his ewe lamb and were making ready to kill her and roast her and eat her.

"Yehuda the sheep-man ran into the clearing, shouting with a great shout, so mighty that half the bandits fell down stunned. The others took up swords to fight Yehuda the sheep-man.

"He had only his staff, but he was filled with a big rage on the bandits. He swung his staff on their swords and broke them all like reeds. He smote those evil men until they all fled or fell before his fury. The ewe lamb cowered before him on account of his rage, but his rage was not on her. His rage was on the bandits.

"He picked up his ewe lamb and kissed her many times and put her on his shoulders and ran all the way home through the howling storm.

"All the village heard his shouting over the rage of the storm. They came out to see this wonder, a sheep-man who left ninety and nine sheep safe at home to find one who was lost.

"Yehuda the sheep-man shouted with a great shout for all the village to see his lost ewe lamb who was found. He said, 'See, this lamb of mine was lost, and now she is found, my dear little Hana, the lamb of my heart.'"

Hana weeps loud. "HaShem is not angry on me?"

"HaShem is angry on those who did evil on you. HaShem loves you more than all the others. HaShem forgives you every sin you ever did."

Hana's body shakes all over. She cries and cries until she is done. When she is done, she looks on me and smiles.

"HaShem tells your bosom to be healed. HaShem tells the swollen part to return to normal. HaShem says you will live and not die."

Hana looks on her bosom. She puts her hand on her bosom, pressing hard. "Rabbi, the swollen part is gone!" She leaps to her feet. She dances for joy. She sings to HaShem.

I stand and give her a kiss and a kiss and a kiss. "You are the lamb of HaShem's heart."

Hana's smile is wide as her face. "Rabbi, you should come to Magdala and tell such a tale to my friends. Please, will you come to Magdala? Please?"

"I will ask HaShem if he will send me to Magdala."

Hana hops up and down for her joy. "HaShem will send you. I know he will send you."

"Go home and tell your friends what HaShem has done for you."

Hana nods and hurries down the hill toward Capernaum.

I sit again and close my eyes for my weariness. My arms feel like water. My legs feel like stone. I wish to sleep for a thousand years.

"Rabbi Yeshua," says a voice. "May I ask you a question?"

CHAPTER FIFTY-FIVE

Yoni of Capernaum

I hurry up the hill toward the olive grove where Rabbi Yeshua sometimes goes to talk to HaShem. I think he will be there now, and I will find him and ask on the matter of telling forgiveness to the man. We do not have much time. The people are angry, and soon all the village will have heard the tale and think Rabbi Yeshua made a scorn on HaShem. It is a good luck he has me to solve the scandal for him.

I see something moving under the olive tree far ahead.

It is a person.

It is two persons.

It is Rabbi Yeshua and a woman.

My head feels faint, and my heart hurts my chest with all its pounding. My feet have forgotten how to walk. There are many grapevines here. I duck down so they cannot see me. I crawl closer, bit by bit, to see what is happening.

The woman is a young woman, no more than twenty. She is very beautiful. Rabbi Yeshua holds her hand and smiles on her.

That is a mighty scandal. If I held the hand of a beautiful young woman, I would wish to lie with her. Big Yaakov and Toma Trouble sneer on me and call me a boy, but they do not know the wicked thoughts I have when I look on a woman. Rabbi Yeshua is a *tsaddik*, but even so, he should not sit alone with a beautiful woman, holding her hand.

I creep closer to see what will happen.

The woman is talking to Rabbi Yeshua.

As I get closer, I hear her words.

She is a *zonah*.

My lungs cannot take in breath. This is a mightier scandal than I thought. I am sick to my heart. I am terrified to see what will happen next. I am dying to see what will happen next. I crawl closer.

The *zonah* cries and cries.

Rabbi Yeshua kisses her hand.

I think I will faint. I cannot bear to watch. I cannot look away.

Rabbi Yeshua tells her a tale of his mother, how she lost a coin. He tells her a tale of some sheep-man in his village, how he lost a ewe lamb.

The *zonah* wails in a loud voice.

Rabbi Yeshua tells her HaShem is not angry on her. He says HaShem loves her. He says HaShem forgives her all her sins she ever did.

Rabbi Yeshua tells healing to her.

She jumps to her feet, laughing, crying, shouting, dancing, giving glory to HaShem.

Rabbi Yeshua gives her a kiss and a kiss and a kiss and then sends her away.

She passes by the row of grapevines where I am hiding and smiles on me.

I never had such a beautiful woman smile on me. My face feels hot and sweat rushes down my sides and my blood rises inside me. Wicked thoughts shout loud in my mind.

Rabbi Yeshua still sits under the tree. His eyes are closed, and he looks like a mighty warrior who has fought a great battle and fainted for weariness.

I should leave him alone to rest. But I cannot leave him alone to rest. He made a scandal in the village today, and it is on my shoulders to unmake the scandal.

I stand quietly and move on silent feet toward him. I think he is asleep. His face is peaceful. I hate myself, but I must wake him.

"Rabbi Yeshua, may I ask you a question?"

His eyelids flicker open, and he stares on me like a man in a fog. At last his eyes show signs that he knows me. "Not … now, Yoni."

I should leave him alone, but I have my duty. I sit beside him. "Rabbi, all the village has heard of the scandal you made."

"I … yes, I made a scandal."

"How is it that you told forgiveness to the cripple-man? Only HaShem can forgive sins."

Rabbi Yeshua says nothing.

I look on his face. His eyebrows hunch together, and his mouth is a straight line. I think he does not have an answer.

"I told the others you are a prophet. HaShem showed you the man had repented. HaShem told you the man was forgiven. So you told forgiveness to the man, because HaShem told it to you. That is not making a scorn on HaShem. That is only doing the work of a prophet. But the others do not believe me. They want to know if that is the way of it."

Rabbi Yeshua thinks for a long time. "That was well said, Yoni. Yes, I think that is the way of it."

"I liked the way you told forgiveness to the *zonah*. You showed her forgiveness first in a tale. Then she could believe when you told her forgiveness after. When you tell a tale of forgiveness, nobody will say you make a scorn on HaShem, because it is only a tale. But a tale sneaks in through a man's ears and hides in his heart and makes him think it is all his own idea, even if it is yours. That is a good way to tell forgiveness."

Rabbi Yeshua's mouth falls open. He stares on me as I have told him I went walking on the lake this morning to dig fish for my sister Caesar. "That was very well said, Yoni."

I am so happy I cannot sit still. I jump up and run back toward the village.

I will tell the others I was right.

I will tell them Rabbi Yeshua does not make a scorn on HaShem, because he only tells forgiveness when HaShem tells him to, not on his own authority.

And I will tell them Rabbi Yeshua told me twice in a row that I said a thing well.

I want to see Toma Trouble's face when I tell him that.

Yeshua of Nazareth

I sit quietly, thinking on what Yoni said. HaShem showed me a new thing today.

I knew the kingdom of HaShem is freedom. Freedom from sickness. Freedom from evil spirits.

But HaShem showed me it is also freedom from the Accuser, which stabs a man with his guilt over and over.

I see now that the man could not be set free from his sickness until he was first set free from his guilt. The Accuser would not allow it. The Accuser would rub his face in his guilt. Only forgiveness from HaShem can break the power of the Accuser.

That is a great matter, and if that were the only thing I learned, it would be a mighty victory.

But see how it terrified the village to hear me tell forgiveness. They thought I made a scorn on HaShem, and their teeth were set on edge.

I must continue to tell forgiveness.

HaShem says I must tell forgiveness.

Forgiveness is the coin of the kingdom.

But Yoni showed me an even greater thing. The better way to tell forgiveness is through a tale. A tale does not set a man's teeth on edge, for he thinks it is only some idle tale.

But no tale is an idle tale. That is a lie of the Accuser. The scriptures are full of many tales. If they seem like idle tales to some, that is the wisdom of HaShem to hide his truth in idle tales.

A moldy purse may hold a golden coin.

From now on, I will tell more idle tales.

CHAPTER FIFTY-SIX

Yaakov of Nazareth

"Little Yaakov, stop! There is some man to see you."

I do not wish to stop to see some man. My brothers and I worked in Tsipori today, and then I haggled long in the market for a thing that will make my woman's heart dance for joy. I got a mighty bargain, and now I wish to give it to her.

"Little Yaakov, there is news on your brother!"

I stop. I am very tired, for we were doing stonework in the hot sun all day, and then I bargained hard, and then we came home by a walk of one hour, and last of all we made the steep climb up to Nazareth. But I must know what Yeshua is doing.

Old Yonatan the leather-man sits just inside the village gate with the other elders, scowling on me. He points down the hill to the giant rock by the side of the road at a distance of fifty paces. "Your friend is under the shade of that rock."

I wonder what friend would wait outside the village when he could go to my house and wait in comfort.

My brothers and I walk back down the path toward the rock and go around it to the far side.

A man wearing rags lies in the shade napping. He wakes when he hears us and grunts and stands. His face is a great mass of bumps, bigger than boils. His fingers are worn down to stumps.

I step back a pace. "Who are you?"

"Where is Yeshua the healer? I heard he lives in Nazareth."

I point to his hands. "Stand back!"

"I heard Yeshua healed a man with the mighty leprosy. Where is he?"

My face feels hot. Yeshua should be raising up an army, not wasting his time healing the mighty leprosy. "I … we do not know where is Yeshua. He left here two months ago to tell the kingdom of HaShem."

"Can you heal me?" The leper makes a step toward us.

I leap back. "When Yeshua returns, then will be a good time for you to ask after him."

"When will Yeshua return?" The leper makes another step.

"Stand back, man! Yeshua will return here soon. That is all I know."

"Tomorrow? Next week? Can you give a hungry man a round of bread?"

I point to Yosi. "Run to Shimon the baker and get two rounds of bread. And ask Uncle Halfai for some raisins and bring them here."

Yosi hurries off.

Thin Shimon and Yehuda Dreamhead run after him.

I did not tell them to go too. Now I am left alone with this leper.

"Perhaps you can heal me?" The leper stretches his hands toward me.

I step backward. "When Yeshua returns, you can ask him to heal you."

All the hope runs out of the man's face. "I came here by a walk of one day because I heard Yeshua of Nazareth heals lepers."

"From where do you come?"

"Bethlehem of Galilee. I was begging for bread outside the village gate, and a man told me he had been a leper and a prophet named Yeshua of Nazareth healed him."

I try to think what Yeshua would do. He would ask the man his story and they would sit together quietly and the man would tell him everything he ever did. In the fourth part of an hour, Yeshua would be the man's best friend. I have seen Yeshua do that a hundred times. He would do it even for a leper.

I am not Yeshua, but I can hear a man's tale. My brothers will take time to buy food for the man. I point to the shade. "Sit, friend, and tell me who you are and where you come from and how you came to be a leper."

Within the fourth part of an hour, I have heard his story.

"Little Yaakov!" Yosi shouts from the village gate. "We have the rounds of bread and some raisins! And Old Hana the cheese-woman gave us some cheese for a kindness."

"Stay here," I tell the leper. I hurry back to the gate to get the food.

My brothers do not wish to come outside the village. They hand me the food wrapped in a large fig leaf. Their eyes are huge and they look past me.

I turn around and see the leper has followed me.

There is a hiss of anger inside the gate. The village elders stand and point fingers on the leper. "You, man! Stand back!"

The leper scowls on them. "When is Yeshua of Nazareth to return? I met a man he healed who was a leper. He told how Yeshua sends away evil spirits and healed a man with a withered arm and a woman with the summer fever."

Old Yonatan the leather-man curls his lip in a sneer. "Yeshua is gone and we do not know when he will return, and it is a lying tale that he can heal. If he could heal, he would not dishonor us by healing other villages when he should do it here first. You go somewhere else."

The leper shakes his head and points to me. "This man is his brother and says Yeshua is telling the kingdom of HaShem and will return here soon. Do you call him a liar?"

Old Yonatan the leather-man spits the ground. "I call him the son of a spreadlegs. Why should Yeshua tell the kingdom of HaShem? Does he think he is somebody? He is a *mamzer*, and that is a *haryo*. If he tries to make himself somebody in other villages, we will tell them what we know on the matter. You, man, go to some other village. We do not welcome lepers here."

My hands curl in fists. If Old Yonatan were not an elder of the village, I would break his teeth in his jaw. I put the food on the ground and step away from it and face the leper. "Friend, here is some food. There is a cave down the road two hundred paces where you can sleep. When Yeshua returns—"

"Yeshua will not return," says Old Yonatan.

I cross my arms on my chest. "Yeshua will return soon. He will heal the man. And he will call down fire from HaShem to destroy you and your house."

Old Yonatan sneers on me. He puts a finger over one nostril and blows the foul refuse of the other at me.

I leap back and twist away.

My legs tangle beneath me.

I land hard on my belly.

Yosi and Thin Shimon and Yehuda Dreamhead crowd around me.

"Come away with us."

"He is a fool."

"Do not smite an old man."

I stand slowly and spit Old Yonatan's feet. "I do not smite *haryo*. I throw it in the leather-man's piss-pool."

Old Yonatan's face turns purple. He takes a step toward me.

I should break his teeth, even if he is a village elder.

My brothers pull me back. "Do not think on him. Think what joy your woman will have when you show her the thing you bought her."

I am angry on Old Yonatan, but he is *haryo* and only a fool thinks on *haryo*. My woman will be glad when she sees the gift I bought her —a tiny bottle of Roman glass, filled with a few drops of perfume. When you hold it in the sun, it shines with many colors. My woman will make a big delight in it.

When we come to our house, I reach inside my cloth belt where I carry my things.

I feel a dampness there.

Something sharp.

I jerk my hand back.

A drop of blood wells up from my fingertip.

My heart skips. I stop and peer inside my belt.

The bottle has become shards.

When I fell on my belly, I must have broken it.

The perfume is all leaked out, and the beautiful glass is destroyed.

My brothers crowd around me, staring on my loss. It cost me half a *dinar* and an hour of hard bargaining.

All my body is hot.

All my mind is cold.

"What are you going to do?" Yosi asks.

We stand alone in the street at our end of the village. Nobody is watching us.

Thin Shimon grins. "Yehuda Dreamhead, bring out the piss pot from the house."

Yehuda Dreamhead goes in the house and comes out with an earthen jar. I hear the slosh of piss and smell its reek.

"Give Yehuda the bottle," Thin Shimon says.

Then I see what he has in mind, and I grin on his cleverness.

I shake out the broken bits of glass into the piss pot.

My brothers grin on me.

Yehuda Dreamhead takes the piss pot away up the street.

It is a sight we see every day in our village. The youngest son of every house carries the piss pot to the north end of the village and then outside the village fifty paces to the leather-man's pool, where hides are always soaking.

I would not be a leather-man for all the gold in Egypt and all the ivory in Ethiopia.

A leather-man always reeks of piss because he wades in his piss-pool, kneading the hides with his bare feet.

The pool is large and filled to the level of a man's knees, and one cannot see the bottom.

This month or the next or the next, Yoseph the leather-man will step on a shard of broken glass.

And I will be avenged.

CHAPTER FIFTY-SEVEN

Yoni of Capernaum

"I never saw you so quiet, Yoni. Are you sick?" Shimon the Rock takes my hand in his.

I do not know what to say. I did not talk much last night or this morning. I am afraid if I open my mouth, my mighty secret will fall out, that Rabbi Yeshua was alone with a *zonah* yesterday. He did not do anything wrong, but still it will make another big scandal, on top of telling forgiveness to the cripple-man.

We are walking along the road on the north side of the Lake of Ginosar. Rabbi Yeshua walks ahead of us, holding hands with his mother. He did not say where we are going, but this road will take us by a walk of one hour to Bethsaida, which is across the border in the territory of King Herod's brother Philip. I think Rabbi Yeshua means to leave Capernaum for a few days. People are still angry on him for telling forgiveness to the cripple-man.

My father was angry also, even after I explained the matter. He said Rabbi Yeshua did not make a scorn on HaShem, but still he made a big confusion, and he should go away until the village cools down. My father is a priest and a man of honor, and when he explains the matter to the village, they will accept. But he needs time to explain the matter, for he is only one man.

I do not know where we are going. We could go beyond Bethsaida and down the other side of the lake, but all the villages on that side are goy. We would have to sleep in some cave or out in the open field, for we will never take lodging from goyim.

I think we could stay in Bethsaida, if the scandal has not got there ahead of us. Bethsaida is a big village, big as Capernaum. Shimon the Rock and Andre were born there, but their father brought their family to Capernaum seven years ago on account of the overgreed of the tax-farmer at the border.

"The village will be talking on this scandal for many days," Shimon the Rock says.

My hand feels damp and my tongue sticks to the roof of my mouth, for I am afraid he is right. And I am sick for my fear that someone else saw the *zonah*.

Andre shakes his head. "Our fathers will make the matter straight. But it would have been better if Rabbi Yeshua did not tell forgiveness to the cripple-man. He should have just healed him and sent him to the Temple to repent."

"Someone should explain the matter to Rabbi Yeshua," Shimon the Rock says. His voice sounds tight in his throat.

"I wonder who would be so bold as to explain the matter to the rabbi?" Big Yaakov says. "If only we knew some talkative boy who never worries on the matter of dishonoring his elders."

"There was a talkative boy here once," says Toma Trouble. "He used to speak many words about the deep things of HaShem. But I think we lost him. I have not heard a word from him since yesterday."

They are all thick as mud. I cannot bear to hear them jabber any longer. "You would not know a deep thing of HaShem if you fell in it to the level of your nose."

Shimon the Rock makes a big laughter. "So you are not lost, Yoni! We thought you had run away or been stolen or fallen in some deep thing of HaShem and drowned."

The other men laugh.

I am sick to my death of them laughing on me. I did think of a deep thing of HaShem last night. I was going to ask Rabbi Yeshua about it today, but I think I will throw it in their faces now.

Andre squints hard on me. "Oy, I know that look. See, Yoni has a deep thing of HaShem to tell us. He has been silent, trying to make us beg. Shall we beg?"

Big Yaakov falls on his knees in front of me. "Yoni, I beg! Tell me your deep thing of HaShem!"

I kick hard at his underparts.

He stops my foot with both hands. He stands and raises my foot to the level of my waist.

I scowl on him. "Let go of my foot."

He begins walking while holding my foot.

I have to hop after him to keep up.

Rabbi Yeshua has been walking far ahead. He turns to look back on us.

Big Yaakov lets go of my foot. "Rabbi Yeshua, Yoni has a deep thing of HaShem he wishes to tell."

Rabbi Yeshua's eyebrows rise. "Then I wish to hear it. Yoni sees many deep things of HaShem."

Big Yaakov's mouth falls open.

We walk until we reach the rabbi and his mother. I had thought to tell the matter only to Rabbi Yeshua. It would be a waste of good breath to tell the matter to these dull-wits.

"Come walk with me and Imma and tell what is the deep thing of HaShem you saw," Rabbi Yeshua says. "But hurry. There is a thing we must do, and it will not wait."

I follow after him. "Yesterday, you said the kingdom is breaking in on us. And then what broke in on us?"

"An iron bar." Andre makes a big grin.

"That is not deep."

"A very deep iron bar," Big Yaakov says.

"Now you are making idle talk. What was behind the iron bar?"

"Four men," says Toma Trouble. "Four is a deep number, yes?"

"And what was behind the four men with the iron bar?"

"A cripple-man," Shimon the Rock says.

"And what happened with the cripple-man?"

A silence falls all around, for they do not wish to talk on the matter of the scandal Rabbi Yeshua made.

Big Yaakov coughs on the back of his hand. That is what he does when he thinks I should stop talking.

I hope he coughs his lips off. "Rabbi Yeshua healed the cripple-man, yes?"

Toma Trouble makes a big scowl on me.

"That is all your deep thing of HaShem?" Shimon the Rock asks.

"Rabbi Yeshua has healed many cripple-men," Big Yaakov says.

"We expect better from the Genius of Capernaum," Andre says.

Toma Trouble says, "Rabbi Yeshua, what do you think on the matter Yohanan the son of Zavdai tells?"

Rabbi Yeshua acts as he did not hear Toma Trouble. He makes quick steps, like a man who thinks only on the place he is going.

I will have to explain the matter myself, and that is a hard labor to explain a deep thing to dull-wits. They are all like my father, who only cares that the men paid for the damage to the roof and that it will be repaired before Shabbat. He did not see that a deep thing happened in our house. People will be talking on this deep thing for many weeks. Maybe a whole year.

"You are all blind! Did you not see? Rabbi Yeshua said the kingdom of HaShem was breaking in. The cripple-man broke in, and then Rabbi Yeshua made him whole! When Rabbi Yeshua heals a man, *that is the in-breaking of the kingdom of HaShem.*"

Big Yaakov grins on me. "Yoni, you are not making a good sense. Did our genius run away? Has some dream on a woman dulled your wits?"

"I ... that is foolishness." Heat rises in my cheeks.

The men laugh.

"Do not be ashamed," Andre says. "They are only dreams, and it means you are a man at last. It is past time that you should begin having such—"

"I did not dream on a woman! The kingdom of HaShem is a large matter, and none of you see it. You are all fools, and Rabbi Yeshua should throw you off. Wherever we go, Rabbi Yeshua tells tales of the kingdom of HaShem. Then he sends away evil spirits. What does that mean?"

"It means evil spirits fear the coming of the kingdom of HaShem," Shimon the Rock says.

"No, fool! It means sending away evil spirits is the beginning of the kingdom of HaShem."

"That is not the kingdom of HaShem," says Andre.

"When Rabbi Yeshua healed the mighty leper, that is the beginning of the kingdom of HaShem."

"That is a bad logic you make," says Toma Trouble.

Shimon the Rock frowns. "The mighty works of Rabbi Yeshua are good works, but mighty works have been seen before in Israel. The kingdom of HaShem has not been seen before in Israel. When the kingdom of HaShem comes, HaShem himself will return in power and crush the goyim. When the kingdom of HaShem comes, every eye will see it."

"No, you are wrong. The tales Rabbi Yeshua tells are tales of a kingdom of HaShem that is hidden. It is among us, but not seen. Rabbi Yeshua's mighty works *are* the beginning of the kingdom of HaShem, only hidden."

Big Yaakov picks up a stone and throws it in the Lake of Ginosar. It makes a big splash, and ripples go out from it. Then it lies hidden. "I think a hidden kingdom of HaShem is not the one we look for."

"That is not the kingdom of HaShem the prophets have told." Shimon the Rock gives me a look as I am a fool.

I am used to this look, but I do not mind being thought a fool by a dull-wit. "You should let Rabbi Yeshua's words and his actions tell you what is the kingdom of HaShem. You should not tell him what is the kingdom of HaShem. His actions and his words tell the same tale, if you only had eyes to see it."

Shimon's hand tightens on mine. "So you think Rabbi Yeshua's tales of the kingdom *are* the kingdom?"

For a moment, I am unable to breathe. Shimon the Rock has seen a thing even I did not see—that the telling of a tale could be part of the kingdom of HaShem. That is a very deep thing of HaShem. I am sure Shimon does not even know what he said.

Shimon grins on me. "A tale of the kingdom is not the kingdom. A dream on a woman is not a woman."

The other men laugh, for Shimon the Rock makes my deep thing of HaShem sound like a big foolishness.

I do not laugh.

It is not a big foolishness.

If Shimon the Rock thinks to shame me when I tell the deep things of HaShem, then I will not tell any more deep things of HaShem.

It is not my fault if I do not understand all the meaning of the deep things of HaShem. I will. At least I see there is a deep thing to be understood.

Shimon the Rock is a fool and does not see there is a deep thing here.

I am twice a fool if I try to tell the matter to him.

I throw off Shimon's hand from mine.

Shimon the Rock is not my friend.

A friend does not mock his friend for trying to know the deep things of HaShem.

CHAPTER FIFTY-EIGHT

Yeshua of Nazareth

'You waste your time healing the sick, when you could be bringing in the kingdom of HaShem.'
            'Healing the sick is the kingdom of HaShem.'
'You waste your time telling tales.'
'Telling tales is also the kingdom of HaShem.'
'You waste your time with these men.'
'These men are also the kingdom of HaShem.'
'You waste your time on Yoni, for he is conceited and he spies on you.'
'Yoni is a lamb in the heart of HaShem.'
'You waste your time.'
'Do I waste my time sending away evil spirits?'
Silence.
'My men are the men Abba gave me.'
Silence.
'My tales are the tales Abba gave me.'
Silence.
'I heal with the power Abba gave me.'
'Where are you going today? There is nothing this way but a long line

of oxcart drivers and a tax-farmer's booth and a border and beyond it some village.'

'Abba sends me this way.'

'You waste time waiting here with the oxcart drivers. A man with no cart can walk through the border crossing free.'

'Abba tells me to wait.'

'Surely you do not think to—'

'HaShem commands that you will leave me now.'

❦

Silence.

I stand in line at the tax-farmer's booth, just before the bridge over the river. Many oxcart drivers wait to pay the tax-farmer so they can pass from Herod's lands into Philip's lands. The tollbooth is well made of fine stone. I have not come to see the booth.

Outside the booth are two soldiers of King Herod who guard the tolls collected here. I have not come to see the soldiers.

Inside the booth sits a man with a stylus and a wax tablet on a lapboard across his knees. He wears a white linen tunic and a fine belt of red-dyed linen. A gold chain hangs on his neck. I have not come to see his fine clothing or his gold chain.

I have come to see this man.

He looks on me and his eyes widen to the size of Temple shekels and his mouth drops.

I think today is a good day for HaShem to set this man free, but I do not know if he will choose to be set free. "Friend, do you know my name?"

It is a foolish question. Of course he knows my name. Everybody in these parts knows my name.

"You are Rabbi Yeshua of Nazareth, who lives here with us in Capernaum." His voice sounds parched like the desert sands.

It cuts my heart that he should fear me. I smile on him. "I am looking for a man in these parts. Do you know all the men around here?"

He nods, and the fear runs out of his eyes. "Who do you look for?"

I squat on the floor like a peasant, so I am looking up on him. Perhaps he will feel I am no threat this way. "I do not know the man's name. I will tell you his tale, and perhaps you will know of him. Once there was a boy, the son of a Levite, who was a scribe. This boy learned to read and write and do sums from his father. He excelled in Torah and wished to study with a great sage of Israel. Then his father died of the belly-fever, and his mother drowned herself in despair, and the boy was thrown out in the streets hungry."

The tax-farmer's face has become pale, and his forehead is damp, though he sits in the shade of cool stone.

I hear the Accuser whisper in his ear how this boy died long ago.

I think of the boy he was. I wish I could hold that boy and comfort him now. I love that boy who once was, and I love this man who now is.

"This boy found work doing sums for a corrupt tax-farmer who paid him almost nothing, but at least he could eat. He hated his work, but he was not free to leave, for he had no other way to earn bread."

The tax-farmer leans back, and his breath rasps like a man carrying a great weight a long way up a steep hill. "What do you want, Rabbi Yeshua?"

I hear the Accuser complain on him how Rabbi Yeshua has come to call him a sinner.

I have not come to call him a sinner. I have come to call him my brother.

"This boy grew to be a man, and his master died, and he rose to the position of tax-farmer himself. He learned he could charge men two *dinars* and pay the king one. He learned that bread tastes like ashes when all men scorn him. He learned that sleep has no sweetness when a man is not free. He learned that a man can walk unchained beneath the sun and yet be held captive by the Accuser. This man cried out to HaShem for freedom, and HaShem heard his cry."

The tax-farmer cannot look my eye.

I hear the Accuser shout the tax-farmer to call the soldiers to send me away, for I am here to plunder the king.

I am here to take plunder, but not from the king.

"Friend, I must find this man, for I have a word from HaShem for him."

Tears pool in the tax-farmer's eyes, but his face is set hard and tight against me.

The Accuser sings to him a song of easy wealth, of sinful women, of fine wine. It sings how I am a destroyer of joy.

"Friend, do you know this man I look for?"

The tax-farmer's chin quivers and his whole body shakes. "This man's name is called … Mattityahu the son of Halfai. His friends call him Mattai."

I hear the Accuser rage on him, screaming how HaShem hates him, how his sins reach up to heaven, how he can never be free of his guilt.

I know he can be free. I want freedom for him, but this man cannot be given freedom.

He must take it.

"Friend, I have a tale for this man Mattai, if you should see him. In the days of King David, his own son Absalom rose up against him. Absalom used his father's concubines on the palace roof for a pleasure. He roused all Israel against his father. He made a big war on his father in hope to kill him and rule in his place. First the war went ill against David, and he fled for his life on foot. Then the war went ill against Absalom, and he fled for his life on a mule. His hair caught in the branches of an oak tree. King David's commander Joab found Absalom and put a javelin through his heart. That was what Absalom expected, for that was what he deserved. But when King David heard the news, he fell on his face and wept. He threw dirt in his own hair. He mourned his son with many tears. King David would have forgiven his son. But his son fled before him and was killed without need by the Accuser."

I stand, and my heart beats hard and fast, for now comes my final throw. "Friend, I beg you. If you see this Mattai, please, you will tell him Rabbi Yeshua longs to call him brother. Rabbi Yeshua calls him to live and not die. Rabbi Yeshua calls him into the kingdom of HaShem."

The tax-farmer's face is stone.

I have said all I can say. I cannot command freedom.

Abba says I must go now.

I turn and walk out of the tollbooth.

Yoni and Shimon the Rock and Big Yaakov and the others all stare on me as I am a leper.

They are right, for I am a leper, I am a *zonah*, I am a *mamzer*, I am a tax-farmer, I am all who cry out to Abba for freedom.

The Accuser sneers me for a fool. The Accusers says if I would plunder it, I must take its captives by force.

I walk, but I hear nothing.

I walk more, but still I hear nothing.

I walk more, and my heart feels as it is balanced on the edge of a knife, but still—

"Rabbi, wait!"

I spin to look.

Mattai has come out of the tollbooth. He throws his wax tablet and stylus on the ground. He stares after me, frozen, his eyes begging for mercy.

My heart rises and joy floods my veins, for it is enough. I hear the sound of the Messengers shouting around the Throne. I hear the music of HaShem dancing.

I run to Mattai and throw my arms around him and give him a kiss and a kiss and a kiss. "My brother, do you wish to be free?"

His arms seize me. "Leave me, Rabbi, for … I am a sinful man."

"HaShem forgives you all that you ever did." My heart swims in joy, and I laugh with a great laugh.

High up and far away, the Accuser shrieks as it flees.

Mattai laughs for his freedom. He laughs for his joy. He laughs for the in-breaking of the kingdom of HaShem. At last he releases me from his grip. "Rabbi, there is a poor, foolish man who wishes to follow after you, only he is not worthy—"

"HaShem says you are worthy. Follow me. I will give you a mighty work to do."

I hear a hiss of disbelief behind me.

I turn to look on my men, for I have made a new scandal.

Shimon's face is stone.

Andre and Big Yaakov cross their arms on their chests.

Toma the boat maker's mouth hangs open as he cannot believe what his eyes tell.

Imma stares on me as I am a tax-farmer.

Philip and Natanel cannot look my eye.

Yoni's eyes gleam with a big shock.

I take Mattai's hand in mine, and I smile on Yoni, for he is my hope. If he understands, then the rest will also. "When a man is set free, *that* is the in-breaking of the kingdom of HaShem. Those with eyes will see this deep thing of HaShem."

Yoni's face does not move, and his scowl says he does not accept.

My chest aches. I do not wish to lose Yoni. I do not wish to lose any of them.

I have plundered the Accuser's storehouse. I beg Abba that the Accuser will not plunder mine.

CHAPTER FIFTY-NINE

Shimon of Capernaum

'It is an outrage beyond bearing. You should throw off the rabbi.'

'I ... I promised to follow after him, wherever he goes, until forever.'

'You were tricked. He is a deceiver. He tells tales of the kingdom of HaShem, but where is the kingdom of HaShem?'

'Yes, but—'

'He calls lepers clean, when only a priest can call a leper clean.'

'Yes, but—'

'He tells forgiveness to a man, when only HaShem can forgive sins.'

'Yes, but—'

'Now he walks with this tax-farmer, this *haryo*. He gave him a kiss and a kiss and a kiss! He holds hands with him now as he walks! Rabbi Yeshua is a friend of your enemy. You must throw him off, or you are a friend of a tax-farmer.'

~

My head is filled with a big fog. My heart aches for its pounding. Bile rises in my throat. I would vomit if it would give me relief, but nothing will give me relief. I do not know what to do. I should throw off Rabbi Yeshua, but I made a promise, and I am a man of my word. But have I not been deceived? Rabbi Yeshua is not what I thought he was.

A small hand takes mine.

Yoni's hand.

His face is tortured and sad. "You are angry on the rabbi, yes?"

"He did a big foolishness." I spit the road.

"Very deep foolishness," Yoni says.

"He says the tax-farmer is forgiven by HaShem of all he ever did."

"It is more foolish than yesterday, when he told forgiveness to the cripple-man," Yoni says.

"That was …" I do not know what to think. If the rabbi had no authority to tell forgiveness to the cripple-man, how did he make the man whole?

"It is more foolish than when he told forgiveness to the *zonah*."

I turn to stare on Yoni. "What *zonah*?"

Yoni's hand flies up to his mouth, and his face turns the color of wine. "I … Rabbi Yeshua told me once that a *zonah* repented and he told forgiveness to her."

I am more shocked than I ever was. A man should not speak with a woman, for women are full of lewdness and idle talk. Rabbi Yeshua is a *tsaddik*, and he sometimes speaks with the women of our family. Perhaps HaShem winks on a *tsaddik* who speaks with women of good family.

But even a *tsaddik* does not make words with a *zonah*. It is not done.

Yoni's face turns dark and hard as the stones we use to build our homes. "But I have not told you the most foolish thing Rabbi Yeshua ever did."

"You should not say it. Guard yourself from the Evil Tongue, for that is a sin—"

"You would not believe who Rabbi Yeshua once told forgiveness to."

"I do not wish to hear it."

"Rabbi Yeshua once told forgiveness to men who were his own friends, men who threw him off and ran like women."

All my body is ice.

I cannot walk.

I cannot think.

A knife is in my heart.

Yoni is impudent and conceited and talks overmuch.

But even an impudent, conceited, talkative boy can tell a true word.

The others are walking ahead of us. Yoni still holds my hand. He looks on me with eyes I cannot look back on.

I hurry after the others. I do not run. A man of honor does not run. I walk speedily.

I pass Andre.

I pass Big Yaakov.

I pass Toma the boat maker and Philip and Natanel the hireling.

I pass Rabbi Yeshua's mother, who walks with heavy steps.

I come up behind Rabbi Yeshua. He still holds hands and talks with the tax-farmer and laughs. He seems to have forgotten me, but I know in my heart he will never forget me, not if I live to be as old as our prophet Moses.

I seize his free hand in mine.

Rabbi Yeshua looks on me, and his eyes are the eyes of a friend.

He smiles on me. "Shimon, my brother."

Far above us, beyond the range of hearing, some bird of prey screams a cry of rage.

Miryam of Nazareth

Your son makes another scandal.'

'My son has his reasons.'

'What reasons? He called a tax-farmer his brother.'

'I ... that is a hard thing.'

'It is a thing that cannot be forgiven.'

'He must have his reasons.'

'What reasons? Tax-farmers are wicked and make a theft on the people. What will Little Yaakov say when he hears your son call a tax-farmer his brother?'

'He will be very angry. I am glad Yeshua refused to let him come, for he would fight Yeshua on the matter.'

'Yeshua would not fight back. He is weak.'

'He is kind.'

'Kind is the same as weak. Your son will never make a war on the Great Satan.'

'He will.'

'He will never make a freedom on the land.'

'He will.'

'He will never crush your village and make a justice on your name.'

'He ...' I cannot say my son will crush our village.

'You know I speak true.'

'My son will make a justice on me. He said he will.'

'He means to, for he loves you, but he is kind and he will not. He will never confront. He will never tell them their sin. That is his weakness. You know I speak true.'

'He is kind. I thank HaShem every day in the year that my son is kind.'

'That is a good thing when he is kind on you. It is a weakness when he is kind on the village, when he will not defend. And you know he will never defend. When the Evil Boy kicked Little Yaakov in the underparts, did Yeshua defend?'

'He was only a child.'

'When the Evil Boy threw haryo on you and squeezed your bosoms and reached for your woman parts, did your son defend?'

'He was not yet a man.'

'Your son will never defend.'

'He is a man now. He will defend.'

'When will he defend?'

'He will defend when he wears the Ring of Justice. And Thin Shimon will find it for him. I know he will.'

'Even if he wears the Ring of Justice, he will not defend.'

'He will defend if he must.'

'What would make him defend?'

'If all the village attacks him, he will defend.'

'You are sure on that?'

'He must defend, or he will die.'

'What will make the village attack him?'

'How should I know?'

'So you will let him go all his life grinning on the village elders and doing nothing to confront the village and never making a justice on your name because he is kind. You do not care if he never defends, do you?'

'I care. I wish more than anything that he will smite the village.'

'Then make the village smite him first. That will force him to defend.'

'How?'

'Make a scandal on the village.'

'How?'

'Make two scandals. Make five. Make a hundred.'

'How?'

'You see that tax-farmer he walks with now?'

'How can I not see him? It makes me sick on my stomach to see him walk with a tax-farmer, holding hands with him as he is a friend.'

'Will it make your village sick on its stomach to hear of this tax-farmer?'

'How should they ever hear of a tax-farmer?'

'Do you know nothing? What can a tax-farmer do that most men cannot?'

'He can steal by permission of the king.'

'That will not make your village hear of him. What else can a tax-farmer do?'

'He can do sums.'

'That gets near the boil, but it will not lance it.'

'He can write.'

'That is well said, that a tax-farmer can write. What would you do if you could write?'

'I would write a letter home to my sons to tell them the news.'

'If you make a friend on this tax-farmer, what could he do for you?'

'I will never make a friend on a tax-farmer!'

'Think on the matter.'

'I only wish my son to smite the village.'

'Think on the matter.'

'My son will never smite the village unless they smite him first.'

'Think on the matter.'

'The village will never smite my son unless he makes a scandal.'

'Make a scandal, Miryam Beautiful. Make a mighty scandal.'

'How?'

'Think on the matter.'

PART 4: THE PRECIPICE

Summer, AD 30

We must kill the mamzer boy
The mamzer boy
The mamzer boy.
We must kill the mamzer boy
The son of Miryam.

CHAPTER SIXTY

Miryam of Nazareth

"But how are we to send the letter?" I ask Mattai the tax-farmer. I never sent a letter in my life.

Mattai the tax-farmer grins on me. "Come and see."

I have made a friend on the tax-farmer. It burns my heart to say so, but I did it. I need him. None of the other men can make fine letters in ink with a reed pen on papyrus. Even my son cannot do it, for he never had anyone to teach him fine writing. Yoni can write a little on a wax tablet, but he does not know the matter of fine writing on papyrus. But the tax-farmer can do it in his sleep, and he also has money to buy papyrus.

Mattai the tax-farmer is grateful to have one friend, even if I am only an old woman.

Last night, I asked him to write a letter to my sons. I told him all my sons can read. He was surprised to hear it and said I must be a proud mother to have five sons who can read. They cannot read well, except Thin Shimon, but my lord Yoseph learned to read from Yaakov Mega, and he made all my sons learn before he died.

When my sons get my letter, they will read it many times and then take it to the village square and tell the news. I told the tax-farmer all we did since we left Nazareth, and he wrote it down in beautiful letters, and it is a mighty tale.

We came to Magdala yesterday, which is a big town. My son went out early this morning before anyone was awake. Yoni went also, and they are both still gone. Now is a good time to send my letter.

I follow Mattai the tax-farmer through the streets. He knows the town well, for he grew up here. He told me it is the chief town of this toparchy. I do not know what is a toparchy, but I see Magdala is bigger than Nazareth and even Capernaum.

Mattai told me his father was a scribe here. He told me after his father died he was starving until he found work with a tax-farmer.

I am in a big confusion on the matter. A tax-farmer is a wicked who cheats the people. HaShem hates tax-farmers. But Mattai was starving. If my sons all died and I was starving, what would I do? I could not be a tax-farmer, for that is a man's work.

I could be a *zonah*, or I could starve, and that is not a choice.

The synagogue sits in the center of the town. When we arrive there, it looks to me like a big confusion, for there are many hundred people outside, all going a different way. There are more people here in this one street than we have in all Nazareth! It makes me dizzy to see so many people.

Mattai the tax-farmer cups hands to his mouth and shouts, "Who travels to Caesarea and will carry a letter?"

That sounds like foolishness, for I want my letter to go to Nazareth. Caesarea is a big city beside the Great Sea, far from Nazareth.

Three men move toward us, grinning with big grins.

Mattai the tax-farmer smiles on them all. "I have a letter for a man in Nazareth. It is south from Tsipori by a walk of one hour on the road to Caesarea. The village is only just off the road a little."

"How far off the road?" asks one of the men. He looks like an oxcart driver.

Mattai the tax-farmer turns to me.

I shrug. "It is not the fourth part of an hour's walk, up a small hill."

"That is not far," Mattai the tax-farmer says.

"It is very far if the hill is steep," says the oxcart driver.

The second man looks like a peddler, for he has a pack of wares on his back. "I have seen that hill. It is not more steep than the road from here to Tsipori. But the path is narrow and twists like a snake and has big ruts. It is hard for a man with a pack. Too hard for an oxcart."

The third man looks like a beggar. His face is dirty, and he smells like three-days-old fish. "I will take the letter for two *dinars*."

I do not want him to take my letter. And anyway, I do not have two *dinars*.

"The man who receives the letter will give hospitality one night," Mattai the tax-farmer says.

The oxcart driver shakes his head. "I do not like the sound of that path."

"One *dinar* and a half," says the peddler.

Mattai the tax-farmer taps his nose. "If you can tell news to the village, you might get hospitality a second night. If you tell a good news, they will feast you, for Nazareth is a small village."

The beggar shifts his weight. "One *dinar*."

The oxcart driver and the peddler scowl and say nothing.

Mattai the tax-farmer looks hard on each of the men. "Is it one *dinar*, then?"

They all look on each other and nod.

Some filthy beggar is going to take my letter away! What if he is a liar who takes our *dinar* and then does not give the letter to Little Yaakov? I feel as I will faint.

Mattai the tax-farmer tilts his head toward the synagogue. "Come with me," he says to the beggar.

I follow them into the synagogue. Mattai the tax-farmer goes to a small side room where there is a wooden writing table with an inkwell and reed pens. He unrolls my letter and writes something at the end. He blows softly on the ink to dry it, then rolls up the papyrus and seals it with a glob of wax from a small metal pot hanging over an oil lamp.

He presses his signet ring into the soft wax and hands the letter to the beggar. "Take this only to Little Yaakov the *tekton*, who lives in

Nazareth. I have written him to pay you one *dinar* and feed you well and give you hospitality one night. Also, he will take you to the village square if you can tell any news."

The beggar makes a big grin and gives a strong right hand to Mattai the tax-farmer. "I swear by The Name that Little Yaakov will read this letter tonight."

We go outside in the bright sun. I am astonished it was so easy. I never knew how to send a letter before. It never mattered, because I cannot write. I cannot read either, but I have sons for that.

Now I know how it is done, I will send a letter every week.

Only now I am in debt to this tax-farmer. I feel unclean. I do not like pretending to be a friend on a man I scorn.

I think it is how a *zonah* feels, who pretends to take a pleasure with a man she hates.

I think I am not so wicked as a *zonah*, but still I feel unclean.

～

Miryam of Magdala

I am walking from my salting house to the fish market when the voice of my dead son rises up from the deep places in my heart.

'Imma! Turn now and go another way! There is a man of scandal just ahead of you.'

'I do not see a man of scandal.'

'That man walking toward you with purpose in his stride. He has men with him, half a dozen lowborn men. He gives you an evil eye.'

'Who is that man? He does not look wicked, and anyway it is a public street. What can he do in the broad daylight?'

'He will make a scandal on you for all Magdala to see. If you love me, turn now!'

I do not want a scandal, and I trust my son to guide me. I am about to turn away, but then I see the man of scandal stop to give alms to the blind beggar who sits in front of the synagogue.

Every day I give this beggar a coin, for it is a commandment of HaShem to give alms.

The beggar calls out, "Give to HaShem!"

The man of scandal squats in the dust of the street in front of the beggar.

I am scandalized. A respectable man does not squat before a beggar.

The man of scandal puts dust from the street in his hand and spits the dust and mixes with his finger.

I am beyond scandalized. My friends Yohana and Shoshanna will demand a full report on this dreadful thing. I move closer.

The man of scandal puts the mud in the eyes of the blind beggar.

I wish I had a stick to beat this man of scandal! It is not done, to put mud of dishonor in the eyes of a helpless man.

The blind beggar cries out with a great cry.

That was ill done! I press closer to give the man of scandal hard words.

The man of scandal seizes the hand of the beggar and pulls him to his feet.

The blind beggar smiles. He shouts. He falls on his face before the man of scandal and kisses his feet.

He looks on me.

The blind beggar looks on me with eyes that see.

I am undone.

My head is hot and my hands are cold. This man of scandal must be that Rabbi Yeshua we hear tales on. Out of Capernaum. At first, we thought they were idle tales of foolish fish-men. But now all Magdala tells these tales, and some even believe them.

I do not know what to think.

The man of scandal gives the beggar a kiss and a kiss and a kiss.

He has no honor, if he kisses some beggar in the street. I have seen enough. This tale will shock my friends beyond all they ever heard. I turn to move away.

"Woman, wait!" There is command in Rabbi Yeshua's voice.

I wish to rush away fast, but my feet are stones, and I have no strength to walk. I look back.

Rabbi Yeshua is running toward me.

I never saw a grown man run. It is dishonor to run. A man of honor walks with dignity.

He runs to meet me. "Woman, I have a word of HaShem for you."

'Imma! Send him away! He has evil intent. Why else would he speak to a woman in the street? He will make a scandal on you.'

My mouth falls open, but my words crumble to dust. "I ..."

"Woman, HaShem says you are invited to a big feast this evening."

'Imma! That is a lie. This man has no house, nor money, nor servants. How can he make a big feast? Tell him away.'

My heart drums in my chest. I am a woman of high family, even if all my family is dead. I will not allow this man to make a scandal on me.

A crowd gathers around us.

I read their faces. They envy me. Any one of them would pay a hundred *dinars* to dine at the feast of Rabbi Yeshua. There will be shocking tales to tell from this feast. Never and never will I go to his feast. Although if I did, Yohana and Shoshanna would be begging for every detail. They would be furious they were not invited. But of course I will refuse it.

"Woman, HaShem begs favor of you, that you come to my feast."

The crowd murmurs, and there is scorn in their voices. A man of honor does not beg favor of a woman. It is beyond foolishness that HaShem should beg favor of a woman.

I am dying to know why HaShem begs favor that I will come to a feast. "Where and at what time is this feast?"

'Imma! No! Tell the man away at once! If you love me, Imma, do as I say!'

Rabbi Yeshua points to a boy of the age of ten. "My servant Yoni will bring you to the place this evening at the going out of the day."

Yoni smiles on me. He reminds me of my own son long ago, before he became a man, before the wasting disease took him.

'Imma! Father says no.'

My breath catches in my throat. I do not dare disobey my lord, the father of my son.

The voice of my lord wakens from the abyss.

'*Miryam Magdala, I command that you will not go with this man of scandal. You will not.*'

I shake my head, for to disobey my lord is death. My voice has lost its breath in the dryness of my throat, and I do not know if the rabbi will even hear me. I lean close to him and force out my words in a broken whisper. "Rabbi, I thank you, but I will not come."

A smile spreads across Rabbi Yeshua's face, and he shouts with a big shout of joy. "Blessed be HaShem! You honor me! My servant will find you at the appointed time and bring you to the place."

I am stunned at his impudence, for now all these people think I said yes. This man is wily.

'*Imma, see what a deceiver he is!*'

'*Miryam Magdala, I command that you tell him no. Backhand the man for making a deception.*'

I wish to strike the rabbi, but my arms have no strength. Already he is turning away.

All around me, the men of the town scowl on me with eyes of envy.

I try to take a step after the rabbi, but my legs refuse me.

The boy Yoni looks on me, and his smile is kind and innocent.

Yohana and Shoshanna will never forgive me if I fail to go to this feast.

My son and my lord will never forgive me if I do.

'*Imma! No good can come of this!*'

'*Miryam Magdala, I command that you will not go. This man will make a scandal.*'

I do not know what to think. My son guides me. My lord commands me. Without their strength, how would I have kept their salting house in business after they went down to Sheol?

I dare not go to this feast of Rabbi Yeshua.

But now all Magdala thinks I will.

Rabbi Yeshua is wily. I must be wary on this man.

Dreadful things are certain to befall at his feast.

I must see them.

I must.

CHAPTER SIXTY-ONE

Miryam of Magdala

The sun has dropped behind Mount Arbel, high above Magdala, when the boy Yoni comes to my salting house to take me to the feast of Rabbi Yeshua.

He is a talkative boy, and before we have walked a hundred paces, I know the names of his father and mother and brother and five sisters. I know that his village *hazzan* calls him the Genius of Capernaum. I know that he has followed Rabbi Yeshua since last fall, and he claims to have seen many mighty works of HaShem.

Boys are gullible, that is what I think. I make a scowl on him. "Some idle tale tells that Rabbi Yeshua healed a man with *tsaraat*."

Yoni shakes his head. "It was not *tsaraat*, it was the mighty leprosy. I saw it with these eyes."

"Never and never will I believe this tale! Did you know the man before? How do you know he had the mighty leprosy? Perhaps it was some other disease."

"I … no, I did not know the man. But I also saw Rabbi Yeshua heal Fat Miryam, who had the summer fever. She is my father's cousin and the mother of Shimon's—"

"Never and never will I believe this tale either! How do you know she had the summer fever, or did you merely hear report? Perhaps it was some other kind of fever."

"I … I saw her myself, and she sweated through her tunic so it clung to her body like skin, but I only heard report that it was the summer fever. But I also saw Rabbi Yeshua send away the evil spirit of Yoseph the Rage. I have known Yoseph long, and I know he had a spirit of rage because I saw him bite off a man's ear once."

My hands turn cold. I do not wish to hear lies on the matter of spirits. Fools and simples think all spirits are evil.

That is a false tale. A familiar spirit is not evil. The shade of one you loved who went down to Sheol is not evil.

'Imma! You must not go to this feast! The man will make a scandal on you.'

'It is dishonor to the host to agree to a feast and then turn away.'

'Imma! You did not agree to the feast. The man tricked you.'

'I will not be shamed before all Magdala by turning away.'

'Miryam Magdala! I command that you turn back. The man means to shame you at the feast.'

'The man seems kind. I will not dishonor him. But I will be wary on him, for he is wily.'

Yoni studies me with large eyes. "Are you well, Savta?"

My heart is warmed that he calls me grandmother. I never had a grandchild and never will. "I feel faint. Where is the place we are going?"

"Rabbi Yeshua said it is to be a surprise. But it is not far."

We walk down the wide and bending street above the synagogue, where there are many houses that are considered large and fine. Merchants live here. Also owners of fishing fleets. Also tax-farmers. I do not consider these houses large or fine, and I would not live among such middleborn people, but at least these are not the huts of fish-men. The feast will be adequate.

Yoni talks and talks as we walk.

I learn that he is older than he looks, for he is thirteen, a man. He shows intelligence. I can believe he is thought a genius in a fish village. I do not think Yoni would be the Genius of Magdala, but my friend Shoshanna has a son who is a scribe and could examine his merit.

Yoni is conceited, but I like him. If he is the tenth part as wise as he thinks he is, then he is the greatest mind in a hundred generations and I will pay to send him to Jerusalem to study Torah with Rabbi Shammai, who is the wisest sage of Israel.

Yoni stops. "Savta, now you must close your eyes and take my arm, and I will guide you the rest of the way. Rabbi Yeshua says it is to be a big surprise."

I close my eyes, and I close my heart to the voices of my familiars. I already know they do not like the matter. I do not like the matter either. I will attend the feast and not shame myself before the town, and then I will be done with this Rabbi Yeshua until forever.

I take Yoni's arm and follow after him. I feel like the blind beggar Rabbi Yeshua healed in the street today. At least that is a tale I believe.

Yoni leads me left, and then right, and then left.

"Now you may open your eyes, Savta."

I open. Heat floods my chest. No, never! It is the home of that tax-farmer—that wicked Alexander. He cheats me on every cart of salted fish I send from our toparchy. I hate the man and would spit his eye, only then he would cheat me double.

'Imma! I told you not to come! We are dishonored!'

'Miryam Magdala! I command that you go home at once.'

I am so angry, I want to beat Rabbi Yeshua with my fists. I should turn back on this tax-farmer. But it is not done to accept a feast and then turn back. If I dishonor this man, nobody will ever invite me to a feast again. I must go through with the matter. This Rabbi Yeshua is a deceiver and a cheat. I will give him hard words.

Rabbi Yeshua stands near the door, surrounded by five women, lowborn by the look of them. I cannot believe he makes words with women in public. The man has no honor. What man ever came to a feast and spoke to—

My heart jumps to double. There is choice gossip here! Those are not ordinary lowborn women. Those are sinful women, or I am a catfish. Sinful women, speaking with Rabbi Yeshua as they mean to offer business!

One *zonah* points to her belly and speaks to Rabbi Yeshua.

She must have some sickness of the woman parts. That is a justice. It is a curse from HaShem on account of her sin.

This matter is vile beyond imagining. My friends will faint for the shock of it. I must see more.

Yoni takes my arm and tries to pull me away from looking on Rabbi Yeshua. "Savta, perhaps this way? There is our host just inside."

I fling Yoni off and move closer. This is too horrible to watch.

I must watch.

Rabbi Yeshua puts his hand on the *zonah's* belly and speaks to it.

It is not done in Israel, for a man of honor to touch a woman. Not even a *tsaddik* should do it.

The *zonah* screams for her pain.

I am mad with delight. My friends will never forgive me, that I have seen this great scandal and they have not.

The *zonah* screams again, but no—it is not for her pain. She laughs. She weeps. She shouts. She dances. Either she is healed or she is gone mad and walks beside herself.

Rabbi Yeshua gives the *zonah* a kiss and a kiss and ... a kiss.

This is beyond madness. Never and never would I have dreamed to see such a horror. I shall be telling this gossip until I die. My friends will call me liar, but I know what I see.

Rabbi Yeshua is a mighty scandal. I am more glad than I ever was that I came to this feast.

The tax-farmer's woman comes out to greet me. I know who she is, a middleborn daughter of some fig farmer. She thinks to be my hostess? I am dizzy with the audacity of the matter.

I put on a strong face and pretend to be at ease.

She leads me in to the feast. A servant brings water and washes my feet. Another brings olive oil to dip my hands and a towel to wipe. At last the tax-farmer's woman shows me where I am to recline.

I am appalled. I will recline at table with the women of tax-farmers and the women of merchants and the women of scribes. There is one woman I do not know who looks as she is some peasant and hangs her head in silence. At least she knows she is nothing. The others have a little wealth and think they are something. There are nine of us, and we recline on three couches around a table in an alcove where we cannot be seen by the men. Of course, I am in the chief place at the table, for I am above all the others in age and wealth. Still, it chafes me to rub shoulders with women so common. I will be brief when I tell this part of the tale to Yohana and Shoshanna.

The meal is only seven courses. In truth, I did not expect so many from a tax-farmer. The women chatter among themselves and attempt to make words with me, but what do I have in common with such folk? Still, I do my best, for a woman of respect does not shame middleborn women for no cause. I learn that the peasant woman is Rabbi Yeshua's mother. She looks out of her place, more than a sow in a synagogue.

I hear Rabbi Yeshua's voice in the central courtyard, loud with wine, making jest with the tax-farmer who owns this house. There are several tax-farmers here. I hear the voice of that dreadful Mattityahu, the tax-farmer who has the booth at the border. He is wicked, even for a tax-farmer. I should warn Rabbi Yeshua to watch his purse when that man is around. But I will not. If he loses all his *dinars*, I will laugh him to scorn, because he tricked me here.

What man of honor would jest with tax-farmers? It is a scandal and worse than a scandal.

I wonder if this tax-farmer and his woman will expect me to feast them at my own house. Never and never! Rather I should dance in the street naked at noontime. If Rabbi Yeshua invites me to another feast, I will take off my sandal and smite his face and spit his eye.

When the feast draws near an end, Rabbi Yeshua stands to tell a tale. He comes to the end of the courtyard, where we women in the alcove can see him. He tells a strange tale of some peasant woman who lost a coin and made a big dust in the house to search it out. Then when she found it, she made a big joy in all the village.

Never and never did I hear such a big foolishness.

He tells another tale of some sheep-man who left ninety and nine sheep in the pen to search for one lost ewe lamb in a storm. Then he fought bandits and took her back home on his shoulders, and he shouted the whole village to come see his lost sheep that was found.

I do not see what is the point of this tale. It is less than pig sense to me.

When he is done, Rabbi Yeshua gives orders that food should be taken out to the street and served to the beggars. Of course, there are always beggars at the door of a feast, but one does not serve food to them. One throws out the leavings in a pile beside the house, and the beggars fight for the scraps. That is a good sport.

There is muttering on the matter among the women at my table. I hear it even in the courtyard, for there are six tables of men there, and men are noisy even when they try to be quiet.

There is more wine to be served, and there will be some sweet thing to tickle the tongue before the feast is ended. People of quality serve apples, but I fear that is too much to hope for. My teeth will complain on me if they serve dried figs. I am eager to be gone, for I have enough gossip now for many days of telling, and I am weary of these middleborn women and their middleborn talk.

Suddenly, silence.

The silk merchant's woman nudges me and points with her chin.

Rabbi Yeshua stands outside the alcove, motioning me with his hand.

I do not know which is worse. That he wishes to speak with me, or that he makes a commotion for all to see.

'Imma! You should ignore him, and he will leave off the matter.'

'Miryam Magdala, I command that you tell him away. Put on your strong face and give him hard words.'

'Imma, do not allow him to speak, for he is a deceiver.'

Rabbi Yeshua continues to motion me with his hand.

Fool of a fool! He makes a spectacle on me.

I rise from my couch and put on a face stronger than I ever did. When my lord and my son died, I was weak. But when I went down to Sheol and found their spirits, they taught me to be strong, to be a woman of respect in the world of men. I am respected now, for all men respect age and fear power. I am in the sixty-first year of my age, and I am more mighty than any woman. I am not afraid of this teller of tales.

I walk to Rabbi Yeshua with bold foot and strong face.

'Imma, do not look his eyes.'

'Miryam Magdala, I command that you tell him away before he can speak!'

I open my mouth to tell him away.

Rabbi Yeshua leans forward and gives me a kiss and a kiss.

My cheeks burn and my words turn to dust. Yohana and Shoshanna will faint for the shock of it, that some common man kissed my face.

I call up a big indignation in my soul. "Rabbi Yeshua—"

He kisses me again on both cheeks.

My soul is undone, and my indignation turns to smoke. I cannot speak, nor breathe, nor think.

He kisses my lips.

I feel as I will faint. My head rings. This is not done! Rabbi Yeshua treats me as a friend, as a man. I wait for the whirling to pass. My strong face must look like a weak face now.

I do not wish to look Rabbi Yeshua's eyes, but he wishes to look my eyes, and he kisses me again and again. Each time he kisses me, he looks deep in my eyes, and I know he sees every secret I ever had.

Fear rises like a storm. My soul loses its strength.

'Imma, he sees us! What have you done?'

'Miryam Magdala, I command that you run away fast!'

Rabbi Yeshua leans close to my ear. "Friend, do you wish to be free?"

"I … do not know what you mean. I am more free than any woman ever was."

'Miryam Magdala, I command that you say no more. Turn and flee!'

'Imma, he will destroy us! If you love us, run away fast!'

Rabbi Yeshua holds both my arms and peers on me with strong eyes. "They are not who you think they are."

'Imma! Tell him away!'

'Miryam Magdala, I command that you smite his face!'

My son and my lord are in a rage now, more furious than any woman ever endured. We have storms here in Magdala, great storms of wind and rain and wave and thunder and lightning. But they are nothing to the storm between my ears. I cannot hear. I cannot think. I am going mad with the fury of it.

Rabbi Yeshua blows in my face and whispers, "You storm, be silent."

Silence.

I am damp with the sweat of my trembling. My familiars are silent. My heart hammers on my ribs as it will crack them, and I want to faint for the pain. I am terrified that Rabbi Yeshua has sent my familiars away. Who will be my strength, if I lose my son and my lord?

"Are they ... gone?" My voice is a thin breeze.

He shakes his head, and his eyes are gentle as a mother looking on her only child. "No, but they will be silent for a moment, while we talk."

"And then?"

"Then they will punish you. What you heard was the first birth pangs of that punishment. Do you wish for me to help?"

"Never and never!"

"Are you sure?"

"Leave me!"

He gives me a kiss and a kiss and a kiss. "I beg favor of you, let me help."

I cannot bear the kindness in his eyes. "Maybe."

"Only maybe?"

"Y-yes."

The smile of Rabbi Yeshua is like sunlight on gold. "You spirits, leave her!" he says in a whisper.

I feel a rushing in my soul.

I am cold, naked, destroyed.

I am alone.

I have lost my lord and my son, whom I lost once to Death and pursued to Sheol at great cost. Now they are gone again, forever and forever. Rabbi Yeshua has stolen my strength.

I scream. I give Rabbi Yeshua the backhand of dishonor hard across his right cheek. "Do not touch me, you evil man!"

A gash of red rises on his cheek, for I wear three gold rings on that hand, and one of them is heavy.

Rabbi Yeshua's eyes water, and they lose their seeing for a moment.

I am glad, for he stole what I loved most.

He turns his head so his left cheek is toward me. "And this one also, friend."

All my strength goes out of me. It is not done to give the left backhand, for that is the hand one uses for wiping away *haryo*. The left hand is vile. I would shame myself to give him the left backhand. Never and never will I do it. My knees fold.

Rabbi Yeshua catches me before I can fall. He gives me a kiss and a kiss and a kiss and speaks softly in my ear. "They are not who you think they are. You are free from them for as long as you will. Do not ask them back, or it will go worse."

I feel more lonely than I ever did.

I pull away from Rabbi Yeshua and stagger to my couch.

I thought I was strong.

I am strong.

I have strength to deal with honorable men.

I do not have strength to deal with a man of scandal. When a man is so low that he cannot be dishonored, what power do I have on him?

I slide onto my dining couch. My body is hot, and I am sick to my bones with emptiness, and I do not know what to do. Rabbi Yeshua has sent away my familiars. If I ask them back, they will make a rage on me.

The silk merchant's woman leans close to my ear. "Why did you slap the rabbi? He loves you like his own mother. He kissed you many times. What did he say to you? We tried to hear, but he spoke his secrets softly."

Yes, softly, while he ruined my life. Now I am alone, forever and forever. I am naked without my lord and my son. Rabbi Yeshua is at blame for this.

I hate him more than I ever hated any man.

I do not wish to see Rabbi Yeshua ever again.

CHAPTER SIXTY-TWO

Yoni of Capernaum

Rabbi Yeshua is a paradox, and I mean to solve him.

Before the feast, I saw him talking with the *zonah* we met two weeks ago. She lives here in Magdala, and she brought other *zonahs* to see Rabbi Yeshua. It turned my face hot to look on them. But Rabbi Yeshua's face did not turn hot when he spoke with them.

Also, he laid hands on one of the *zonahs* and healed her. A man of honor does not speak to a *zonah*, nor look on her. How is it that Rabbi Yeshua laid hands on a *zonah's* belly in public, and nobody said no? Then he kissed her, as she is a man and a friend.

Just now, I saw him talking with the old woman I led to the feast. Our tax-farmer says this woman is the wealthiest woman in Magdala, which is a big town. Rabbi Yeshua kissed her also, as she is a man and a friend.

Rabbi Yeshua treats a wealthy woman as a man. He treats a *zonah* as a wealthy woman. He treats a leper as a clean man. He treats a tax-farmer as one of us.

That is a paradox, and I do not see the meaning of it, but at least Shimon the Rock and the others see it too and agree it is a paradox.

But there is a deeper thing. Lately, I saw another paradox.

I wish I could ask Rabbi Yeshua on the matter, but he reclines at the main table with the host, and I recline at a side table with Shimon the Rock and all our other men.

I am very pleased with the matter, for it is a mighty paradox, and I have seen it first in all the world. I saw it in a loose word Shimon the Rock said on the way to Bethsaida. I hope it was a loose word. I would be shamed to think Shimon saw this paradox before me. I must know for certain.

"Shimon the Rock!" I poke him hard, for he has eaten and drunk much tonight and is sleepy.

He gives me a groggy eye. "What now, Yoni? I saw you staring on that serving girl who brings our wine. Did you frighten her away with your lewd eyes? If we get no more wine, we will make a blame on you."

The other men around our table laugh.

I do not think it is funny.

I say, "No, I told her you are a wicked man who pinches the hind parts of serving girls when you have drunk too much. If we get no more wine, we will make a blame on you."

The other men roar.

Shimon the Rock laughs too. "Well said, Yoni. You have given me back double. Now what thing did you wish to ask me? If it has to do with women, I will not tell you. If it has to do with the deep things of HaShem, you should ask Rabbi Yeshua, and he will also not tell you. Whatever you ask, there is someone who will not tell you."

I shake my head. "You asked once if Rabbi Yeshua's tales are part of the kingdom of HaShem."

Shimon the Rock peers into the bottom of his wine cup. He is deep into that cup tonight. "I never asked on the matter. Why would I ask such a big foolishness? When did I ask it? Was I drunk on a bad wine?"

I never felt so happy in all my life. I was afraid Shimon had seen this deep thing first. But he does not even know what he said, so I am sure he did not see it first. Therefore, I saw it first.

Toma Trouble looks on me with hard eyes. "Yohanan Talk-Talk, why are you grinning and not talking?"

I make a shrug on my shoulders. "I made a mistake on the matter."

Toma Trouble's eyebrows crowd together. "I doubt you made a mistake. If it was true you made a mistake, you would never admit. Therefore, you did not make a mistake. Do you deny my logic? What did you see and what do you know?"

I make a big scowl on him. Toma Trouble has more wits than all the others together, but even so, he is no more than the village fool, and why should I explain the matter to the village fool?

Big Yaakov returns to the table. He was talking to the serving girl, and now he wears a fat grin.

I think his woman will twist his ears off when I tell how he made words with some serving girl who is a big-eyes and a slim-waist.

Shimon the Rock calls to the girl for more wine.

I know he is trying to distract me. I will ignore the girl, although she is very beautiful. I like to watch her walk, for she is graceful.

She comes to our table and pours wine for Big Yaakov very skillfully.

She pours wine for Shimon the Rock very skillfully.

"And more for Yoni, also." Big Yaakov points on me.

I do not want more wine. My head will ache in the morning. I take my stone cup away from the table so she cannot pour more.

The girl smiles and comes around behind the dining couches and stands at my feet and stretches her hand for my cup.

I do not give it.

She stretches more and leans toward me.

I shake my head.

She stretches more and leans far over me.

I am angry. "No! I do not want—"

Her foot slips.

She falls forward.

She falls on top of me.

All my body is in a big shock.

I try to push her away.

She laughs on me and tries to kiss me.

I push harder on her.

She leans on me with all her weight. Her body is soft and warm.

My arms lose their strength.

She presses against me, pushing her bosoms in my face.

The men shout with a big laughter.

I wish to die of my dishonor.

The girl takes long to climb off me, and all the time she smiles and winks on Big Yaakov.

My heart thumps in my chest, and my face is so hot I could light fire with it.

She has not spilled a drop of the wine from her pitcher. That is the proof it was no accident.

My mind is numb with the shock of it. My hands still tingle with the feel of her softness. I often have wicked thoughts when I look on a woman. Now I will have more wicked thoughts, for now I know the feel of a woman.

The girl goes around on Big Yaakov's side of the table.

He passes her a bronze coin and makes a big smirk on me.

Shimon the Rock laughs so hard I think he will choke.

I hope he sucks his tongue down his throat and dies.

I should put *haryo* in Big Yaakov's ear while he sleeps.

My *yetzer hara* shouts in my ear that I should find some *zonah* and pay her a *dinar* and learn what it is to lie with a woman.

I think I am further than ever from solving the paradox of Rabbi Yeshua.

~

Yoni of Capernaum

"Rabbi Yeshua!" shouts a voice. "Please, you will come to our aid!"

I know that voice. We are coming out of Alexander the tax-farmer's house, staggering with full bellies, sleepy with wine. And now that terrible man has come, begging for help.

Hananyah the nail maker falls on his knees before Rabbi Yeshua. "You must help us, Rabbi!"

Rabbi Yeshua's eyebrows rise high. "Who must I help, and why must I help them?"

Two other men come forward and stand beside Hananyah the nail maker. They were with Yohanan the immerser last winter when we told repentance to Israel.

Hananyah the nail maker says, "We have been fasting and praying that HaShem will release our master from prison. We heard tales that you were doing mighty works in Galilee, so we came to Tiberias. People there said you were doing mighty works in Magdala, so we came here. You must come with us and throw down Herod's fortress at Mikhvar and bring out Yohanan the prophet."

"Why must I?" Rabbi Yeshua says.

Hananyah's lips press into a thin line. "Because he is your master."

"HaShem is my master."

"You follow after Yohanan the prophet."

"I follow after HaShem."

"Ask HaShem how you are to bring out Yohanan."

"I have asked HaShem already."

"Then why have you not brought out Yohanan?" Hananyah the nail maker narrows his eyes. "Do you think to take his place?"

Rabbi Yeshua sighs. "I have asked HaShem many times how to set Yohanan free. I have not heard an answer."

"You must ask again! You must come with us to Herod's fortress at Mikhvar. You should command the walls to be thrown down, and they will be thrown down."

"You will not tell me what I must do. HaShem tells me what to do, and I do it. I have asked after Yohanan, and HaShem has not told me what to do. Therefore, I will do nothing."

I am sick to my death of this Hananyah the nail maker. I push forward through the people gathered around Rabbi Yeshua, and I point a finger on Hananyah. "You are a hypocrite. When Yohanan was arrested, you ran like a woman to escape Herod's men."

"Yoni," says Rabbi Yeshua.

I am angry and I do not wish to listen. "Rabbi Yeshua, this man could have fought and defended Yohanan, but he ran. Now he thinks he can make you fight—"

"Yoni."

I stamp my foot. "If he wishes to fight, let him go fight. But he has no right—"

"Yoni."

I am dizzy with my rage, and I fear I will vomit. I lean forward and put my hands on my knees. My belly is angry on me. It feels like a storm on the Lake of Ginosar. It feels—

I retch. A great stream of wine-mixed food comes rushing out of my mouth. I retch and I retch until everything I ate lies on the ground.

Hananyah the nail maker stabs his finger at me. "I know you. You are that wicked boy who speaks with lewd women and thinks he is a genius and talks overmuch. And here you are feasting and drinking wine, when your master is in prison. For shame! Rabbi Yeshua, tell him shame!"

"His master is not in prison," Rabbi Yeshua says.

Hananyah puts his hands on his hips and glares on Rabbi Yeshua. "Does he deny his master now?"

"Yoni follows after me," Rabbi Yeshua says.

Hananyah's face turns pale as the moon. Rage curls his lip. "He follows after you, and not Yohanan? You think you are greater than your master Yohanan?"

"Yohanan is not my master. HaShem is my master. Yoni and these other men follow after me. They feast and drink because I feast and drink. I feast and drink because HaShem calls me to feast and drink. HaShem calls me to feast and drink because the kingdom of HaShem is breaking in on us."

"And you leave your master to rot in prison, when you could come and do a mighty wonder?"

Rabbi Yeshua sighs. "I told you many times already, Yohanan is not my master, HaShem is. If HaShem tells me to do a mighty wonder, I will do a mighty wonder."

"You should ask him again," Hananyah the nail maker says.

Rabbi Yeshua closes his eyes.

I see the Shekinah all around him.

People are still coming out of Alexander the tax-farmer's house, talking loudly, shouting. Three of them had too much wine and are singing a song about smiting the Great Satan.

Their voices grate my ears.

Hananyah the nail maker scowls on them.

Rabbi Yeshua opens his eyes. "I heard a word from HaShem."

Hananyah rubs his hands together. "So you will come with us and destroy Herod's prison and bring out Yohanan the immerser?"

"I will stay in Galilee and destroy the works of the Accuser and bring in the kingdom of HaShem. You will go to Yohanan the immerser in prison and give him comfort and tell him the kingdom of HaShem is beginning. Take him food and drink, for he is hungry."

"But ... we would be killed if we went to his prison."

"HaShem says you will not be killed."

"We would be put in prison."

"HaShem says you will come away safe."

"You should come with us."

"HaShem says I will do what he has called me to do, and you will do what he has called *you* to do."

Hananyah's mouth hangs open like the mouth of a fish.

One of his friends says, "The fortress Mikhvar is far from here, a walk of six days or seven."

"HaShem says if you start now, you will come there safely in a week. Give Yohanan a kiss and a kiss and a kiss, for HaShem loves him and I love him."

I am glad Rabbi Yeshua did not tell me to visit Yohanan the immerser in prison and give him a kiss and a kiss and a kiss.

He has been there three months now, and I think he will smell worse than a camel.

CHAPTER SIXTY-THREE

Yaakov of Nazareth

"Little Yaakov, stop! There is some man to see you."

I do not stop to speak to the elders in the village gate. My brothers and I worked hard all day in Tsipori, and we are tired. If that vile leper has come back—

"Little Yaakov, the man brings a letter from your brother."

I stop. We have waited long to hear news from Yeshua. "Where is this man?"

Old Yonatan the leather-man leers on me. "At Shimon the baker's house. He asked for Little Yaakov the *tekton* of Nazareth, but we did not send him to your house, because only women are there."

My brothers and I hurry to the house of Shimon the baker.

He grins on us when we arrive. "Little Yaakov, if you do not wish to give hospitality to the stranger—"

"We will give hospitality. Where is he?"

"Taking his ease inside. He walked from Magdala today." Shimon the baker shows us inside his house.

A filthy beggar sits on a wooden bench in the courtyard, eating dried figs and sipping beer from a stone cup.

Shimon says, "Here is Little Yaakov the *tekton* of Nazareth."

The beggar stands. "My name is called Theudas, and I was in Magdala this morning. A man asked who goes to Caesarea who would carry a letter for two *dinars*."

My face feels hot. I never sent a letter, so I did not know it costs two *dinars* to send. The news must be a big news if Yeshua paid so much. "Where is the letter?"

Theudas pulls a rolled papyrus from his cloth belt. "Where are the two *dinars*?"

My heart thumps hard in my chest. I must pay the two *dinars*? I did not know that is how it is done. I worked hard all day and got a *dinar* for my labor. My brothers worked hard and each got a *dinar*. We brought home four *dinars*, and this man should have two?

Thin Shimon steps up beside me. "How do we know this letter is from Yeshua?"

Theudas shakes his head. "Did I say it was from Yeshua? I did not speak to any Yeshua. It was sent by an old woman, almost fifty years old, who said her name was called Miryam of Nazareth."

Thin Shimon says, "Our mother cannot write."

"Did I say this woman wrote the letter? She was with some man. He wrote the letter and put it in my own hands this morning in Magdala. If you do not want the letter, I can give it to this baker who showed hospitality—"

"Give me my letter." I reach out my hand.

"Give me my two *dinars*." Theudas reaches out his hand.

I shake my head. "Prove to me the letter is from my mother."

Shimon the baker steps forward. "Little Yaakov, give me the two *dinars* to hold. Then take the letter and read it. I swear by The Name that if it is a false letter, I will return your two *dinars*, but if it is a true letter, I will give the *dinars* to this Theudas. This is fair to both of you, yes?"

I study Theudas.

His forehead gleams, and he does not look my eye.

I think there is a fish in the matter. I take out a *dinar* from my belt. Yosi takes out a *dinar* from his belt. We give them to Shimon the baker.

Theudas scowls on us and Shimon the baker. At last he gives me the letter.

The wax seal bears some impression, but it is so crushed I cannot read it.

I peel off the seal and unroll the papyrus and hand it to Thin Shimon. "Read it to us."

He reads in a loud, clear voice, "Miryam, mother of Yeshua the *tsaddik*, to Little Yaakov, Yosi, Thin Shimon, and Yehuda Dreamhead, shalom!"

"There, you see?" Theudas says. "You four men, are you Little Yaakov and Yosi and Thin Shimon and Yehuda Dreamhead?"

We all nod.

"Then give me my two *dinars*."

Shimon the baker gives him a hard look and closes his fingers on the *dinars*. "I had a letter once, and the price was told at the tail of the letter. Read the last words."

Thin Shimon scans down to the end and reads it aloud.

"I, Mattityahu, a tax-farmer of Capernaum and friend of Rabbi Yeshua of Nazareth, write this letter with my own hand. Pay the bearer of this letter one *dinar* and give hospitality one night, for that is what was promised."

My whole body is in a big sweat and my hands shake and I think my heart will pop in my chest. I never felt such a big rage. Yeshua is friend to some tax-farmer?

Shimon the baker frowns on Theudas. "You are a liar and a thief. Here is the *dinar* you were promised. Little Yaakov, here is your other *dinar*. Do you still wish to show him hospitality?"

"Never." I turn and stalk out of Shimon the baker's house with my brothers.

Half a dozen men stand there with mouths hanging open. Their faces tell that they heard what Thin Shimon read from the tax-farmer.

Yoseph the leather-man grins such a big grin as I never saw. He steps into the house of Shimon the baker. "I will give hospitality to this man. Friend, what is the news from Magdala?"

I do not wait to hear more. I march down the street toward our house. My head buzzes as it is filled with hornets. We must read this whole letter, but not out here on the street. I will take my brothers into an inner chamber and Thin Shimon will read it to us in a quiet voice.

But I already know what we will hear.

Yeshua is making a scandal.

And now all Nazareth knows it.

CHAPTER SIXTY-FOUR

Yoni of Capernaum

When I wake, it is still dark. My heart beats three times too fast. I have done a bad wickedness.

I would blame Big Yaakov for this, but it is my own wickedness. Rabbi Yeshua will be ashamed on me when he finds out.

Shimon the Rock snores near me, and also Big Yaakov and Toma the boat maker. A little light comes in the window slits of the house where we are staying. I think dawn will come in an hour. When Rabbi Yeshua wakes, HaShem will tell him what I did, and he will call me a sinner and send me home to Capernaum.

My hands still tingle with the feel of the serving girl's softness. It has been almost two months since we went to that feast in Magdala, but not one day has passed that I have forgotten what happened there, how the girl fell on me and pressed her body on me. We have walked all through Galilee for those two months, telling the good news that the kingdom of HaShem is beginning, but all that time, I have been thinking on that girl.

Yesterday, we came to Tsipori, and Rabbi Yeshua healed a few sick and sent away an unclean spirit. A wine merchant offered hospitality, and we ate a big evening meal and slept all night on fine mats in the main room of his house.

The village *hazzan* told me once that when a man dreams, his soul goes out of his body and walks the earth doing good things or wicked things. Last night, my soul did a wicked thing.

I listen long to know who is awake. I think they are all asleep.

I raise my head and look to see.

Even Rabbi Yeshua is asleep. Sometimes he goes out early to speak to HaShem, but I see him lying on his back now, breathing softly. We walked far yesterday, and he must be very tired.

Slowly, slowly, I push to a sitting position.

Nobody says no.

Slowly, slowly, I push to a standing position.

Nobody says no.

Slowly, slowly, I take up my cloak and my belt and my pack. I put on my sandals. I walk on silent feet through the door into the middle courtyard of the great house. I walk through the courtyard to the iron gate.

A gate-man sits on a stone bench. He looks on me with sleepy eyes.

I say, "I wish to see the king's palace. Which way is it?"

He looks on me as I am some ignorant child from a small village. "There is no king in Tsipori since ten years. King Herod lives in Tiberias now."

I make a big scowl on him. "Yes, I know, and I have seen his palace in Tiberias. But I wish to see the palace he left here in Tsipori. Tales tell it is a big palace."

He makes a shrug as I am a fool. "Walk downhill. The king's palace is in the lowest part of the city."

I know that is a lie, but all I want is for him to unlock the gate. I grin on him and make a move to go out.

He unlocks the gate.

I go out and look all around. There is a pink glow in the east, toward the Lake of Ginosar. Home is that way by a walk of one day. I will not dare go that way ever again.

To the west, in the middle of the city, at the top of the hill, there is a fortress with large walls around it and tall stone buildings inside. That is the king's palace. The gate-man thought I am a fool who will believe a king would put a palace in the lowest spot of a city. I will show him who is the fool. I lift my tunic and make a piss on the iron gate.

The gate-man shouts on me, "You! Boy!"

I turn and run away fast toward the city center. The streets of Tsipori are wide and straight and paved with flat stones. Rabbi Yeshua told me yesterday that he helped make some of these buildings, he and his father and brothers, for they live near here, only the walk of one hour to the south and east. I think Rabbi Yeshua means to go home soon. We have not been to Nazareth all summer, and I do not know why. Rabbi Yeshua says we will go to Nazareth when HaShem tells him to go to Nazareth. I think he means to do a big thing in Nazareth and is waiting his chance.

I was hoping to see his brothers soon, for they will be fierce warriors in the battle with the Great Satan. Now I will not see them ever again.

I catch up to an oxcart driver in the street and ask him, "Which way is the *mikveh*?"

He scowls on me and points with his chin toward the avenue we are approaching. "Turn south there and go a hundred paces. What do you need a *mikveh* for?"

He knows well enough why I need a *mikveh*. He knows I did a wickedness. I hurry ahead and turn left on the broad avenue. There are large homes on the left and right. A hundred paces up, I see the *mikveh* on the right side. I push on the door, but it is locked. There is a bench across the avenue, facing south. I sit and wait.

Rabbi Yeshua will be sad when he learns I am gone. I will not tell him why I left. I will not tell him I am leaving. I will just go. If Big Yaakov finds out what I have done, he will mock me to scorn. And he will tell my sisters. If he tells them, I will die of my dishonor.

I sit waiting, trying not to think of the wickedness, but it is no use.

Last night, when I dreamed, my soul went to Magdala. It wandered the dark streets. It found the house of that tax-farmer where we ate the feast. It searched all through the house. It found the room where the serving girls sleep. It found the girl I think on all the time, the big-eyes slim-waist girl. My soul looked on her with hungry eyes until she woke. She gave me lewd eyes and said she was glad on seeing me. She took off her tunic. She took off my tunic. She—

"It is a fine morning for thinking, yes?"

My head spins around. "Rabbi Yeshua! You … are awake early." My heart beats fast as a hummingbird's wings. My face feels as it has a bad sun-scorch.

Rabbi Yeshua sits on the bench beside me.

I wish to crawl down in some hole in the ground like a snake. He must see there is a *mikveh* just here. He must know why I have come. At least I can trust him not to tell Big Yaakov. But now it will be hard to leave without telling him I am going. He will wish to sit here talking with me. After I go in the *mikveh*, he will wait for me, and he will wish to return to the house where we are staying. Then the men will see my wet hair and my wet clothes and know where I was.

I stand as I mean to go walking.

Rabbi Yeshua looks on me with raised eyebrows that ask where I am going when my business is here.

I sit.

My heart thumps in my chest like a war drum. I think it might break my ribs. I think my cheeks will burn up with my shame. I think—

A clinking of metal.

An old man stands at the door of the *mikveh* with a great ring of iron keys. He finds one, inserts it in the iron lock, twists it around, and pulls until the latch inside clicks. He turns to look on us. He looks on Rabbi Yeshua. He looks on my burning cheeks. A crafty grin spreads across his face. He knows this is my first time to use the *mikveh*. He reads my face like I read a line from the Torah. "You are here for the *mikveh*?"

I cannot speak. My tongue is the size of a rat. I am frozen in my place. I cannot move. I will die from my big shame. If I could move, I would tear that mocking grin off his—

"Yes." Rabbi Yeshua stands. "I had a dream on a woman last night, and now I am unclean."

My mouth falls open and I cannot breathe.

Rabbi Yeshua takes a coin out of his belt and hands it to the old man. "For me and also for my friend after me."

I watch him go in the *mikveh*. I do not know how this can be. Rabbi Yeshua is a *tsaddik*. How is it he dreamed on a woman? A *tsaddik* should not dream on a woman. I thought a *tsaddik* was pure in heart. I thought …

I lean forward, for I am dizzy with all my thinking. I am more shocked than I ever was.

Shortly, the door opens. Rabbi Yeshua comes out. His hair and his beard are wet. His tunic is wet all through. He smiles on me. "Blessed be HaShem, yes?"

I stand and walk past him into the *mikveh*. My feet feel as they are wooden blocks. I step out of my sandals. I take off my pack and my cloak and my belt and lay them on the stone bench. I take off my tunic and look to see where I spilled seed on it. I do not see it, but I must have spilled seed. That is what they say will happen, and that is why it must be immersed with me.

I walk down the steps on the right side of the stone divider into the *mikveh*. I lower myself into the water until my head is covered. I come up from the water clean. I wring out the water from my tunic. It takes many times to wring it all out.

I walk up the steps on the clean side. I put on my tunic. It clings to my skin wet. I take up my belt and my cloak and my pack. I put on my sandals and go outside.

Rabbi Yeshua has been waiting for me. He takes my hand. "We should walk and let the sun dry us, yes? I will show you a place I helped build."

We walk for the fourth part of an hour until we reach a large stone house. Two stone benches sit across from it, facing east. We sit on the benches until the sun rises. We say the morning prayer. We sit again and wait for the sun to warm us. Finally, I make my courage strong to ask the question burning a hole in my heart.

"Rabbi Yeshua …?" My tongue refuses to speak.

He smiles on me. "Did Big Yaakov tell you some idle tale about dreaming on a woman?"

"I ..." My ears turn hot. I nod my head.

"Did he tell you it is a wickedness to dream on a woman who is not yours?"

I cannot look his eyes.

"Once there was a man who went on a far journey. His donkey went lame, so he had to walk. He met a hungry beggar and gave him some of his bread and cheese. A big storm blew and delayed him. Two days before his journey's end, his food ran out. He was in a desert place and could not glean from the edges of a field or vineyard. There was no town or farm to ask for bread. The man spent all day thinking on food and wishing for food. When night came, he went to sleep hungry. In the night, HaShem gave him a dream on a rich feast with figs and cheese and grapes and stewed lentils and bread and fine wine and a whole fatted calf. The man ate and ate until he could not eat any more. In the morning, he woke and knew it was only a dream. Do you know what he did?"

I stare on Rabbi Yeshua with my mouth hanging open.

He grins on me. "The man said the blessing after bread. He blessed HaShem for sending him a kindness, a promise of good things in days to come. Blessed be HaShem, yes?"

I think I am only beginning to understand what is a *tsaddik*.

CHAPTER SIXTY-FIVE

Miryam of Nazareth

I am going home for one night! We spent three days in Tsipori.
Yesterday was Shabbat, and we all went to the synagogue. Tsipori
has a mighty synagogue, for it is a large city. They asked my son
to read from the prophets and expound on them. He read it well and
told some tales. Then some man with an evil spirit spoiled it all by
shouting curses on him.

My son sent away the evil spirit, and now all the city knows Rabbi
Yeshua is a mighty man of HaShem. He was busy all today healing
people.

Of course, Little Yaakov and Yosi and Thin Shimon and Yehuda
Dreamhead heard the matter. They work in Tsipori most days, and
they heard the talk in the street today and came to find us.

They said we should come home to Nazareth.

Yeshua was too busy—there were many hundred people waiting to
be healed—but he said I could go home to see my grandchildren
tonight.

I said I was not sure if I should go.

Little Yaakov said I should come.

I said maybe.

Yosi said I should come.

I said maybe.

Yehuda Dreamhead said I should come.

I said maybe.

Thin Shimon tapped his nose and said his little son longs for me to come home.

I said yes.

I never thought I would be eager to go back to Nazareth, but now I am eager. Now I am brave of the village. I wish to see—

"Explain the matter of the tax-farmer," Little Yaakov says.

I do not know where to begin. "Two months ago, Yeshua made a scandal in Capernaum and—"

"What scandal?" Yosi asks.

"They brought a sick man to be healed, but Yeshua did not heal him at the first. He told forgiveness to the man, and people thought he made a scorn on HaShem."

Little Yaakov sucks in his breath through his teeth. "That is a bad matter."

"Yeshua is a prophet," I say. "HaShem told him the man was forgiven, so he told the man he was forgiven. That is not a scorn on HaShem."

My sons say nothing, but I hear a big disapproval in their silence.

At last Little Yaakov says, "What has this to do with the tax-farmer?"

"There was a big scandal in Capernaum on the matter of telling forgiveness, so we went away from there toward Bethsaida. When we reached the border, there was a tax-farmer's booth. Yeshua waited in line with the oxcart drivers as he had something to pay. Then he spoke kindly to the tax-farmer and asked him to come with us and help destroy the Great Satan."

"Tax-farmers *are* the Great Satan," Yosi says.

I do not know what to say to that.

"So now Yeshua has this tax-farmer in his army," Little Yaakov says. "That is more foolish than I ever heard."

My cheeks feel as they are on fire. "You should be glad on the matter. Mattai is the one who wrote letters all the summer long for me. Without him, you would not know what Yeshua has been doing."

"Without him, all Nazareth would not know what Yeshua has been doing. Do you know how angry the village is on the matter?"

"I ..." Suddenly, I cannot breathe.

"Do you know how angry *we* are on the matter?" Yehuda Dream-head says.

I stop and look on my sons.

Their faces are red with their fury.

I do not know if they are angry on me, but I am sure they are angry on Yeshua. "Mattai is not a tax-farmer anymore. You should meet him. He is a kind man."

"Kind?" Yosi glares on me. "He is a thief and a liar and a finger in the hand of the Great Satan. Do you think none of that matters, only because he is *kind*?"

I cross my arms on my chest and glare back on him. "Yes, kind. He wrote many letters for me all summer, one in each week, and never called me a foolish old woman. He bought papyrus and ink and reed pens with his own money, for a kindness on me. And he loves HaShem. When he was a small boy, he was strong in Torah. He wished to go to Jerusalem to study with a sage. He—"

"What sage would have a tax-farmer?" Little Yaakov spits in the dust.

"He was not a tax-farmer yet! He was the son of a scribe in Magdala, and his father taught him to read and write and even do sums! He was mighty in Torah already as a boy, and Rabbi Shammai wished to have him in his school when he came of age, only—"

"Rabbi Shammai?" Thin Shimon looks as he will faint. "Rabbi Shammai wished to have a tax-farmer in his school?"

"He was not a tax-farmer yet! I keep telling you, and why will you not listen? Mattai would have gone to Jerusalem when he became a man, but before that, his father died, and he was starving, and he agreed to do sums for a tax-farmer to put bread in his mouth."

"Bread in his mouth." Little Yaakov's lips curl. "That is no good—"

"Hush, fool!" I stab a finger on his chest. "Your woman was once a *zonah* to put bread in her mouth. Do you sneer on your woman because she chose not to starve?"

Little Yaakov's face is stone. He loves his woman, even if she is only a concubine.

I say, "I like the tax-farmer, and you will not speak ill on him."

My four sons stare on me as I am a dead woman.

I am still shocked to say such a thing, but it is true. I like the tax-farmer. At first, I pretended to like him so he would write letters for me. But then I saw he is kind and loves Torah and gives alms to the poor, even when no one is looking. I am only a foolish old woman, but he does not treat me as a foolish old woman. After one month, I realized I liked him. Now it is two months, and he is like a son to me.

I stand to my tallest height, but still I do not come as high as Little Yaakov's chin. "Mattai is a good man, and he loves Yeshua."

"If he comes to our village, he will be killed," Yosi says.

I do not say anything to that. Maybe that is why my son has delayed to go to Nazareth. I know he longs to go there. We walked past it three times, but he never made a move to go up the hill.

We walk the rest of the way to our village in silence. My sons are angry on me. I am angry on them. The sun hangs low in the sky behind us when we reach the village gate.

The village elders stop their chatter when they see us.

We march through the gate.

Old Yonatan the leather-man hawks loud and spits the dust. He sings the wicked song he made long ago.

> "Once there was an evil tale
> An evil tale
> An evil—"

I scoop up a fistful of dust from the street and fling it in his face. "You old fool!"

He gags and stands, retching in the street. He coughs and coughs and coughs. At last, he spits out something black. He wipes his mouth on the sleeve of his tunic. "Filthy *zonah*."

"You did not think I was a *zonah* when you tried to buy me many years ago."

His face fills with hate. "I—"

"I thank HaShem every day that my father refused you."

"I—"

"You stink of piss and your woman is ugly and your son is *haryo*, and I wish your granddaughters will be barren. I wish you will die in your sins. I wish the tales are true that evil men go to Gehenna when they die. I wish you will feel the fire there for the whole twelve months appointed for wicked men. I wish—"

"Imma." Little Yaakov pulls me away. "Imma, come home with us."

"If your son comes here, we will crush him," says Old Yonatan. "Tell the *mamzer* that—we will crush him."

I spit in his direction.

He spits back at me. "Spreadlegs!"

"Imma, enough!" Little Yaakov picks me up and turns toward home.

I let him carry me. All my body burns with my hate. When we reach our house, I collapse on a bench and cry for my rage. But I also feel glad on one thing.

I stood up to my tormentor. I never did that before in all my life. His scorn still burns me like fire, but I gave him back my own scorn, twice as much.

I am not a weak old woman anymore.

I am a strong old woman.

I am brave of the village.

When Yeshua comes here, I will ask him to call down fire from heaven on them.

When he sees how strong and brave I am, he will do it.

∽

Miryam of Nazareth

When we reach the village spring, I put down my waterpot and sit on a large stone. "Show me."

Thin Shimon looks back down the path toward the village. He looks all around us. He sits beside me and reaches in his belt and takes out a leather pouch.

He pours it into my open hand.

The Ring of Justice gleams bright like a sword.

A rush of joy runs all through my body. All the world becomes a blur. "Where did you find it, you clever boy?"

Thin Shimon hides the Ring back in the pouch and puts it in his belt. "In a secret place where I will hide it again until Yeshua comes back to make a justice on you."

"Do your brothers know you found it?"

"Only you, Imma. Little Yaakov would take it for himself, if he knew."

"You are the cleverest boy that ever was."

Thin Shimon grins on me. "When will Yeshua come back to the village?"

"He means to go to Cana tomorrow to see Shlomi Dancefeet and then back to Capernaum before Shabbat. After Shabbat, he leaves for Jerusalem for Sukkot."

"We could take the Ring to him in Jerusalem."

I shake my head. "It is not safe to take it so far. Not on the Samaritan Road. I will make a beg on him to come here after Sukkot. That will be a good time to make a justice on me."

"The village is angry on him. The leather-man says he will crush him."

"The moment Yeshua comes in the village, find the Ring and then stay close to Yeshua. When you see he is in a big danger, put it in his hand in that moment. He will know what to do."

"What if he refuses it?"

"He will not refuse it if he knows he is about to die."

Thin Shimon wears a grim face. "If he refuses it, I will give it to Little Yaakov."

I thank HaShem for my clever son, for he saw a thing I did not. I wish Yeshua will make a justice on me. He is my firstborn, and that is his duty and his honor.

But if he will not do it, Little Yaakov will.

By one son or another, I will have my justice.

CHAPTER SIXTY-SIX

Shimon of Capernaum

The day is growing late, and we are just reaching the edges of Magdala, and I know we will reach Capernaum tonight if we hurry, and I am on fire to get there. We were gone two whole weeks this time, and it is a sore trial to be away from my woman so long.

It is not a good sense, what we have been doing. We walked to the far end of Galilee and back, to no gain. We stayed long in Tsipori, which is the chief city of Galilee. We could have raised up an army there to fight the Great Satan. Instead, Rabbi Yeshua healed many people and sent away evil spirits and told tales of the kingdom of HaShem.

Only he made no move to bring in the kingdom of HaShem.

Now we are going home, and I am sick in my heart. It feels as we have done nothing all the summer. When Rabbi Yeshua called us to follow him last spring, I thought we would instantly raise up a mighty army and attack the Great Satan. But now after four months, we are still only eight men who follow the rabbi. That is not an army. Someone should explain the matter to the rabbi, only not me.

I walk beside Rabbi Yeshua, thinking on my woman.

Only it is hard to think on her, because Yoni keeps asking many questions.

"Rabbi Yeshua, why did we not go to Nazareth when we were so close? Why did your mother stay there, instead of coming back with us? When will you make a big army and fight the Great Satan? Will Little Yaakov command your army? What did you tell your brothers, to make them so angry? Will we reach Capernaum tonight? I think Shimon the Rock is eager to see his woman, what do you think? He looks eager. Can you teach me how to heal people as you do?"

I hear the hiss of Big Yaakov's breath behind us. "Yoni, hush your impudent questions, or I will box your ears."

Yoni covers his ears with his hands. "I do not see why it is impudent to wish to do what my master does."

Rabbi Yeshua stops and stares on Yoni for a moment. A smile creases his face. He begins laughing.

I do not think it is funny. He smiles on Yoni's foolishness, when he should give him a good beating. My father always says a boy needs a thousand beatings to grow into a man. I say an impudent boy needs more.

I look behind us at the sun. It is two hours above the mountains in the west. "Rabbi, we stayed long in Cana, but if we hurry, we will reach Capernaum just at sunset, and that will be a good end on our trip, yes?"

I do not add that we stayed long in Cana because many hundred people came to be healed and Rabbi Yeshua was kind on them. Kindness is good, but there is such a thing as too much kindness.

Rabbi Yeshua says nothing, but he quickens his pace.

If we reach Capernaum tonight, that will be a good kindness on me. A *tsaddik* does not need a woman, but I am not a *tsaddik*.

"There he is! There is the rabbi!"

The voices come from the direction of the synagogue. Three men hurry toward us. They look ragged and dirty, and their cloaks are stained as they have been on some long journey. Behind them, others from the town are pointing and shouting and following.

Rabbi Yeshua waits.

The three men arrive.

Rabbi Yeshua greets each of them with a kiss and a kiss and a kiss. "Brother Shmuel! Brother Hananyah! Brother Yoseph! It is good to see you."

They do not look as they think it is good to see Rabbi Yeshua. That is anger shining in their eyes, or I am a *zonah*.

Yoni tugs on my sleeve. "Those are the men from Yohanan the immerser. Remember them?"

I do not remember them, except the thick-built one, that Hananyah the nail maker, who told us some lying tale last Pesach to make us run like women. Rabbi Yeshua should tell him away.

"My brothers, you will come with us to Capernaum, yes?" Rabbi Yeshua says.

The three men pass dark looks among themselves. Hananyah the nail maker steps forward. "Rabbi, all the countryside is making rumor on you, even as far as Jericho. We have gone three times now to visit Yohanan in prison, and we told him all that we heard on you, and he sends us to ask what is the meaning of these things. When will you make a move? If you think you are something, why do you leave HaShem's prophet in the prison of the evil king?"

I do not like Hananyah the nail maker, but he asks the same questions I ask. We have waited overlong for Rabbi Yeshua to make a move.

There is a big murmuring all around us.

Many hundred men of Magdala have surrounded us. All of them are asking the same questions.

Yoni's small hand takes mine. His eyes shine.

I know what he thinks. He thinks that soon will come the Day of Vengeance. Last Shabbat we were in Tsipori, and they asked Rabbi Yeshua to expound on the prophets. He read from the scroll of Isaiah, but he stopped before the Day of Vengeance. That is where he always stops. I am sick to my death of waiting for him to read the Day of Vengeance.

I want the Day of Vengeance to fall on the earth. I want it now.

Rabbi Yeshua says nothing. His head tilts and his eyes close halfway.

I know this means he is listening to the voice of HaShem. My belly tightens into a hard knot. I wish HaShem would tell him to do some sensible thing.

Rabbi Yeshua's eyes open. He rises up on his toes and looks all around. He points at a man and walks toward him. "You!"

The crowd parts before Rabbi Yeshua.

The man trembles as Rabbi Yeshua approaches. He crouches down tight, covering his head.

Rabbi Yeshua stops before him. "Friend—"

The man leaps at Rabbi Yeshua's throat, snarling, snapping with his teeth.

Rabbi Yeshua twists right.

The man's teeth sink into Rabbi Yeshua's left shoulder.

Rabbi Yeshua staggers backward. "Shalom!"

The man screams and falls in the dirt.

Rabbi Yeshua kneels beside him. "Leave him, all you unclean spirits. Go now, and never come back."

The man screams again and shakes like a boat in a great storm and then …

He falls still.

There is no sound but the man's weeping.

Rabbi Yeshua bends down and whispers long in his ear. At last, he stands and helps the man to his feet and gives him a kiss and a kiss and a kiss.

Everyone begins shouting all at once.

"Rabbi! I have a broken finger!"

"Rabbi! My son at home has the belly-fever!"

"Rabbi! My mother has the wasting disease!"

I am sick to my death on all these many people. Now is a good time for Rabbi Yeshua to make a move. He should break open the prison where Yohanan the prophet is held. Yohanan immersed many ten thousand men, and they would all join our army if Rabbi Yeshua broke him out.

Now is the time for men of violence to rise up. Now is the time to throw down the evil king, Herod, and the Great Satan, Caesar. The wicked goyim call Caesar the son of HaShem, but that is a lie. Caesar is not the anointed king of Israel. Caesar is a false king.

Now is not the time for Rabbi Yeshua to waste strength on sick folk of no account. After we crush the Great Satan, the sick can come and be healed. That is the right order of things—call up the men of violence now, and then heal the men of weakness after. Rabbi Yeshua is a good man, but he has a kind spot for these men of weakness. If he misses his chance, it will be because he is too kindhearted.

I touch Rabbi Yeshua's shoulder. "Rabbi, a word, please."

He grins on me. "Shimon, my brother, I need your help. Place hands on this man's arm and tell it to be whole."

I reach for the arm and then see the spots of whiteness. My heart seizes in my chest, and I pull back. "Rabbi … the man has the look of …"

I do not dare say he has the look of *tsaraat*, or the crowd will hear and make a big rushing and people will be crushed.

Yoni pushes his way in. "Rabbi Yeshua, what are you doing?"

Rabbi Yeshua says, "Place hands on the man's arm and tell it to be whole."

Yoni places hands on the man's arm.

I hate that Yoni pushes in where he has no place.

"Tell it to be whole, Yoni."

Yoni says, "Be whole."

I do not see anything happening, and I am glad. Yoni is impudent, more than any boy ever was.

"Be whole," Yoni says again.

I am hot in all my parts. That would be the worst thing, if the man should be made whole. Then we will never hear the end of Yoni's boasting.

"Be whole," Yoni says.

All my body is in a big sweat.

Rabbi Yeshua grins. "Lift your hands, Yoni."

Yoni lifts his hands.

The man's arm is whole.

For a moment I cannot breathe. Did Yoni make the man whole? No, that is not a good sense. Rabbi Yeshua made the man whole. He told what words to say. All Yoni did was repeat. That is not the same as knowing what words to say. But Yoni will not see it, and now he will be more conceited than ever.

Toma Trouble tries to crowd in. "Move aside, Yohanan Talk-Talk. We cannot see what the rabbi is doing when you and Shimon crowd all together."

All the three of us step back from the man who had *tsaraat*.

Now I see what is the reason for the matter. Rabbi Yeshua did not need our help to heal the man. That would be a big foolishness, for we are only fish-men, not prophets. Rabbi Yeshua only needed us to make a fence for prying eyes, so no one would see that the man had *tsaraat*. That makes a good sense.

Rabbi Yeshua grins on me and Yoni. "That was a good help."

Yoni grins like a wolf.

I do not grin. I should speak to the rabbi on the matter of giving the boy a good beating. If he will not do it, I will.

Behind Rabbi Yeshua, I see the men from Yohanan the immerser scowling on us.

I only wish we will make an end on this healing foolishness and leave now. If we hurry, we can still reach Capernaum.

But Rabbi Yeshua does not make an end on it. He finds a blind man and heals him. He finds an old woman with an evil spirit and sends it away. He finds a deaf boy and heals him. He does not make an end on his healing until the sun falls down behind the mountains.

We will not reach Capernaum tonight.

The men from Yohanan the immerser stand with arms crossed on chests.

Rabbi Yeshua looks more tired than I ever saw him, but he gives a smile to the men. "Go to Yohanan the prophet and tell him what you have seen. The blind see. The lame walk. The lepers are made clean. The deaf hear. The kingdom of HaShem is breaking in on us."

The men scowl on him. They turn and stomp away in a big rage.

They should be angry. I am angry too.

That is not a good sense, what the rabbi said.

Yes, he healed the blind and lame and deaf.

Yes, he purified *tsaraat*.

Yes, he sent away evil spirits.

No, the kingdom of HaShem is not breaking in.

The kingdom of HaShem will not break in until we raise up an army.

We could have gone to the city square and called for an army and raised up a thousand men of violence.

Instead, we missed our chance and wasted time on sick people, old people, weak people.

The sick and the old and the weak are no use for an army.

We missed a chance for the kingdom of HaShem to break in.

Rabbi Yeshua never misses a chance to miss a chance.

I will not dishonor him by asking him on this matter.

Instead, I will tell Yoni to do it.

CHAPTER SIXTY-SEVEN

Yoni of Capernaum

"Rabbi Yeshua, may I ask you a question?"

The rabbi laughs out loud. "Yoni, no day goes by that you fail to ask many ten thousand questions. Ask."

Shimon the Rock has been begging me now for a whole week to ask the rabbi on this matter. I have been stalling, because when Shimon wants a favor from me, he does not tease me about women. But I am dying from my curiosity, and now is a good time to ask.

I hear the others drawing close behind us. We are on the way to Jerusalem for Sukkot. Only the eight men who follow Rabbi Yeshua. Our families are coming a day behind us, on account of all the rabbi's scandals. We walked all day from Jericho up the steep road toward Jerusalem, and we are tired, and now that it comes to the point, I am afraid.

Rabbi Yeshua looks on me with laughing eyes. "So, you will ask me this question that burns a hole in your tongue, yes?"

I take a large breath and rush forward before my courage runs away from me. "The … men who came from Yohanan the immerser. They wanted you to make a move, and yet you did not make a move.

When will you make a move? Will it be at the feast? Will you make a big army at Rosh HaShanah? Will you send away the evil priests from the Temple on Yom Kippur? Will this be the year of liberation? What is the meaning of what you do? Why do you wait to make a move? Do you not see we are all dying for the Day of Vengeance to come?"

"That is only eight questions. You are not up to your usual mark, Yoni!"

The other men laugh, but it is a nervous laugh.

I grin on him. "That is not even the eighth part of an answer, Rabbi. You are not up to your usual mark, either!"

The others roar.

Rabbi Yeshua laughs too. He laughs so hard, he stops and bends over and slaps his thighs.

He honors me, to laugh on my jest, but still I wish he will make an answer.

Rabbi Yeshua takes my hand and we continue walking. "When you first went to see Yohanan the immerser, what did you go to see? Some reed swaying in the wind?"

"No, I looked for a man who fears HaShem."

"Did you go to see a rich man wearing soft clothes?"

"No, I looked for a man who does not fear rich men who wear soft clothes."

"What else did you go to see?"

"A prophet."

"And more than a prophet, yes? You went to see the one the prophet Malachi told tale on, the messenger of HaShem, who makes a way before the coming of HaShem, yes?"

"If Yohanan made a way before the coming of HaShem, then where is the coming of HaShem?"

"And I tell you true, no man born of women is greater than Yohanan the immerser. Yet the weakest man in the kingdom of HaShem will be greater than Yohanan the immerser."

My heart beats many times in my chest. That is not a good logic. If that is a good logic, then no man is worthy to enter the kingdom of HaShem. But I do not think it is a logic at all. I think it is a paradox. "When will the kingdom of HaShem come?"

"Since the prophet Yohanan appeared, the kingdom of HaShem has been advancing. But it is hidden, and men of violence wish to lay hold on it before the time."

My ears feel hot. I wish to be a man of violence. Shimon the Rock wishes to be a man of violence. We all wish to be men of violence. We all wish to lay hold on the kingdom of HaShem. But Rabbi Yeshua makes it sound as we wish for a wrong thing.

Rabbi Yeshua smiles on me with kindness. "The men of violence, the men of this generation, they are like children in the market who think to make the village do as they wish. The children play their flutes and are amazed the village does not dance. Then they sing a dirge and are amazed the village does not mourn."

"But—"

"Yohanan the immerser fasted, and they said he had an evil spirit."

"But—"

"The son of Adam eats and drinks, and they say he is a glutton and a drunkard and a friend of tax-farmers and sinful women."

I do not know what to say. Rabbi Yeshua *is* a friend of tax-farmers and sinful women. Every time I think he will make a move, he makes a scandal instead. Our families are coming to Jerusalem a day behind us, only because they think Rabbi Yeshua is a scandal, and they do not wish to be seen with him.

"Blessed is the man who is not scandalized on me."

I think my eyes will bulge out of my head. Sometimes I think he hears the words I say in my heart before I do.

Rabbi Yeshua smiles on me. "Are you answered, Yoni?"

I am not answered. I am more confused than I ever was. I do not see what making a scandal has to do with the kingdom of HaShem.

We are close to the last village before Bethany, and I am eager to see Aunt Miryam and tell her all that has happened since Pesach, when we ran like fearful women from King Herod. We do not run like fearful women now. We went all through Galilee this whole summer, and King Herod never—

"Rabbi!" A woman shrieks and runs toward us from the village.

My heart flutters for fear for a moment. Then I see it is only some *zonah*. A *zonah* is nothing to be afraid on.

The woman falls at Rabbi Yeshua's feet wailing. "Rabbi! Help me!"

The village is two hundred paces away. I hope it is too far for them to hear her big noise.

Rabbi Yeshua squats in the dust beside her and speaks softly to her.

The woman screams louder than any woman ever did, more than six wild dogs barking on the moon.

I wish to beat her with my fists. She will make a big scandal on us, and then how will Rabbi Yeshua make a move?

Rabbi Yeshua strokes her head gently. She wears a silk hair covering. It is bought with the wages of her sin, or I am Mashiach.

The woman weeps and wails, and her head flops around until her hair covering comes off. Her hair is very long and beautiful.

Rabbi Yeshua says, "Yoni, place hands on the woman's head."

I wish to run away. Shimon the Rock and Big Yaakov will mock me to scorn if I touch a *zonah's* hair.

"Yoni, place hands on the woman's head."

I squat beside Rabbi Yeshua.

Big Yaakov says, "Yoni, think on what you are doing."

I wish to do what Rabbi Yeshua said. But I am terrified to do what Rabbi Yeshua said.

Rabbi Yeshua says, "Yoni, place hands on the woman's head."

I reach forward and place hands on the woman's head. Her hair is soft and warm. For a moment, I cannot think.

Rabbi Yeshua says, "Tell the spirit of adultery to go."

My whole body feels hot. I never touched a woman's hair before. I never touched a *zonah* before. I feel as I am unclean.

"Tell the spirit of adultery to go," Rabbi Yeshua says.

My voice is a ragged whisper. "You … you spirit of adultery, go away."

The woman screams with a big scream.

"Tell it away, Yoni."

"Go, you spirit of adultery."

The woman pulls and rips at her tunic as she will tear it off.

"Speak with authority, Yoni! Quickly!"

For a moment I do not see a *zonah*. I see a small girl, screaming and screaming while some big man holds her down and does a wickedness on her. I feel her terror. I know her heart. I am enraged on this man of wickedness.

"Go!" I shout. "Leave this daughter of HaShem in peace! I command it by The Name. Go!"

She stops screaming in the middle of a big scream. She stops tearing at her tunic. She smiles.

All my body is in a big sweat. I placed hands on a *zonah*. If I never do that again, it will be too soon.

The woman begins crying, softly at first, then louder, then a big wailing. It is the wailing of repentance, and I think she has much to repent.

Rabbi Yeshua leans down and whispers in her ear. "HaShem says your sins are forgiven. HaShem says he loves you like his own daughter. HaShem calls you to come home to Abba."

The *zonah* cries and cries and cries.

Shimon the Rock and Big Yaakov and the others are standing in the road, making a wall between Rabbi Yeshua and the village. In case there are idle eyes, they will only see a group of men standing in the road. That is not a scandal.

At last Rabbi Yeshua stands. That is not a scandal.

The *zonah* stands. That is not a scandal.

Rabbi Yeshua gives her a kiss and a kiss and a kiss.

That is a scandal.

The *zonah* smiles on me and gives me a kiss and a kiss and a kiss.

That is a mighty scandal. All my body feels numb from the scandal.

If Big Yaakov makes a joke on me later about this *zonah*, I will put my thumb in his eye.

CHAPTER SIXTY-EIGHT

Miryam of Bethany

I am in the kitchen piling rounds of bread on a platter when I hear Marta's voice in the courtyard.

"They are here! The rabbi and his men are here. Miryam Big-Eyes, be quick!" Marta bursts in and clucks tongue at me and seizes the platter and scuttles out.

I take a bowl of crushed chickpeas and hurry after her.

It is not quite dark yet, and we have been expecting the rabbi and his men all day, and now they are here, and I am sure I will make a fool on myself. But little Yoni will be with him, and I would make a fool on myself ten times if only I can see him again. I wonder if he is grown any since Pesach.

The men sit on benches against the wall in our large receiving room. We have a big house with many rooms. The rabbi has eight men with him, but they are not too many for us.

Marta offers bread to the rabbi.

He takes and gives her a large smile. "Marta, you outdo yourself!"

Marta blushes and does not look on the rabbi, but I know she is pleased. She offers bread to the rabbi's men and last to little Yoni, who is youngest.

I offer chickpeas to the rabbi.

He dips bread and eats.

I do not know if he smiles on me, for of course I do not look a man in the eye.

"Miryam Big-Heart, you are beautiful as my own mother, who is also called Miryam. I thank HaShem, who made you more beautiful than all the flowers of the field."

My hands feel numb and my heart dances like a drunkard. I was not sure if the rabbi would even remember my name. It is long since he was here, more than five months, but it is longer since any man said I was beautiful.

I do not feel beautiful. The women of the village look on me as I am *haryo*, for I am barren and cursed by HaShem and divorced. I feel as I am ugly.

Marta clucks tongue at me and hisses. "Miryam Big-Eyes, the serving!"

Of course. I am a fool. Marta will say I am making a scandal, to make words with the rabbi, but it is not my fault. I did not speak to him. He spoke to me.

I offer chickpeas to Shimon the Rock, who is a friend on our family.

Shimon the Rock dips bread and eats and does not speak to me.

I offer chickpeas to the other men.

Each of them dips bread and eats and does not speak to me.

I offer chickpeas to Yoni.

He dips bread and eats. "Aunt Miryam, you will not believe what happened this summer! Rabbi Yeshua healed a man with the mighty leprosy! I saw it with these eyes. And he healed a blind man, several of them. And he sent away many evil spirits, more than I can count, and I can count past a hundred. He healed a boil on the arm of an old man, and it was more vile than—"

Marta hisses again. "Miryam Big-Eyes, some wine for the rabbi, yes?"

My face feels as I have been sitting next to the firepit. I hurry to the kitchen and pour wine in stone cups and bring them out on a great platter. I walk carefully, for if I drop the platter, Marta will skin me with her teeth.

I offer wine to Rabbi Yeshua.

He takes and sips.

I dare to look on him.

He smiles on me. "Blessed be HaShem, who lights up this house with your kindness, little sister."

I cannot breathe. I have a brother, Elazar, but he does not call me little sister, and he does not say I light up the house.

I offer wine to Shimon the Rock.

He takes and sips, but he does not speak to me.

I offer wine to each of the men.

They take and sip, but none of them speaks to me.

I offer wine to Yoni.

He takes and sips. "Aunt Miryam, when Rabbi Yeshua makes his move, HaShem will return to Israel and live again in the Temple, and men of Israel will feel the Shekinah, as in days of old! I think even women will feel the Shekinah. Rabbi Yeshua, what do you think? When HaShem comes back, will women feel the Shekinah also, and not men only?"

I long for this to be true, but I know it is a big foolishness.

The other men mutter behind their hands.

Marta clucks tongue. "We must eat soon! Miryam Big-Eyes, I need you in the kitchen!"

Rabbi Yeshua stands and goes to Marta and gives her a kiss and a kiss. "Marta, there was never a woman like you for excellence in hospitality. I think King Solomon wrote of you in the book of his proverbs."

Marta blushes like a sunrise, for he kissed her on each cheek, like a man, like a friend. I never saw her so confused. All the words are frozen in her mouth. She hurries to the kitchen like a fluttering hen.

Marta has forgotten me for a moment.

Rabbi Yeshua looks on me.

He smiles on me.

He walks to me and gives me a kiss and a kiss.

And a kiss.

All the strength goes out of my knees.

"When the kingdom of HaShem comes, you will feel the Shekinah every moment in the day, Miryam Big-Heart. You will bathe in it. You will swim in it. You will hold the Shekinah in your heart like a secret fire, and it will never leave you."

If I had any cups of wine left, I would drop them all on the floor.

I look on the rabbi.

He looks deep in my eyes, deeper than any man ever did.

He pierces my heart.

I come to my senses and see that I am a fool, and I hurry to the kitchen.

I am more foolish than any woman ever was, for now I have done a thing no respectable woman ever should.

If anyone finds out, I will be a scandal in the whole village, until forever.

I have fallen in love with Rabbi Yeshua.

CHAPTER SIXTY-NINE

Miryam of Bethany

I am bringing more wine to serve the men when I see Yoni begin choking.

It is four days since Rabbi Yeshua came to stay with us, and tonight we are having a feast with many guests. We have five whole tables, with nine dining couches at each one, and I am run off my feet trying to serve my table, which is the fifth.

I look to see if my little Yoni has enough.

He is talking to his brother, but Big Yaakov ignores him. Yoni makes a loud jest and bites off a piece of choice roast kid and laughs too hard on his own joke, and the meat catches in his throat.

I see it all in an instant that seems like an hour.

Yoni clutches at his throat, and his face pinches tight, and he writhes on the dining couch, and nobody sees.

I drop my pitcher of wine and run to him, screaming for my fear. "Yoni!"

Big Yaakov turns and nudges him with his elbow. "Spit it out, Yoni. Spit, spit, spit!"

That is foolishness. Tears blur all my eyes, for I know Yoni cannot spit, and he will die if I do not do something.

Shimon the Rock leaps off the dining couch and pushes past me. "Yoni!"

My heart feels as I am running off a cliff, and my mind spins like a great top, and I do not know what to do, and I cannot catch breath. I wring my hands and scream in a big despair.

Now all the feast is in a roar.

Yoni's face turns blue. He rolls wildly and beats his hands on the dining couch.

If he dies, I will die also. I scream louder than I ever did. "Rabbi Yeshua!"

Feet come running on the flagstones of our courtyard.

"Fools, out of the way!" Marta seizes Yoni's feet and pulls with a big pull.

Yoni slides almost all the way off the dining couch.

Marta tries to lift him, but he is too big for her.

She screams on Shimon. "Lift him by the feet, fool!"

Shimon the Rock seizes Yoni's ankles and raises him in the air upside down.

Yoni flops like a fish, and his face is purple.

Marta hits him hard on the back, once, twice, three times.

A chunk of meat pops out of Yoni's mouth.

He sucks in air.

I can breathe again, but I can hardly see for my tears.

Shimon the Rock puts Yoni on his feet.

I push past them all to Yoni and smother him with a hug. "Little brother! You are alive!"

"You did well, Marta. That was quick thinking and quick work." It is the voice of Rabbi Yeshua. He was reclining far away at the head table with my brother Elazar and the important guests.

Marta's face cracks into a smile.

I am so happy, I kiss the top of Yoni's head many times.

"Is the boy well? You lewd woman, you, stop crushing him against your bosoms. You will shame yourself and dishonor Elazar."

I know that voice, and it turns all my joy to ashes.

My ears turn red. I push Yoni away and turn to look on the man I hate most in all the world. The man who divorced me and sent me home in a big shame.

He scowls on me with mouth turned down and eyebrows knotted and lips curled. His name is called Shimon, and people say he is a good man, for he is a Pharisee. He is a man of honor and has flocks and vineyards and olive groves, and people said HaShem smiled on me, to marry such a man.

At the time, I thought so, for he is rich as my brother Elazar, and he can read and write. Most men of the village cannot read, and those who can must labor over each word before they say it. But Shimon the Pharisee can read the Torah straight off as fast as a man can talk. I have seen him do it. He can even write, not only with a wax tablet, but also with a reed pen. He does not hire a letter-man to write his letters for him, like my brother Elazar.

If only I was not barren, I would have been happy with such a man.

But I am barren, and a man of honor needs sons, so Shimon the Pharisee was not happy with me. He sent me back home with a writ of divorce and married some other woman of good family. That was six years ago, and now that other woman is already nineteen, and it seems she is barren too.

I am glad on it.

I hope Shimon the Pharisee never has sons.

I hope his vineyards get the blight and his sheep die of the hoof disease and his olive trees wither in the summer sun.

I would make *haryo* on his meat. I would piss his wine. I would serve it to him on a gold platter.

Rabbi Yeshua looks from me to Shimon the Pharisee and back to me. His face tells that he must have heard something on the evils Shimon the Pharisee has done on me, for his eyes are sad.

Rabbi Yeshua smiles on me. "Miryam Big-Heart, you love Yoni like your own son, and you saved him, for you were first to see him choking."

I wonder how he knows this, for he was far across the courtyard when it happened. Rabbi Yeshua sees much.

Yoni's eyes shine. "Aunt Miryam, I am glad you will be at the feast tomorrow, in case I will choke again."

I do not know what he is talking on. "What feast?"

Marta takes my arm and pulls me away. "Come, Miryam Big-Eyes, there is work to be done. You dropped a pitcher of wine, and we must—"

"What feast?"

Marta pulls me fast toward the kitchen. "There is to be another feast tomorrow at another house, and the host has need of help. Elazar promised our help."

"What feast? Who is the host?"

Marta pulls me as fast as she ever did. "A friend of Elazar."

My heart feels as it is crushed in a fist of iron. "What friend of Elazar?"

But I know what friend of Elazar. There are not many men of wealth in Bethany.

Marta pulls me into the kitchen. "There is to be a feast to honor Rabbi Yeshua tomorrow. Pharisees from Jerusalem wish to meet the rabbi. It is a big honor for him to meet Pharisees from Jerusalem, yes?"

Pharisees. Yes, it is a big honor. Pharisees are men of honor. If I had a son, I would wish him to grow up to be a Pharisee, for they are the most righteous of all men.

Except for one.

Bile rises in my throat.

Shimon the Pharisee will hold a feast tomorrow.

And I am required to serve at it.

I will not do it.

I would rather eat my own *haryo* than serve at a feast given by the wicked man who sent me away in shame.

CHAPTER SEVENTY

Miryam of Bethany

"Aunt Miryam, Rabbi Yeshua wishes you will go walk with him!" Yoni's face shines.

It is the morning, and I did not sleep all night for my rage on the matter of the feast that will come tonight.

"I ..." My face feels hot, and something makes wiggles in my stomach, and my heart wishes to climb up out of my throat and fall on the stone floor of our kitchen and shatter.

"Miryam Big-Eyes is busy," Marta says. "Yoni, tell the rabbi she is busy. We must go soon to see to the preparations for the feast."

"I am not going to the feast." I set my mouth in a thin, hard line. Never will I go to the feast of Shimon the Pharisee. Never.

Rabbi Yeshua comes into the kitchen. "Marta, I would not beg favor unless I had a big need. There is a matter I am concerned on, and I think only Miryam Big-Heart can explain it to me. Please, you will give me this favor, yes?"

Marta's hands twitch.

I never saw her hands twitch.

Elazar comes in. He is eight years younger than Marta, and usually he is cowed by her, but today he has a face that says he is the man and he will tell what will be. "Marta, you will give Miryam Big-Eyes leave. Miryam, you will go with the rabbi."

Marta opens her mouth, but no words come out.

I never saw her without ten thousand words sharp on her tongue.

Rabbi Yeshua takes my hand and tugs me away.

I follow him into the courtyard and through the receiving room and out.

We walk down the street together, side by side, as we are friends. My heart beats in my ears, and my eyes sting, and my mind whirls.

I never heard such a thing, that a rabbi walked alone together with a woman, and a shamed woman at that. Any other man would be dishonored to walk with a woman, for they say women are full of lewdness, but I do not think I am full of lewdness, but it must be so, for everyone says so, but Rabbi Yeshua is a *tsaddik*, and he does not fear to walk and talk with a woman, whether she is full of lewdness or not full of lewdness, and all my heart is a big confusion.

We reach the brow of the Mount of Olives. All Jerusalem spreads out before us. The golden Temple gleams like fire in the morning light.

"I wish to go to Elazar's olive press, if you will walk so far with me," Rabbi Yeshua says. He still holds my hand.

I would walk many ten thousand miles with him. I clutch on his hand, and we begin our descent. I can hardly breathe. I think I might faint. I wish …

I am a fool. A rabbi would never marry a divorced woman who is barren.

But he could take me as concubine. He should take a woman. I do not understand why he has no woman. It must be on account of the smirch on his name, the cruel tale his village tells, that his mother played the *zonah*. Yoni told me the smirch is a foolishness, for Rabbi Yeshua is not a *mamzer* according to the rulings of the rabbis. I would long for him to take me for his woman, even if he was a *mamzer*. He is a good man, and kind. He is not a eunuch. He is a man, and a man needs a woman. I would give him a good happiness. I am barren, so I could not give him sons, but a man does not take a concubine to get sons.

We walk in silence all the way down the hill. The road is packed with people, for tonight begins Rosh HaShanah, and this is the best time of year, and all Israel is here for the holidays. Nobody says no that the rabbi holds my hand.

At the bottom of the hill, we turn off the main road on a path through Elazar's olive grove. Quickly, we are a hundred paces from the road, and it is quiet. It is still a month until the olive harvest, and there are no workmen about. We are alone.

We come to the olive press. There is a cave near it, and a stone bench beside the cave. Inside the cave, my brother has another olive press to do the second pressing.

We sit in the cool shade. My heart beats faster than a sparrow's wings.

Rabbi Yeshua still holds my hand. "Elazar says you know the man who gives the feast tonight, this man Shimon the Pharisee."

"Elazar knows him also. He is Elazar's friend. You should ask Elazar on him."

"Elazar speaks well on him. But when I look on Shimon's face, I do not see the things Elazar tells."

"He is a Pharisee. Pharisees are good men. What more is there to tell?"

Rabbi Yeshua looks on me with sad eyes. "Perhaps I read this man wrong, but let me tell you what I see in his face when he looks on me.

"He sees a man who comes from a small village of no account. Nazareth is a village of sheep-men and farmers and leather-men and men who work in stone and wood and metal. It is a village where no Pharisee ever set foot. A village where even a man who can only read halting and slow is asked to read the scroll on Shabbat. A village where not one man can write his own name.

"That is what I see in his eyes when Shimon the Pharisee looks on me. I do not know why he invites me to a feast at his house. I asked Elazar, and he says all men speak well on Shimon the Pharisee. I asked if all women speak well on Shimon the Pharisee. Elazar said that all do except one. He said that you have words to say against the man. I have heard parts of the matter from others, but I never heard it from you. Tell me the whole matter."

"I ..." Tears bubble out of my eyes. I cover my face with my hands and lean forward and wail.

Rabbi Yeshua leans close to me. He wraps his arm around me. I hear him weeping with me. I feel his body shaking.

I never heard such a thing, that a man would cry with a woman. I cry and I cry until all the tears have come out of my head.

Then I tell the whole matter to Rabbi Yeshua. How I was married to Shimon the Pharisee. How he threw me off like an old rag because I was barren. How he married some other woman. How I have lived six years in shame on account of this man.

Rabbi Yeshua listens until I have told him all. "This man is a hard man, yes?"

"You should be wary on him. If he thinks you are some low person, he will dishonor you."

Rabbi Yeshua's breath hisses in his throat.

My heart seizes. I do not know if Shimon the Pharisee knows the matter of the smirch on Rabbi Yeshua's name. But if he knows it—

Rabbi Yeshua says, "Elazar is a good man, yes?"

"Yes."

"Is he a man brave of speech?"

"He is not."

"Marta is a woman brave of speech, yes?"

"She is."

"Is she brave of speech to women only, or to men?"

"To women and to most men."

"Most men?"

"She is not brave of speech to Shimon the Pharisee."

Rabbi Yeshua sighs deeply. "I gave promise to go to this feast. I would not dishonor Shimon the Pharisee by going back on my promise. But I do not wish to walk into a trap. And I am not brave of speech."

I am shocked. He speaks as he does not know what to do. But he is a prophet. I thought prophets always knew what to do. I thought all prophets were brave of speech, like Yohanan the immerser.

"I do not think you are brave of speech," Rabbi Yeshua says.

I shake my head. If I am brave of speech, then a mouse is a lion.

"And yet last night when Yoni choked, you were brave of speech."

"I had to, for my love of Yoni. Nobody saw except me. Big Yaakov treats my little Yoni as he is a fool and was paying no mind to him. If I had not shouted—"

"But you did shout. You did. And so I still have Yoni, who is a big help to me. You did a mighty thing last night. Yoni will be great in the kingdom of HaShem, and I am in your debt. But I have a thing to ask you."

My belly pulls itself into a knot. I know what he will ask me.

No. I cannot do it.

Never, ever, ever will I serve at the feast of Shimon the Pharisee.

Rabbi Yeshua looks on my face. His eyes are kind, but as they look on me, they pull together in sad lines. "I am sorry. I should not ask such a—"

"Yeshua!" shouts a voice from the direction of the road.

Four men walk toward us. Four men run toward us.

Rabbi Yeshua stands. "Little Yaakov! Yosi! Thin Shimon! Yehuda Dreamhead!" He runs to them and hugs them and gives them each a kiss and a kiss and a kiss.

He leads them back to me. "This is my friend Miryam Big-Heart. I was asking her advice on a matter."

The four men look on me in amaze.

I do not know what to say. My face must be the color of fire. I look on the ground and wish I could hide.

The biggest of the men tugs on Rabbi Yeshua's arm. "Come with us. We arrived last night in Jerusalem. Imma sent us to find you."

Rabbi Yeshua nods. "One moment."

He takes my hand and makes me stand. He gives me a kiss and a kiss and a kiss. "I should not have thought to ask you to do what you cannot. Please forgive me."

I cannot see for my tears. I never heard that a man should ask a woman to forgive. I kiss my fingers and touch them to his cheek. "You say you are not brave of speech, but I think you could be. Not for yourself, but you could be brave of speech for one you love, yes?"

A shudder runs all through Rabbi Yeshua's body. He wipes away the tears from my cheeks and looks deep in my eyes. There is a new thing on his face. "I am glad Yoni has such a friend as you. Blessed be HaShem."

His brothers pull him away.

I sit and watch them go, and my heart feels crushed.

I should have told him I would go to the feast.

Now it is too late.

If Shimon the Pharisee makes a mock on him, who will say no?

Yeshua of Nazareth

"I mma!" I run to see my mother, who stands out in the street waiting.

Her face lights like the sun, and she runs to me.

I seize her in my arms and lift her up and give her a kiss and a kiss and a kiss.

"Yeshua!" Shlomi Dancefeet tugs on my sleeve.

I give her a kiss and a kiss and a kiss and then hold her back to look on her. "You are well?"

Her face glows.

Her lord stands behind her wearing a big grin.

I guess they have a thing to tell me. "You have a good news?"

"I missed my bleeding!" Shlomi says. "I was not sure last week when you came through Cana. Now I am sure."

I hug her to myself. It seems only yesterday she was a baby, and I held her on my knee and played with her and kissed her fat cheeks. Now she is a grown woman of fourteen years, and soon she will be a mother in Israel. My heart is full with my joy.

We go in the house, which is the same one we always rent for the big feasts.

There is a stone bench there, and they make me sit on it, and they all gather around on the floor.

I pull Shlomi Dancefeet up to sit on my lap. She is the only one of us who never knew our father Yoseph, for he died before she was born.

I am her brother, but I am also the father she never knew, and I will not be denied one last chance to show her a father's love.

Shlomi Dancefeet nestles against my chest. "I was glad of seeing you when you came to Cana. Why have you not gone to Nazareth also?"

I sigh with a deep sigh. I do not know why I have not gone to Nazareth. I have asked HaShem many times if I could go to Nazareth, and always the answer was no. But last night HaShem said I could go after Sukkot.

Yehuda Dreamhead says, "A leper came to Nazareth three times asking after you. The last time, we told him you were in Tsipori. He went there, and we never saw him again."

I remember the man. He told me a good tale of Little Yaakov. It made my heart warm to hear that Little Yaakov did a kindness on a stranger.

Thin Shimon says, "Imma sent us many letters all summer. The men who brought the letters told news on you in the village square. All Nazareth has heard big tales on what you did in Capernaum and Magdala and Bethsaida and Yodefat and Tsipori and Bethlehem and Cana."

My breath catches in my throat. "And what does the village say of those tales?"

Yosi says, "They are angry on you on account of the tax-farmer. And because you never came to the village. They know you went to Tsipori, but you did not come to Nazareth. They say you think you have grown too big for your own village. They say you pretend in other villages that you have no smirch, but they know you have a smirch."

Thin Shimon says, "What will you do when they raise a stench on the matter? You should have done big things in our village before you made a name in other villages. Why did you not come and make a flattery on the village and show honor to them?"

I do not have an answer. I did what HaShem told me, and I did not do what HaShem forbade me.

Little Yaakov says, "Old Yonatan the leather-man says if you come to Nazareth, he will crush you. And his son says the same."

My stomach feels as I am in a small boat on a large lake. Old Yonatan the leather-man and his son mean what they say.

Imma's face is hard and dark as the black stones of Capernaum. I never saw her with such an angry look. "You should come and punish them. You should call down fire on them. If you do not crush them, they will crush you."

All my body is on fire. I cannot crush my village. But I do not wish my village to crush me. And now I remember the words of Yohanan the immerser. It was a year ago, after Sukkot, when I asked him how to be Mashiach.

HaShem will show you the first Power, and you must destroy it or be killed.

Since then, HaShem has been showing me what is the first Power.

I am certain the first Power has a mighty hold on my village.

My battle against the first Power will be in Nazareth.

I do not know how to destroy the first Power.

I do not know what I should do.

But I know one thing.

I will never destroy my own village.

CHAPTER SEVENTY-ONE

Miryam of Bethany

I am serving at the feast of Shimon the Pharisee.

Rabbi Yeshua did not ask me to.

If he had asked, I would have said no.

But he did not ask. That crushed my heart.

That is why I decided to come.

I cannot bear to let him come to the feast without anyone to speak for him. His men are strangers here and Galileans, and they have no voice. Elazar is a long friend of Shimon the Pharisee, and he will not speak. Marta is only a woman, and she will not speak.

I am only a woman too. Worse than that, I am a shamed woman. I am nothing. I am *haryo*. Therefore, I have nothing I can lose. I have one thing only, and that will be enough.

I have my rage. My rage will make me brave of speech for Rabbi Yeshua.

So here I am now, with Marta and the servants of the house of Shimon the Pharisee, waiting for the feast to begin.

We stand outside the house keeping watch for the guests.

"Are you well?" Marta looks me over with sharp eyes.

I shake my head. "Rabbi Yeshua wished for me to come."

"You were gone long this morning."

"Rabbi Yeshua and I talked long."

"Some idle women in the village saw you go and had much chatter on why the rabbi walks together with a big-eyes—"

"If idle women think lewdness on a *tsaddik*, they are fools and worse than fools."

Three men turn the far corner of the street and walk toward us. Even so far away, I can see they wear black leather *tefillin* strapped to their foreheads. Pharisees.

As they come nearer, I recognize them from years ago, when I was woman of this house. They are good men and honest, although they do not make words with women. Pharisees are wary on lewd women, and everyone says a big-eyes is a lewd woman.

Marta sends a boy into the house to fetch Shimon the Pharisee.

Shimon comes from the house and calls out to the guests.

They call out to him.

He goes out to greet them.

He gives each man a kiss and a kiss and a kiss.

He calls for three servants to bring water to wash their feet.

Their feet are not dirty, for they have come only from Jerusalem, but it shows honor to a guest, to wash his feet.

Another servant brings olive oil in a bowl, and the men dip hands in oil and anoint their hair and dry their hands on fresh towels.

Marta takes them in to find place at table.

My brother Elazar and Rabbi Yeshua and his men come around the far corner.

Elazar holds hands with Rabbi Yeshua, for they are friends.

Shimon the Pharisee calls out to Elazar.

Elazar calls out to him.

Shimon the Pharisee does not call out to Rabbi Yeshua.

Rabbi Yeshua's face does not show his dishonor.

Shimon the Pharisee goes to give Elazar a kiss and a kiss and a kiss. He does not give Rabbi Yeshua even one kiss.

My hands have made themselves fists, and my heart thumps for its anger.

Shimon the Pharisee calls for a servant to wash feet. One servant. For Elazar.

I never saw such a thing, to ignore a guest!

I run in the house and fetch water and towel.

I hurry back.

The servant is finishing Elazar's feet.

I kneel before Rabbi Yeshua and wash his feet.

The heat of Shimon's anger scorches my back.

I do not care. If he invites a man as guest, he should show honor. It is not done, to dishonor a guest. I hate him now more than I ever did.

Shimon calls for olive oil for Elazar.

Elazar dips his hands in oil and anoints his hair and wipes his hands on a towel.

The servant makes to go away.

I seize the bowl and offer it to Rabbi Yeshua.

He dips his hands in oil and anoints his hair and wipes his hands on the same towel Elazar used.

Shimon's face is stone, but his eyes shoot fire on me.

Marta takes Elazar and Rabbi Yeshua in to find place at table.

I return the bowl of water and towel to the house, but I do not come back out. I am afraid I will scratch out Shimon's eyes if I look on him again.

The feast is set in the courtyard of the house. It is a large courtyard, and there are six tables for all the guests, and nine guests at each table. I do not know how many guests that is, but it must be more than a hundred, or I am a virgin.

Soon all the guests have arrived. There is a whole table just for the men of Rabbi Yeshua. There is a table in a hidden alcove for Shimon the Pharisee's woman and her friends. The Pharisees that Shimon invited are in the highest place at his table. Rabbi Yeshua reclines at Shimon's table in the lowest place.

I am in a rage that Shimon the Pharisee shows him such a big dishonor.

Rabbi Yeshua smiles and nods to the others, but I see in his eyes a deep pain.

I wish he had not come, if it is only to be dishonored.

I wish I had not come, if it is only to see him dishonored.

Tales tell that in days of old, there was an evil man, King Herod who was called Magnificent. HaShem made Herod's man parts shrivel and go rotten, and he died in a big agony. I wish Shimon's man parts will shrivel and go rotten. I wish Shimon will get the mighty leprosy and have to live in a graveyard. I wish Shimon will get the belly-fever and die in a big agony.

Marta shakes me. "Miryam Big-Eyes! Miryam Big-Eyes! Wake up from your dreaming and help with the serving."

I follow her to the kitchen.

It is a big feast, for Shimon has money and is not afraid to spend it. He spends much time speaking with his guests, the Pharisees from Jerusalem. He does not spend time speaking with Rabbi Yeshua.

After the third course of the meal, I see what is Shimon's purpose. He thinks to gain honor with the men of Jerusalem by showing dishonor to Rabbi Yeshua. We have all heard big tales on Rabbi Yeshua from far away in the villages of Galilee. Some believe the tales and some do not.

Shimon the Pharisee shows that he does not. He shows that he is a big man and Rabbi Yeshua is a small man. That is why he dishonored Rabbi Yeshua outside his house, where everyone could see. By now, the whole village knows that Shimon the Pharisee dishonored Rabbi Yeshua to his face. Shimon's honor is more, and Rabbi Yeshua's is less.

I wish I were serving at Rabbi Yeshua's table, but I am serving the women's table. If I were at Rabbi Yeshua's table, I would shout on Shimon the Pharisee and make a big rage and call him wicked.

Marta crooks finger for me to go with her.

I follow her to the kitchen.

The servants have opened a new amphora of wine from Shimon the Pharisee's vineyard.

I taste some to be sure it has not soured. It is a good wine.

Marta draws a pitcher, and I draw a pitcher, and we return to the feast. Marta goes to the far end of the courtyard. I serve the women in their alcove.

When I return to the courtyard, I see a *zonah* hiding in the shadows near the gate of the courtyard that leads to the street. Of course, the gate is open for the feast, and there are beggars outside hoping for food afterward.

But this *zonah* is no beggar. I have seen her many times, for she lives in the next village and comes here to seduce our men. She is young and very beautiful, with large eyes and skin to the smoothness of milk, and she dresses in soft clothing and wears a silk hair covering. I hate her, for *zonahs* are wicked women and full of lewdness.

I should throw her out in the street, but I do not move. If this *zonah* makes a scandal at the feast of Shimon the Pharisee, it will make a big dishonor on him.

I will laugh to see it.

The sun has long gone down, and there are torches at spaces along the wall, but the *zonah* hides in a pool of darkness. She looks as she is waiting for something.

I wait.

I watch.

I hope she takes off her clothes and throws herself naked on Shimon the Pharisee and makes a scandal on him in front of the men from Jerusalem. I would laugh him to scorn. All the village would make a mock on him.

There comes a moment when all the servants have returned to the kitchen. Even Marta is returned there. She is probably wondering where I am.

The *zonah* makes her move. She walks in a crouch, but even so, she is lithe and quick on her feet.

I watch.

She is halfway to Shimon's table.

I see her weeping.

She is at Shimon's table.

I hear her weeping.

She kneels at the foot of the couch where Rabbi Yeshua reclines at table.

My heart seizes. This wicked woman will make a scandal on Rabbi Yeshua!

I want to run, I want to beat her with fists, I want to tear her away from him. But now I am too late. My legs feel as they are wood, and I cannot move.

The *zonah* weeps big tears on the rabbi's feet.

All the people look, craning necks to see.

The *zonah* tears off her hair covering. Her hair hangs like a great sheet of black silk.

I cannot believe what my eyes are telling. It is not done, for a woman to show hair in public!

She wipes Rabbi Yeshua's feet with her hair covering.

She wipes his feet with her hair.

She kisses his feet.

At last I think to do my duty. My clumsy legs carry me toward the woman. The rabbi trusted me to keep a watch on him, and I have failed. I have allowed this wicked woman to make a scandal on him.

The *zonah* pulls out some small jar from her belt.

She breaks the jar.

She pours out perfume on Rabbi Yeshua's feet.

I stagger toward her, but I feel as I am in a dream, running and running, but never moving.

I see the rabbi's face.

He smiles on the *zonah*.

How can he smile? She has done a wicked thing, to dishonor him with her lewdness.

All the table stares on the *zonah*.

Shimon's face is pale as leprosy, for it is dishonor on him for some lewd woman to make a scandal at his feast. The village will whisper on the matter for a week.

Shimon sees me, and his eyes shrink to points of rage.

He thinks I could have prevented the scandal, and he is right.

The *zonah* kneads the perfume on Rabbi Yeshua's feet. She kisses his feet.

Rabbi Yeshua closes his eyes and breathes deep.

I see he delights on the smell of the perfume, even though it is bought with the price of her sin. I see he delights on the feel of her hair on his feet. I see he delights on the beautiful face of this lewd woman.

"Rabbi Yeshua!" Several of his men hiss on him from the far table.

The Pharisees who came from Jerusalem stare on the *zonah*, and their mouths hang open like fat fish.

Rabbi Yeshua does not seem to care that she makes a scandal on him.

Shimon points finger on the *zonah* and shouts, "Out!"

The *zonah* cringes, but she does not move.

On a sudden, Rabbi Yeshua looks all around and sees many scowls and knows the woman is making a scandal. She shames herself. Shimon will shame her more.

I think he does not know what to do.

His eye catches mine from across the table.

I kiss my fingers and make a motion as I could touch his cheek from far away.

I mouth one word. *Brave.*

A shudder goes through Rabbi Yeshua's body.

Shimon the Pharisee points finger on the *zonah* again. "Out, you spreadlegs!"

The *zonah* weeps for her big shame.

A light burns in Rabbi Yeshua's eyes. He holds up his hand. "No, she will not be told away."

All the courtyard looks aghast.

Shimon glares on him. "If you knew who is this woman and what she—"

"Friend." Rabbi Yeshua's face has become calm. And brave. "Friend, I have a matter to discuss with you."

All the feast goes silent as Sheol. When a man says he has a "matter to discuss," he does not mean some small matter. He means some large matter. But I never heard such a thing, to discuss a large matter at a feast. It is not done. Men discuss large matters in private.

Shimon's face is tight and hard. "T-tell me this matter … Rabbi."

I am more happy than I ever was. Rabbi Yeshua will tell dishonor on Shimon. He will make him small in the eyes of his friends. Rabbi Yeshua will crush Shimon like dust between his toes.

"Shimon, two men of Tsipori owed money to Honi the silver-man. A poor sheep-man owed five hundred *dinars*. A rich merchant owed only fifty. When the seventh year came around, Honi the silver-man heard the Torah read, to forgive every man his debts. He went to the poor sheep-man and forgave him the five hundred. Then he went to the rich merchant and forgave him the fifty.

"When a tree fell on Honi the silver-man's house in the storm, who do you think worked longest and hardest to build his house back?"

Shimon says, "The poor sheep-man who owed the five hundreds."

I never heard Shimon speak in such a small voice.

"You judge the matter correctly," says Rabbi Yeshua.

All the guests stare on Rabbi Yeshua.

"Shimon, when I came to your house, you gave me no water nor towel for my feet. This woman wet my feet with her own tears of repentance, and she dried them with her own hair of shame. You gave me no kiss of friendship, but she has not stopped kissing my feet. You gave me no oil to anoint, but she anoints me with perfume of a big price. You think I do not know this woman, but I do. I met her in the road last week, and she had a mighty evil spirit, and I sent it away. Her sins are great, but her repentance is greater, and her forgiveness is greatest of all, for it comes from HaShem."

Shimon's face is so pale, he looks like a dead man.

"She who was forgiven much loves me much. He who was forgiven nothing loves me not at all. I tell you the truth, this woman will be higher in the kingdom of HaShem than he who was forgiven nothing."

All the feast stares on Rabbi Yeshua, for it is not done to speak so plainly to the man who is host.

My heart leaps inside me for my joy. Rabbi Yeshua was brave of speech to Shimon the Pharisee. Now Shimon will be his enemy. When Rabbi Yeshua comes into his kingdom, Shimon will have no place. That will punish him for the evil he has done.

I look across the courtyard for Yoni. He knows how Shimon the Pharisee has ill-used me. Yoni will be happy to see this man dishonored.

I see Yoni at last, reclining next to Big Yaakov.

Yoni's eyebrows pop up high, as they will disappear into his hair. His mouth opens round. He stares on Rabbi Yeshua's table.

But he is not looking on the rabbi.

I hear a loud wailing behind me.

I know that voice, but I never heard it wailing.

I look on Shimon the Pharisee.

He is not reclining on the couch.

He is not on the couch at all.

He is on the ground.

He is on his face.

He weeps tears of repentance.

He begs forgiveness of the rabbi.

I rush out of the courtyard into the kitchen.

If Shimon the Pharisee repents, Rabbi Yeshua will forgive him, for he is kind.

That is the problem with kindness.

It is good when it falls on me.

It is not so good when it falls on the man I hate.

CHAPTER SEVENTY-TWO

Miryam of Nazareth

"Yeshua is coming this way, and he is bringing a woman!" Shlomi Dancefeet rushes into our rented house wearing a big grin. "The woman does not look like a *zonah*. She looks respectable. Do you think …?"

I do not know what to think. I have waited long for my son to take a woman. I have asked him many times when he will give me grandchildren, and he always smiles and says it is not time. He never mentions the smirch, but I think that is the reason. Perhaps now it is time. Here in Jerusalem, far from Nazareth, they do not know of the smirch.

My sons and my son-in-law all went to the Temple this morning, so it is only Little Yaakov's woman and Yehuda Dreamhead's woman and me and Shlomi Dancefeet here. I take a deep breath and walk out to meet this new woman.

Yeshua is deep in talk with the woman. Her mouth makes a thin line and her eyes are hard. Shlomi Dancefeet is right—this woman does not wear the lewd smile of a *zonah*.

Yeshua points to me and smiles on the woman and tugs on her hand.

I wish he would not walk with women in public. I wish he would not talk with women in public. I wish he would not hold hands with women in public. But it is like speaking to a wall to tell him not to do these strange things.

"Imma!" Yeshua rushes forward to greet me. He gives me a kiss and a kiss and a kiss. He wraps his arms around me. His eyes smile on me as I am a queen.

For this, I forgive him every strange thing he ever did.

"Imma, here is my friend Miryam Big-Heart, who lives in Bethany. Her brother Elazar owns a big house where all my men can stay with me, and her sister Marta is a fine woman who is spoken well by everyone. My friend Miryam served at the feast last night, to watch over me. She did me a great kindness."

I look on this woman Miryam Big-Heart to see what sort of daughter-in-law she would make. That is a strange nickname, Big-Heart. In our village, we would call her Big-Eyes. She loves my son—any fool can see that by the blush on her cheeks and the way she looks on him. She seems respectable, and I am glad. If Yeshua married a *zonah*, I do not know what I would do.

Miryam Big-Heart is not young. I am sure she is past fifteen, and she might be more than twenty. That is too old, but I cannot afford to be choosy. There are tight lines around her eyes that tell she is angry on something. But I also read fear in her eyes, and that is natural, for every woman fears a bad mother-in-law. I lived in dread of my own, for she always thought I played the *zonah* on my lord Yoseph, and she never forgave me. I must not do such an evil on this Miryam Big-Heart.

I step toward her and make a big smile. "Shalom, Miryam Big-Heart, I am glad on meeting you. Are you well? Would you like wine? Come in the house and sit with us and talk!"

Yeshua hugs my daughter Shlomi Dancefeet and kisses her many times. I push him in the house so he will not make a scandal. That boy has no sense.

Miryam Big-Heart follows us in.

Yeshua goes to get wine and brings us each a stone cup, filled with goodness.

I make Miryam Big-Heart sit on the stone bench, and we all sit on the floor.

Yeshua looks all around. "Where are my brothers?"

I point up the street. "They went to the Temple to listen to the rabbis expound Torah. Little Yaakov said you should come find them. He said there is a new rabbi he wishes to hear, Rabbi Tsadduk, who follows after Rabbi Shammai."

Yeshua sits beside Miryam Big-Heart on the bench. "I ... we have a guest."

I will never learn anything from this woman with Yeshua hovering like a hen. "Go, go to the Temple! How do you think we can talk to Miryam Big-Heart with some man around? Come back in a few hours with your brothers, and we will have food."

Yeshua looks on Miryam Big-Heart. "I wish—"

"Go!" There is a knife-edge in her voice.

Yeshua sighs and goes out the door.

He rushes back in and gives Miryam Big-Heart a kiss and a kiss and a kiss and then hurries out again.

I look on Miryam Big-Heart with a searching eye.

She looks on me with a fearful eye.

"Tell me how you came to know my son."

"My nephew Yoni is one of his men."

"I know Yoni." I like that boy, except he is conceited. But he is kind and cheerful, and he is a big help on my son. There are worse things than being conceited.

Miryam Big-Heart tells about last winter when Yeshua went to tell repentance to Israel by the Jordan River, and how he and Yoni and my son Yehuda Dreamhead came sometimes to the house of her brother Elazar to rest a few days.

I am glad to hear this Elazar has money, for Yeshua has none. When Miryam Big-Heart says Yeshua's name, I see a softness in her eyes and a hot glow on her cheeks that tells she loves him. That is good. I have seen a woman marry a man she hated.

I keep waiting to hear if Yeshua has asked Elazar for Miryam Big-Heart, but she does not say so, and I would not shame her by asking. I am dying to know the facts on the matter.

Finally, Miryam Big-Heart stops talking. Something in her eyes tells that she has more to say, but I do not know what it is.

I lean forward. "Yeshua told us yesterday he was going to the feast of some rich man, a Pharisee. Tell us about this feast!"

Miryam's face looks as I have stabbed her. Tears well up in her eyes.

I have stepped in a pit of *haryo* without knowing.

Shlomi Dancefeet moves up to sit on the bench with Miryam Big-Heart and kisses her cheek. "You do not have to tell the matter if you do not wish to. But thank you for making a big help on my brother. He is more kind than any man ever was, yes?"

Miryam Big-Heart covers her face with her hands and wails.

That is good. Now we will hear all.

She tells us all, but her tale is not so good.

Miryam Big-Heart is divorced! I should have known, for she is beautiful and too old to be a virgin.

Worse than that, she is barren and cursed by HaShem! She will not be giving me grandchildren after all. I do not know why Yeshua would bring home a woman cursed by HaShem. I will talk sense on him. I hope he has not made an offer to her brother yet.

Miryam Big-Heart tells how she hates the man who threw her off.

I hate him too, hearing her tale. Little Yaakov says all Pharisees are good men, but I see it is not so. Here is one who did a cruel thing.

Miryam Big-Heart tells how this man ill-treated my son last night. How he gave Yeshua dishonor out in the street. How he gave him the worst place at the table. How he ignored him during the feast.

That is a bad Pharisee, and now I hate him more. I will tell Little Yaakov on the matter. He will be angry when he hears it, for he counts on the Pharisees to help when Yeshua makes his move. The Pharisees hate the Great Satan, and they long for the day when HaShem will free us. Everyone knows the Pharisees will rise up to join Mashiach when it is time. The Pharisees will be the sword in the hand of Mashiach. It is an evil thing to hear that one of them is a bad man.

Miryam Big-Heart tells how some lewd woman came in the feast and made a scandal on my son. How Yeshua took delight in the woman and thanked her for her kindness. How he shamed Shimon the Pharisee.

That is no surprise, that he turned aside this sinful woman's scandal. No lewd woman can dishonor a *tsaddik*.

Miryam Big-Heart tells how Shimon the Pharisee repented, and how Yeshua forgave him.

I am glad on the matter. That is my son's wisdom, to make a wicked man repent.

Miryam Big-Heart cries and cries. She is angry on the matter. She is angry on my son. She is angry he forgave this wicked man.

Shlomi Dancefeet tries to comfort her, but she will not be comforted.

Shlomzion Lewd tries to comfort her, but she will not be comforted.

I do not try to comfort her. She is the wrong woman for my son. She is bitter and angry. Yeshua can do better. He should do better.

I will speak to him privately on the matter when he returns.

Miryam Big-Heart cries many tears of rage. She hates this man who did her wrong. I am sick to my death on her crying. I wish she would set the matter aside. I do not know what to do with her. She is more bitter than any woman ever was.

My heart begins beating fast.

I know how she feels, a little, for I also hate a man who did me wrong, and I cannot set the matter aside.

I cannot. I will not.

Now I see why Yeshua brought this woman to meet me.

He wishes to show me a thing.

Fine, he has shown me a thing.

She is bitter and angry.

I am bitter and angry.

I am ashamed that I am bitter and angry.

But that does not change the fact that I am bitter and angry.

I would set the matter aside if I could, but the knife cuts too deep. I will never set the matter aside.

I would if I could. Yes, I would. But I cannot. There is a thing in my heart that is twisted, and I cannot untwist it.

Nobody can untwist it. Not even HaShem can untwist it.

But … I wish that he could.

CHAPTER SEVENTY-THREE

Miryam of Nazareth

I do not like weeping women. We have been in Jerusalem a whole month, first for Rosh HaShanah, then for Yom Kippur, then for the feast of Sukkot, and finally for Shabbat. Today we leave for Nazareth with my son and his men.

We stayed overnight in Bethany with Yeshua's friend Elazar, who is a very rich man. His parents are dead, but his sister Marta is a wise woman and runs a good house. His sister Miryam Big-Heart is not so wise. Right now, she is weeping and clinging on Yeshua and making a fool on herself.

I am glad Yeshua has not made an offer to her brother. I do not think she is a right woman for him. A woman with rage in her heart will burn every man she touches. I do not want her scorching my son.

Besides that, she is twenty-six! I found it out yesterday. She could almost be a grandmother. That is too old for my son, even if she looks no more than twenty.

Yeshua gives her a kiss and a kiss and a kiss. "Thank you for your kindness, little sister."

Her face crumples when he says *little sister*.

I do not think Yeshua knows anything about women or he would see how she longs for him. When we are gone far from here, I will explain the matter. Or I will make Shlomi Dancefeet do it.

At last we pick up our packs and leave to join up with the Jericho Road. We are a big group. We have my five sons and two of their women who do not have small children. We have one of my daughters and my son-in-law. We have Yeshua's eight men. Usually, we go by the Samaritan Road, but there has been trouble that way lately, so this time we will go around. We will join with some large group going down the Jericho Road and will not fear bandits. There are many thousand people leaving Jerusalem for Galilee.

Yeshua finds me and takes my hand.

My heart feels warmed. My son is strong. We have been gone long from Nazareth, a whole month, and now we are going back, all of us.

And Yeshua is going with us to Nazareth.

I do not know what will happen when we get there. The men of Nazareth always loved my son, for he is kind. Most of them did, anyway. Not Old Yonatan the leather-man. Not his wicked son. But most of them.

That changed this summer. They all heard tale on the big things he did in other villages, and their hearts became angry on him, for he never came. They heard tale on this tax-farmer, and their anger turned to rage, like a boil on their heart. They have some plan to hurt him. He means to show kindness to them, and he thinks they will love him again. Not the leather-man and his son, but the others will. That is what he thinks.

I think he is wrong. I think their hate is too great. I think they will try to smite him.

I wish they will try to smite him. I wish they will force him to fight back. I wish he will punish them. I wish he will burn their houses down. I wish he will crush their bones to dust. He will have the Power now to do it. When they put his back against the wall, he will use it.

"Rabbi Yeshua, tell us a tale!" says Yoni.

I like that boy. He is cheerful and makes everyone laugh. His brother Big Yaakov acts as Yoni is a fool, but Yeshua says the boy is a genius. That is a good praise. I think Big Yaakov is the fool.

"What tale should I tell?" Yeshua asks.

"Daniel and the lions!" says Yoni.

"Father Abraham and the wicked men of Sodom!" says Little Yaakov.

"Jonah and the big fish!" says Shlomi Dancefeet.

Nobody tells tales like my son. His tales will make the road go faster.

First, he tells the tale of our prophet Daniel, who was stolen away to Babylon when the wicked king came and destroyed our Temple and burned our city and left our people dead in the Hinnom Valley. But Daniel was wise, and the king saw he was honest and made him his chief prince. The other princes were jealous on Daniel and fooled the king to make a law that for thirty days no man should pray to any but the king. Daniel saw it was a trap, but he prayed to HaShem anyway.

They came and threw him in the den with many hungry lions, but HaShem shut their mouths and they could not eat Daniel. In the morning, the king came to see if any bones of Daniel remained, and he had a big joy when he saw Daniel alive. The king was angry on his other princes and threw them all in with the lions.

I see them in my mind as clear as they are right here before me. The evil men cower in a corner.

The lions rush on them, roaring in their rage.

The evil men shout for their fear.

I am glad to see their fear.

The lions fall on them and tear them apart. They eat them until nothing is left.

I am glad, for they are wicked men and deserve it.

But there is more. It is not only the evil men who were thrown in. Their women and children were put in with the lions too. I had forgot that part of the tale.

The women wail and wail for their grief. The children shriek and shriek for their terror. I see a little girl of the age of three, holding a small doll. She clings to her brothers and her mother. She is screaming.

I see the lions pounce again. They tear apart the women. They tear apart the children. Last of all is the little girl, hiding in the corner.

A lion comes to her, snarling for his fury.

She screams.

The lion claws her face.

She begs for Imma and Abba, but they are dead.

The lion eats her left leg while she is still alive.

She screams and cries in a big agony.

The lion eats her right leg.

She calls out to HaShem for help.

The lion eats her left arm. He eats her right arm. He eats her belly.

All the while she screams and begs.

Last of all he eats her face.

There is nothing left of her but the terrible screaming in my head. I do not think it will ever end.

When Yeshua finishes the tale, I am shaking. I never heard it told this way. I do not like this tale. Yoni did a bad thing to ask for this tale. I do not wish to hear this tale again.

Next, Yeshua tells the tale of Father Abraham and the wicked men of Sodom. HaShem came to Father Abraham in the shape of three men. Father Abraham told his woman, Sarah, to make a big feast. She made bread from three measures of flour, which is enough for a hundred men. Father Abraham killed a fat calf. They fed the men.

Then HaShem told how he would crush the city of Sodom on account of its wickedness. Father Abraham begged mercy in case there were fifty righteous men in the city, and HaShem promised mercy if there were fifty. Then he begged mercy in case there were forty-five, and HaShem promised mercy. Then he begged mercy in case of forty. Then thirty. Then twenty. Last of all, ten. HaShem promised mercy each time.

But there were not ten righteous men in Sodom. There was only one—Father Abraham's nephew Lot. When HaShem sent two Messengers to visit Sodom, Lot gave them hospitality in his own house. The wicked men of the city came to the house after dark and asked for the visiting men, to lie with them as a man lies with a woman. That is a big dishonor on a man, to use him like a woman. Lot told them no. The wicked men cried out for their rage. Lot offered them his own virgin daughters.

I would not offer my virgin daughters to save the honor of a man.

I do not think Lot was so righteous. But the wicked men refused the girls. All night they howled for the men. The Messengers put blind eyes on them all and took Lot and his woman and his daughters, and they ran away fast from that evil city, and HaShem burned it with fire.

I see the city burn. The flames are so hot they are white, as when you burn pitch. I see the evil men shriek for their agony. I see their women roll on the ground in big flames, screaming and screaming. I see a small boy in a pit of pitch up to his waist. He has a beautiful face like my Yeshua when he was a child.

His face twists, and he screams and screams while the fire burns hot around him. He begs HaShem for mercy. His skin turns black from the fire. He claws at his skin until it rips. Watching him gives me a big agony. His voice rises higher and higher to heaven until it rings in my head.

I would tear off my ears to make that voice go away, but it will not. Tears run down my cheeks. I would vomit if I had food in my belly.

I wish to beat Little Yaakov for asking for this tale. It is a bad tale. It is an evil tale. I do not care if it is in the Torah. I hate this tale.

When Yeshua finishes the tale, I think I will never breathe again.

Yoni says, "Rabbi Yeshua, what would have happened if Father Abraham begged mercy on account of five righteous men, and then three, and then two, and then one?"

Yeshua says, "What do you think, Yoni?"

Yoni says, "Also, if HaShem is righteous, why did Father Abraham have to beg mercy to make HaShem do right? That is not a good logic."

Yeshua says, "What do you think, Yoni?"

I am no genius, but I wish Father Abraham had begged mercy more, whether it is a good logic or no.

Yeshua tells the tale of Jonah and the big fish. Jonah was a prophet, and HaShem told him to tell repentance to the great city of Nineveh.

I do not know where is Nineveh, but it was a wicked city and its sins reached up to heaven.

Jonah hated Nineveh and did not wish to tell it repentance, so he ran away from HaShem on a boat.

That was foolish, for you cannot run away from HaShem.

HaShem made a big storm on the boat, and the sailors cried out for their fear. They sacrificed to their false gods, but the storm howled more. Finally, Jonah told them the storm was on account of his sin, and they threw him in the sea and he drowned and a big fish ate him.

I do not like the tale told this way, that Jonah died. I like it told that the fish took Jonah in his mouth and saved him from dying. I wish Yeshua would tell the tale that way, but Shlomi Dancefeet likes it this way, and she asked for the tale.

Jonah's shade was in Sheol, and it cried out to HaShem. After three days, the fish came up on dry land and vomited out his bones, and HaShem made him live again.

Jonah went to Nineveh and told them repentance forty days, that the wrath of HaShem would fall on them. The people of Nineveh made a mock on Jonah, but there was one man who did not, and that was the king. He repented his sins, and he made all the people repent. They fasted and threw off their fine clothes and wore *saq* and begged mercy on HaShem.

At the end of forty days, Jonah went out of the city to watch the wrath of HaShem fall on the city. HaShem made a gourd spring up and shade Jonah, and he was glad, for it was hot. Jonah watched all day, but the wrath of HaShem did not fall on the city. The sun blazed like fire, and it dried up the gourd, and all the shade went away. Jonah looked up at the sky and shook his fist on the sun and complained to HaShem.

He told his rage to HaShem. The wicked people repented their sin and begged mercy, and HaShem repented his wrath and did not destroy them. That was not fair, to escape wrath for their sins, only because they repented and begged mercy.

Jonah complained and complained to HaShem on the matter, but HaShem only said he wished to show mercy on those who repent.

I do not understand this story.

Yoni says, "Rabbi, why did HaShem show mercy on Nineveh? It was the greatest city of Assyria. After this tale, Assyria grew mighty and destroyed Samaria and took away the ten tribes of Israel and laid siege to Jerusalem and would have destroyed it, only good King Hezekiah outfoxed them."

I do not know how Yoni knows all these things.

He makes it sound as HaShem did a wrong thing to show mercy.

I do not know what to think on the matter.

Father Abraham begged mercy on Sodom, but not enough, and little children were burned with fire. Jonah did not beg mercy on Nineveh, but they repented and escaped fire, and their children lived to destroy ten tribes of Israel.

That is not fair.

I think there is a time to show mercy and a time not to show mercy.

I wish HaShem will send his wrath on Nazareth.

But I will not beg mercy on them.

Never, ever, ever.

CHAPTER SEVENTY-FOUR

Yaakov of Nazareth

We have been on the road five full days and a little extra. When we arrive home to Nazareth, it is late morning on the day before Shabbat. I have told Yeshua the village is angry. Until now, I have not told Yeshua what he must do. First I must show him his great danger. Then I must persuade him to fight.

If he will not fight, then I will, because that is what a man does, but it will not be enough.

If he will not fight, he will be killed.

The village elders sit inside the gate. None of them rise to greet us, nor say a word of welcome to Yeshua, who has been gone many months. Old Yonatan the leather-man makes a cruel grin like a hawk. None of the others smile.

Fear twists in my belly. We are five brothers, all strong men. Yeshua has eight men with him. We have Uncle Halfai the winemaker and my cousin, Fat Shimon. They live in this village and did not go to the feast because they must tend their farm. They will stand with us. That is fifteen men. It is just enough, if we all fight. But I do not know if Yeshua will fight.

We walk through the village square.

I call greeting to Shimon the baker.

He turns his back.

My woman calls greeting to our neighbor Marta.

She scowls and goes in her house.

Three small girls see us and begin singing that song about Imma. They are too young to know what is a *zonah*, yet they sing it with hate in their eyes.

When we reach our house, Yosi's woman and Thin Shimon's woman come out to greet us with their children. They stayed here all this time we were gone to the feast, but the village does not hate them. It hates Imma. And now it hates Yeshua.

We all take off our packs and put them in our house.

Yeshua shows his men the rooftop where they will sleep. The weather is still fine, and they will sleep well there.

The women set to work to make food, for we are all hungry.

Thin Shimon goes out of the house wearing a hard smile.

I do not know what that means.

Yeshua catches my eye. "Come walk with me, Little Yaakov."

I take his hand and we walk.

That boy Yoni makes a move to follow us.

Yeshua shakes his head. "Yoni, please, you will stay here and make a watch over my house. If there is trouble, run fast to find us. We are going south to the lookout place. It is far, but you will not lose your way if you follow the path."

Yoni grins as he has been given a big job.

Yeshua and I walk in silence.

The path is more than a mile, but it goes downhill most of the way and is easy. We do not talk. The sun beats down on us all the way.

We sit on a large stone at the edge of the precipice and look south over the broad green Jezreel Valley. Far to our right is a mountain range that leads to the Great Sea. Straight ahead in the distance, the hill country of Samaria. To our left, Mount Tabor, shimmering in the sun, and beyond the range of seeing, the Lake of Ginosar and the Jordan Valley. Beneath us, slanting down to the valley, is a steep slope studded with jagged boulders.

"The village has an angry look," Yeshua says. "Nobody called shalom as we walked to our house. I smiled on two children, and they ran away as I was a wolf."

"I tried to explain the matter on the road, but you would not hear."

"I heard. I did not realize—"

"You should have made a move this summer."

"I did make—"

"You should have raised up an army."

"HaShem said—"

"You should have come back to Nazareth."

"I never—"

"You should have called your own village to join with you."

"But—"

"All summer, we heard tales on you from travelers, how you did a big thing in other villages. We waited and waited, and what did we see?"

"I did not promise—"

"Nothing! We heard tales how you sent away evil spirits in other villages, but we never saw you do it in your own. We heard tales how you healed sick in other villages, but we never saw you do it in your own. We heard tales how you said the kingdom of HaShem is coming in other villages, but we never heard you say it in your own. You called men of Capernaum your friends. You called men of Bethsaida friends. You called men of Cana friends. You called a tax-farmer friend! But you did not come to your own village and call them friends. You have dishonored yourself, and you have dishonored the village. And now you are surprised they are angry on you."

"I did only what HaShem—"

"All the village is in a rage on you now."

Yeshua says nothing.

The whole long summer runs before my mind. The village is angry on Yeshua, and they should be angry, for he dishonored them. My blood burns hot in my veins. "What do you have to say?"

Yeshua says nothing.

I feel as I am crushed between two great stones. The village always hated Imma, and why? Because she played the *zonah* with one of their men. They all know it, but she will not admit. If she would admit and tell who the man was, they would forgive. But they will never forgive if she will not admit. And on account of her sin, all our family suffers. Yeshua suffers. My father suffered. I suffer. And yet none of us ever speak on the matter.

I remember long ago, I fought the five boys to defend Yeshua because I thought they lied about Imma. But they spoke true. Abba denied it. Imma denied it. But it is a fact. My mother spread her legs for some man of the village. Our grandfather forbade me to speak on the matter. He said one does not speak on a matter of shame on a woman. I was four years old—who was I to say no to the great and mighty Yaakov Mega? So I have kept silent all my life, even after Yaakov Mega was gone, even after Abba was gone. I should not have kept silent. I should have told Imma to confess she played the *zonah*.

And now the village hates not only Imma but also Yeshua. They never hated him before. A few made a smirch on his name, but most thought that was a small matter, for Yeshua was only a *tekton*. But then he went out to other villages and made a big name for himself there, when his own village knows what he is. He dishonored them by not coming here to do mighty wonders. He dishonored them by not telling the kingdom of HaShem here. He dishonored himself by calling a tax-farmer friend. The village was angry on him a month ago when we left for Sukkot. Now Yeshua has come home, and they are in a rage.

"What do you think I should do?" Yeshua asks.

I shake my head. "You could beg mercy."

"I only did what HaShem told—"

"Or you could fight."

Yeshua says nothing. It is like when I fought the five boys and he stood by and did nothing, and they kicked me in the underparts until my world went dark for my agony.

I leap to my feet and begin pacing. "If they come for us, you will have to fight. Our brothers and I will fight, whether you do or no, but your men will fight only if you do. Our brothers and I are not enough against fifty villagers. If you do not fight, we will be killed. Imma will be killed. Do you want Imma killed?"

"I want ..." A shadow passes over Yeshua's face. "They killed Imma already many years ago."

I do not know what he means by that. The village did not kill Imma. What she has become, she did to herself because she refused to confess her sin.

I cannot see how to save him if he will not save himself. And now I think he will not. Yeshua will not beg mercy. He will not fight. He will not run. He will be killed.

My only hope is that the rest of us are not killed also.

"Rabbi Yeshua!" shouts a thin, squeaky voice behind us. "Rabbi, you must come!"

It is that boy, that foolish little Yoni. I do not see why Yeshua gives ear to him. The boy is conceited and constantly prattles nonsense.

Yoni arrives panting. "Rabbi, there are a few sick folk in the village who have come to ask help. One has an unclean spirit, and there is a boy who is blind, and another has a festered wound."

Yeshua stands and tugs on my arm. "Come see what HaShem will do, and then we will talk more on this matter."

He will kill us all with his kindness, to no gain.

CHAPTER SEVENTY-FIVE

Yoni of Capernaum

Rabbi Yeshua's brother terrifies me. His face is set like stone, and there is a darkness around his eyes when he looks on me. I think I interrupted some large matter, but that is not my fault. Rabbi Yeshua's mother told me to run find him.

Rabbi Yeshua smiles on me. "It is good that you came, Yoni. Tell me who it is that needs help."

I take his hand and we walk. I feel Little Yaakov's hard eyes on my back, like an icy wind, but I am safe with Rabbi Yeshua. "There is an old woman named Hana who has a spirit of sadness."

"I know Old Hana the cheese-woman. She was kind to me when I was a boy."

"And there is a boy who is lately blind from the eye-fever. His grandfather brought him, a big man with a white beard, and his name is called Shimon."

"I know Shimon the baker. He called on me often to tell tales in the village square when I was a boy."

"And there is a man with a wound on his foot that festered. His name is called Yoseph, and he stinks like piss."

"I know Yoseph the leather-man. He …" Rabbi Yeshua's voice breaks.

I look hard on Rabbi Yeshua and think on the evil tale Yehuda Dreamhead told on the leather-man's son. I think there is more than one tale to be told. I think this leather-man is a cruel man.

Rabbi Yeshua smiles on me. "Yoseph the leather-man loves HaShem."

I do not wish to know all that Yoseph the leather-man did to Rabbi Yeshua. I do not like this village. There is a dark feel about the place. The village elders did not stand when we came in the gate. The women hovered in the doorways of their houses giving us angry eyes. I want to go home to Capernaum, but Rabbi Yeshua said we are to stay for a week and make the village glad. I do not think we can make this village glad.

After a long walk uphill, we arrive back at Rabbi Yeshua's house.

His brothers stand out in the street waiting for us. The women must be inside making food.

The woman, Old Hana, hobbles toward us. Her eyes are set tight and her mouth is made small and I think she is afraid on something.

Rabbi Yeshua runs to meet her. He throws his arms around her and gives her a kiss and a kiss and a kiss. "Savta, what troubles you?"

She weeps and speaks in a small, cracked voice.

Rabbi Yeshua leans close.

She speaks long in his ear.

Tears grow in his eyes. He nods and speaks quietly to her. Then he lays hands on her head. "Go, you spirit of sadness, go!"

It is as HaShem draws her face again, without so many sad lines.

Old Hana wraps her arms around Rabbi Yeshua and weeps. It is what women call weeping for joy. I do not understand women.

Rabbi Yeshua rocks her gently. At last he gives her a kiss and a kiss and a kiss. "HaShem loves you much, Savta."

"You were always a kind boy, and you have grown to be a kind man." Old Hana looks over her shoulder at the village and shudders. "There are wicked lies told—"

Rabbi Yeshua touches his finger to her lips. "Beware the Evil Tongue, Savta. HaShem loves our village."

"You should be wary on the village."

"I will be wary, Savta."

Old Hana walks back toward the village square.

Her step is lighter than when she came.

Rabbi Yeshua turns to the large man with the white beard. "Shimon, my father! Tell me what has befallen."

Shimon the baker does not smile. "My grandson had the eye-fever six weeks ago. Now he is blind in the right eye. Tales tell that you have healed such things in other villages. I have come to see if they are idle tales."

Rabbi Yeshua sits on a stone bench in front of his house and takes the boy on his lap.

The boy is young. I have a nephew just his size, in the fourth year of his age. This boy's right eye is vacant and lost.

Rabbi Yeshua speaks quietly to him for a time.

The boy smiles and grows calm and still.

"Shimon, my father, please take dust from the street and put it in my hand."

Shimon the baker's eyes grow wide. For a moment, it seems that he wishes to go, but he cannot leave without his grandson. At last, he pinches dust between his fingers and puts it in Rabbi Yeshua's hand.

"A little more, friend." Rabbi Yeshua's voice is kind, but behind it, I hear tears.

Shimon scowls and adds more dust to Rabbi Yeshua's open palm.

Rabbi Yeshua spits in his hand and mixes with his finger to make mud.

I remember he did this in Magdala, and the blind beggar was healed. My heart thumps. Shimon the baker will not be so rude when Rabbi Yeshua makes the boy see.

"Shimon, my friend, please, you will put mud on the eye."

Shimon's face turns red. He stands frozen like some stone idol of the goyim.

Rabbi Yeshua's brothers gather close to watch. Our men stand farther back, for they have seen this before and they know what is to happen next.

Rabbi Yeshua smiles on Shimon the baker. "HaShem says to put mud on the boy's eye."

Shimon the baker grunts and takes mud and puts it on the eye.

Rabbi Yeshua does nothing. He holds the boy quietly for the fourth part of an hour. Finally, he sets him on his feet and gives him a kiss and a kiss and a kiss. "Shimon, my friend, HaShem says to take the boy to the village spring and wash the eye."

Shimon the baker's eyes narrow to thin slits, and his face turns black with anger. "And … does HaShem say washing the mud will heal the boy?"

Rabbi Yeshua stands. He looks more weary than I ever saw him. "HaShem says to take the boy to the village spring and wash the eye."

For a moment, I think Shimon the baker will give Rabbi Yeshua the backhand of dishonor.

Rabbi Yeshua says, "Shimon, my long friend. If you love me, please, you will do as HaShem says."

Shimon the baker takes the boy's hand and tugs him away.

I watch them go.

They march toward the village square.

Just beyond it, they turn aside.

I think to run after them, for they went the wrong way. Rabbi Yeshua's mother already told me the spring is outside the far end of the village.

Rabbi Yeshua clutches my arm. "Shimon the baker is a son of Nazareth sixty years. He knows which way is the village spring."

The leather-man makes a clearing of his throat.

Rabbi Yeshua turns to him and smiles. "Yoseph, my friend! Tell me your troubles."

Yoseph has a hard face.

I would too if I had to wade in a tanning pool full of piss to knead hides with my feet. I would not be a leather-man for all the sweet-smelling myrrh in Arabia.

Yoseph points to his right foot. "I stepped on some sharp thing in my piss-pool two weeks ago, and now the wound has festered."

Rabbi Yeshua leads Yoseph the leather-man to the bench. "Sit here, friend."

Yoseph sits and scowls on him and pulls up his tunic above the right knee.

His leg is red and swollen from the ankle all to the knee.

That is an evil sign. Six years ago, my father's cousin had a wound fester in his foot. I saw it with these eyes. A spirit of death came in through the wound and filled up his leg and turned it red as a sun-scorch. After two weeks, the spirit gave him a dizziness in his head and a racing in his heart and a weakness in all his muscles. After two days more, he died of it.

Rabbi Yeshua kneels before Yoseph the leather-man and takes the foot in his hands.

Yoseph's foot is filthy with the fouls of a tanning pool. At the base of the heel is an angry wound, ugly and festered.

The smell of piss gags me.

Rabbi Yeshua licks his own finger and puts it on the wound. "You wound, give up your evil."

Nothing happens for a moment and then …

White pus squirts out of the wound onto Rabbi Yeshua's finger.

My stomach lurches inside me.

Rabbi Yeshua wipes his finger in the dirt. He calls into the house, "Imma, please you will bring me a cup of water."

Little Yaakov sucks in his breath.

Rabbi Yeshua's other brothers look on each other with wide eyes.

We wait.

Rabbi Yeshua's mother comes out of the house with a stone cup.

She stops as she is frozen.

She stares on the leather-man.

She looks as she wants to run away fast.

I do not think she likes this leather-man.

The leather-man looks on her as she is *haryo*.

Slowly, slowly, she brings the cup to Rabbi Yeshua.

He smiles on her and takes the cup and pours water on the foot.

I step in to see.

All the festering around the wound has gone away.

That is good, but it is not enough. The right leg is still red, still swollen to twice the size of the left. The spirit of death means to grow stronger and stronger until it kills Yoseph the leather-man.

Now the rabbi will send it away.

Rabbi Yeshua puts his hand on the thickest part of the leg. "You spirit of death, leave him."

Nothing happens.

"You spirit of death, leave him!"

Nothing happens.

Rabbi Yeshua looks on the leg and waits. His eyes turn inward as he is listening. "Friend, HaShem says that at this time tomorrow, the spirit of death will leave you. Also, HaShem says …"

Yoseph the leather-man's eyes pierce him like knives. "Yes?" He spits out the word as it is poison.

I think Yoseph the leather-man does not like Rabbi Yeshua.

Rabbi Yeshua thinks long. "Ask me tomorrow, and I will tell you what else HaShem says."

Yoseph the leather-man stands and tries to put weight on his bad leg. He winces. A jagged smile creeps across his face.

I do not understand this matter. His smile looks more festered than any wound I ever saw.

A tremor runs through him.

Yoseph the leather-man blinks twice and puts out a shaky hand to touch the wall. He sits again on the bench and leans forward, breathing hard.

I think the spirit of death gave him a dizziness just now.

Rabbi Yeshua says, "Friend, let me walk with you to your house."

Yoseph the leather-man shakes his head and puts his hands on his knees and stands up slow, wearing the look I used to see on the face of Yoseph the Rage.

Rabbi Yeshua says, "Friend, take my arm."

Yoseph the leather-man pushes him away and limps up the street without looking back.

All my belly is in a big knot.

CHAPTER SEVENTY-SIX

Miryam of Nazareth

We have finished the evening meal and welcomed in Queen Shabbat. The heat of the day is gone, and I should feel happy. But I am afraid. All the village feels tense as a viper coiled to strike. Nobody came to make a welcome on my son. Nobody asked him to come tell a tale in the village square tomorrow night after the going out of Shabbat. Sometime this week will be a big fight, I am sure of it.

Yeshua wears the face of a man who does not know what to do.

My sons' women look like they wish we can run away fast and hide. Only we do not have anywhere to go.

My sons look like they wish to fight, all except Yeshua.

Yeshua's men look like they wish to fight. Only none of them will fight unless Yeshua fights.

Yeshua must fight the village. He has a big Power in him, only he does not know it. A man who can heal the mighty leprosy can call down fire from heaven to destroy his enemies. Elijah the prophet called down fire from heaven. He killed four hundred false prophets with one sword. Our village is no more than two hundreds. HaShem can kill them all with one blast from his nose.

If Yeshua knew he had the Power, he would fight. When Thin Shimon puts the Ring of Justice in his hand, he will know it. He will see that the Ring was given for such a time as this. Like when the King of Persia put his signet ring in the hand of Mordecai, the cousin of Queen Esther, and Mordecai used it to save our people.

"Rabbi Yeshua, tell us a tale!" Yoni says.

A tale would be good, to help us forget our troubles.

"What tale should I tell?" Yeshua says.

"The tale of Father Noah and the big boat!" says Toma the boat maker.

I like that tale, for it is a tale of judgment on wicked men. Today is a good day for such a tale.

All our family and all Yeshua's men gather around him.

The stars are winking awake, one after another, tiny dots in the deep blue sky. A thin crescent moon hangs in the sky, for we are three days past the new moon. There is no breeze, and I feel as a giant weight hangs over the village, waiting to crush it.

"In days of old, wicked men flourished in all the lands under heaven," Yeshua says. "Men stole their enemies' gold. They forced their enemies' women to spread their legs. They murdered their enemies' children in the light of day. There was no judge to make a justice on the weak and the powerless."

He stops and his face looks puzzled, as he has forgotten something.

"And there were giants in the land," says the tax-farmer. "Our father Enoch wrote a book on the matter, how mighty spirits came down to earth and took women who were daughters of men and used them for a pleasure and begat sons, giants and champions and evil men of renown."

I never heard of this book Father Enoch wrote, but if it tells these things, they must be true.

Yoni says, "The book of Enoch is one of the doubtful writings. Rabbi Yeshua, do you believe this tale of the mighty Nephilim? That sounds like a Greekish tale."

My son shrugs. "The first book of Moses tells also of the Nephilim. Do you say the books of Moses are a Greekish tale?"

Yoni says, "But it is a paradox, that invisible spirits could use women for a pleasure and beget visible sons. It is not even a paradox. It is a foolishness. How do you explain the matter?"

"What do you think, Yoni?"

Yoni thinks long on the matter. "I think there are invisible Powers for evil in the world, whether I can explain the matter or no."

My son makes a big grin on him. "That is well said, Yoni."

I do not know what Yoni means by invisible Powers for evil. When my sons speak of Powers, they mean Syria and Egypt and Babylon and Rome.

But I know there is evil in the world. I know there is evil in my own village. I know I am afraid. I know my only hope is that HaShem will punish the wicked. That is what I like about the tale of Father Noah.

Yeshua continues his tale.

I close my eyes, and I see the tale as it happens. It is here and now, and not some tale from far away and long ago.

～

The Tale of Father Noah

I see Father Noah cutting down many trees outside our village. He clears a place on his land and stacks wood for a big boat.

His enemies come to ask on the matter. They make a mock on him, for we live on a hill and far from the sea.

Father Noah says nothing and works on his boat.

Years pass. Five. Ten. Twenty. A son is born to Father Noah, and then another, and then another. The boys grow to be men and work with Father Noah on the boat.

Their enemies gather around to make a mock on them. They laugh them to scorn. They call them fools and simples. They throw *haryo* on them and run away.

Those evil men should die. I hate them. HaShem hates them.

Father Noah says nothing and works on his boat.

More years pass, and the frame of the boat is done.

More years pass, and the shell of the boat is done.

More years pass, and the inside of the boat is done.

Father Noah and his sons spend a whole year sealing up all the outside with pitch.

Their enemies come with torches to burn the boat.

Father Noah and his sons fight them off with clubs.

I am glad they do not sit idle while their enemies come to destroy.

At last, the boat is done all over. Father Noah has worked a hundred and twenty years to build the boat. He sends his sons all around the land to find animals. They bring sheep and goats and horses and cows and camels and donkeys and pigs. I wish they had not brought pigs, for they are unclean and vile. I cannot count all the animals they bring. I will ask Yoni how many, but I think it is more than a hundred. I feel sorry for Father Noah and his sons, for all those animals will make *haryo*. That will make a big stink in the boat, with only one window. I never thought on that until now.

Father Noah brings his woman and his three sons and their women, and they go in the boat. They close the door and seal it up.

All Father Noah's enemies gather around the boat to laugh on it and make a mock on him.

I laugh to see those wicked men, for they do not know what is to come. They do not believe HaShem will punish them for their sins.

They shout Father Noah for a fool. They throw *haryo* on the boat. They make a piss on the boat.

I smell the stink of the *haryo* and the piss. It is a bad stink.

I am angry on them, but I do not shout them for fools. HaShem will punish them, and then I will laugh.

One day passes, and they shout Father Noah for a fool.

Two days pass.

Three days, four days, five days, six pass, and every day they shout Father Noah for a fool.

On the seventh day, I know they will be punished. They do not know it, but I do, for I have heard this tale many times. The seventh day will bring the wrath of HaShem to smite them.

The seventh day dawns clear and hot.

Father Noah's enemies gather around and shout him for a fool.

Something dark appears above the horizon, small and black. It creeps across the sky toward the boat.

Father Noah's enemies see it and make a mock on it. They do not know what is a cloud, for they never saw one.

Another cloud comes, and then another.

Soon all the sky is black with clouds. The air has a wet smell. I can feel it myself—cold and sharp. A breeze springs up, and it makes me shiver. It grows to a wind, and I wrap my cloak tight around my shoulders. It begins to howl, and my ears hurt.

I am beginning to mislike this tale.

A fat drop falls on my head.

Another one.

More.

Many.

I am wet. My whole head is drenched.

This is a bad tale. There is a thing wrong with this tale.

I am watching from inside the tale.

But I am watching from outside the boat.

All Father Noah's enemies are angry on him. They beat on the sides of the boat. They shout on Father Noah for mercy.

I shout on Father Noah for mercy.

The rain falls harder now. I see it falling in sheets. Lightning shoots down from heaven. Lightning is when HaShem is angry on people. The thunder follows, so loud it makes me deaf. That is the sound of HaShem shouting. HaShem has made a mistake, for he should not be angry on me. A wrong thing has befallen.

I beat with my hands on the boat, shouting for Father Noah to open.

He does not open.

All the ground is wet to the level of my ankles.

I should climb a tree, but I think that is not enough.

I know there is a hill not far from here, Mount Tabor. That is a big hill. I run for that hill, faster than I ever did.

All around me, others run.

When one falls, I step on him and keep running and do not look back.

It is the walk of two hours to reach Mount Tabor, and I run all the way in a white flame of fear. When I reach the mountain, my side aches and my heart hurts and I wheeze like the bellows of Shmuel the iron-man.

Many others have come here. We all run up the mountain. It is steep and rugged. The winds blow on me. The rains drench me. All around, I hear men shrieking. Women wailing. Children crying.

I run and I run and I run. Once, I look back and see the boat Father Noah made, floating on the water.

I climb higher.

Two men are at the top, each trying to climb on the same tall rock. They beat each other with fists. They scratch. They bite. They gouge eyes. One kicks the other in the underparts and makes him fall. He smashes the man's head with a club and then climbs up on the rock. There is room for another. I climb up after him. The waters lap up behind me.

I stand on the rock with that wicked man.

He looks on me with hate.

I look on him with hate.

The waters climb to our feet.

We are forced close together.

He smells like piss.

I smell like rage.

I see in his eyes he means to kill me.

He sees in my eyes I mean to kill him.

The water licks my ankles.

I rush on the wicked man.

He rushes on me.

I scream with the righteous rage of HaShem, for this man is a wicked murderer.

We smash together.

He knots his hands around my throat and spits my face. "Now you will die, you spreadlegs!"

I shove my thumbs in his eyes.

He screams and falls off the rock, pulling me with him in the water.

I scream more than I ever did. I am so cold I cannot think. I sink under the water, sucking water in my lungs.

It stings like death.

∼

Miryam of Nazareth

"Imma! Imma!" Yeshua's arms wrap tight around me.

I am weeping. All my face is wet.

He pulls me onto his lap and holds me.

I cannot see for all my tears.

I weep and I weep for my terror.

I hear the sounds of the others stepping away. They mutter things I cannot hear.

I do not care what they say. They do not know what I have suffered.

I clutch Yeshua and breathe in his warmth. I am safe with my son. Yeshua will protect me. Yeshua will defend.

But I do not know why he told such an evil tale.

If Toma the boat maker ever asks for this tale again, I will box his ears until they fall off.

CHAPTER SEVENTY-SEVEN

Yoni of Capernaum

I am lying awake on the roof of Rabbi Yeshua's house, trying hard to sleep. Shimon the Rock snores loud. Big Yaakov snores louder. The others sleep like dead men—Andre and Philip and Natanel the hireling and Toma Trouble and the tax-farmer.

I do not see how they can sleep at such a bad time. Tomorrow will be a big trouble. Little Yaakov says it is Rabbi Yeshua's fault.

I wish we were far from here, only Little Yaakov says being far from here is what made the trouble. He says the village is angry on Rabbi Yeshua for doing big things in other places.

I do not see why that is his fault. He comes here to do big things, and they make a rage on him, so why should he not do big things in other villages, where they do not make a rage on him?

Tomorrow, Rabbi Yeshua must find a way to lance the boil.

Only I do not see how he will lance the boil.

The silence down below in the street disturbs me.

Why should silence disturb me?

That is a strange matter.

I think on it and then I see what is the trouble.

The silence is too much. The silence is the silence of men trying to be silent.

I rise to a sitting position.

I rise to a crawling position.

I crawl on silent hands and knees to the parapet of the roof.

I look up at the sky. We are three days past the new moon, and now the moon has gone down. I do not think the night is old. I think it is near midnight. If I make a caution and raise my head slowly, I will not be seen against the stars. Perhaps I will not see anything either, but I must try.

I listen with both ears.

Men are moving on the street below. Men in bare feet, not speaking.

I think I smell the sweat of their rage.

Or else that is the sweat of my fear.

Slowly, slowly, I raise my head to the level of the parapet and look out.

They brought oil lamps, several of them.

That is good—I can see them. But it is bad—they might see me if I make a sudden move.

Something gleams in the light. They brought metal tools, or weapons, I cannot be sure. Also leather buckets, only I cannot see what is in the buckets.

Slowly, slowly, I lower my head. I feel faint and I cannot catch breath. My heart runs fast in my chest, faster than it ever did.

If they came to kill us all in the night, I should shout the alarm.

Only if I shout the alarm, our men will rush out in the street, sleepy and unaware, and there will be a big fight, and we are overnumbered, and that will go ill on us.

Little Yaakov says there are fifty men of the village. I think they are all below me in the street. They carried weapons and buckets here, which means they do not care that they break Shabbat. That means they have a big rage, for a man does not break Shabbat without a mighty reason.

We are thirteen men, and the only way out of this house is through the door that goes out on the street from the courtyard. That is a narrow door. Only one man can go through at a time. If our men rush out in the street, it will not be fifty angry men against thirteen. It will be fifty angry men against one man alone, thirteen times.

I must not shout the alarm, not yet, for that will make a warning on the men below, and it will terrify our men, and they will act and not think.

I must think first.

Why did they bring weapons?

To kill us, of course.

But why did they bring buckets?

Buckets are no use for killing.

I must look again to understand the matter.

Slowly, slowly, I raise my head.

I do not see anyone.

I see the glow of oil lamps.

I see the shadows of men stretching long out into the street.

They must be all pressed up close to the wall of the house.

What is the meaning of that?

I hear the soft rasp of metal on stone, slow and slow, at the edge of my hearing.

I wait.

I think the men are spread all along the front of the house. I think some must have gone around the sides. They are doing something to the walls, that is all I can say.

I do not hear them preparing to attack.

I think this is a bad matter.

They do not mean to kill us.

They mean to do something worse, only I do not know what.

I wait and I wait.

After the fourth part of an hour, the lights below move out into the street again.

I lower my head and listen.

Silent feet pad away from the house.

Silent feet pad up the street toward the village square.

I raise my head and look.

I see oil lamps.

I see men walking with light feet and light buckets.

I see something smeared on one of the buckets, brilliant white in the light of the oil lamps.

Plaster.

White plaster.

They plastered the house.

That is a very bad matter.

The days of the smirch are over.

The village has decided that Rabbi Yeshua is a *mamzer*.

Yaakov of Nazareth

I slept like a stone last night, and that is good. Today will be a hard day. We will go to the synagogue, and Yeshua will try to reason with the village, and they will make a scorn on him. They will not make a fight on him, because it is Shabbat, and a man does not make a fight on Shabbat. But tonight, after the going out of Shabbat, the village will gather in the village square for songs and tales. The weather is fine, and they will wish to celebrate. Then, I do not know what will befall. If we go to the square tonight, there will be hard words. Sometime in this week, there will be a fight. Yeshua is not ready for it.

But I am ready.

We eat the morning meal in a big silence.

Yeshua's eyes are turned inward.

Shimon the Rock looks from side to side as he is unsure on himself. This is not his village and he does not know how he should act.

That boy Yoni looks as he knows something.

Thin Shimon looks as he knows something.

I do not think either of them know anything. They both of them think they are clever, but I piss on their cleverness.

After we eat, we prepare to go to the synagogue. Yosi's woman and Thin Shimon's woman have their children to attend to, so they will not go. Imma never goes. My woman makes to go with us, for she loves a crowd. Also, Yehuda Dreamhead's woman makes to go.

Yeshua walks out first to the street. He sucks in his breath.

I go out just after.

The wall of the house is all plastered over, white as a tomb.

I suck in my breath.

My woman sucks in her breath.

Shimon the Rock comes out and sucks in his breath.

All our men come out and suck in their breath.

That boy Yoni does not suck in his breath.

My woman takes hold on my arm. All her body is shaking.

"You will stay home today," I tell her.

Yehuda Dreamhead's woman falls down in the street shrieking in her fear.

It takes me and Yehuda Dreamhead both to lift her up.

Yehuda Dreamhead takes her to the house and pushes her in the door.

My woman clutches on my arm. "Stay home with us and defend."

I shake my head. "You are not in danger. It is Yeshua I should defend."

I turn to see where is Yeshua.

He stands a few paces away with his back to us. Thin Shimon is in front of him, grinning.

That is a foolish thing, to be grinning on such a time as this. Thin Shimon is not so clever as they say, if he does not see what a big danger we are in.

My woman calls out, "Yeshua, stay home with us today."

Yeshua turns and looks on her. "Shlomzion, my sister, please you will watch over Imma." He comes and takes her hand and speaks softly in her ear and leads her back in the house.

When he comes out, he pulls the door tight behind him and shouts, "Bar the door and do not open except for one of us!"

The iron bar scrapes the door on the inside.

We walk to the village square with eyes hard open.

I think there will be a bad trouble sooner than I expected. I think the village will not allow Yeshua in the synagogue. They have declared him *mamzer*, and Torah says a *mamzer* cannot go in the assembly.

When we reach the square, men are going in the synagogue.

I do not see any women.

I expected to see Old Yonatan standing at the door of the synagogue to tell Yeshua no. Old Yonatan is president of the synagogue now. It was him, many years ago, who told Yeshua no, on the day all the rest of the village told him yes.

Today, all the village will tell Yeshua no.

But Old Yonatan is not standing at the door.

Yoseph the leather-man is not standing at the door.

Nobody is standing at the door.

I do not like the look on this matter.

I hurry to come level with Yeshua, to tell him what I think, that we walk into a trap.

His face is set hard, and his steps are quick.

He gives me a strong face.

I never saw such a face on my brother. Bold and fierce.

We march across the village square.

We march to the door of the synagogue.

We march inside the synagogue.

Three rows of stone benches go up in steps on all sides to the walls.

The synagogue is mostly full, but there is a place near the front, on the left side, three rows clear, enough for all of us.

I do not like the look of this. Usually, the last places are near the door. I would have wished to take place near the door.

All the places near the door are taken.

We all take seats. I go up to the farthest row and put my back against the wall. I smell a trap. When you walk in a trap, you should protect your own back.

Yeshua takes place on the front row. The tax-farmer sits beside him.

That is a bad matter. I will protect Yeshua's back, for he is my brother.

I will not protect the tax-farmer's back.

The last men of the village come in and take place.

I do not see one woman here.

Usually there are boys to the age of four who come, but today there is only one.

Shimon the baker brought his grandson.

The boy's right eye is still empty and blind.

All the synagogue is silent as Sheol.

Old Yonatan rises and makes a cruel grin. "Thin Shimon, come, you will lead the prayers and read Torah."

They always ask Thin Shimon to read Torah, for he is the only man of the village who reads well.

Thin Shimon goes forward.

I see what will befall, and I am glad on it.

Today there will be a big fight.

I will fight the village.

Shimon the Rock will fight the village.

All our men will fight the village.

Yeshua has lived all his life without ever once making a fight.

But today he will fight the village.

CHAPTER SEVENTY-EIGHT

Yeshua of Nazareth

'What do you think you are doing, to come in the synagogue? All the village hates you.'

'They love HaShem.'

'They broke Shabbat to plaster your house. You are mamzer to them.'

'I am not mamzer in the eyes of HaShem.'

'Do you not wonder why they let you come in the synagogue? You have walked in a trap, fool.'

'HaShem said to come in the synagogue, so I came in.'

'You were a fool to have stayed away from the village so many months. That is why the village hates you.'

'I came when HaShem gave the word.'

'You were a fool to bring the tax-farmer to the village.'

'He is no tax-farmer, he is my friend.'

'You were a fool yesterday not to heal the boy at a touch.'

'I healed him the way HaShem told to heal him.'

'What do you mean, you healed him? See, he is blind still. And the leather-man still has the spirit of death, more than he did yesterday. If he dies here in this place, they will say you put a curse on him.'

'HaShem said he would heal the boy and the leather-man both.'

'That is a lie, for see they are not healed. You are a liar or deceived or a fool. No wonder the village is angry on you. You should run away fast.'

'I will not run. I will confront the village.'

'Confront? After thirty years, at last you will stand and fight? You will be killed.'

'I did not say I will fight. I will confront.'

'You should call down fire from heaven.'

'I will confront.'

'The prophet said you must destroy the first Power or be killed.'

'The village is not the first Power. The village is slaved by the first Power.'

'It is a gift of HaShem that Thin Shimon found the Ring of Justice for such a time as this. Use it for a Power of HaShem to defeat the first Power, and blessed be HaShem!'

'The Ring of Justice is not a Power.'

'The village thinks it is a Power. If they think it is a Power, you can use it to defeat them, even if it is not a Power.'

'It is a lie to say a thing made with hands is a Power.'

'It is no sin to use a lie to save your life.'

'If I use a lie to defeat the first Power, then I will be the one slaved by the first Power.'

'You will be killed unless you use it, fool.'

'HaShem says you must be silent.'

~

Silence.

The synagogue is full today, and hope makes my heart tremble. Fear presses in on me also, for I have a deep thing to say to Nazareth. I have longed all summer to come home. Now the time is ripe. If they will listen to my words ever and repent, it is today. But their hearts are fenced in by their long cruelty. If they will not tear down this fence, there will be no room to receive the words of the kingdom, which are life.

We have finished the prayers. We have finished the Torah. The time of Nazareth's judgment or her redemption is now. My brothers sit here with me. My men sit here with me. The men of Nazareth sit here, but they are not with me.

Abba, I beg that my village will repent and make a righteous justice and enter the kingdom of HaShem.

Old Yonatan the leather-man stands and points to me. "Yeshua, son of Miryam, they say big things on you in other villages. Let us see if those big things are smoke. You will expound from the prophets."

I rise and go to the *bema* in the center.

Our synagogue is small and reeks of sweat and rage. On all sides are three rows of stone benches rising up in steps. The men on the first row are near enough to spit my eye.

When I was a boy, I felt warm and safe to have a small synagogue where all the village sat packed close together. Now I do not feel warm and safe.

My heart thumps in my chest, and I smell the stink of my own fear.

I could take three big leaps and reach the door and run away fast. Except HaShem did not tell me to run away fast.

HaShem told me to confront. HaShem told me to speak truth. HaShem told me to smite the first Power that slaves my village.

The scroll of Isaiah lies on the table. I know the portion I should read today, and I pray it is life for my village. Life or death, they must choose. *Please, Abba, may they choose life.*

All the village scowls on me with dark faces.

I look to my brothers.

Little Yaakov and Yosi and Thin Shimon and Yehuda Dreamhead scowl on the village with dark faces.

Uncle Halfai and his son, Fat Shimon, scowl with dark faces.

Shimon the Rock and Andre and Big Yaakov sit together with dark faces.

Mattai huddles alone with fear in his eyes.

Toma the boat maker and Natanel the hireling look as they think we should run away fast.

Yoni grins on me and takes the hand of Philip.

Philip sits up tall and gives me a strong smile.

I remember the tale of his sister Rivka, how Philip took a beating from his father, and took more and more and more until he wore his father down.

I feel a big courage well up in me. Philip is a quiet man and says little, but today I feel his strength. Kindness is stronger than rage.

I find my place in the scroll of Isaiah.

All the synagogue falls silent.

I read with my strongest voice the Hebrew words, translating to Aramaic as I go.

"The Spirit of the Lord,
The Spirit of Yah
Is upon me.
For Yah has anointed me
To tell good news,
To tell good news to the meek.
For Yah has sent me
To bind up wounds,
To heal the brokenhearted,
To cry freedom to the captives,
To open the eyes of the blind,
To shout the Year of Favor
Of the Lord Yah."

I stop at a place that is no stopping place.

I look up.

The men of the village sit with backs straight and mouths open, waiting for the next, for all know this saying of Isaiah. They wish to hear me say today is the Day of Vengeance of HaShem.

I will not say it.

I close the scroll.

I sit in the Seat of Moses to expound.

The silence feels thick and heavy all around.

I say, "Today, this word from HaShem is fulfilled in your sight. The kingdom of HaShem has begun here today, as it has begun already through all Galilee."

I hear the voice of murmuring at the edge of hearing.

"Who is he, if not the *tekton* we know?"

"Who is he, if not the son of Miryam Spreadlegs?"

"Those are his brothers, Little Yaakov and Yosi and Thin Shimon and Yehuda Dreamhead, day laborers without land."

"He says he heals people in other villages, but he cannot heal one man here."

"He makes a friend on a tax-farmer, but we will never be a friend on a friend of a tax-farmer."

"He looks for a big honor in other villages, but we turned our back on his father's claim and called him *mamzer*, and see how weak he is, he can do nothing."

"We gave him a chance to expound the prophets, and he even twists the words of the prophet."

My brothers and my men fidget. Little Yaakov's face is hard with rage. Yoni looks ready to tell them all fools. Shimon the Rock fingers his cloth belt where he usually carries a fish knife—only not on Shabbat. Thin Shimon grins on me and taps his nose.

Philip gives me a strong face.

I must try again. "You think in your hearts that Rabbi Yeshua heals the blind in Capernaum, but he cannot heal the blind in Nazareth, which is his own home. You think the physician cannot heal himself, and therefore he is no physician."

Shimon the baker sits with straight back and arms crossed on his chest. His hard face tells that I made a scandal, to say I give sight to the blind, when here is his grandson beside him still blind in one eye.

It is a scandal, but it is not my scandal. If the boy lived in Capernaum, he would be seeing today. For a moment, I cannot breathe for the injustice of it. The boy would see today, if Shimon the baker trusted HaShem to obey.

My whole body is wet with sweat. Today is the appointed day for release from oppression. But there is no release without repentance. Nazareth will repent today, or it will never repent. "My brothers, I have a matter to discuss with you."

All the men lean forward to hear.

The air crackles like before a lightning.

I feel the cold breath of the Accuser on my neck.

I refuse the Accuser.

Today, I accuse the Accuser.

Today, I confront my village. *Please, Abba, soften their thick hearts.*

"With the same measure that you measure others, HaShem will measure you. If you put a smirch on an innocent child, HaShem will put a smirch on you. If you accuse a spotless woman for a *zonah*, HaShem will accuse you for a *zonah*. If you smear dishonor on the house of a prophet, HaShem will smear dishonor on your house."

I wait, and I hear the Accuser shrieking. I refuse to listen. *Please, my brothers, repent and measure out mercy. Turn to HaShem and measure out kindness. Enter the kingdom and measure out trust.*

Shimon the baker's face is hard and cold. He looks on his grandson, and anger lights up in his eyes. The Accuser clutches at him, searching for a hold.

My heart burns at the Accuser, for I love Shimon the baker as I love Shimon the Rock. I love Shimon the baker as I love Little Yaakov. I love Shimon the baker as I love Imma.

Shimon the baker stands and takes his grandson's hand and walks out.

His footsteps are a slap across my face.

The men of Nazareth watch him, and their faces are stone.

I must be more blunt, for they resist gentle words. "Many poor widows in Israel could have fed Elijah the prophet, but they did not, and they were not saved from the famine. Only a widow of Zarephath fed him, and she was saved."

The room grows hot with the lies of the Accuser.

I must outshout the Accuser with truth. There is no harder word than to call a Jew a leper. This word will break their pride, or it will break their honor. I pray it will break their pride.

"There were many lepers in Israel who could have come to Elisha the prophet, but only a Syrian came to him and was saved. Please, my brothers, turn to HaShem and trust in his prophet and be saved, or else you will die in your leprosy."

Yoseph the leather-man stands up slow. His face is red and he looks shaky on his feet. He points an angry finger at me. "You are a *mamzer* and a liar and a false prophet!"

Old Yonatan stands up fast and shakes his fist at me. "You lead Israel astray, you son of a spreadlegs!"

Others stand, a dozen of them, two dozens, three dozens, all the village.

"False prophet!"

"Leper!"

"Samaritan!"

My heart seizes, and I want to weep, for I have lost these men of my village, my brothers.

I think I have lost them all.

CHAPTER SEVENTY-NINE

Shimon of Capernaum

I am sitting on the third row beside Little Yaakov. A big storm rages in my heart.

'*He should have read more from the scroll of Isaiah. He stopped before the Day of Vengeance.*'

'*Rabbi Yeshua had his reasons.*'

'*What were his reasons?*'

'*How should I know? I will ask him, or Yoni will.*'

'*Rabbi Yeshua does not know what he is doing.*'

'*He knows. I think he knows.*'

'*Rabbi Yeshua is a fool.*'

I am sick in my soul. Things have gone ill since we came to Nazareth. Little Yaakov looked afraid when we came in the village gate yesterday. Rabbi Yeshua's mother melted into a weeping puddle last night during the tale of Father Noah. Some in the village broke Shabbat last night to come and plaster his house. The villagers this morning had darkness around their eyes when we came in the synagogue. And now—

Men stand all around the synagogue.

I am so shocked I cannot think.

"False prophet!"

"Leper!"

"Samaritan!"

The men of the village leap to attack.

I leap to defend, only I am in the third row.

I push past Toma Trouble and Natanel the hireling.

I push past Philip and the tax farmer.

I fly to defend Rabbi Yeshua.

I should have sat on the first row. Already, many men surround Rabbi Yeshua.

I am outside the circle.

Rabbi Yeshua is inside.

The men shout their rage on Rabbi Yeshua. They slap his face with the backhand of dishonor.

I drive my fist into the lower back of some man in front of me.

He screams in a big agony.

I know he will be pissing blood tomorrow.

I hear Yoni shouting something.

My heart beats triple time. I seize the tunic of the villager before me and pull with my biggest strength.

His tunic rips in my hands.

Two strong men take vise holds on my arms.

I twist like a bull in the battle.

One strong man takes grip on the back of my tunic.

I lunge forward, or try to.

All three pull me back.

I kick with my biggest kick.

I shout with my biggest shout.

A fourth man with an iron fist punches me hard in the belly.

All my breath is stolen away.

He hits me in the face, twice as hard.

I feel as the sun has dimmed.

He kicks me in the underparts.

I scream like a woman.

He kicks me again.

I never felt such a big agony.

He kicks me a third time.

I cannot see or hear or think. All I know is the big agony in my underparts.

The three men drop me to the floor.

I clutch on my underparts and wish I will die.

All my mind is in a big rage. They caught me unawares, three of them. Then a fourth hit me. They overnumbered me, that is how they beat me.

All around me is shouting. The smell of sweat fills my nose. Blood clogs my throat.

My own weight crushes me against the floor. I hear the sounds of a mighty battle all around, but I am weak and blind as a lamb. My pride stings me like a hornet, that I am beaten before I broke any man's teeth. Only because they overnumbered me.

"Stone him!"

My heart seizes in my chest. I cannot see for the sweat in my eyes. I cannot think for the pain in my underparts.

"To the precipice!"

All the men shout louder than I ever heard. They push Rabbi Yeshua toward the door.

I do not hear our men fighting.

They all must have been caught unawares.

I hear the men of the village leave.

All my hope runs away like smoke.

They will take him to some precipice somewhere.

They will push him off onto the rocks below.

They will throw big stones on him until he is dead.

Unless our men fight to defend.

Only I do not know where our men have gone.

I do not know if they will fight to defend.

So I must fight to defend, whether I have hope or no hope.

My underparts are still in a big agony.

I feel as I am crushed under a mighty weight.

I put both my hands on the floor.

I push on the floor with all my strength.

Slowly, slowly, I rise to my hands and knees.

The synagogue is empty. There is a big noise outside, but fifty paces away.

Slowly, slowly, I crawl to the nearest stone bench.

Slowly, slowly, I push myself to stand on two feet.

I am bent over in a mighty agony, hunched like a man of a hundred years.

Yoni screams somewhere outside. "Shimon the Rock!"

I hobble toward the door. Every step is a knife in my underparts. All the world is a blur. I wipe my eyes with the sleeve of my tunic. I lean against the doorpost and look out.

Yoni runs toward me. "Shimon the Rock, you must find your fish knife! Our men are scattered. Even Little Yaakov ran away."

I will show myself better than Little Yaakov. I throw my left arm over Yoni's shoulder. "Help me walk."

We stagger like drunkards through the village square.

I still hear the noise of the villagers, very far ahead, dying in the distance.

Andre comes out from behind a house and joins us.

I throw my right arm over his shoulder, and we go faster.

Big Yaakov joins us and pushes Yoni aside to support me. We go faster.

Philip and Natanel the hireling and Toma Trouble appear. Then the tax-farmer.

"Where are Rabbi Yeshua's brothers?" I ask.

The tax-farmer points toward Rabbi Yeshua's house. "See them carrying his youngest brother slow? His leg was broken."

"Which way did the villagers take Rabbi Yeshua?"

Yoni points straight ahead of us, far south. "They were shouting about the precipice. The place I found Rabbi Yeshua and Little Yaakov yesterday."

"How far is this precipice?"

"More than a mile. Can you run, Shimon?"

I cannot run. Every step feels like a hammer smashing on my underparts.

I listen for the shouts of the village.

They have died away to silence.

I run.

Yaakov of Nazareth

Yosi and I carry Yehuda Dreamhead slow down our street. I am in a fever to run, but I know every step is a big agony on him.

Thin Shimon limps behind us, grunting for his pain.

Uncle Halfai shouts, "We must stay calm!"

Our cousin, Fat Shimon, wrings his hands foolishly.

All my body is in a big sweat. We have knives in our house. We have iron bars. We have hammers. That is not much against a mob of fifty, but it is something.

We lower Yehuda Dreamhead to the bench in front of our house.

His leg is bent at an angle I never saw. That knee will never be right again.

Yosi sits beside him. Blood streams from his left foot.

I pound on the door of our house. "Open!"

The sound of an iron bar scrapes on wood.

The heavy door creaks inward.

Yosi's woman stares out on us with huge eyes.

I rush through into our courtyard.

My woman and Thin Shimon's woman have their arms wrapped around Imma, struggling to hold her.

Imma's eyes are wild, and she twists and pulls to break loose. "Where is Yeshua?"

Uncle Halfai shouts on Fat Shimon to find weapons in our workshop.

Imma waves a fist at me. "Where is Yeshua?"

I know she will do something foolish. "Stay here. We will chase after them."

"Chase where?" Imma writhes like a rabbit caught in a snare.

Fat Shimon comes out of the workshop with a hammer.

I rush to him and tear it out of his hands. "Find more! That is not enough!"

Thin Shimon says, "They took him to the precipice."

"Yeshua!" Imma rips loose from the women. She bounces off Thin Shimon. She runs out into the street. "Yeshua!"

Thin Shimon staggers after her.

I crash into his back.

We both fall in the dirt.

I roll free and leap to my feet.

That boy Yoni stands outside with the others.

Shimon the Rock hangs limp between two of them. He will be no use in a fight, and the others are nothing without him.

My heart is ready to explode. I knew this would befall. They will kill Yeshua. They will kill Imma. And I alone am left to defend. With only a hammer.

I run.

"Follow me!" I shout.

Imma is already fifty paces down the path, flying fast as a mother rabbit to defend her cub.

I run like the wind.

But Imma runs faster.

~

Yeshua of Nazareth

A big sweat pours down my back. The stink of the villagers' rage fills my nose. Shouts beat on my ears like hammers.

Two men walk behind me, twisting my arms hard.

Yoseph the leather-man holds my beard tight, pulling me forward as fast as he can stagger. I see how his leg pains him, how he groans in a big agony, but his rage drives him on.

It feels as we walk for many miles, but I know that the way to the precipice is not so far.

Yoseph the leather-man keeps us at his quickest pace, jerking harder and harder on my beard.

The Accuser shouts in my ears. '*You have power to destroy these men. Call down fire from heaven.*'

'*HaShem loves these men.*'

'*HaShem loves you more. Call down fire from heaven.*'

'*HaShem loves them like his own children.*'

'*HaShem cannot love you both. If he loves you, he hates them. If he loves them, he hates you. Call down fire from heaven.*'

'*HaShem loves all his children.*'

'*HaShem destroyed all his wicked children in the flood. Call down fire from heaven.*'

'*These men are slaves to sin.*'

'*Then destroy them. Sin is the first Power. The prophet told that you must destroy the first Power or be killed. Call down fire from heaven.*'

'*Destroying sinners is not the same as destroying sin. These men are my brothers.*'

'*Then you will be killed, to no gain.*'

⁓

At last, we arrive at the stony field before the precipice. Here is where Imma played as a child. Here is where I played as a child. The sweat of my fear fills my whole head. I quiver in all my bones.

We stop a few paces before the edge.

The men tie my hands behind me with leather cords. They stand around me in a circle, all shouting on me for their rage.

Shimon the baker gives me the backhand of dishonor.

Old Yonatan the village elder spits my face.

Yoseph the leather-man pisses my feet.

All the men of the village give me the backhand of dishonor or spit my face or piss my feet.

My heart breaks for these men, my brothers.

Yoseph the leather-man pulls up his tunic to show his leg, still red and swollen. Now it looks shiny with sweat. "You said HaShem would heal my leg. You are a liar and a *mamzer* and a false prophet."

He drives his fist into my belly with all his force.

I cannot breathe. Black spots dance before my eyes. My heart misses a beat. Two beats. Three.

I stagger to one knee.

~

I am before the Throne.

    All the Messengers are silent, staring on me. They call out to HaShem.

'Avenge this innocent man!'

'Make a justice on him!'

'Destroy these evil men!'

HaShem comes down off the Throne.

I feel the Shekinah all around me.

I feel the love of HaShem for me.

I feel the love of HaShem for my village, stronger than fire, stronger than flood, stronger than fear.

There is no time in the Presence of HaShem. It feels as many ten thousand years pass while I rest in the comfort of his Presence.

The Throne fades.

~

I am back in the circle of rage. No time has passed.

    Yoseph the leather-man breathes fast and shallow. His face is dark with the spirit of death and he looks as he will fall over any moment. He says, "Stand him at the edge of the precipice."

A dozen hands seize hold on me, forcing me toward the edge.

I am three paces from the edge.

Two paces.

One.

They have me circled, all screaming on me in their rage.

There is Shimon the baker, whom I love like a father. I repaired his ovens when the tree fell on them.

There is Yehuda the sheep-man, whom I love like a brother. I built the pen where he shelters his sheep.

There is Hananyah the winemaker, whom I love like a son. I carved toys out of olive wood for him when he was a boy.

Yoseph the leather-man stands before me, weak and shaky. His eyes are half-closed. He rubs his fist slow, gathering his strength.

I see what he means to do. He means to hit me again in the belly. To drive me over the edge.

I will fall twice the height of a man onto the big rock below.

Then they will drop stones on me until I am dead.

Yoseph the leather-man looks on me with the rage of a man who knows he has the spirit of death on him. He waits for the other men to go silent. "What do you have to say, you son of Miryam! You son of Spreadlegs!"

I have a word from HaShem to say.

I open my mouth to say it.

But before I can speak, I hear the sound of a mighty wailing.

Louder and louder, like an avenging spirit.

Like the Messenger of Death that killed all the firstborn of Egypt.

Imma bursts through the circle of men.

Her face blazes with the wrath of the Accuser.

She points a finger on Yoseph the leather-man and screams, "Die, you Evil Boy! I call on the wrath of HaShem! I call on him now to destroy you! I call on him to burn you with fire!"

That is the worst thing she could say.

Now they will not only kill me.

They will also kill her.

CHAPTER EIGHTY

Miryam of Nazareth

I fly down the path on wings of rage, clutching the Ring of Justice. My son refused it this morning. He put it in the hand of Shlomzion Lewd when he brought her back in the house. He will not refuse it now. He will use it or he will die. He will use it or I will die.

I see a half circle of men, just at the edge of the precipice. I hear their shouts of anger.

Their anger is nothing to my rage.

I scream louder than any woman ever did.

Heads turn to look on me. Their faces melt with fear before me. They fall away in their terror.

I burst into the circle in my rage.

My son stands on the lip of the precipice with his hands tied behind him.

The Evil Boy spins to look on me.

I hate that Evil Boy, who is now grown into a wicked man.

He smells like piss and sweat and rage.

He smells like *haryo*.

I point my finger on him and scream, "Die, you Evil Boy! I call on the wrath of HaShem! I call on him now to destroy you! I call on him to burn you with fire!"

His face is dark with a mighty rage. "Spreadlegs!"

I open my fist and show him the Ring of Justice. I put it on my finger. A thrill of power runs through me. I point my finger on him. "I curse you with the Ring of Justice! I curse you to die! I curse you to burn!"

The Evil Boy screams.

He falls to the ground, clutching his leg in a big agony.

He tears at his tunic, pulling it up.

All his leg is red like fire.

The heat of it smites me in the face.

"Fire!" he screams. "My leg! On fire!"

All my heart fills with joy. I knew the Ring of Justice was a mighty Power. HaShem is judging the Evil Boy. I called down the wrath of HaShem on him, and HaShem heard my cry.

The men of the village drop back for their terror. They fall on their faces in the dust.

The Evil Boy screams and screams and screams, writhing in the flames of his torment.

I feel glad of his screaming. I hope HaShem tortures him many days. I hope HaShem tortures him many years. I hope HaShem tortures him until forever.

Yeshua turns and shows me his bound hands. "Imma! Quickly, you will untie me." His voice is frantic.

I look on what those evil men did to him. They spat his face. They pissed his feet. They would have pushed him off the edge if I had not come to save him.

The Evil Boy screams again and again and again.

I wish he would stop his screaming so loud, for it hurts my ears.

I fumble with the leather cords that bind my son. They are tied with many knots of rage. I pluck and pluck until all the cords are undone.

All the while, the Evil Boy screams and screams and screams.

The screams of the Evil Boy hurt my heart. I take my Yeshua's hand and pull. "We should run away fast."

Yeshua stares on the Evil Boy.

"Yeshua, come away with me!"

Tears run down my son's face.

I pull hard on his hand. "Run away fast, or they will hurt you again!"

Yeshua kneels beside the Evil Boy.

The Evil Boy screams in a big agony.

He screams like Thin Hana, the iron-man's woman, who died last year in childbed. Her baby was too big in her belly and would not come out, and the midwife could do nothing. Thin Hana screamed her agony three days and two nights until she died, while all the village wept. That is how loud the wicked leather-man screams.

I am sick in my soul. There are some things too terrible even for the wicked.

The leather-man's leg glows brighter and redder than any log we ever put in the fire.

The heat of it makes my eyes burn. My face sweats for the fury of that fire.

My Yeshua puts his hand on the leather-man's leg.

His hand jerks back for the pain of it.

He puts his hand on the leg again.

Tears rush out of his eyes. "HaShem, forgive my brother! Forgive!"

HaShem will never forgive. Never, ever, ever. HaShem is just.

Yoseph the leather-man screams. His voice rises higher and higher and higher, loud as the cry of some terrible bird of prey.

I think I will weep for the sound of it. HaShem cannot forgive such a big evil as the leather-man has done on me. Only ... I wish HaShem could forgive it. HaShem would forgive if he could, but that is not a justice. HaShem must make a justice.

The Evil Boy made me cry. HaShem has no choice but to make him cry.

Tears for tears. A big agony for a big agony.

That is what I always wanted, only now it makes a piercing in my ears. But HaShem must do it anyway. That is a justice.

I close my eyes so I will not have to see the leather-man writhing in the wrath of HaShem.

Another scream, more terrible than any so far.

My heart twists in a big knot, and my eyes spring open. That is not Yoseph the leather-man's voice.

That is my son.

Yeshua's hand holds fast on the leather-man's leg. His hand glows white for its heat. His whole arm glows white.

Yeshua screams and screams and screams.

I am frantic for my fear. I tear at his body, desperate to pull him away.

He is heavy as an ox.

"Yeshua!" I scream.

My Yeshua's face twists in a big agony. He screams again. His voice mixes with the leather-man's voice.

A sword pierces my heart. "HaShem, help us!"

Yeshua screams again, a long rising cry more terrible than death.

"Mercy, HaShem! Have mercy on my son!" I tug on Yeshua to pull him away.

I cannot move him, no more than I can move a mountain.

All my rage is turned to sorrow.

I called down the wrath of HaShem, and he made a justice on me.

Now my son has turned my justice into mercy.

I fall on my knees and clutch my son to my heart.

His arm burns with a blinding heat.

I scream for my terror. "HaShem, forgive!"

A bolt, bright as lightning.

A clap, loud as thunder.

A lightness in my soul, sweet as the smell of morning in springtime.

Yeshua stops his screaming.

His arm fades from its fiery brightness. It returns to cool flesh.

The silence smites me like a hammerfall. The leather-man has stopped his screaming also. The leather-man's leg no longer burns. HaShem has forgiven the leather-man his great sin.

I breathe faster than I ever did, as I had run all the way from

Mount Tabor. My heart thumps louder than the running of a herd of goats.

Yeshua pulls back his hand from the leg of Yoseph the leather-man.

The red is gone.

The spirit of death is gone.

Yoseph the leather-man is healed.

His face is like the face of a baby. Like my son Yeshua when I nursed him as a newborn.

All the world is a blur for my tears.

All is silence for many thousand years of sorrow.

At last, Yeshua stands. "Yoseph, my brother, HaShem says he loves you like his own son."

I never heard such a thick silence from the men of the village. They cower for their terror before my son.

They should cower. There was never a man like my son in all the earth.

Yeshua leans down to me. He gives me a kiss and a kiss and a kiss. "Imma, you look more beautiful than any woman ever did."

He has told me so many ten thousand times.

Only I never believed him.

Until now.

He takes my hand. He takes the Ring of Justice from off my finger and puts it in his belt. There is a big sadness in his eyes.

I do not understand the matter. We won a mighty victory.

But Yeshua does not wear the face of a man who won a mighty victory.

We walk out from the circle of men.

The villagers tremble on their faces in the dust.

All my family stands at a distance of twenty paces, frozen, staring on us.

There is Little Yaakov with a hammer in his hand. His mouth hangs open.

There is Yosi. There is Thin Shimon. There is my brother-in-law, Halfai, and my nephew, Fat Shimon. There are all Yeshua's men.

Toma the boat maker's eyes bulge out of his head. Tomorrow, he will say he does not believe it. Today, he believes it.

Yoni comes running from the village, and his eyes are huge and gleaming white. "Rabbi Yeshua! I am afraid I did a wrong thing."

Yeshua looks around on all my family and all his men. "Where is Yehuda Dreamhead?"

"He was hurt," Little Yaakov says. "We left him at the house. You boy, Yoni, you should have stayed with him."

Yeshua walks swiftly toward the village. "What wrong thing did you do, Yoni?"

I run fast to keep up with my son.

Yoni runs fast to keep up with us both. "I ... did what I have seen you do many ten thousand times, Rabbi Yeshua. I laid my hands—"

A shout from far up the path.

The dust of someone walking.

A large man is coming this way.

My son Yehuda Dreamhead is walking this way.

My son Yehuda Dreamhead is running this way.

My heart shouts for joy within me.

But Yeshua walks heavy beside me. He thinks I have done a wrong thing.

I did a right thing. I saved him with the Ring of Justice.

I proved the Ring of Justice is a mighty Power in the world.

But I did not get all my justice. I cursed the Evil Boy, but only him. There is still the rest of the village.

Now Yeshua knows the Power of the Ring of Justice. He should tell a judgment on the whole village, every man, every woman, every child who was cruel on me.

If he does not see that, he is a fool and a simple.

CHAPTER EIGHTY-ONE

Yoni of Capernaum

I wake in the night, thinking I heard some noise.

I listen with my biggest ears.

I do not hear a noise.

It is nothing. I should sleep more. Today was a day of terror. They would have killed Rabbi Yeshua at the precipice, only he did a mighty wonder at the last moment, and put them all on their faces in the dust. I wish I could have seen it, but it took me long to heal his brother. By the time I got there, Rabbi Yeshua did not need my help.

I think the matter would have gone better with my advice, but I will not say so, or Little Yaakov will make a big scowl on me, and Big Yaakov will tell my mother to box my ears when we get home.

Now I wonder what will happen next.

All the village was silent today. When they came back from the precipice, they walked past Rabbi Yeshua's house on silent feet, wearing terrified faces.

They should be terrified. I think Rabbi Yeshua called down fire from heaven on the leather-man and made him repent. All the men were on their faces when I got there, quivering for their fear.

They will fear him all their lives, and that is good. They know if they do a wrong thing on him ever again, he will call down fire from heaven and destroy the whole village. Only I do not think they will join his army when he comes into his power, and that is not so good.

At least they will not raise a stench in the other villages of Galilee when he makes his move. They are too afraid on him to do that. They have a big terror of Rabbi Yeshua, and that is enough.

Fear is a greater Power than rage.

Rabbi Yeshua has put the fear of HaShem in them, until forever.

They were so terrified, none of them went to the village square at the going out of Shabbat. Little Yaakov's woman went out to see, but she came back and said all the village was silent as Sheol. She looked sad when she said it, for I think she likes going to the village square.

I was not sad to hear it. I was glad, for it means the village lives in fear. They should live in fear all the rest of their lives.

I should sleep more.

It is too quiet to sleep.

There is a mighty stillness in the street below.

I do not like the sound of such a stillness.

Slowly, slowly, I sit up.

Slowly, slowly, I crawl to the parapet.

Slowly, slowly, I peer over the edge.

Men stand in the street holding hammers and stones and chisels.

For an instant, I think they came to kill us all, only they look small and frightened and weak. They look like the sails on the boats when there is no wind.

Women stand in the street holding oil lamps. Also baskets. Also brooms.

That old leather-man, the one who is president of the synagogue, points people where they should go.

Fear is written all over their faces. They move toward the house on silent feet.

Soon I hear the sound of stones grinding against plaster, very light.

I hear the crunch of iron hammers crushing plaster.

I hear the hiss of chisels scraping.

I hear the whisper of brooms sweeping.

They work slow, for they are terrified to make a noise.

I go back to my place and roll up in my cloak.

I try to sleep, but it is impossible when you can just hear a faint noise at the edge of your hearing, grinding and crushing and scraping and sweeping.

It is the sound of a smirch being erased.

It is the sound of an agony of fear.

Rabbi Yeshua has won a mighty victory, to put such a big terror on the village.

Now that he knows he can do it, he will put a big terror on the first Power, and the second, and the third, and the fourth.

Last of all, he will put a big terror on the Great Satan, and that will be the kingdom of HaShem.

That will be the mightiest victory of all.

I sleep.

$\sim$

Miryam of Nazareth

I go out early with my son and Shlomzion Lewd to get water. When we see how the wall of our house is scrubbed clean of the smirch, my son smiles.

Shlomzion Lewd smiles.

I do not smile. They took away the smirch from Yeshua's name. But he still has not made a justice on me.

When we walk up the long street to the spring, it feels as we walk through a village of dead people. Shimon the baker makes a weak grin on us, but then looks shamed and puts his eyes to the ground. Two small girls playing in the street see us and run away fast. The leather-man treads hides in his piss-pool, wearing a fearful face.

We come home and eat our morning meal. Little Yaakov and Yosi and Thin Shimon and Yehuda Dreamhead go away to Tsipori for the day to look for work.

Yeshua takes a walk with Shlomzion Lewd and little Yoni. They go south toward the precipice and are gone long. When they return,

Yeshua comes in the house and tells me I am beautiful and sits with me and tells me tales all the day.

Shlomzion Lewd does not come in the house. She goes to the village wearing that look on her face.

Yoni and the rest of Yeshua's men sit in the courtyard doing nothing. Yoni wears a big grin, enough to make Big Yaakov scowl for a week.

The house feels as it is ready to explode.

Late in the afternoon, my sons came home from Tsipori with grumpy faces. They found work, but only half a day, so they earned two *dinars* for the four of them. I think that is a good money, only they do not think so.

We eat the evening meal in a big gloom. It feels as there is a mighty cloud over the village.

"We should go to the village square tonight," Yeshua says.

Little Yaakov stares on him as he is a fool. "Tonight is not a good night to go to the village square. Nobody will come."

"They will come," says Shlomzion Lewd.

Yosi says, "We saw the look on them when we came in the village gate. The elders looked fearful and shamed. All the village looked fearful and shamed. They will not come."

"They will come," says Shlomzion Lewd.

Thin Shimon says, "That is a big foolishness. Why should they come to the village square when they are terrified on us?"

Shlomzion Lewd says, "They will come because I told them Yeshua son of David commands that they should come. All the village will be there. And all of us will go also."

Yehuda Dreamhead says, "That is a wrong thing, Yeshua. We should not leave Imma alone in the house while we all go to the village square."

"Imma will come with us." Yeshua looks on me and smiles. "Yes, Imma? You will come to the village square and hear the judgment I make on the village?"

My head feels light and my heart leaps in my chest. I do not think I will ever breathe again. My son will make a justice on me!

I smile back on him. "Yes."

All my sons look on me in amaze.

They do not understand yet that I am brave of the village now.

And I want my justice. The village made a scorn on me all my life. Now my son will make a scorn on them.

So we go. All my sons. All their women. All their children. All Yeshua's men. And me.

The villagers sit huddled in the village square.

Yehuda the sheep-man sits with his woman and seven children, looking fearful and shamed.

Shmuel the iron-man sits with his children and that new woman he got from Yodefat, looking fearful and shamed.

Old Hana the cheese-woman sits with her daughters and their lords and their children. Old Hana does not look fearful and shamed. The rest of her family does, but she smiles on my son with a hopeful look in her eye. My son will be kind on her when he makes a judgment on the rest, for she was always kind on him.

Shimon the baker sits with his woman and his daughter and his sons and all his grandchildren. They all wear fearful faces, except the youngest grandson, who is too young to be afraid.

We all take places in the very front.

Yeshua stands to face the village.

Shimon the baker's little grandson runs to my son and smiles on him. "Run with me in circles!"

My son grins and takes the boy's hand. "Show me how fast you can run, friend!"

The boy runs around my son fast. He runs fast and faster. He runs until he loses his feet. My son makes him fly and fly and fly. The boy shouts for his big joy. He would not shout for joy if he knew what is to happen.

When my son sets him back on his feet, I see that the boy is still blind in one eye. That is a good justice. My son should make him blind in both eyes. That would be a better justice.

My son looks all around the village square as he is looking for someone.

He waits.

From far up the street, the last family is coming.

Yonatan the old leather-man walks slow with his woman. Also, Yoseph the leather-man walks slow with his woman and three daughters. They all look fearful and shamed. They take place at the very back of the crowd.

My son looks all around the village square. There is a look on his face of a mighty judge, come to make a judgment on a wicked people.

"Tell us a tale, Yeshua!" says Shlomzion Lewd.

I am shocked she would say such a thing. Now is not a good time for a tale. Now is a good time for a justice.

"What tale shall I tell?" Yeshua says.

I cannot believe he would even think of telling a tale. That is a wrong thing. He should have more sense than that.

Yoni says, "Tell that new tale we heard from the Babylonish traveler last winter when we told repentance to Israel. The tale of Shoshanna."

I never heard any tale of a woman named Shoshanna. I do not wish to hear a tale. I wish to hear a judgment on the village. I wish my son will make a justice on me.

All the village stares on Yeshua in amaze. They came to receive their judgment. They wish to receive it quickly and endure their punishment, for they deserve it. They did not come to hear some Babylonish tale of a woman they never heard of.

Yeshua grins and nods. "That is a good tale, the tale of Shoshanna Beautiful."

I think it must be a tale of judgment. A tale of vengeance. If that is the way of this tale, that will be a good tale.

The village will think it is an evil tale, but that is what they deserve.

Yeshua waits until all the village is silent.

My heart thumps.

Yeshua says, "In the days of Daniel the prophet, there lived in the city of Babylon a great and wealthy man named Yeho-Yakim. He married a woman more beautiful than any woman ever was, and her name was called Shoshanna Beautiful."

My son looks on me, and I see in his eyes he thinks I am beautiful. When he looks on me with those eyes, my heart feels full. I feel as HaShem thinks I am beautiful. I feel as men think I am beautiful.

I feel as I am … Shoshanna Beautiful.

CHAPTER EIGHTY-TWO

The Tale of Shoshanna Beautiful

My name is Shoshanna, and all my people call me Beautiful.

I live in a great house in Babylon, and my lord is a rich and mighty man, a judge over Israel, which is in exile.

My lord holds court in our great garden every morning in the week except Shabbat. Men of Israel come from every district of Babylon to bring their cases before the elders. My lord presides over them all. Whenever he hears a case, he wears a Ring of Justice as a sign that he will make a righteous justice.

In the afternoon, in the heat of the day, all go home to sleep, for the heat of Babylon is more fierce than the heat of any land.

One afternoon, the heat is too fierce for me to bear. I call my maidservants to shunt in fresh water to the bathing pool in our walled garden. They bring me sweet resin of the mastic tree to soothe my heart. I send them away so I may bathe alone in peace.

I take off my hair covering and shake out my hair, which hangs to the level of my knees. I lay aside my tunic. I recline in the water, enjoying its coolness. The sun beats down on me. I feel free and calm and alone.

Only I am not alone!

Two men leap out from behind a tree—two elders, judges in my lord's court.

My heart seizes in my chest. All my head feels light as fog. I cannot breathe. I spring for my tunic, squeaking in my terror.

They are too quick for me. Before I can cover myself, they seize hold on my arms and tear away my tunic. They grin on my nakedness and squeeze my bosoms.

I catch my breath.

I open my mouth to scream for help.

They cover my mouth with my own hair covering. "You will lie with us, you *zonah*."

"Never!" My voice is so muffled I can hardly hear myself. I shake my head.

They pinch my hind parts. "Lie with us, or we will accuse you before the court of playing the *zonah* with some young man."

"Never and never!" I struggle to pull free.

They are too strong.

They force me to the ground.

They stuff my hair covering between my jaws.

One pins my arms.

The other tries to spread my legs.

I kick and writhe and bite at my hair covering.

They say, "Lie with us now, or we will accuse you in the court, and the court will condemn you, and you will be stoned."

I shake and cry for my rage. They have me in a box. If I say no, they will accuse me, and I will die. If I say yes ...

No, never. To live in guilt is a death that never ends. Rather I should die innocent than live guilty.

I kick with my legs harder than I ever kicked. I tear my hands free. I pull away the hair covering that gags my voice. "Never! Help! Evil—"

Their thick hands cover my mouth again. "*Zonah*! Wickedness! Sin! Men of Israel, come and see this great sin!"

They shout their lies many times.

My maidservants come running.

Our manservants come running.

My lord comes running.

They all stare on my nakedness and hear the evil tale, how I played the *zonah* with some young man.

Rage fills my lord's eyes. He was always a jealous lord, and he believes the evil tale.

The next morning, my lord holds court in my garden.

I stand trial for my life.

The evil elders bear false witness on me. "We think this is the woman we saw, but we cannot be sure, on account of her veils."

My lord says, "Remove her veils."

The bailiffs rip away my veils.

The evil elders stare on me and say, "We think it is her, but we have a doubt. The woman we saw had long hair that hung to her knees."

My lord says, "Remove her hair covering."

The bailiffs tear away my hair covering.

The evil elders grin and say, "Still we cannot be sure. The wicked woman we saw had a mole on her left bosom."

My lord says, "Remove her tunic."

The bailiffs slit the seams of my tunic with a knife and tear it from my body.

I try to cover my bosoms and woman parts with my hands.

My lord says, "Pull away her hands."

The bailiffs seize my hands and stretch out my arms on both sides.

I hang my head and shake out my hair in front of me to cover my nakedness.

My lord says, "Pull back her hair."

My own maidservants gather my hair and pull it back.

All the court leans forward to see my nakedness.

All the court grins and points with long fingers. "She has a mole on her left bosom!"

I cry and cry for my shame.

The evil elders say, "We saw this wicked woman spread her legs for some young man under a tree in the garden. We shouted *zonah* and tried to seize them both, only we are old men, and the young man was too strong for us, and he ran away fast. Ask this *zonah*, and she will tell his name."

I stamp my foot for my fury. "They lie. There was no young man. These men came on me unawares while I bathed and begged me to lie with them."

"She lies! We are elders in Israel and honest men. We swear by The Name that we saw the matter just as we have told. Some young man used her for a pleasure under a tree in the garden. We see it clear in our minds. Such a big sin can never be unseen. We name her Shoshanna Spreadlegs, and we say she deserves death."

All the judges gather together with my lord. They speak long in soft voices.

My lord's eyes fill with anguish, for he loves me. They fill with rage, for he is dishonored.

At last my lord raises his right hand to show his Ring of Justice. "Here is my judgment, and it is a righteous justice. The woman played the *zonah*, and she will die."

All my breath is stolen away. That is not a righteous justice! The Ring of Justice is twisted into evil. The lies of my accusers have made it a Ring of Vengeance.

The bailiffs seize my hands to take me away.

I beg for my clothes, so I can cover my nakedness.

The judges refuse. They say I will be thrown naked in the stoning pit, and the witnesses will drop the first stones on me.

I weep and scream for my shame. Nothing is more terrible than this.

Nothing except that I should have sinned.

They drag me out of the garden. They drag me down the street. They drag me through the city market.

All the while I scream and cry for my shame.

People point fingers on my nakedness.

I wish I will die quickly.

A young boy runs to stand in our way. His face looks more angry than the face of our prophet Moses when he saw the golden bull-god. "Stop, you fools! What is this madness?"

"Who are you to say stop, you conceited boy?" My lord's face is purple for his rage.

"My name is called Daniel, and I am a prophet of Yah. Why are you shaming this woman?"

"She played the *zonah* with some young man."

"Where is the young man?"

"He ran away fast."

"Then how do you know she played the *zonah*?"

"We have witnesses."

"What witnesses?"

"These two elders."

The boy Daniel looks on my accusers. He looks on me.

I shake and cry for my shame, that a prophet of Yah sees my nakedness.

But the boy looks only on my face. "Yah says there is a big evil here. Yah says to put clothes on the woman. Yah says I will make a justice on the matter."

A light burns in Daniel's eyes, more fierce than I ever saw. He is only a boy, but his voice is command to all the judges.

"Put clothes on her," my lord says in a thick voice.

The boy Daniel snaps his fingers at the merchants in the market.

The merchants come running with clothes.

My maidservants put a tunic on me. They wrap my hair in a hair covering. They put veils on my face.

At last, I am clothed again. But still I cannot breathe. My accusers have Torah on their side, and Torah says that any matter is proved at the word of two witnesses who are men. The word of a woman is nothing. I am dead unless Daniel can find three witnesses who are men. And there are no witnesses except the trees of my garden.

If trees can speak, then I am an eagle.

My lord commands that we return to our garden.

When we are all returned to the judgment place, he says, "You boy, Daniel, say what you have to say."

"What was the testimony against the woman?" Daniel asks.

"These two elders swore by The Name that they saw this woman playing the *zonah* with a young man under a tree in this very garden."

Daniel's face shows no fear. He looks on the two elders. He looks on me. He looks all around the garden. His eyes turn inward, as he is hearing a song no mortal man can hear. A thin smile splits his face.

"You are all fools," he says in a voice bitter as bile. "Let me question each witness alone."

The two elders look on each other in amaze and alarm.

My lord points to a bailiff.

The bailiff seizes one elder and leads him away.

The other has the look of an ox hit on the head with a hammer before it is sacrificed to the Babylonish gods.

Daniel looks on him without pity. "Under which tree did you see the woman playing the *zonah*?"

The elder's face seems frozen for his fear. He looks all around the garden. "It is not so clear in my mind—"

"Then you lied," says my lord. "You swore by The Name that you saw it clear in your mind."

"I …" The elder looks here and there. He points on a mastic tree that is twice my height. "That one! That very tree. I see it clear in my mind. She lay on the ground and spread her legs for the young man under that tree."

"Liar!" I scream.

Daniel makes a fierce grin on the elder and commands that he be led away and the other one brought.

Bailiffs take him away and bring the other back.

Daniel stabs his finger at the elder. "Under which tree did you see the woman playing the *zonah*?"

The elder's face is gray as death. He says nothing.

"Under which tree?"

The elder looks all around and shakes his head. "It is not—"

"You swore by The Name it was clear! Under which tree?"

"That one!" The elder points on the giant oak behind my lord. It stands twenty times the height of a man. "I see it clear in my mind. She stood against that tree and spread her legs for the young man—"

"Liar!" shouts my lord. He stands from his judgment seat, and his face gleams with rage.

All the judges stand from their judgment seats and spit the eye of the elder.

My lord spits his eye.

The bailiff brings in the other elder.

All the judges spit his eye.

My lord spits his eye. He holds up his right hand to show the Ring of Justice. "Here is my judgment, and it is a righteous justice. He who bears false witness is condemned with the death of the one he would have killed unjustly."

The two elders fall on their faces, begging mercy.

My lord calls for his bailiffs. "Take them away and stone them."

The bailiffs take hold on my accusers.

I do not know what to feel.

I was lost, and now I am free.

I was shamed, and now Yah made a justice on me.

But a voice in my heart says I should beg mercy on the men.

I run to my lord. I take his hands in mine. I cover the Ring of Justice with my own fingers. "Make a mercy on them, I beg you."

My lord looks on me long in a mighty wonder. "Why should I make a mercy on them? They are wicked and cruel, and they made a big injustice on you. They would have killed you, and now you beg mercy on them? What reason should I make a mercy on them?"

I do not know a reason my lord should make a mercy on them.

I know it is a foolishness, only my heart says that even if they are wicked and cruel and made injustice on me and would have killed me, still they are children of HaShem. I think HaShem loves them and hopes they will repent.

Love is not a reason.

Hope is not a reason.

So I do not have a reason, and I do not know what to say.

Still I think my lord should make a mercy on them, even if I can give no reason.

Mercy is its own reason, more than justice ever was.

My name is Shoshanna, and all my people call me Beautiful.

Miryam of Nazareth

nd all the people of Babylon praised Shoshanna Beautiful, the righteous woman, who did right in the eyes of HaShem," Yeshua says.

I blink once, twice, three times.

I am not Shoshanna Beautiful.

It was all just a tale, more wonderful and terrible than any tale I ever heard.

Only a tale.

I am Miryam Beautiful.

My son looks on me and smiles.

My son looks on the village and smiles.

I had forgot the village. I look behind me.

Yehuda the sheep-man and his family are on their faces, weeping.

Shmuel the iron-man and his family. Old Hana and her family. Shimon the baker and his family. On their faces, weeping.

Old Yonatan and his family, on their faces.

Weeping.

I do not need to see more.

Tonight, they weep. Tomorrow, perhaps they will be kind, and perhaps they will be cruel, I do not know.

It does not matter.

I am brave of the village now, but more than brave.

I do not care what the village thinks on me, any more, forever.

I am free of the village, and free is more than brave.

My son grins on me. "Come here, Imma, there is a thing we must do."

I do not know what thing we must do. I feel weak in all my body.

Yeshua comes to me and pulls me to a standing. "Walk with me, Imma. This way."

I walk with him.

He leads me down the street toward our house.

I look back toward the village square.

Nobody follows after us.

We are alone.

"Run in circles with me, Imma."

"I … that is a big foolishness."

He takes my hand and makes me walk in circles around him.

He makes me run in circles around him.

He makes me run fast.

I laugh. I shout. I scream for my joy.

I run fast and faster. I never ran so fast in all my life.

He takes both my hands in his.

I run so fast, I lose my feet.

He holds my wrists in his strong hands, and he spins and spins and spins.

I feel as I am flying. I feel as I am soaring like an eagle. I feel as I am riding on the wings of HaShem.

It is a big foolishness, for I am an old woman, almost fifty.

It is not done in Israel.

It is not done in Egypt.

It is not done in Babylon.

It is not done in Rome.

It is not done anywhere in all the earth.

My son Yeshua is making a scandal again.

I love him more than I ever did.

CONTINUE THE ADVENTURE

Shimon the Rock says:

"The tale you have read is the first of four scrolls in the long tale called **Crown of Thorns**.

"The second scroll will be called **Son of David**, and it is a mighty tale, how Rabbi Yeshua fights the second Power with a big help from me.

"I hope it will also tell the secret how my brother died. I was there and I should remember the matter, only some Samaritan smote me on the head, and I lost the memory on it. I have dreams on the matter now and again, only I wake up shouting in a big sweat and never learn the truth. If some man knows how it befell, I will have the secret out of him, if I have to break his teeth.

"Also, Rabbi Yeshua must do battle with the Greatest Satan. I do not understand the matter, only I know the Greatest Satan is mightier than the Great Satan. It has to do with the evils done by Rabbi Yeshua's father David. I think it is a hard thing to ask a *tsaddik* to step into the sandals of a bloody man like David the king. The man who would be Mashiach should think three times whether he can take up David's sword and not destroy his own soul.

"But the scribe who writes the tale of **Son of David** is a dull-wit and slow with his reed pen, and the tale is not yet all put on papyrus. I have set Miryam Magdala to hound the scribe. She has sharp teeth and will see the thing done at a good speed.

"This same scribe wrote another tale, a set of three scrolls that can be bought now. The tale is called **City of God**, and it tells about that matter we heard from Yohanan the prophet, how the Great Satan will make a bad war on our people. Yoni says it is the wrath of HaShem, but I say that is a big foolishness. I heard the tale once, and it is a mighty tale, better than any tale Yoni ever told, only not so good as a tale by Rabbi Yeshua. The first scroll is called **Transgression**."

IF YOU ENJOYED THIS BOOK

Yoni says:

"Did you like this tale of Rabbi Yeshua? What do you think will happen next? I am dying of my curiosity to find out. When the tale began, I thought the first Power was Egypt, only I was wrong.

"Toma Trouble says there is another mighty Power in the world, and that is the Power of word-of-mouth. I do not know what he means by that.

"I wish I could write letters with a reed pen on a papyrus, but I am not such a big genius as that. Do you know how to write? Rabbi Yeshua will be very angry on me for saying so, but I think you should write a review on this tale, so your whole village will know the matter of the first Power.

"If I could write, I would make a review of many ten thousand words, but Miryam Magdala says that is a big foolishness. She says a review should be one sentence or two, to tell how the tale made you feel, and that is all.

"Anyway, there is a good place where you can write a review, and that is the place you bought the scroll of this tale."

ABOUT THE AUTHOR

Miryam Magdala says:

"The scribe who wrote this tale is some man from a far country. His name is called Randy son of Carl of the House of Ingemar, only he does not write it that way.

"I heard he is a *philosophos*, so you should be wary on him. He made a study on a thing called physics in a far country called Berkeley. I do not know what is physics, but it sounds like a mighty foolishness. Also, I do not know what is the meaning of the letters PhD. He said it was important, so it probably is not.

"This man says he lives in a place called ingermanson.com and that you would know how to find it.

"Also, he says if you go to that place, you can sign your name to get emails to learn when his next tale will be written on a scroll. The man is more lowborn than even a fish-man, but I like him, and if I knew how to sign my name, I would do it, for my heart beats fast when I hear words from him. Only do not tell him I said so, or he will be more conceited than that little Yoni, and that will be a bad matter."

www.ingermanson.com/mary

facebook.com/RandyIngermansonFiction

amazon.com/author/rsingermanson

bookbub.com/authors/r-s-ingermanson

goodreads.com/randyingermanson

STANDARD DISCLAIMER

Toma Trouble says:

"The tale you have read is a thing called a fiction. The plain meaning is that it is not quite a lie, but almost, and you should not believe the matter without making investigation on it yourself. What did you see, and what do you know?

"If you did not see the matter yourself, then how can you know that was the way of it? That is a hard matter, and I think you should ask someone who was there. Only do not ask Yohanan ben Zavdai, for he bends his tales overmuch, and anyway he uses too many ten thousand words. Also, you should not ask Shimon the Rock, who is a thick-head and a dull-wit.

"Now that I think on the matter, it is not so easy to know who to ask. I think even a *philosophos* will make a big work to understand the matter. All the people in the tale are dead, and the matter is written by many scribes in many books, mostly Greekish people, and it is not so easy to put sensible Aramaic words in the foolish Greekish language.

"Here is what I know, that the scribe who put this tale on papyrus spent many thousand hours to make a study on the matter, and still you should not believe he got his tale right. I think you would have a good luck if a tenth part of his tale is true.

"But only HaShem knows which is the tenth part that is true, and which are the nine parts that are guesses and foolishness."

20 QUESTIONS TO THINK ON

1. **Emotions**: How did this story make you feel? What did you like most in the story?
2. **Characters**: Which characters did you identify with most?
3. **Plot**: Want to take the #SonOfMaryChallenge? Try to explain the storyline of the book in 25 words or less.
4. **Setting**: What surprised you most about the geography of first-century Palestine? How does geography affect the story? Would you like to get the maps in the book as free downloads? For a limited time, you can get them at ingermanson.com/maps.
5. **You**: How did this story change you? Did it make you think about Yeshua in a different way? Is he the same Yeshua you've always imagined? Is he a different Yeshua? Is he a little of both?
6. **Theme**: Yeshua and Yoni make several guesses about the first Power. What do you think is the first Power? How many different facets of the first Power can you find in the story?
7. **The Ring of Justice**: Is the Ring of Justice a Power for good? A Power for evil? Is it a Power at all?
8. **Miryam's Story Goal**: Miryam desperately wants justice. Is there more than one kind of justice? How many kinds of justice can you think of? What kind of justice does she want? Do you think she deserves justice? Does she receive justice in the end, and if so, what kind? Does the village receive justice?
9. **Yeshua's Story Goal**: Yeshua wants to destroy the first Power. In what sense does he succeed? In what sense is humanity's battle with the first Power still going on? Do you think this battle will end?
10. **Patriarchy**: Most societies in the ancient world were

shockingly patriarchal. In what ways does Yeshua subvert this system? In what ways does he work within the system? Why do you think he deals with patriarchy the way he does?

11. **Family**: There are three different theories on the "brothers of Yeshua" mentioned in Mark 6:3 and Matthew 13:55. Some say they were sons of both Miryam and Yoseph. Some say they were sons of Yoseph by a previous wife. Some say they were cousins of Yeshua. Which theory makes the most sense to you? What reason do you have for accepting the theory you prefer? Do you think we have enough information to prove any of the theories?

12. **Miryam's Secret**: If you had a twelve-year-old daughter who told you she was pregnant by a miracle of God, would you believe her? Do you think Miryam's parents would have believed such a story? What would you do if you were Miryam? Would you tell anyone, ever? Would you tell even the child born from that miracle? If so, how would you prove your claim?

13. **Son of God**: In the Bible, the term "son of God" is used with several different meanings. How many can you think of? In what sense was Adam the "son of God?" In what sense was Israel the "son of God?" In what sense was the king of Israel the "son of God?" In what sense are all humans "sons and daughters of God?" In what sense was Yeshua the "son of God?"

14. **Paradoxes**: Yoni is obsessed with paradoxes. Do you agree with all the solutions he comes up for his paradoxes? Are you able to live with paradox in your own life?

15. **Obedience**: Hebrews 5:8 says that Yeshua "learned obedience from the things he suffered." What does that mean to you? Why would he need to learn obedience? Can you think of any gospel stories that say Jesus learned things or asked questions to get information?

16. **Yeshua's Humanity**: The Council of Chalcedon ruled in AD 451 that Yeshua had two natures in one person—a

human nature and a divine nature. The Confession of Chalcedon says that Yeshua was truly God and truly man, both at the same time. Do you agree with the Council's decision? What does it mean to be truly God? What does it mean to be truly man? Do you find it a paradox? How do you think Yoni would resolve this paradox?

17. **Omnipresence**: God is said to be omnipresent—present everywhere throughout the universe. Do you believe Yeshua was omnipresent in his human nature? Why or why not? Do you think there is a paradox here?

18. **Omnipotence**: God is also said to be omnipotent—all-powerful, able to do anything. But Hebrews 6:18 says it is impossible for God to lie. Are there other things God can't do? Were there things Yeshua was not able to do? Was he ever tired, hungry, thirsty, or sleepy? Did he ever cry out in agony? Did he ever need strengthening from angels? Do you believe Yeshua was omnipotent in his human nature? Why or why not? Do you think there is a paradox here?

19. **Omniscience**: God is said to be omniscient—knowing all things. Can you think of some occasions in the gospels where Yeshua appears to not know something? Do you think Yeshua was born able to speak Aramaic? What about English? Elvish? As an unborn fetus, did he know the plays Shakespeare would write sixteen centuries later? As a one-celled embryo, did he know the number of carbon atoms in the planet Mars? Do you believe Yeshua was omniscient in his human nature? Why or why not? Do you think there is a paradox here?

20. **Yeshua's Self-Knowledge**: What do you think Yeshua believed about himself and his relationship to God? Did he believe this as a one-celled embryo? As an unborn fetus? As a growing child? When do you think he came to his belief? How do you think he came to his belief? What are your reasons for thinking so?

GLOSSARY

Abba: Father.

amphora: a ceramic container for holding liquids or dry goods.

ba'al: literally "lord." A *ba'al* can be either human or supernatural. A common word for husband is "*ba'al.*"

bema: the podium from which the Torah or prophets were read.

borit: any of a number of plants having a high saponin content that could be used as a primitive soap.

dinar: a silver coin, the standard payment for a day's wage for a working man. Often rendered as "denarius."

Gehenna: literally "Valley of Hinnom," the valley on the south and east sides of Jerusalem. This was the site of child-sacrifices in ancient Israel, and was the dump site where bodies were thrown after Babylon destroyed Jerusalem in the sixth century BC. The word signifies horror and desolation. At some point, it came to also mean a place of punishment after death, not necessarily for all eternity.

goy: gentile.

haryo: dung.

HaShem: literally "The Name." Used out of respect in place of the actual name of God, which is typically written Yah or Yahveh.

hazzan: cantor.

Imma: Mother.

logos: literally "word" in Greek, but used to refer to the divine Reason behind the universe. In Jewish circles, "Wisdom" played a similar role.

mamzer: the exact definition is hard to pin down and seems to have varied over the centuries. In the first century, a *mamzer* was probably the offspring of a man and woman who could not legally marry. This was more severe than mere illegitimacy. If a child was the result of sexual relations between a man and woman who later married, the child was not a *mamzer*.

mikveh: a ritual bath, used for purification rites as described in Leviticus.

Nephilim: legendary superhuman offspring of divine male spirits with human women.

Pesach: the feast of Passover, celebrated in the spring after the barley harvest.

phantasm: ghost.

philosophos: philosopher.

Purim: a feast celebrating the victory of Queen Esther and her cousin Mordecai over their genocidal enemies in Persia.

Rosh HaShanah: literally "head of the year," the New Year, celebrated in the fall.

saq: a coarse cloth made of animal hair, traditionally worn during mourning or repentance.

satan: literally "enemy," often translated "accuser." A *satan* could be any adversary, human or supernatural, and either individual or a group.

Savta: Grandmother.

shalom: literally "peace," often used as a greeting.

Shavuot: the feast of Pentecost, celebrated in early summer after the wheat harvest.

Shekinah: literally "Presence," often used for the actual Presence of God on earth.

Sheol: literally "the grave," the abode of the dead, traditionally a dismal place, with its occupants having little or no consciousness.

Sukkot: the feast of Tabernacles, celebrated in the fall.

tekton: a worker in wood, metal, or stone. This was the occupation of Jesus, traditionally translated as "carpenter."

tsaddik: literally "righteous one," a traditional term for an exceptionally good, kind, and holy man.

tsaraat: originally any of several skin diseases, but this later came to be used for Hansen's disease (modern leprosy).

wadi: a desert gulley.

yetzer hara: the evil inclination, traditionally considered to be one of two warring inclinations in every person.

Yom Kippur: the Day of Atonement, ten days after the New Year.

zekhut: righteousness as shown by generosity to the poor.

zonah: prostitute.

FOR FURTHER READING

Sometime in the spring of 1983, I walked into the library at UC Berkeley "to find a book or two as research for my novel." I discovered a world vastly bigger than I ever imagined. I have lost count of all the books, articles, and websites I've read since then. Some I agreed with; some not.

Here are a few I found especially interesting, surprising, or shocking:

Nahman Avigad, *Discovering Jerusalem*. Kenneth E. Bailey, *Jesus Through Middle Eastern Eyes*. Richard Bauckham, *Jesus and the Eyewitnesses*. Meir Ben-Dov, *In the Shadow of the Temple*. F. F. Bruce, *New Testament History*. F. F. Bruce, *Peter, Stephen, James & John*. Bruce Chilton, *Rabbi Jesus*. Shaye J. D. Cohen, *From the Maccabees to the Mishnah*. Gaalya Cornfeld, *Josephus: The Jewish War*. John Dominic Crossan, *The Historical Jesus*. Henri Daniel-Rops, *Daily Life in the Time of Jesus*. Paula Fredriksen, *Jesus of Nazareth, King of the Jews*. Rene Girard, *I See Satan Fall Like Lightning*. Joachim Jeremias, *Jerusalem in the Time of Jesus*. Chris Keith, *Jesus Against the Scribal Elite*. Richard M. Mackowski, S.J., *Jerusalem, City of Jesus*. Bruce J. Malina, *The New Testament World*. Jacob Neusner, *First Century Judaism in Crisis*. Jonathan L. Reed, *Archaeology and the Galilean Jesus*. David M. Rhoads, *Israel in Revolution 6-74 C.E.*. Jane Schaberg, *The Illegitimacy of Jesus*. Emil Schurer, *The History of the Jewish People in the Age of Jesus Christ*, revised and edited by Geza Vermes, Fergus Millar and Matthew Black. James D. Tabor, *The Jesus Dynasty*. Joan Taylor, *The Immerser*. Joan Taylor, *What Did Jesus Look Like?* Walter Wink, *The Powers That Be*. N.T. Wright, *The New Testament and the People of God*. N.T. Wright, *Jesus and the Victory of God*.

ABOUT THE CITY OF GOD SERIES

When I began writing fiction, I had a dream to write a particular kind of suspense novel. It would be similar to the historical suspense Ken Follett writes, and somewhat like the historical action-adventure fiction of Wilbur Smith's *River God*, but it would be set in first-century Jerusalem.

Why first-century Jerusalem? Because that place and time set the direction for the next twenty centuries of western civilization. Something big happened in Jerusalem in the first century.

Not just one big thing. Not even two big things. Three big things —the Jesus movement, the Jewish revolt, and the birth of rabbinic Judaism.

And they were related.

My gut instincts told me that the Sunday-School version of those three things wasn't quite right.

As I dived into research, I found that my instincts were correct. I discovered an amazing and exciting world. I felt sure that many people would care about this world if only they could see it the way I did.

My first published novel was book 1 in what became my *City of God* series, an epic tale of the Jewish revolt. After three books in *City of God*, I interrupted work on it.

Why? Because the epic tale of the Jewish revolt is closely tied in with the epic tale of Jesus. So I began work on a project that would go deeper into this strange and mysterious world—the *Crown of Thorn* series—the life and death of Jesus of Nazareth.

Crown of Thorns is planned to have four books.

When those are done, I plan to return to the *City of God* series and finish it. Here are the books that I've written so far in *City of God*:

Book 1: *Transgression* (AD 57)
Book 2: *Premonition* (AD 57-62)
Book 3: *Retribution* (AD 62-66)

Made in the USA
Monee, IL
22 April 2022

95128968R00343